Stepping Across the Desert

KAT CALDWELL

LADWELL PUBLISHING

To the man who stuck by me, through
thick and thin.
Because of your faith in me I have gotten
this far.

I thank God for you every day.

Chapter One

TIARET, ALGERIA, MAY, 1832

THE WIND BLEW SOFTLY through the trees as Rowena dropped the dress back into the sudsy water. From downriver, she could hear the soft chant of the male slaves resting against the cedars. No time to rest for her.

Rowena closed her eyes as she ran her calloused hands up and down the cloth, the movement slow and gentle. While the garment must surely be out of style in Paris by now, it was still one of Mistress Nadira's favorites. The fine silk had to be washed with care.

Selma grunted loudly from where she was pulling wet clothes out of the river—a warning to focus. There were guests tonight at the grand house and under no circumstances could they delay with the clothes. Rowena considered the dark-skinned woman her adopted mother, but love as a slave was harsh. No one was willing to take a beating for another person's badly done work. Selma's love could include swift slaps to the face, but a warning slap from Selma was better than a whipping.

Rowena unconsciously touched her cheek, remembering the first slap Selma had given her, then wrapped her thin, muslin scarf over her head as a shield. Her heart began to race, and she noticed the throbbing in her feet again. Gently she pushed the silk dress back into the water, singing to herself in hopes she could calm herself down. There was no need to waste energy on anxiety.

"Slow, methodical," Selma said in Berber, the language they both had in common. "Breathe. I'll tell you a story."

Rowena looked up with a smile for her adopted mother. "About your brothers?" she asked.

Selma grunted in mock disapproval but began the well-worn story of her brother the warrior as Rowena hung the yellow dress from a tree branch to start the time-consuming task of wringing out the water.

"Come, sit down here," Rowena said in Berber when she saw Selma stretch out her back. "I will finish the wash while you tell the part about your brother saving your mother from the lion. Sit here and wring out the water."

Selma started to protest, but shouts down the river cut her words short. She turned her head with pursed lips and narrowed eyes, but sat down in the seat without a word. Rowena tried to concentrate on the shouted words as she picked up a long, black silk vest embroidered with gold thread.

"Hurry, child," Selma said wearily. Her story now forgotten, she started to hum a tune in her mother tongue.

"What are they saying?" Rowena asked.

"Keep your eyes down, Fatia," Selma replied sharply. "It doesn't involve us."

Rowena obeyed immediately. The afternoon was still young, and the sun would only get more intense. They must work faster to get the clothes dried and pressed before dinner; Rowena willed her fingers to go quickly as she delicately rubbed a stain out of the embroidery. When shouts floated to them from the river again, she stole a glance at Selma with concern, but Selma simply continued singing.

It was a sad song about a child being taken away—a story that rang all too true to both women. Rowena shook her head sharply and stared at the water. With even breathing, her heart had slowed, and the tears that threatened finally receded.

Thanks to persistence and a little luck, the stubborn stain in the embroidery started to fade. Two years before, when she had begun living here, the tips of her fingers would tingle at the end of the day, sometimes cracking and bleeding. Now her callouses worked much like hardened sponges without nerves.

A sigh escaped her as she rolled back her aching shoulders. Selma clicked her tongue to chivvy her along, but Rowena didn't need it. She was already dipping the tunic back into the water. Nadira had beautiful garments, just like those Rowena had once worn. They were all made of silk and dyed to perfection. Nadira's legendary beauty did not keep Saed from having other wives, but it was clear that she was his favorite, his first. The only wife that had ever traveled to France for her clothes.

"Have you thought on Sara's offer?" Selma asked in Berber.

Rowena looked sharply at her, but Selma didn't take notice of her glare. "I will not become a concubine."

"It is more secure."

"No."

Selma gave one nod, then continued with her work.

Now that Nadira could not have any more sons for him, Saed seemed to expand his harem every month. Just a few days ago Sara, Mistress Nadira's personal maid, had offered to train Rowena into being a concubine, an offer that she had received with horror.

As grotesque as it seemed to Rowena, with her English upbringing, entering Saed's harem was considered an honor. Some woman tried to be chosen well past their prime years. Selma encouraged her to enter it, saying it would provide a luxurious life. But it also meant no escape. No one ever left the harem.

Still, if Rowena was to be a slave the rest of her life, Selma argued that she should not risk going to the slave market. To Rowena's fortune, she had been privately bought and sold since the moment she had been kidnapped five years ago. The slave market was something she had never experienced and never wished to.

"Balik A'brid!"

The fierce command echoed through the trees. Surprised, Rowena scrambled to obey. She grabbed the basket and threw herself onto the bank before realizing that the command was not for her. Instead, it was directed at Saed's head slave, Mohammed, by a tall man with shoulders twice as wide as even Saed's personal guards. He appeared from the forest as though by magic, his red burnous flying about him like a sandstorm, yet never daring to hinder his long, determined strides. Mohammed obediently fell into step behind the man, trying to maintain long enough strides to keep ahead of the other slaves. An aura of panic surrounded the entire group. Even the lowest slaves could not seem to focus on their tasks.

Rowena squinted, trying to find the reason for such strange behavior. Some in the group were house slaves, which added to the incongruity. Selma gasped just as Rowena's eyes fell on the bundle the man carried. In them was Youssef, Nadira's eldest son. The boy bounced like a limp fish to the rhythm of the stranger's steps, his eyes closed, his soaked clothing leaving Rowena and Selma to think the worst. Youssef was nearing his fifteenth birthday, but in this man's arms, he looked like a child.

A long stick poked into her ribs. Rowena turned around abruptly to find Selma looking steadily at her.

"It is none of our business."

Rowena sent a silent prayer towards the boy before reluctantly turning back to her work. As she did so, she noticed the stranger was wearing black, English-style boots over tight brown riding trousers underneath his burnous.

For the first time in years, tiny bubbles of excitement popped within her. If an Englishman was here, it was possible—but—no. No. She shook the hope away. Even if the French soldiers were here, they would not bother to rescue slaves.

When Selma and Rowena arrived that evening, the entire household was buzzing with the story about Youssef. He had been thrown into the river by his horse, and before Mohammed had been able to do anything, the stranger in red had appeared from nowhere to fish the boy from the rocky waters.

It was a miracle Youssef was alive, and for that Saed wished to celebrate. Already the smell of lamb and couscous and dates wafted through the air, along with honey cakes and strong tea. Rowena entered the female baignoires, where she slept with forty-four other female slaves, and heaved a sigh. Her stomach growled as she listened to the story being told once again, the weight of her exhaustion intensifying the moment she sat down.

"Fatia! Come! Mistress is asking that you perform for the man who saved Youssef's life. You must bathe!" commanded Sara from the tent opening. The urgency in the command pushed Rowena to her feet.

"Coming!" she called out in Berber, grabbing her soap before running from the tent towards the female bathing house. Before she went far, Sara grabbed her hand.

"Mistress wished you to bathe in our quarters. You are to put on perfume and a silk dress. I was told to make you look as beautiful as Venus."

"A-a silk dress?" Rowena sputtered. "I have no such dress."

Sara smiled. "Come. You must hurry."

Rowena kept herself only one step behind Sara until they entered the cool, marbled bathroom reserved for Nadira's personal maids and slaves. She slowed to take in the sight. The green marble seemed to transform the room into a stone pond. On the eastern wall hung a life-sized oil painting of the mistress with kind, golden eyes.

Truthfully, Nadira was the kindest woman Rowena remembered knowing, though she knew that might be due to her not having known very many women in her life. Although everyone described her as a jealous wife, Nadira radiated an energy of kindness and love to those around her. Every Saturday she gave out dates and cakes to the slave children, and she always made sure each worker was given proper clothing. Often, she spoke with the elder slaves to make certain the pregnant women didn't work past their eighth month or that every child saw the doctor when they fell sick.

To those who had never known anything but misery or cruelty, Nadira's kindness was easy to accept—but Rowena had known luxury. She knew there was more to the world than working for Nadira, and she couldn't give her heart to loving the woman who owned her, who kept her from going home, who kept her from the future she was entitled to.

Or rather, had been entitled to a long time ago.

"You should practice. Perhaps if tonight's performance pleases Mistress Nadira she will move you permanently into the house quarters."

"Yes, Sara," Rowena said, managing to suppress a shudder.

Swallowing hard, she began to warm her voice as her vocal teacher had once taught her. Like bees, the other slaves swarmed around her, carefully removing her dirty clothes, clicking their tongues at the line that divided her skin into two very distinct colors. Rowena continued her scales, closing her eyes against the veiled women who washed her body and hair. She stopped her practice only to wash her face, beginning again as oil was poured over her hair and an ivory comb ran through the strands.

"Come now with the dress," Sara commanded a young girl as Rowena stopped her voice exercises. The slave combing perfume through her hair stepped away as a pink silk, empire-waist ball gown was presented to Rowena. The style must have been about twenty years out of date, which was why she was allowed to wear it.

Still, as she stepped into the gown and that unmistakable rustling of silk reached her ears, Rowena could not help feeling beautiful. It took much of her strength to keep from crying at the familiar touch against her skin as she smoothed the silk down her concave abdomen. Sara molded her hair into a spiral, smiling at her from the large mirror. Rowena smiled back, knowing Sara couldn't possibly understand the pain that silk against her skin caused her.

For years, she had denied herself the pleasure or pain of remembering her old life. Carefree afternoons in the garden; dinner parties where she sang for her father's friends and business partners —it seemed a world away. But now the memory of standing in a pale blue dress with her hair pinned in ringlets was too vivid to dismiss. It was her seventeenth birthday, and she had her future planned out down to the very moment when all of London would shiver with awe at the sound of her voice.

The image that now looked back at her was nothing like the pampered girl she remembered. Instead, she was a woman in an overworked body with darkened, callused hands and gnarled feet.

A self-pitying sigh escaped her as Sara finished the placement of her hair. The older servant raised her brows in a warning. It was an honor to perform for Saed and his guests. An honor to wear a silk ball gown. Rowena didn't bother explaining herself. She hadn't spoken in confidence to anyone in so long that she wasn't sure she knew how anymore.

"You look very beautiful," Sara whispered with finality in Arabic.

"*Shokran Gazillan,*" Rowena answered. Her Arabic had improved greatly since Saed had bought her, but it was still heavily accented. Berber, the language she had used to speak to her own servants, was what she spoke in the baignoires. Sara used to speak to Rowena in French, proud that she knew the language fluently, but since the invasion of the French army, Saed had forbidden it from being spoken in his house. Not even Nadira dared to speak it, though it was her mother's language.

"Master Saed wants you to sing only European songs tonight," Sara instructed her. "He wishes to impress this man."

She stepped away to admire Rowena, scrutinizing her with a critical eye. When Rowena received approval with a firm nod, she once again warmed her voice, this time with a song. The bathhouse fell silent as Rowena sang *Ave Maria*. It was the last song she had learned before her life had changed forever.

Audible sighs of pleasure filled the room. Rowena closed her eyes, pretending she was singing in an opera house in London, with her father watching from the front row. As the last note rang out, she felt something cold placed around her neck. She recoiled and opened her eyes. Sara smiled at her again through the mirror.

"But why?" Rowena asked as she gazed at the heavy, intricate detail of the traditional Algerian necklace. The necklace contained four large rubies, each surrounded by small diamonds. Rowena had never worn anything like this, not even when she had performed for Saed's brothers just a few months before.

"Nadira told me you should wear it," Sara answered. "Now, it is time to go. Are you ready?"

"The most beautiful voice you have ever heard is right here in our very own home," Saed announced. "And she is here tonight to honor you, my friend."

The words gave Rowena no pleasure. Saed would say anything to impress his guest; it did not mean he thought anything of her. She was a slave, here to do his bidding.

At Saed's signal, the boy slave standing near Rowena tapped his large stick. Immediately, Rowena raised her head and began *Auld Lang Syne*, the first song her German teacher had ever taught her. As she sang, the young boys sat together on the floor eating dates while the two men smoked. Their manners were relaxed. The

Englishman seemed at ease with the local traditions of eating with fingers and passing food to one another, something she had seen many Europeans struggle with when coming to Northern Africa.

Saed was dark, slightly taller than Rowena herself, and although he was strong, there was little build to him. He reminded Rowena always of the men her father used to describe after coming home from a boxing fight. The Englishman was much taller. His skin was tan, and he had a build that was more like those of the slaves who did the heaviest labor. For a moment she found herself lost in the difference of the English man, which caused her to repeat too many verses of an opera she couldn't quite remember. Noticing a flicker of amusement in his eye, she quickly focused on the top of the curtains as she finished the ballad and began a different song.

After just three more songs, Saed made an impatient gesture for her to stop. He looked grim, which was never a good sign.

"Mr. Sutton, we are honored tonight not only by your presence and company," he said gravely. His voice lifted the sleepy silence from the room, instantly bringing the family to attention. "But also because you have, by the grace of Allah, saved my first son."

Saed placed his hands on the young boy's shoulders and squeezed them with love.

"You have honored me, Saed, with your hospitality and your generosity. I did only what one does for a brother."

While no one paid attention to her, Rowena dared to look again at the stranger. When she heard his English name, her heart raced. With so much adrenaline running through her veins, she had to fight the urge to faint.

"I grow weary of this concert because it is not enough for what you have done, my friend," said Saed. "Nadira wishes to give you a gift. One we hope will please you and comfort you, as we are comforted with our son safe and alive."

He flipped his robes back dramatically. Mohammed stepped up, holding a small, golden box towards Saed. Rowena shrank back, but found a man standing directly behind her, forcing her to stay put. Saed presented the box to Mr. Sutton with ceremonious words that Rowena had trouble understanding. Then Nadira stepped forward, kissing Mr. Sutton's hands.

Something pushed her forward. She tried to plant her feet firmly onto the floor, but a second later a large staff struck the back of her knees, forcing her to kneel.

"In gratitude, my wife would like to present to you the most beautiful virgin of all our slaves. It is a small payment to the enormous debt that we owe you," Saed announced as Rowena tried desperately to scramble to her feet, to get out of the way before someone noticed her clumsiness. It was not until Mohammed swiftly kicked her in the side that she understood.

She was the gift.

Anger built up in her chest, but she ground her teeth against it and continued to stay still. Five years ago she might have screamed at them, shouting that she was not cattle to be given away as a present, but now she knew it was of no use. From her kneeling position, the flicker of light from her silver bracelet reminded her she was not Rowena Brayemore now, but Fatia, the slave.

"I am honored by these splendid gifts, my brother," Mr. Sutton said. A coldness in his voice that hadn't been there before sent a shiver through Rowena.

Saed laughed. "Tomorrow we will talk more about the business. For now, we should all rest."

With that, two men whisked Rowena away through the opposite door, where Sara waited.

"Sara!" Rowena gasped as the other woman dragged her through the hallways towards the servant's quarters.

"Hush," Sara commanded as they entered the green marbled bathroom.

"*La afham!*" Rowena whispered. "I don't understand!"

Sara gently took the pins from Rowena's hair before quickly pulling a comb through it. Rowena swallowed hard against her tears, but could not stop shaking.

"Stop," Sara said forcefully. "You are not to cry. Allah has sent you here. This is your life now."

Rowena shook her head, snatching her chin from Sara's fingers. "I do not believe in Allah, Sara."

"Whoever your god is, he has sent you here and made you Saed's slave. And now Saed has given you to this Englishman. Now! Listen to me!"

Rowena focused her attention on Sara's stern brown eyes. The severity in them kept her from fainting.

"Listen to me," she repeated. "You make sure this man likes you. Make sure he understands you are not to be left behind. Saed has given you to him, and if he doesn't take you with him Saed will see it as a disgrace. He will think that you did something to displease this man and will probably sell you."

"But I do not want to be this man's slave. I do not know him."

"Listen, Fatia! Do not allow fear to swallow you. Think about if this Englishman takes you with him. Perhaps he will take you back to Europe with him and then you will find your life again there. Perhaps he is kind and will do that for you. Won't he have no choice but to set you free?" Sara turned Rowena around and took up her hair again. "Do whatever you must, Fatia, to make certain this man takes you with him."

The plan was so clear it shocked her senseless. Perhaps being given to an Englishman as a concubine was not how she had planned it, but it was the only option she had. This was her chance to go home.

Chapter Two

ROWENA FOLLOWED A HOUSE slave through the eerily quiet halls, each more exquisitely decorated than the last. The light from the candle cast her shadow high, twisting it at the angle where the wall met the ceiling and curving it over her head. If only she could be so tall, her life would be different.

A strange tremor of fear and anticipation overcame her at the gruff reply to the knock. The house slave opened the door and glared at Rowena to enter. Inside, Mr. Sutton was sitting at an ebony desk too small to fit his large frame, his back to her. Rowena waited near the door for him to recognize her presence.

But the Englishman only continued writing furiously in his book. Rowena looked around at the silk cushions, the blazing fire, and then to the mountain of food on silver trays on the low table. The idea of eating something drew her forward, but she stopped short after only a few steps. She was uncertain if the food was for her. Or the cushions, for that matter. What a concubine's rights were, she did not know.

A movement caught her attention. The ebony desk was now empty. Being left alone brought both relief and fear until the sound of tea being poured into cups penetrated the silence. Feeling much like a caged animal, she snapped her head to the right, finding Mr. Sutton across the room.

"I thought you might be hungry," he said in Arabic.

Rowena found her heartbeat slowing at the man's gentle voice, though her hands began to sweat when he looked straight at her.

"Master," she said, bowing her head.

After a moment of silence, the tips of his black boots appeared before her. Cool fingers lifted her chin to force her to look into his eyes.

"Please, don't lower your head," he told her. "You are not my slave. I do not own slaves. What is your name?"

"Fatia," Rowena answered, her throat dry and scratchy.

"Fatia," he repeated, the name falling gently from his lips. "Please sit down and eat something before you waste away."

Shame flooded her cheeks at his playful words, but his admittance to not owning slaves troubled her more than her pride. She needed to convince him to take her away from Algeria.

"My lord, in Algeria it is still legal to give people as a gift. To not take me would be a dishonor to Saed." The moment the words spilled out of her, she gulped in fear.

Much to her dismay, she watched his face fill with anger instead of sympathy. The man marched towards the fireplace and violently deposited his goblet on the mantel.

"Damn it!" he growled in English. "This whole situation disgusts me."

For the first time in her life, Rowena's heart sank at hearing English words. She disgusted him. A slave. A woman who spent all day scrubbing or mending clothes. She looked at the traces of green streaked across her palms from the last vat of dye. A refined gentleman would not want to bother with her.

But he must take her. That much Sara had made clear. Renewed determination filled her, brushing aside her shame. She must do everything possible to convince him to take her away. This would be her last chance.

"Sit and eat," Mr. Sutton said. It was obvious he was struggling to hold his irritation at bay.

Still, the small hint of sympathy in him made Rowena happy to comply. It seemed sincere enough. Perhaps if she could show him obedience, she could convince him to take her away.

She could feel his eyes on her as she chewed quietly, and was suddenly aware of how low the nightdress was cut. She squirmed on the cushion, keeping her eyes down as she finished her three dates. The man moved about in front of her, but she did not look up—not until he thrust a silver plate piled high with food at her.

"Eat a proper meal," he said, his Arabic betraying his English grammar.

When she took the plate, their fingers grazed against each other subtly. The tension in the air, her revealing nightgown, and the knowledge of the duties expected of her all made her nerves crackle like a lit candle wick.

Mr. Sutton displayed no emotion as he leaned back, quietly smoking his cigarillo. His calm only spurned her nerves into a frenzy, making her breath catch and her fingers shake.

In all his years of doing business in North Africa, Christophe had never been in a situation like this before. A virgin. As a gift for doing what anyone would have done. Christophe blew the smoke out forcefully as he looked towards the fire. If only he had let the boy drown.

But, of course, that wasn't a solution either.

He rose to pace back and forth, but being so close to the fire was suffocating, and he needed to think. In a fit of annoyance, he opted for the window and the vast desert night sky. The moon and all the millions of stars shone brightly everywhere he looked. It was an image he always missed whenever he was in London; nothing soothed more than the expanse of the black sky and the twinkling stars. Nothing made a man, or his troubles, feel smaller.

The calm of the night at least soothed his head. He was weary after the rather stressful day and needed sleep. Ignoring the girl and his predicament, he began the task of undressing, leaving himself in only the thin muslin shirt and silk dinner trousers. The nights were cool in the mountains, yet he still found the English-style clothing asphyxiating. He had worn them at dinner only because he knew Saed would wear the same. His gifts for Saed had included a few jackets and trousers from the latest styles in Europe. Since the French invasion, European-style clothing was scarce in Algeria.

A stirring near the fire reminded Christophe of his inconvenient reality. He looked to the stars for an answer, but heard nothing. For the next few weeks, he must once again travel over the mountains into Morocco with his fresh supplies. To get there safely, he would need to travel partway with a band of desert pirates who would guarantee his protection in return for a hefty payment. Bringing a girl with him was impossible.

Christophe turned to find the sofa empty. Before he could sigh with relief, he noticed candlelight moving towards him from the dressing room. He had been so deep in his thoughts that he hadn't even noticed her entering it. Now she came out wearing only a simple white gown. The oil lamp she held out to light her way gleamed off the folds in the sheer fabric formed by her small breasts and curved hips. Her brown hair, glowing with red streaks in the light, cascaded in waves down her shoulders and back. Christophe noticed that her thin shoulders shook slightly.

When he said nothing, she stopped in front of the fireplace. There the light burst through her dressing gown, leaving almost nothing to the imagination. Christophe immediately retreated to the window, disgusted at his body's weak reaction.

"I will ring for someone to come and make another bed for me in the dressing room," he said coolly, keeping her out of his line of sight.

"No!"

The force of the word stunned him into freezing mid-step. He turned to her and within five long strides; he stood in front of her, glaring down into her eyes.

"Do not say no to me," he said in a low, controlled voice. Anger boiled within him at the situation of suddenly owning a slave, but he did not know how to explain something so complicated in Arabic.

"Please, my lord," she whispered, throwing herself at his feet with a whimper. "I am sure I can please you, my lord. Please don't throw me out. Just tell me what I am to do. I will do anything you ask. Please, give me a chance to please you."

"Get up," Christophe said, lowering his voice to what he hoped sounded gentler. "I cannot accept a gift like this. It is not my culture, but your own."

He grasped her arm, noticing at once that she was thinner than a starving child, and pulled her to her feet. The thin fabric of the nightgown ripped, and she shivered in fear at the sound. Again, he cursed his dilemma.

"My lord, although it is not your culture, Master Saed has given me to you and you must take me," she said. Her courage faltered soon enough, though, and she immediately lowered her head. "It would please my master and myself if you would take me as your servant."

Christophe's deep laughter surprised even himself. What a situation he was in.

"Would it please you, my dear, really?" he asked as he lifted her chin to see her expression. "Why are you begging me to do this to you? Do you really want a stranger to strip you of your innocence?"

"I am now yours," she answered stubbornly.

Christophe noticed the anxious set of her shoulders and the ripple in her throat at the words. Fear and longing filled her eyes, as well as determination. Everything about her confounded him.

"I cannot do this to you," he whispered as he let go of her chin.

To his surprise, the girl relaxed her face and rolled back her shoulders. She turned her lips up, and then took a step closer. He stood still as she took another, then another, until she stood just a few inches from him. Slowly she placed her palms on his chest, then leaned in and placed her lips on his mouth.

His traitorous body reacted immediately to that light touch. Almost instantly his breathing became heavy, and the desire to do the unthinkable flashed through him.

No! He could not.

And yet he could not move away. She closed the gap between them, her small breasts now touching his chest, her hands now moving up his neck. Without thinking, he opened his mouth and drew her lips closer with his own. Undoubtedly, she had no experience in the matter. But when his hands closed around her thin hips and his mouth pressed harder against hers, she responded with timid human instinct.

Just as the girl became soft and malleable, Christophe came to his senses. With more force than was needed for her slight frame, he pushed her away. He grimaced when she fell softly into the large pillows and cushions placed around the table.

"I cannot do this," he repeated. The entire situation was too much. Traveling through the desert with a woman would be extremely dangerous. It would be much easier to leave her here.

"Please, sir," she pleaded with him in Berber. "Saed will think there is something wrong with me."

In spite of himself, his eyes roamed the silhouette of her naked form visible beneath the gown, taking in where she was soft and where she was angled from lack of food. From her collarbone up, her skin was dark, but below that, she had paler skin than he. It was not uncommon on the great Barbary Coast to find white slaves. Pirates had sold captured and sold European slaves for centuries, and he had seen many in his years traveling through here. Still, her paleness surprised him.

He looked into her eyes. They were brown, ringed with a bit of green. Like copper, oxidized on the edges. In them, willpower outweighed her fear of the unknown. The fear of her master punishing her was clearly more than the shame of her innocence being taken. Saed was a good man, but he still had to preserve his dignity. Sutton reached out to finger the torn material of her gown and sighed.

"Get dressed, Fatia," he whispered, but before she could protest, he continued. "I will not allow Saed to think you displeased me, but I cannot do this to you. I will sleep at the foot of the bed tonight. In the morning, before the servants come in, I will lie next to you so there will be no rumors."

He turned away from her to give her some semblance of privacy as she gathered the torn gown together. When he dared to turn around again, he found that she had gathered blankets from the large bed and made a small bed next to it.

"I think that might be too small for me," Christophe chuckled. Strangely enough, he had laughed twice already with her.

"You will sleep on the bed, my lord," Fatia mumbled. "It is more certain that I will wake up before another person comes in here than you."

There was no use in arguing with the girl, who had already snuggled deep into the blankets. With a sigh, he lay down on the bed, feeling like a cad. A gentleman would never accept the bed and allow a lady to sleep on the floor. But then again, he was only a gentleman in name—and she was not a lady, but a slave. It didn't seem to be a problem with a solution. Not a suitable solution, at any rate.

Christophe turned on his side. He watched the bundle of blankets rise and fall rhythmically until his eyelids closed and his own breathing slowly matched hers.

"Have a good night, Sutton?" José asked, leaning against a large tree. His attention moved to a slave nearby, packing dye in a trunk, before Christophe could answer. "Drop that, and I will see that you pay for it."

Christophe sighed audibly at his business partner, choosing to ignore the earlier comment altogether.

"What?" José shrugged. "If they do not have someone yelling at them they do not do it correctly. Will you be ready to leave tomorrow morning, or will you be too *busy*?"

The glint in José's eye turned Christophe's stomach. He glanced at the window where he had left Fatia before taking the paperwork from Mohammed.

"Ah, she must be good, then," José laughed, this time in Arabic for Mohammed's benefit. "She kept you up all night and you still want more, eh?"

"*Cállate,* José," Christophe retorted, looking over the numbers one more time. "Where is the aquamarine dye?"

Mohammed's smile faded instantly.

"It will come in this afternoon, my lord," the man said nervously. "Saed sent some of his men to make certain it will arrive."

"Everything should have been here yesterday already. We need it properly packed in straw before we leave," Christophe drawled, stepping closer to the shorter man. "And we leave tomorrow morning. Early."

For a moment Mohammed looked back at him, his eyes shuttering every emotion.

"Yes, my lord. It will be here. Saed was very sorry to learn that it was delayed."

José clapped Christophe on the back with a laugh. "Do not worry, Sutton. It will be here. Already the other dyes and materials are being packed. We should still be able to leave when we wish. You, wrap those tightly and make certain to put much straw around inside the crate. If I find one silver piece missing I will have your hand."

"José," Christophe warned.

"Do not worry, Sutton," José said, flashing his yellow teeth. "I am not so serious. I do not wish to cut off another man's hand. Come, look at this beautiful colt I bought for us from Saed."

"Is he broken in? Perhaps Fatia could ride him."

José's brown eyes turned black at the mention of the girl. Knowing an argument was coming, Christophe turned his nose to the young horse, petting his black neck rhythmically to keep his pulse steady.

"She is coming? With us?"

Christophe tried to smile at his friend, but his attempt faded upon seeing José's pursed lips.

"The desert is no place for a girl. She is just a slave. Leave her here."

"Saed would be insulted. I do not know what will become of her if I leave her here."

"Bah! Nothing will become of her more than her staying in Saed's harems or being married to another slave. It is their plight. It is none of your business, and you should not make it your business."

"She is coming with us."

"Why?" José asked, leaning against the stall door.

"It's already decided, José. I pay you to help me with the journey. I do not pay you for opinions on what I should or should not bring with me."

"Of course, Mr. Sutton," José said with a mocking bow. "But she will not ride this horse. I will keep the stallion for myself. Look, there is Youssef. Let us go talk to Saed."

Saed paced from one argan tree to another, scowling at the goats stuck within the branches.

"Farouk!" he yelled, dashing his whip against the trunk where the loudest goat was bleating. "Get these ridiculous creatures out of this tree! Then make certain all the oil that Sutton wished to buy is properly accounted for and packed. Now!"

"Yes, Master," panted Farouk, out of breath from running a group of goats down the trail. "Simon and Zahir are back, Master. They are coming up the long road."

Saed left Farouk and the bleating goat to look down the road to his mansion. Two slaves were walking towards the houses, immediately changing direction and pace the moment they saw him. Farther down the road came a lumbering wagon, laden down with crates of dyes and other supplies he had ordered the slaves to find.

"A good trip?" Saed asked, grabbing the cypress paper scroll from Zahir.

The slave only gave a slight nod before stepping farther back— an experienced movement. When Saed's eyes dropped to where the price of the dye was written, his whip rose and fell with a crash against the rock, skimming Simon's foot. Simon jumped back in pain but chose to bite his lip instead of crying out.

Saed waited, watching. Simon knew what his master expected. He straightened himself up, shifting his weight evenly onto both feet.

Pleased, Saed turned back to Zahir. "Zahir. An explanation, please."

The tall, dark-skinned man stepped forward, his eyes warily watching Saed's whip. "The French, Master. They burned down a factory in Saida. Master Rachid says if you have the opportunity to sell yours out of the country, to do so. The price to smuggle it out of the country has also gone up. Right there, a note at the bottom, Master Saed."

Saed waved his slaves away from his sight and cursed again—in Berber and Arabic for good measure. Sutton would not like this. Not at all. He must change the price from what they had agreed on. There was a good reason, but Sutton would not like it.

"Salam, brother," Sutton said steadily. Saed looked up to find the Englishman atop a magnificent stallion and Saed's son Amir next to him on his own. "Will you ride with us?"

"Yes, brother," Saed said, his smile not quite staying on his lips. "But I think perhaps we should talk first. I have news from the village. And your dyes, you see?"

Sutton's gaze followed Saed's hand, waving towards the road. Several slaves now worked to carry the crates into a large building to package them correctly for the journey.

"The oil should be finished and packed as well, Sutton," Saed said, his breath quivering, knowing he had to deliver the bad news. "But the price has changed. For the dyes, you see."

Sutton turned his dark blue eyes to him, and Saed resisted the powerful urge to pull back.

"You think I am cheating you. I can see it in your face," Saed said, his voice much calmer than his heart. "But I am not, you see. The slaves came back with the aquamarine dye and with news that prices are soaring everywhere. The French, they are to blame for all of this. They are making these prices rise."

"Yes, I heard that a factory was burned down," Sutton said slowly. "But then I heard that several smuggling ships were also burned. Getting the dye out of the country will become very expensive as well, brother."

Saed stiffened, his hope that Sutton would not be so well informed now snuffed out. High prices were worthless if the dyes sat in his storage houses. Sutton was here, ready to take much of his inventory for a price that was already fair. And yet Saed could not resist negotiating. If the Englishman paid more, Saed would not have to worry about money for a long time.

"I wish things were different these days, my friend," Saed said. "If they were, I would be preparing to leave for Paris soon. My wife would be happier there, buying new dresses and spending time drinking English tea with her cousins, and I would be smoking cigarettes and cigars imported from the Indies while making new business partners. If only the French were more comprehensive of the situation – if only they would simply pay back the debt they owe to Algeria for the wheat that they ate."

Sutton only gave a noncommittal grunt. The silence weighed heavily on Saed's chest as he smoked, looking at his English brother through narrowed eyes until the silence exploded within him.

"I must ask four hundred pounds, brother. I cannot go lower."

Sutton leveled his black gaze at Saed, sending lightning bolts through the smaller man's body.

"That," Sutton said evenly, "is a fortune."

Saed swallowed hard, gathering strength from deep within himself before countering. "It is fair. I cannot sell dye to you at one price and turn around to sell to my other friends and neighbors at another price. That would be deceitful. I must keep it fair to everyone. If I set a low price with you, I will not make it through the winter. If the fighting comes here, I might lose everything."

Sutton made no show of surprise, and yet he said nothing for a moment. He took a long drag on his cigarette and looked at the sky. Saed's stomach lurched with anticipation. Sometimes Sutton's anger was worse when quiet.

Finally, he quoted another price.

"But that is so much lower!" cried Saed, wanting to appear dramatic even though the price was still a bit higher than that in town. "But as you are my esteemed brother and the one who saved my son from drowning, I will close the price with a shake of your hand, as we would have in London."

"As you wish, brother," Sutton said, thrusting his hand out.

Saed's small hand disappeared into the Englishman's large hand, and he instantly regretted suggesting the action at all. He eyed his son, who sat upon his horse, patiently watching them. Saed refused to allow his slight build to deflect from his victory in this negotiation.

"Let us ride a bit, Sutton. It is too hot to stay immobile for too long."

Saed threw himself onto his beautiful gelding with grace, though Sutton did so almost as gracefully with his bulk. Still, he refused to keep comparing himself to the Englishman who was so staunch and cold. He had won, and winning always aroused him. The pinpricks running up and down his body brought him to a different topic.

"How did you find your gift, Sutton?"

"She is a beautiful girl," Sutton said, keeping his stallion slightly ahead of Saed's gelding.

"Ah, yes. She is pretty. But perhaps too pretty to travel the desert in the company of so many men?"

"She will be well cared for," Christophe answered carefully.

Saed looked to the sky, thinking on how to convince his friend to leave the girl behind. "I was merely noting that you have a long journey ahead of you, and wondered if it was imprudent of Nadira to give you such a gift. Perhaps it is a gift more trouble than it is worth. How will you accommodate her during your journey? José made mention of the problems she might cause for Omar. If that is the case, I would not think it an insult if you did not want to take her with you. I do not wish to burden you on your journey."

"She will work. There is no need for me to treat her as a wife when she is a slave," Sutton said evenly, not seeming to notice how his answer affected Saed.

When the slave girl had stepped forward as Nadira's gift, jealousy had instantly penetrated his bones, just as it was doing again at this moment. Nadira knew her place enough to never complain about Saed satisfying his appetite elsewhere, but he now knew that she did not truly love or understand him. If she did, she would have given *him* the slave girl to enjoy, not an Englishman. No matter his saving Youssef. A visit to the harem for Sutton would have been sufficient.

"Sutton, please. Do not try to tell me she is not a burden. I apologize for Nadira's thoughtless gift. We will not be insulted if you must leave her here. She is still very useful to us."

"I have already made arrangements to bring her along with us," Sutton said smoothly. "If she works, she will not be a burden."

"Do you think she is strong enough to work all day in the desert sun, sleeping little at night and affronting, perhaps, attacks from French soldiers or other tribes at the border of Morocco?"

"I expect no trouble, my friend, neither from the French nor from the native tribes on the border," Christophe said with a smile. "It will be good to have someone else working with us, and I am eternally grateful to you for giving me an extra worker— something I would not have understood that I needed until it was too late. Besides, a female's touch at the end of a long day is always welcome, is it not?"

Saed masked his disappointment with indifference. He could not push the subject further. He spurred his horse to a run, trying to bide his time until he could visit his harem.

Chapter Three

THE FIRST RAYS OF sunlight streamed through the windows, waking Rowena to the day she would leave Saed's house. The day before, the Englishman had left her alone in the room; the door locked against her leaving. No one had come except one boy to leave her some food at midday. When Mr. Sutton had come back to the room, he had said nothing except that they would leave in the morning.

Now Rowena jumped out of her makeshift bed and looked about the room. The giant bed was empty.

Panic rose in her throat, but it quickly dissipated at the noise coming from the bath. Realizing she was holding her breath, she let the air out slowly and finished folding the blanket. A smile dared to creep across her lips as the sun pressed its way up beyond the horizon. Today was her last day here. She was leaving half free. For a moment, the urge to hug herself and scream with joy overcame Rowena, but years of being held in slavery soon rebuked her for believing too soon.

"England," she whispered to herself in English, and cringed. The word was foreign to her ears. After five years of only Berber,

Arabic and a little French, Rowena wasn't certain she would ever get her English back properly.

"Are you ready?"

Rowena turned around to face the man she was now unable to see as anything other than the one who was taking her away from slavery.

"Take some food, if you wish," he said, pointing to the tray from the night before. "We won't be stopping to eat for a few hours. There are clean clothes, along with a headscarf, here for you. I will meet you in the courtyard in fifteen minutes. Don't be late."

"Yes, Master."

Once the door shut behind Sutton, Rowena scrambled to stuff food into two different bags: one for her and one for Selma. If she ran quickly, she could be in the slave quarters and back to the courtyard in well under fifteen minutes.

The day had already begun for many in the slave quarters, but Rowena found Selma still there, slowly wrapping a scarf around her hair. She stood when Rowena entered the tent, a strange look washing over her face. They stood separated by several beds, looking at each other, knowing it would be the last time they ever saw each other. Desperate sadness overwhelmed Rowena as she approached her adopted mother.

"I am leaving, Mother. Saed has given me to the Englishman."

Selma nodded. She kept her face stoic, but sadness flashed in her eyes.

"I wish I could take you with me," Rowena told her, practically admitting to her hope that the Englishman would set her free.

Selma took Rowena's hand in her own and squeezed it. "I hope he is kind to you," she said. "But you leave me behind, in your past. I am here with my son and husband."

Time was running out. Rowena must leave the slave quarters now, but something kept her staring at the woman who had taken the place of a nurturer to her during the last three years. Selma's eyes glistened, as though she herself were holding back tears. At the sight, Rowena threw herself towards Selma and enveloped her in a hug.

"Oh, Mother," she whispered, allowing her agony to show.

Selma squeezed Rowena tightly for a second, then pushed her gently away.

"Goodbye, Fatia," she said, her voice deep with sorrow, and then turned away.

Rowena ran out as fast as she could. She couldn't let her guilt keep her from her only chance at escaping.

<hr />

The first day of the journey passed quickly. Fatia had kept the pace well enough, but fell asleep the moment she lay down. Christophe ignored José's quips about her uselessness and endured his friend's ridicule when he covered her with both blankets, leaving himself with nothing.

Without the protection of a tent, it was the early morning cold that woke him more than Fatia stirring close by. He watched her make coffee over the fire embers before greeting her softly. A beautiful pink covered her cheeks, though she said nothing.

The moment was ruined when José awoke.

"Let's go," he growled as he marched off to the privy hole. "We can be at the site by late afternoon."

"No coffee, José?" Christophe asked on his return. "Fatia went to the trouble to make some."

José grabbed the mug, grumbling, as Fatia set about giving each of the camels their grain for the morning. Christophe said nothing, knowing anything he said would be used against her. José had decided not to like Fatia, and his mind wouldn't be changed with any amount of words.

"I will be over there," José declared, indicating no place in particular with a wave of his hand. "Call me when you are ready to go."

Christophe raised his brows at the pink sky, showing the early hour to José, but his business partner only gritted his teeth harder and marched away. Fatia appeared out of nowhere with more coffee and a bowl of bread, cheese, and mutton. She marched behind José, careful to leave the things on a large, fallen tree without saying a word. It was difficult for Christophe not to voice his exasperation when José pointedly ignored Fatia, picking up the food only after she left.

"Sit down," he told her, as they both approached the fire. She obeyed, but when he gathered the breakfast he noticed there was only one other bowl of food. "Aren't you hungry?"

Fatia showed him the bag of two-day-old food she had, as though to say she deserved no more. Christophe's frustration got the best of him, showing in a deep exhalation. "Take some of mine."

"No, Master," Fatia answered.

Christophe breathed slowly through his nose before turning his eyes on the rising sun. Over the last few days he had come to accept that he was taking her to Melilla, where she would automatically become a free woman. A good final solution to the problematic situation he found himself in. What he hadn't considered until now was his responsibility to her once she was free. The way she continued to respond to him, he was starting to wonder if freeing a human from slavery was a bit like sending a domesticated animal back into the wild. The realization that it might take longer than this journey for her to adapt to freedom began to grow alarmingly large within him.

"It is not so easy, is it, Sutton?" José asked. His voice was void of any jest as they saddled the horses together after breakfast. "My sister, she was taken a long time ago. My father tried to buy her back, as his family did for him."

"Where is she now?"

José looked far out into the distance. "She was married and wouldn't come back. So, what do you plan to do with her? Will you take an Algerian slave with you to England?"

"I don't think she is Algerian."

José shrugged, his momentary compassion gone. "Many slaves around here were once from Europe. The Berber pirates are no longer raiding the European port towns, but they do capture the occasional boat. There are many Europeans or half-breeds living in Morocco and Algeria as well. Or perhaps she was sold by her family."

Christophe's stomach flipped. He glanced back at the strange girl, absently petting her camel's leg as though in love with the beast. José was right. The Barbary slave trade had been around for centuries now, with the Berber pirates taking European ships captive and turning all those aboard into slaves in North Africa. The lifespan of a Berber slave was less than ten years if he was kept working on the boat. If they were sold on the slave market, any number of things could happen to them. Some countries, like Spain, organized themselves to pay ransoms and get their people back home. England, though, had a habit of quickly forgetting about its captured people—especially since historically it was poor people living near the coast who were most affected. God forbid the genteel and aristocrats look after their poor countrymen.

Christophe frowned as the caravan set out. Fatia's pretty face was sun-tanned, and her eyes held no more joy of youth, if ever they had, but otherwise she seemed quite young. He remembered the European songs she had sung and her beautiful voice. The Latin songs had been sung without an accent, the words precise and without mistakes. With her pure voice that seemed ready for the opera house, the only explanation could be that she had not been born a slave.

He licked his wind-chapped lips as his horse moved forward, guiding the camels along. The girl might not have been born a slave, but she had been one long enough for the institution to break her.

Christophe stole glances at Fatia throughout the day, but the time passed without a word spoken. She kept her gaze set straight ahead as she walked alongside the camels. When she developed a slight limp, Christophe almost changed places with her. But he knew better than to walk into Omar's camp with a female slave riding on his own horse. Omar wouldn't steal from him, but showing weakness of any sort could bring disaster with Omar's men. Already Christophe was taking a serious risk with so much cargo. If at least two-thirds of the goods made it to England, he would make more in their sales than the whole Parliament made in a year. Still, with the French invading further south and the Algerian people fighting back, he could end up losing his life here in this foreign land. Even before the French had invaded, it had taken a brave man to come here, where trust in Europeans was low.

Looking out into the strange desert spotted with palm trees and ragged, sharp bushes, the familiar heaviness settled in Christophe's chest. He had hoped the sand of Algeria would scrub away the pain of his regret, but it seemed to only uncover it, leaving it vulnerable to the wind. Each time the wind whistled through the trees, sounding just like Dolores' screams of pain, his heart stilled, reminding him vividly that the cry of a baby had never followed hers.

"I'm going to take care of some business," José said.

Before Christophe could say a word, José jumped onto his horse and galloped away. Setting his memories aside, Christophe dismounted and took the leads of the camels. It took much more effort than it was worth to cajole the beasts closer to Fatia, but when he finally did, Christophe was greeted with a low, beautiful melody. As his shadow covered her, she stopped humming and looked away.

During his time working in North Africa, Christophe had seen people treat their slaves worse than animals. There was much cruelty in the world, he knew, but most of it came from people who thought themselves to be better than others. He couldn't understand how, if no one could choose where they were born, one could be so cruel as to believe themselves better than someone born a few seas over, or even a few streets away.

A whistle in the distance drew their attention. Fatia dropped several paces behind him as José and another man appeared atop their horses. Christophe dropped the reins for Fatia to pick up before jogging towards the men.

"Peace be with you, my brother," he called out.

Omar dismounted and grasped Christophe's broad shoulders in his weathered hands. "Peace be with you, my brother!" he laughed.

"It has been so long!"

He kissed Christophe's cheeks, then signaled to a man on another black stallion to take his horse before he wrapped his arm around Christophe's shoulders and laughed again. "How are you, my friend? I have not seen you in a long time."

"Two years is not so long, brother," Christophe said with an answering laugh. "I am well, Omar. Very well."

Omar dipped his head, the weight of his turban bringing his whole torso forward.

"You seem different. Possibly sadder?" he said with narrowed eyes. "You had decided to marry when you last left us. She did not accept?"

Christophe jerked his head back slightly. The usual haunting ache again drenched him.

"She passed on, brother," was all he felt able to say.

"I am sorry to hear it," Omar said, clapping Christophe on the back twice. "Some women get into our hearts."

Dolores had never had his heart, but Christophe didn't wish to discuss her with Omar.

"And your cousin, Albert? I enjoyed his humor when he came with you long ago."

Once again, his heart stilled.

"Also passed on, brother," he said. Albert and he had come to North Africa together to set up business and traveled through the desert and its towns with Omar for almost a year before going on to Spain to connect their business with the continent. "How is your family doing, Omar? Your wife and sons?" Christophe added, keeping his face clear of emotion with great effort.

"They are well," Omar said, his chest puffing with pride. "My oldest is almost a man now. I think the next time we meet, he will be with us. That is a lot of cargo, my brother." His eyes were serious. "Much more than you took the last time. And this time there is a blockade. It is even more dangerous than usual."

"Few would attempt to steal from you, Omar."

"You flatter me, Christophe, but things have changed a bit since the blockade. Many are angry at the French and want to alienate Algeria from any European grasp. They blockade us when it is they who owe us money!"

"I admit that I do not understand their behavior."

"Typical Englishman. I am sorry, my brother, we will not speak more of the politics tonight. Tonight, we will celebrate!"

Christophe paused for a moment and glanced behind to where Fatia and the camels awaited instructions. Omar's man held his master's reins while openly gaping at Fatia. Omar also looked, his curiosity piqued.

"You are taking a slave back with you this time?" José snorted and swore in Spanish. "Perhaps you are looking for a wife here in Algeria? You do not like those white English ladies? Yes—I think I once said you were best suited for one of our beautiful women."

Christophe smiled wryly. "A gift from Saed for saving his boy from drowning."

"I heard rumors of your heroic rescue, but I heard nothing about the prize. It is starting to make sense, then." Omar winked at José.

"What does?" asked José.

"An old friend is working with me. He offered his services just yesterday."

"Who?"

"Yacine," Omar said.

Christophe drew back from the conversation, saying nothing. Yacine never offered anything for free, at least not in Christophe's experience. Something had been set in motion, and he would need to find out what.

With grim determination, he threw himself back onto his horse and signaled Omar and Fatia to folow him into camp.

Chapter Four

THE CAMPSITE WAS IN the enclave of a rocky hillside. Upon arriving, Rowena stood apart from the camels, thinking it better to be out of sight than in the way. Thankfully, the men took no notice of her as they worked.

When the cargo was taken from the camels and the men disappeared, Rowena dared to creep through the campsite. She was hoping to find Sutton, who had left with Omar almost immediately, leaving her alone to tend to the tent. She pulled her hijab across her face as men stopped to leer at her. Though few dared to say anything, nor did they bother to move out of her way: it was she who had to move in the other direction. The freedom she had tasted over the last few days was gone now, replaced by the fear that had kept her company for the last five years.

Rowena faded behind the trees for a time, watching the movement of the camp as an outsider. Every so often, a man from atop the hill gave a signal to another below. Rowena watched over them, trying to figure out their job, but could only assume they were looking out for bandits or thieves. As she continued on, she found more men sitting around a blazing campfire in the center of a semi-circle of six tents. Near a tree facing east, three men stood at the head of prayer rugs, bowing and kneeling in reverence. All of them held guns except those who were praying.

Rowena felt suddenly powerless. If Sutton turned out to be different from what she hoped, she would never escape from this camp. They would shoot her first... which would be more desirable than living in the desert on her own or being a slave to this group of men.

There was no sign of Sutton anywhere, which increased her nervousness. A column of smoke and the smell of roasted lamb floated through the air, apparently coming from behind the largest tent a few meters away. Thinking she might find women as well as food, Rowena crept out of her hiding spot to make her way there. But when she rounded the edge of the tent, she froze. There were no women, just three men. One half-dressed, drying his clothes, one cooking bread on the fire, and another who grabbed her arm before she could back away.

"Salam, sister," the man said, only loud enough for Rowena to hear. His hot breath blew into her ear.

"Salam."

The man loosened his grip, but kept his fingers on the silver band around her wrist that no one had yet bothered to take off.

"A slave from Brother Saed's house. How did you get out?" he teased. "Perhaps you escaped?"

"Master Saed sent me with the Englishman to work for him," Rowena answered in Berber.

The man jerked his head up and leered at her, a strange twinkle in his black eyes. "A Christian slave! This is a surprise. What is your name?"

"Fatia."

"Fatia... hmm. I am Yacine. So, Saed thought it prudent to send you on a dangerous trip through the mountains? Very strange. How will you get home afterward? Perhaps I can escort you."

The man smacked his lips together and laughed. The sound reminded Rowena of the large dog her second master, Fellahi, had trained to bite slaves directly in the neck on command. Fellahi had coddled that dog as anyone else would have a little child. The unnatural affection had surprised no one, though. Fellahi only loved things willing to hurt people as much as he was.

Suddenly, Yacine's hands took her arm in a painful grip. He yanked her farther into the trees so fast that her feet could not keep up.

"Do not make a sound, Fatia. If you do, I will snap your neck and leave you for the animals to feed on."

She stumbled in terror, her body lurching to the ground. Yacine grabbed her by her hijab and hair with a grunt of frustration. The bones in her hips dragged against rough ground, hitting several small rocks even as she tried to catch her feet on something solid. Seeing her attempt, Yacine yanked her to the right, where her breasts caught on a large root. The pain of the rope-like root pulling at her flesh brought tears to her eyes, but Rowena refused to cry out. Finally, Yacine slowed down. Before she could stand, he hauled her up and pressed her face against the large boulder.

Panting from fear and effort, Rowena narrowed her eyes against the threat of fainting. It took some time to calm her heart and even longer for her eyes to adjust to the dark. There was no one else nearby. No one to cry out to. No escape.

"What are you trying to look at, eh?"

Rowena opened her mouth quickly as he pushed her face harder into the boulder to make a small space for her to breathe. The rough surface of the boulder scraped against her lips and cheeks. The metallic smell of blood filled her nose.

There was little time to think about that. The sound of fabric being sliced with a knife filled the air. Rowena gulped in fear as her skin was exposed to the desert night, but still refused to make a sound. He paused for a moment before slashing painfully several times across her thighs. Warm blood trickled down her skin, but it did not seem enough for Yacine. He tipped the end of the blade into the flesh of her buttocks until she whimpered. He grunted his approval, then pushed his fingers into her mouth.

"You think this is the first time I do this? Girl, you do not know. I have perfected this trick from the time I was fifteen. You are stupid enough to think you might get away, but I tell you, you will not. No woman has ever escaped my grasp until I have released her."

His excitement oozed over her, mixing with her revulsion. His fingers tasted of dirt, sweat, and salted lamb in her mouth. She could not stop the shudder thundering through her body. She knew he felt it just as keenly as she did, using the moment to grind his hips into her backside. Rowena pushed her right shoulder back hard, but Yacine only laughed. The sound swirled in her stomach, threatening to release its contents.

"You are an idiotic girl," Yacine whispered, his stale breath covering her face. When she gagged involuntarily, he grabbed a fistful of hair, pulled her head back and smashed it back against the boulder.

Pain shot up through her temples, her eyes exploding with stars. When a groan escaped her throat, the sound only caused her more pain. Yacine slapped the back of her head, and Rowena again gagged. Her stomach settled by sheer will, but for a moment the world went black. A strange wave of relief swept over her. If this was to be her fate, she would rather it happen in darkness.

But full darkness didn't come. Instead, the stars left her vision and the world around her came into focus again. Yacine swore vividly in Berber, and Rowena stiffened. His deep, wicked laugh followed.

"Good to see you didn't hit your head too hard," he whispered. "It isn't enjoyable if I can't feel you squirm underneath me."

Without a sound, Yacine thrust his fist into the center of her. Rowena screamed, but no one heard her. His other hand was back in her mouth to muffle any sound.

"Try to scream again, and I will cut out your tongue."

Tears filled her eyes against her will. She bit her lip until blood came to focus her pain away from Yacine and his feverish hands. She did not wish to give up, but even the strength being a laundry slave had given her was not enough to fight him off.

Yacine drew his hand away, relaxing his grip on her as he gathered up his robes. Rowena knew what would come next. Frantic to escape, she tried to force her mind to focus and not panic.

The opportunity came when a piercing whistle blew from above. Two watchmen yelled out, and a gunshot pierced the desert night. Yacine froze. When a shout came from close behind them, he turned towards it, his hold on Rowena slackening.

Without thinking another second, Rowena tucked her body into a ball and rolled away, her body bruising badly against every stone and root in the path. Yacine cursed behind her, but just as quickly Rowena jumped up and darted through the trees. Footsteps pounded the ground a few yards back. Knowing he would be faster than her, she ran blindly through the camp, looking for any haven amongst the startled men scattered about.

When a strong arm grabbed her suddenly and jerked her to the side, Rowena screamed. But instead of acrid breath mixed with sweat and tobacco, she smelled bergamot and camel.

"Where have you been?" Sutton demanded, reeling away from her screams. "Why the devil are you screaming in my ear? Omar's men captured a man near our camp who they suspect came to rob us. If there is a band of thieves nearby, we need to know where everyone is. You need to stay close by."

"Ye-yes, Master," Rowena whispered, her limbs shaking.

"Stay inside here. I'll be back later."

"No! Take me with you."

Sutton drew back, and Rowena instantly regretted her tone. If she angered him, he might leave her with Omar. With Yacine. She watched his face tighten, but when José appeared, Sutton only muttered under his breath in exasperation.

"I don't have time for this. Stay in the tent and don't leave."

Sutton pushed her inside the tent, although Rowena noticed that he made certain not to let her fall. She peeked through the crack in the tent, relieved to see no one coming from where she had escaped. Silently she stepped back into the interior, finding herself in almost full darkness. One lantern with little oil remaining was the only light. She reached out with shaking hands to fill it, but then changed her mind. Yacine was still in the camp. While she didn't believe him stupid enough to enter this tent, she did not wish to test her faith.

She fumbled blindly about through the piles of rugs and small crates, trying to find her sleeping mat, but her energy gave out before she found it. Rowena collapsed into a weary heap on the dirt floor. Alone in the dark, she pulled her hijab off her head and used it to cover her shaking body, reminding herself once again that she wasn't safe anywhere.

———————

They traveled on the next day in staggered groups. Christophe noticed that Fatia was limping, but each time he asked her about it, she replied that she was fine. The last time José overheard him and went away grumbling about traveling with women. With each passing hour, Fatia seemed to crumble within herself, sidling up to the camel as much as she could. With José's short temper and Fatia seemingly more edgy than normal, Christophe decided it best to leave them both alone.

One afternoon, three days into their journey with Omar, dark clouds rolled over their heads. Quickly the men pitched tents, then unloaded the dyes and perfumes before securing the boxes with precious metals. Once everything was protected from the rain, Christophe pushed back the opening of his tent where he had left Fatia alone earlier. No matter how much the men teased him, Christophe insisted she sleep in his tent, though she always squeezed herself between boxes in order to place herself as far away from him as possible.

Where she had once been cordial and offered some small talk, Fatia now tiptoed about, as though sinking deeper into slavery rather than escaping it. Something compelled him to try to earn her trust. After all, he had to find a solution to the problem of what to do with her once in Melilla. And for that, he preferred her input.

With the sun blocked by the dark, menacing clouds, Christophe found the tent pitch black upon entering. Though crammed with boxes and crates, the space held an eerie feeling of emptiness. He hastily held the lantern up higher to maneuver his way through the piles of rugs and small crates, finally finding Fatia asleep on the cold, hard ground.

The weak lantern light gleamed over her dusty hair, which lay in tangles around her face. She did not wake with the light, but the twitching of her arms and torso told him that her sleep was not peaceful. When he knelt over her, she gave a small whimper and her body jerked violently, as though fighting someone in her dreams. Christophe instinctively caressed away a strand of hair from her face, but the touch didn't seem to soothe her. She looked so small and young as she slept that he couldn't help pulling her closer to him.

He could feel her cold flesh through the thin muslin. She stirred again, her legs jerking in her dreams, and a small cry escaping her mouth. Instead of settling back into blankness, Fatia's face contorted with fear. The evident suffering inside her broke his heart, pushing him to the limits of his compassion. He pulled her closer against his chest, humming softly, and yet still she struggled against her dreams.

"Come now, Fatia, you must relax," he murmured, remembering the way his mother would reassure him when he had hurt himself as a small boy. "The rain will start soon, which is a soothing sound, and I am quite tired myself. You are safe here. Settle down and get your rest so I can get mine."

He spoke to her about the unloading and the men he had observed on Omar's team. He told her about his sister and friend being married and his inability to stop working so much. Christophe spoke with Fatia against his chest until his throat was dry and his back ached from sitting without any support.

When he finally fell silent, Fatia lay limp and relaxed in his arms. Christophe stood up with her in his arms then, and took her to his sleeping mat. The rain was now beating hard against the tent, bringing with it a drop in temperature. While he wanted to respect her boundaries, he wasn't about to allow her to catch a chill. They would be much warmer if they slept side-by-side tonight.

Once he had laid her down, Christophe raised the lantern to assure himself that she was comfortable. Her nightgown had risen up her legs, and he couldn't help staring at her smooth calves and her strong, white thighs. He was ashamed of himself for looking so long as she slept, but just as he was reprimanding himself, Fatia stirred again. There, along the inside of her thighs, were long slashes. Clean, as though made by a knife. And fresh.

Remembering her screams the first night as she wildly ran through the camp, his blood turned cold.

Christophe rocked back on his heels, then cursed in every language he knew. Someone had assaulted her, and she had not bothered to tell him. Certainly she had seemed fearful that night, but he had convinced himself it was about the thief they had caught and shot. A small part of him had suspected there was more to the story, but found it easier not to ask.

He was certain of who the man was. Only Yacine was stupid enough to assault a woman who was legally his.

When Fatia stirred again, Christophe quietly took a camel-hair blanket from a nearby crate and lay next to her. An overwhelming urge to pull her close rose within him, but he reasoned that was simply because she was a woman he had failed to protect.

If he could give her nothing else, he should at least give her his protection. Strange emotions swirled within him as he succumbed to the need to hold her. Gently he wrapped his arms around her shaking body; careful not to wake her, he pulled her against his chest and squeezed until her shaking turned into a staggered sigh.

Within minutes she fell into a deeper slumber and he soon followed, refusing to take notice of how nicely she fit in his arms.

The sound of someone entering the tent awoke Christophe from a fitful slumber; his rifle swiftly caught in his right hand. He had dreamt that Fatia's assailant was foolish enough to come to his tent and was disappointed to find it was not so. Instead of the aggressor, he faced the startled gaze of Fatia herself.

"Where have you been?"

"Getting you some food."

Her answer was brief and spoken into the ground. She set the bowl of meat and rice on a crate near Christophe, then retreated to the furthest corner with her own smaller bowl of food.

"What are you doing?" he asked. "Come here and sit with me."

Fatia obediently came nearer to him. Instead of joining him in using the crate as a table, she balanced the food on her knees. When she sat, Christophe saw where the fabric was jagged near her thighs.

"What happened to your robes?" he asked, motioning to her leg, showing through the cut fabric.

She flushed. "I fell, my lord."

"You—fell?"

She still did not trust him as someone who would care for her. It was not enough that he had brought her out of Saed's house. She still believed he might leave her somewhere.

"A knife cut those," he insisted.

As she looked up, her hijab fell to one side, exposing her hair and a smear of dirt on her cheek. The effect was somehow endearing and almost beautiful.

"Do not worry about me."

"I worry about you because you are a woman," Christophe said firmly.

He stood to rummage through a crate before triumphantly holding up another pair of pantaloons. When he held them out to her, Fatia took off the cut ones without waiting for him to turn around. The reaction his body wished to have at the sight of her bare legs took away all his pride at having been so honorable with her thus far.

He ate his meal quickly, grateful when her legs were once again covered with the dark red cotton.

***

"Have a good night, Sutton?" asked a deep voice as Christophe made his way to the small creek.

Christophe turned to find Yacine leaning against a tree. His lips curled up into a dark smile when their eyes met.

"Will you be leaving today, Yacine?" Christophe asked.

"It depends."

"On what?"

Yacine pushed himself away from the tree. Christophe eyed the knife he flicked between his fingers. He hoisted his rifle higher, pointing it directly at Yacine to make sure the other man saw it.

"I wish to make you an offer for the girl. You have had your fun. Now let someone else have theirs."

"She is not for sale."

"Saed wants her back, and she is slowing you down."

"She is not for sale," Christophe repeated.

"Perhaps she wants to go back to the comforts of her old home. Perhaps one morning you will find that she has run away, disappearing like smoke in the air. Better to make money than to just lose her, no?"

Before he could rationalize with himself, Christophe found that Yacine was dangling off the ground.

"If I find you touching her, even looking in her direction, I will leave you for the vultures. It would be best for you to leave, Yacine. Today."

It wasn't until Yacine fell to the ground that his smile finally vanished from his face.

Chapter Five

ROWENA'S HEAD SPUN. THE sun's rays were so hot, and her thin hijab did little to protect her from it. Ten days had passed since leaving Saed's house and every day she became more a part of the desert. A paste of sweat mixed with the powdery sand covered her body beneath her clothes. The smell of camel mingled with dirt and hot flesh overwhelmed her nose. She had never desired a bath so much in her life. Two days of rain had only made things worse by adding water to the dirt in her clothes until she looked as though dressed in mud.

A timid breeze drifted by, but it wasn't enough to dry the sweat that rolled down her face. Her stomach churned in protest against the brutal sun, her eyes closed against the pounding in her temples. Even as an outdoor slave, she had never experienced the sun like this. Washing laundry had always meant she was somewhere near water, usually under the shade of trees, for most of the day. Rowena sighed at the memories of her last home, then shook her head in disgust. As though a slave could call anywhere home.

Anxiety and bile rising in her, she slowly slid from the camel. Two days ago she had been so grateful to ride the beast, but right now she needed the shade from Betsy's giant hump.

Up ahead, Sutton surveyed the area. He sat straight and handsome on his stallion, his burnous blowing behind him as he galloped back towards the group of camels. He looked much like a desert pirate—nothing like a proper Englishman. As he neared the other men, Sutton pulled the strap connected to his shotgun over his head and threw it to José, who scowled while the others laughed.

Rowena had lost any possibility of humor in the heat. She found it impossible to spend any energy at all, much less in laughter. It took every fibre in her being to just keep moving. Even when her eyes crossed, she refused to stop walking.

"The woman is going to faint."

"How many steps? Two dinars say she falls in twenty steps."

"Fifteen!"

"Thirty!"

Laughter followed the raucous betting, but Rowena ignored all of it. She gripped the leather strap on the camel and gritted her teeth. Fainting would show her as weak.

"Are you not faring well?" asked a gentle voice above her.

Slowly, Rowena turned and dared to look up, only to find her nose but a foot away from the belly of Sutton's black stallion.

"Come," Sutton murmured in Berber, reaching down to her. "Come up and ride with me. Ghazaouet is after the ridge of that mountain there. Would you like to see it?"

Rowena's heart skipped as she raised her calloused hand to his. His fingers glided down to her forearm and bicep, gripping her firmly. She tried to hold on just as tightly to him, but found she could barely get her hand around the flexed muscles of his arms. It did not matter. Sutton plucked her up as though she were a small child and carefully placed her on the horse in front of him.

With a click of his tongue, the huge stallion broke into a gallop, reaching a speed Rowena couldn't ever remember traveling at before. Yet instead of being afraid, she reveled in the feeling of flying through the world. Held tightly in Sutton's arms, she had no fear for the first time in years. Rowena caught herself wanting to relax back into his strong shoulders and close her eyes, to soak in the feeling of freedom from the hot wind whipping into her hijab, drying her sweat from the cloth.

Sutton pulled back on the reins, encouraging the stallion to slow down.

"Master!" Rowena shrieked as her body slipped at the change of pace.

Before the cry was finished, Sutton had his arm around her middle, setting her to rights again.

"Be careful," he murmured, his low voice vibrating in her ear.

A cool shiver shimmied down her spine. "Thank you." Quickly, she turned from him.

"See? That is Ghazaouet. We will board the ship Omar has arranged for us and sail during the night to Melilla."

"Tonight? We will sail?"

"Does that please you?" he asked. His lips spread into a smile at her nod.

They said nothing more as Christophe galloped his stallion back to the other men.

"*No quiero interumpir,* Sutton," José said, his sneer pushing Rowena back into the shadows, wishing she could hide. "We need to get the cargo down the mountainside. Perhaps the girl is done playing?"

Sutton tightened his hand on her middle as Rowena moved to slip down, keeping her in place between the two of them.

"I will take those two camels, and Fatia will help me. Zambia will take the horses down. You can help the two other men with the four that are left," he said.

"*Por supuesto*, Sutton. We will see you at the camp."

Without waiting for a reply, José pulled his reins hard and galloped off, circling the camels before edging them towards the path. Rowena turned to Sutton and gave a weak smile before slipping down the horse's flanks to the sand.

Sutton handed the horse to Zambia before grabbing hold of the most stubborn camel and pulling hard on the reins. The animal took one begrudging step, then stopped. Rowena smiled, coaxing her animal along with a soft song, the notes rising and falling at a rhythmic pace. Soon the other camel followed as she continued singing. She was the Pied Piper of Hamelin, with the camels following her voice.

When the song ended, the first camel halted, sending Sutton colliding into the smelly beast. The oaths that tumbled from his mouth should have made her blush, but laughter bubbled out of her. He seemed bewildered at the sound, staring wide-eyed at her like a disheveled boy.

"You are not used to working with those who have a mind of their own?" she asked.

"No." He smiled slowly, revealing his teeth. "Most of the animals I work with obey my commands."

"A camel follows no one's bidding," she said, more laughter flowing out of her.

He smiled more broadly now.

"Give her to me, and you take this one. She is sweet."

"Perhaps you should continue singing," he suggested, tugging his animal down the narrow path.

Rowena began a chant she had learned from Saed's herders. The melodic words echoed down the small mountainside as they led the camels down. The path was narrow but easy enough, and for an hour they twisted steadily down the mountainside. Rowena sang until her throat was as dry as the desert she walked in. When she stopped to swallow against the discomfort, the camels again stopped, and English curses followed.

"Take this," Sutton said, handing his flask to her from around the second camel. "I'm sorry to ask it of you, but it seems if you do not sing this beast will not continue. I fear she is in love with you."

Rowena smiled and drank the last of his warm tea, the honey in the mixture soothing her throat.

"Come then," she murmured to the animals whose smell permeated her. "Let's be on our way."

The boat from Ghazaouet was old and cumbersome. Rowena tried her best to be of some use as José and Sutton loaded the cargo onto the boat with the other sailors, but finally one young sailor with tattoos scattered across his chest pushed her forcefully aside. She tumbled to the deck before hitting the corners of some of the loaded cargo.

No one bothered to say anything to her; no one bothered to help. Sutton was off the boat, barking commands, and the sailors only cared about doing their work. Some were probably slaves themselves, Rowena noted as she pushed herself back into the dark corner between the cargo boxes. For over an hour she hid there until a small boy popped his head in her space. His toothless grin

made her feel safe enough to come out, though he tried to act
sternly when he spoke to her in a strange language. When she
didn't reply, he switched to Arabic.

"Come, come. Come with me," he said, his demeanor suddenly
harried. "It took me a long time to find you, but then I thought,
where would I go? And so, I remembered where you were in the
beginning and knew where you went. You see? Now, you are to go
to Master Sutton's room. He does not trust the other sailors with a
woman. No, sailors do not like women below. They are bad luck.
This is what Arthur explained to me when I asked why this man
Sutton does not trust us with his slave. You are bad luck, so you
will sleep with this man Sutton. Yes? Let's go. You must come
faster."

He glided with ease through the labyrinth of the ship's belly,
but Rowena had trouble keeping up. More than once the rocking
threw her against the wall.

"Are we sailing now?"

"Yes, yes, we are pushing against the beach. You know this? I do
not know the word in Arabic. You are too stiff to be a sailor. This
is why you fall. Get up, now. I do not have time to wait for you. I
have much work to finish. Come, right here. Yes, here. This is your
room."

Before Rowena could see the room in its entirety, the boy
pushed her in and closed the door with an abrupt click. She cried
out, banging her hands against the door.

"You are bad luck. You stay here. I will bring you dinner soon.
Calm yourself, sister. You are okay. Just do not bring bad luck. We
have three days to sail. I will see you soon."

The ship threw her each time she tried to stand. Once against
the chair, then against the wardrobe, and yet another time straight

onto the floor. That was when she gave up and crawled to the bed.

Before she reached it, Rowena found her stomach cramping and lurching. The pain swept memories of her former sailing trips to the forefront of her thoughts. There had been a reason she had stayed up top for most of the trips, and why her father had demanded a room with a window, no matter how small. When she could no longer control her stomach, Rowena was grateful to find a large bucket clean of any foul odors. When it was full, she banged on the door, but with her body in cold distress and her stomach threatening to revolt again, she knew her cries were too weak. Not wishing to dirty the bed with her filth, Rowena lay down between the wardrobe and desk, wedging herself in tightly. When the tip and tilt of the ship finally stilled, she fell into a restless sleep until awoken by the boy and an old man murmuring over her. Rowena tried to rouse herself when she saw them, but couldn't. She quickly found herself back in a fitful slumber.

In her dreams, Sutton gave commands, but she was too weak to change her position. When she awoke again, the door was open and an old man sat cross-legged on the floor next to her.

"You're awake," he murmured in Arabic. "I have tea for you."

Rowena sat up and took it with shaking hands.

"The sea is not easy for all," the old man said, tipping her cup to get more tea into her. "I bring you a bath. I help you."

"No," Rowena answered quickly.

"Your master tell me to help you. I eunuch, see? I help many women at my old master's palace."

The old man rose gracefully, without the need to support himself. At his clapping, the boy from before brought in a small tub before disappearing and coming back with a folded green dress.

"Ok, you go now," the old man told the boy, who was only too happy to leave her bad-luck presence. Then he turned back to Rowena. "And now you get clean from bad smell."

⚓

Christophe slowly opened the door to the room he occupied with Fatia. Last night, the acrid smell of vomit had almost sent him running to the deck. Drinking with Captain Rhemi had been a bad idea for several reasons—one being unable to keep the contents of his dinner in his stomach, and another that it had kept him from taking care of Fatia. Tonight, he had made certain not to consume too much scotch, something his head thanked him for. His nostrils were thankful for old Jeremiah, who had somehow eradicated the stench of camel and stomach bile and replaced it with a faint scent of cedar.

When his eyes adjusted to the semi-darkness, he found Rowena lying across the bed, tightly lined up with the wall. Jeremiah had dressed her in a green linen dress that Christophe had bought from a port merchant before sailing. The dress covered her feet and looked three sizes too big for her in the waist, but it was a relief to see her slave clothes gone. Sitting on the floor cushions, Christophe couldn't stop watching the gentle way her chest lifted with each breath as he took off his shoes.

A gentleman would look away. A gentleman would retire somewhere else and not stay where he was finding great temptation.

But he was not a gentleman.

Without thinking more, he placed himself on the bed and took one of her feet in his hands. Slowly, he pulled off the cotton stocking and found the heat of her bare skin in his hands overwhelming. Smells of orange blossom wafted to his nose. A strange urge to kiss the foot rose in him, though he didn't act on it. Against his better judgment, Christophe ran his fingers across the line that separated her white calf from the browned ankle. The skin was dry beneath his fingers, the sides of her feet rough, but none of that bothered him.

When his fingers touched the tops of her toes, Fatia's foot jerked from his grasp. He looked up to find her arms flailing, her eyes wild.

"Stop!" she cried out. "Leave me!"

Fatia tried to yank her foot free, but he held fast. Holding her feet fully now, he realized there was something more to them than just dry, worn skin; the sensation was more like cobblestone against his palms. She could not stop him from turning her foot to the light of the candle, revealing bamboo whipping scars.

Curses in all languages escaped him as Christophe ran his fingers over the scars. The tradition of whipping a slave's feet with bamboo rods was a well-known discipline against slaves in Northern Africa. Unfortunately, he had witnessed it before. Staying innocent from these things was impossible when working on the Dark Continent. The glaring reality started to sink in. These marks told a story of pain and hardship. Turning his attention to her scared eyes, he wondered how many more marks were on Fatia's heart and soul.

Instead of letting go as she wished him to, Christophe brought her foot to his lips and kissed the raised lines. Fatia winced visibly, avoiding his gaze as she continued to pull away.

"Fatia, come here," he instructed in a low voice, pulling her foot past him until the two of them were almost intertwined. His fingers skimmed over the exposed skin at her neck and chest to soothe her. Christophe smiled, though his soul reminded him she didn't deserve to be left ruined by an Englishman.

And yet, here in the darkness, the devil voice in his head could almost rationalize taking her to his bed. She deserved to know she was beautiful and desirable, something every woman wished to be. The devil voice grew louder as his fingers plunged into her hair, tugging gently at the curls that fell against her back. Christophe dipped his head towards her neck and gently grazed her skin with his lips. Almond blossoms. Gone was the smell of sweat and camel, but the fresh air still lingered in her hair. When his lips gently sucked at the skin behind her ear, Fatia gasped, sending a surge of urgency through him that Christophe forced himself to ignore.

"Fatia, I don't know how I can leave you. I wish I could bring you back with me to England," he whispered in English, stroking her cheek. "Your nearness gives me a strange comfort."

Fatia shyly kissed the palm of his hand in response.

"You are beautiful," he declared in Arabic.

She slowly shook her head.

To show his sincerity, Christophe lowered his lips to hers in a sweeping kiss. She responded shyly at first, slowly pressing herself forward, opening her lips when he imparted pressure.

A low gasp escaped her when his fingers dared to encircle the side of her breast. Her own fingers worked slow magic against his scalp, digging soothingly into the depths of his long hair. From her lips, he moved up towards her earlobes, where he sucked softly against the sensitive skin.

"Say 'no', Fatia," he pleaded. "Turn away from me."

Fatia pulled away slightly, and he braced himself for her departure, holding his breath to keep his pride and heart from shattering. "*Na'am.*"

Her answer caught the attention of his entire body. 'Yes.' Yes, she was willing. And yet he laughed grimly at her answer. He could see the consequences of his terrible actions even as hurt clouded her eyes.

"I do not laugh at you," he told her, kissing her gently. "It is just that you somehow make me happy. But please, Fatia, you must say no. I would make love to you all night, but there are reasons not to leave you in Melilla ruined by an Englishman. That is why I will say no."

"You could take me with you," she said, her voice so quiet he almost thought he imagined the words.

"Lie down and we will sleep. Tomorrow we arrive in Melilla."

Without another word, Fatia tucked herself under his arm and promptly fell asleep, though he took much longer to find rest.

Just as he was finally nearing sleep, a knock on the door indicated they were approaching land. As Fatia slept, Christophe arranged for José to take her to the house in Melilla when they docked. He would go directly to his office, to convince himself of all the reasons he could not and should not make a former slave from Algeria his wife.

Chapter Six

LONG AFTER SUNRISE ON her second day in Melilla, Rowena lay in a feather bed with no intention of getting out until forced to. She was in Melilla, a Spanish-owned city to the north of Morocco—and according to Spanish laws, she was now a free person. Her journey to freedom was at an end.

The most glorious feeling rose within her at the concept. Instead of getting up to do the bidding of a master, Rowena lay back and allowed her mind to roam where it wished. As she stared at the discolored ceiling of Sutton's house, memories of the past whirled around her.

She spent the morning thinking about her old house in Algeria, trying to remember each inch of the place. When it proved impossible, she moved on to the people who had been important to her there. First there was Sally, who had never picked up her feet but shuffled about, always keeping her wrinkled and spotted face looking at the floor. It was Sally who had spoken to Rowena in Berber, the language that had connected her with Selma and the other slaves at Saed's. While there were many times Sally's chiding had annoyed her as a child, Rowena now smiled at the warm memory.

What erased her smile was the memory of the woman's real name. She had called her 'Sally' because she couldn't be bothered to learn her real name. Her childish thoughtlessness made her flush in shame.

Rowena pushed aside the appalling memory and looked about the room she was now in, trying to imagine Sally being there. She would have scolded her for staying in bed for so long, or for not having eaten much of her breakfast. Rowena pretended to be seventeen again as she followed the imaginary Sally's shuffling feet to the dresser and into the washroom.

Instinctively, Rowena curled her toes under her worn-down, scarred feet. Each night, after hours of dance practice or long walks through the gardens, Sally had rubbed cream on her feet to keep them soft. Rowena remembered whimpering in pain at the blisters, but they had been nothing compared to the pain she had experienced walking on whipped or knotted skin. Now that her feet were no longer swathed in silk slippers but browned, tough and prone to aching, she assumed Sally had suffered the same cane whippings as her, causing her own feet to become deformed.

Sally, Cook Constantine, and almost all the servants who had worked at the house in Algeria had been slaves. The moment he had bought them, her father had set them free, preferring to have servants working for him. Rowena had taken pride in her father not holding slaves, even before she knew what 'abolitionist' meant. Yet, even with that pride in her father, she had never once thought to ask those who worked for him about their former lives. Her life absorbed most of her day, leaving her no room to wonder where Cook Constantine had learned to make dishes with Italian names, or where Aron had learned English.

"*Madame, bonjour*," a busty woman greeted Rowena, bursting into her room. Behind her waltzed in two other girls dressed in silk walking gowns, their hair woven tightly at the sides before ending in identical buns at the top. "*Je suis Madame Benevault. La styliste.*"

The three women exchanged quick conversation in French as Rowena cringed in agony. The French words dripped like thick molasses in her memory. She understood some of the conversation but couldn't find the vocabulary to respond. Her tongue and lips refused to move into any response other than, "*Salam.*"

Madame Benevault raised her left eyebrow with a sigh. Her eyes swept over Rowena's body before returning to her face.

"New clothes. *Ropa? Vêtements?*" Madame Benevault said. "You understand? Mister Sutton told me to come here today. He did not tell you?"

"Ye-yes," Rowena stammered, standing still as the French woman circled her, stepping back occasionally to look critically at one aspect of her body or another. The night before one servant, Maria, had said something about clothes, but Rowena hadn't paid much attention. She hadn't thought for a moment that the person would have anything to do with her. She'd assumed Maria enjoyed talking while working.

As the two young ladies took her measurements and chatted to each other from either side of her, Rowena watched them through the mirror, trying her best to stay still. The moment reminded her of the Roussier twins getting measured for their gowns while she picked up their room, tidied their beds, and scrubbed out the tubs. They had been the daughters of her first owner, Madame Roussier.

The one who had conspired to kidnap Rowena as revenge against her father.

Madame Roussier's grinning face flashed in her memory, and instinctively, she gagged. The movement jerked her body violently away from the girls with their tapes and pins. Within a second, the one with blue eyes held out a clean pot for her to vomit in, but Rowena breathed in shakily and straightened back up. She wouldn't vomit. She had done enough of that during the days after becoming a slave.

From that moment, there was silence until the time came for Rowena to remove her chemise. The mirror reflected the look of horror in the blue-eyed girl's face when she saw Rowena's naked back. The one with brown eyes covered her gasp with her hand, but recovered quicker than her workmate. Madame Benevault also stared. Rowena could have turned around to see for herself, but the others' expressions gave her an answer to the question she had always had. Her marks alone may well make her unsuitable for marriage.

The still room jumped into action when Madame Benevault snapped her fingers. The girls noted down Rowena's measurements, held up fabric, and exchanged silent, meaningful glances. Madame Benevault did not bother to reprimand them. She was too busy sketching out new dresses, her eyes glistening with pride as she showed them to Rowena.

"In one week, you come to me," she said in four languages, holding out a slip of paper with the address.

In less than ten minutes, they had Rowena dressed in a new yellow dress and were gone.

With a sigh of relief, Rowena collapsed onto the bed. The skirts of the day dress billowed out around her, the sight reminiscent of her mother's full skirts. She could recall burying herself in her mother's skirts, the smell of lilacs penetrating the yellow morning gown. As a child, Rowena had believed that lilacs only came in that color.

The memory was comforting, but Rowena shook it away. It wouldn't do to miss someone who had been dead almost twenty years now.

Pushing herself to sit up, she noticed a simple nightgown, a navy-blue walking dress, and a green satin gown hanging in the armoire. She frowned. This was Sutton's house. She was sleeping just across the way from him, dressed in frocks he was paying for. It seemed certain he would expect a payment of some sort.

She knew few men could be trusted, but Sutton was honorable. Not once on their journey had he tried to overpower her, not even at night, as they had slept. He'd stayed near her, sometimes close enough to share each other's heat, but he had never taken advantage of her. Except for that evening on the boat, he had never even suggested it.

The idea had seemed so repulsive to him, back at Saed's...

Rowena chewed her bottom lip. The truth was that she was willing to do almost anything to get home. She had made it this far, but unless Sutton gave her money or she took up work, she would not find passage to England. The only type of work she would find would be prostitution. The truth sent her stomach rolling.

If it came to Sutton paying her or another man, she would take Sutton in a heartbeat.

Christophe trudged up the stairs to the living quarters in the house he had bought in Melilla, a slight throbbing at the back of his neck warning of a migraine attack. He sighed and tried to rub it away. The work that had waited for him in Melilla was more than he had imagined it would be. For four days he had awoken early and arrived home late in order to get ahead of his ship's arrival. There were taxes to pay and bills to sort out, merchandise to protect and officials to bribe. Then there was Fatia and finding her a decent job.

Unfortunately, he was having bad luck with that. No one wanted to hire a former slave. Many openly questioned her virtue, which reminded him that he couldn't trust his servants in Melilla quite as much as he could trust the ones in London. He should have also known that his servants here were not too loyal to spread rumors of a female former slave sleeping at his house.

His mind wandered without warning to the way her loosely twisted hair had bounced ever so slightly with each step she'd taken yesterday as they ascended the stairs. The memory made him flinch. He had ordered to himself to think of her as a sister, but no brother would pay attention to the bounce in his sister's hair. Nor would a brother notice the curve of her breasts and hips or feel a curious need to run his index finger lightly over her collarbone and up her cheek. Certainly not any sane brother.

Christophe poured himself a Spanish rum to help numb his spinning mind. This feeling of being out of control was something he hadn't experienced since Catherine. Although Dolores had liked to think she controlled their relationship, he had been very much at leisure to walk away—and he had, at exactly the wrong moment. Guilt stabbed him for his selfishness. He would forever pay for it.

Undoubtedly, his cynicism with Dolores had been caused by Catherine. With her, he had been young and inexperienced. It was Catherine's blatant unfaithfulness that had dimmed his fire for her.

Now there was Fatia. It seemed the more he tried to resist her, the more he was drawn to her. Strange that a former slave woman could turn his gut into knots, but there it was. The truth was, he didn't even see her as a slave any longer. With clean clothes and the desperate, hungry look in her eyes gone, he had started to see her as... a woman.

Christophe swallowed, the sweet, spicy liquid churning in his gut. She did not need him looking at her as a woman. She was still broken, and needed a job and purpose more than a lover. The heat of his frustration spread through his body as he tugged hard on his cravat, managing only to make a mess of it. How he hated dressing like a pompous Englishman, but doing business and being respected while doing it meant dressing like the second-born of an English marquess that he was, bother though it may be.

Finally, the white linen came loose, and he threw it on the chair. Next came his jacket, then he unbuttoned his cuffs. Released, Christophe sighed contently and poured a second drink. This one he savored, slower than the first.

"*Salam*, Sutton."

Christophe jerked at the sound—a great mistake at the beginning of a migraine. Lightning shot through his eyes, blinding him temporarily. When his eyes focused again, he found *her* standing in a simple yet elegant gown. Her eyes narrowed with concern, the small crease above her nose deepening. He smiled faintly, but she said nothing.

The door burst open then, to a clattering duo of footmen bringing in dinner. The usual wave of nausea rolled over

Christophe at the noise, though he fought it back. Looking down at his rum, his tongue salivated for the taste, but his mind knew it would be a miserable mistake.

With only a little regret, he put it down and made his way to the settee, where Fatia already sat. He sat as far away as he could, right on the edge. Being at a loss for words always wore on his nerves. Their silence made the air dense, thickening even more when the door clicked shut behind the footmen.

"Your head hurts," she said in Berber.

"Yes, but do not worry so. I will be an excellent dinner companion. I know you must be—without much to do. Not happy to be in the house so much, maybe?" he asked, his inability to think of the right words in Berber adding to his frustration.

Turning back to the trays of food, pain shot between his temples before bouncing back again. He breathed out slowly, but knew he had to give in for a moment and rest his head. There was nothing to do about it; he would not be a good dinner companion.

"You need a woman to take care of you, Mr. Sutton, as you do not take care of yourself. Do you not have a wife in England?" Fatia asked, suddenly behind him. Gentle, cool hands wrapped around his head and began a light massage.

Christophe grunted a negative reply. Without a migraine, it would have been tempting to allow Fatia to take care of him. With a migraine, it was impossible not to. The pillow was as hard as stone against his aching head, but her hands moved like magic. When they left him for a second, Christophe couldn't help the small moan that escaped his throat and instantly her hands were back. She began to sing a Mozart composition in a low, hypnotic voice. The melody flowed over him as he tried to relax his shoulders and head.

Ah, but the music was nothing compared to the softness of her lap when she guided his head to it, or the cool of her hands as her thumbs moved in circles against his tense neck. In no time, her singing and the movement of her fingers soothed him into a deep sleep.

Rowena ran her fingers lightly over the red silk that lay across Madame Benevault's counter. It was nearing luncheon and she had yet to be fitted, which seemed to make Sutton uncomfortable. He pushed himself away from the wall and started pacing the small entryway again.

"You do not have to wait for me," Rowena dared to say.

His pacing stopped, his attention shifting towards her.

"It is my duty to make sure you are safe," he answered stiffly.

"I am quite safe. I can make it home if you must do some work."

"I need to go to the shipyard and make a visit to Mr. Watters, as well as stop in to pay José," Sutton said, speaking mostly to himself. Rowena dared to lift her eyes to his face, struck again by how handsome he was. With each passing day, she couldn't seem to stop daydreaming about his face for hours at a time.

"I will be fine."

He met her eyes then, and she froze in place.

"About last night, Fatia, I wanted to thank you. My head was much relieved this morning. I know I have promised you payment. We must speak soon; tonight perhaps—although I have a dinner.

Tomorrow then. We must sort out where you are to go when I must leave."

Rowena's heart stilled. Perhaps he would offer to take her to England without her needing to ask.

"I will tell Pablo to stay with you. He can drive you home. I will see you tomorrow, then," he said, giving her a small bow before he was gone from the store.

In disappointment, she looked at herself in the gold-plated mirror. Even after a week of dressing properly, her image still surprised her. Admiring the gown, running her hands over the soft fabric, helped to soothe away her panic of the unknown future. The clothes went far to give her the appearance of an English lady, but Mr. Sutton still saw her as a slave. Who could blame him, with her sun-darkened skin and empty eyes?

"What do you make of it, Madame Benevault?" An English accent boomed through the store, catching Rowena's attention. "What am I to do? I know that she didn't mean to get sick right before the trip, but it does make things terribly inconvenient. I have hired a nurse to take care of her, for she is the best maid I have ever had, and well worth spending the money to make certain she improves, but two weeks on a ship without a maid to help me get dressed? I will feel barbaric."

Rowena leaned forward as she sat on the soft velvet settee, but the corset she wore cut into her skin, reminding her to sit higher and press down her shoulders. Only then did her discomfort ease.

"You see, Madame, hiring another maid in this manner is quite difficult. I cannot offer her employment once we've arrived. It must be someone who is looking to return to England, but who doesn't need a job once there. And where shall I find a lady's maid like that?"

"Yes, I see the problem, Countess, but you have a few days. And I will keep my ears open for someone."

"I do not see the silver lining as you do," the English voice said with a deep sigh. "But I do thank you, Madame Benevault."

The voices came closer until two women appeared from behind the curtain. Rowena quickly assessed the woman looking for a lady's maid and found her to be near sixty, with kinder eyes than her voice let on.

"Mademoiselle! Right on time. We can fit you now. Come, come," Madame Benevault said, gesturing behind the curtain at Rowena's blank stare.

"Madame," Rowena said in halting French as they passed to the back of the shop. "That woman, before, who she is?"

"The Countess Merville? She is a fine, regal lady, is she not?"

Rowena nodded. As the assistants helped her out of her corset, she repeated the name again and again to herself. It shouldn't prove too hard to find the address of an English countess in Spanish Melilla. Neither would it be difficult to pose as a lady's maid. It would, actually, be a perfect way to get back home safely.

Rowena awoke gasping for breath, her nightgown covered in sweat. The room was cloaked in darkness, with only a few slim trails of moonlight slipping past the branches outside her window and spreading across the wooden floor. She shuddered when the trails of light moved with the wind, slithering like the whip in the sadistic hands of her second owner, Mohammad Fellahi. Another night without sleep because of her dreams. The screams and terror from her dreams were now just echoes in her mind, but the fear was still all around her.

With shaking hands Rowena tried to light the candle, but it proved impossible. Desperation built within her as she crawled to the fire, but there she found only a few coals still slightly orange, giving off little heat. Even when her eyes adjusted to the dark and it was clear that she was in Melilla, she couldn't stop shaking, nor calm her breath. It came in gasps and sputters until her face started to tingle.

She needed to breathe. She needed safety. Without thinking, Rowena opened her door and ran through the common area. Sutton had not come home for two days, but last night she had heard his door open. With all her might she pushed open his door, desperate with hope that he might be there.

"What happened? What is it?" Christophe shouted, as she stumbled to the floor. He sat bolt upright in the bed, a slim knife reflecting moonlight clenched in his hand.

"Su-Sutton," she panted. The sound of metal hitting the floor responded to her pleas.

"Fatia! What's wrong?"

Rowena could not answer. Her breath still came in choking gasps, now mixed with a free-falling river of tears.

"Shh, now. Whatever happened? Breathe. It's all right. It's just me. You can do it. There now, you see? Breathe deeply."

"Please," she whispered, clutching his feet that hung over the bed.

As though she were nothing more than a doll, he picked her up from the ground and gently sat her on his bed. His scent floated around her, fully encircling her when he placed his blanket tightly around her shoulders. She still shivered, but with less intensity than before.

Shame replaced her receding panic in the silence. When she looked up, she found him frowning down at her, his eyes dark. Rowena's cheeks burned with shame.

"Thank you, Sutton," she breathed. "I'm sorry for waking you."

He didn't answer. He simply continued to stare at her. One index finger glided gently across her chin, then pushed back a strand of hair from her face. Panic rolled visibly down her spine, and his frown deepened.

Before she could find words to excuse herself, Sutton swooped down and gently kissed her. His lips nipped at her while his fingers cupped her face. The heat from his hands spread over her like molasses, relaxing every muscle within her.

His fingers moved down from her jawline to her neck. Slowly the blanket fell from her shoulders, allowing him to dust his fingers over her collarbone and then over her thin shoulders—until she felt them hit a bump. A warning jolt shot through Rowena, and she froze.

The feeling of security she felt with him had blinded her to reality. Rowena pushed desperately against him, trying to find a weak spot in his arms, but he had none. A string of curses flowed from her mouth, but Sutton stayed solid, like a rock.

"Turn around," he said, his voice gentle but hoarse.

She shook her head. "I must go back to my bed," she said, her voice cracking.

"Fatia, turn around."

It was a command, and yet there was also an underlying plea emphasized by the agony glistening in his eyes. Hypnotized by his concern, Rowena gathered her hair to one shoulder and turned around. Slowly she lifted her arms, taking her nightgown as she did. Never had she been more exposed. Not even when they had ripped her bodice from her to make the mark.

Her back instinctively stiffened when his warm fingers trailed over the long, raised scars. She had never seen her own, but she could imagine them. She had seen everyone else's.

"Fifteen," Christophe whispered. His strong fingers followed each stripe out, pressing into the ends that would look like exploding stars. "You were Fellahi's slave."

She turned around as he slumped back against the wall away from her. He placed his hands on his knees, his head between them, a deep, painful moan rising in his throat. It echoed off the cold walls before fading into gulps for air. Tears pricked her eyes. She wished she could comfort him, but she did not know how. For years, she had simply watched others live in their own hell. Her years as a slave had stripped every pretty word of comfort she had ever known away from her vocabulary.

"They are ugly," she whispered. "I know. I have seen them on others."

"Fellahi, Fatia!" he said, straightening with a groan. "He was known for so many evil things. For raping girls in the streets, for beating his slaves to death, for going to stonings and hangings for pleasure."

He took her hands in his, staring down at them.

"Fatia, how could I not be there to protect you?" he murmured, pulling her down until she hit his chest.

Shock fixed her in place as his arms enveloped her. It was the first time she had realized that someone might feel pity for her.

"Mr. Sutton, please," she breathed, gulping in courage. "Please take me home with you. Take me back to England. Don't leave me here."

"Fatia," he whispered, then he paused, seemingly unable to say more. Rowena felt all hope of him taking her fade away from her soul. When she slowly turned to take her leave, Christophe gently tugged her back. "Come, it's time to sleep. I will not be dishonorable, but please let me hold you. I understand nightmares. I can do my best to keep them away."

She knew it was more of an apology, a way to make himself feel better for refusing her wish, but she didn't wish to deny herself the feeling of safety just for spite. Though it was lower on her list of wishes, she couldn't deny dreaming of being held by Sutton.

When she acquiesced and moved closer, Christophe picked her up and laid her down as though she were porcelain. She relished his warmth as he kissed her cheeks and neck before settling in at her side and pulling her close. The scent of bergamot, along with his warmth, engulfed her, giving her complete peace. No experience in the last five years told her to trust him. Nothing except her heart and the peace that caused her to immediately fall into a deep sleep.

In the morning, as she mulled over the night before next to a snoring Sutton, Rowena realized with horror that whatever pity, and even responsibility, Sutton felt towards her when he saw her markings, her father would feel tenfold. Going home might cause her father more pain than pleasure. Before she got there, she would need a story and a way to keep her father from ever seeing the scars of her past.

As she tiptoed from Sutton's room, Rowena realized that she could not wait any longer to go home. She needed to see her father again. Convincing Sutton might result in her being left behind with no options left. If the Countess Merville could take her now, it would be better for everyone. Sutton could be rid of her, and she could be on her way back home.

"Miss Fatia, do you understand the character of the job?" Countess Merville asked, looking from Rowena to Madame Benevault as the latter translated English into Arabic. "The circumstances are quite peculiar, but I must admit that I find it strange you are willing to go along with them. What, pray tell, do you plan to do once you are in England?"

Somehow, Rowena had found the strength to come to this grand house in Melilla and rap on the back door. When a maid answered, Rowena had forced herself to ask for Lady Merville. She had had no fear then, only the urgent drive to find a way home. But now, standing in the middle of a room with walls covered in silk paper and furniture detailed with gold leaf, she felt tiny and very unsure of herself. Still, if she wanted a way to England, she knew she must answer the question.

Turning a nervous smile to the countess, Rowena pushed her fear aside and answered without faltering.

"Find a new life," she answered in what she hoped was the right language. The words sounded strange to her ears but when the countess raised her brows, pleased at no longer needing a translator, Rowena realized the words had, in fact, been English.

"You speak English? I like that your accent is not too strong. I'm not good with accents. They seem to muddle everything up. Where did you learn and why didn't you tell me before?"

"I learned as a... a child, but I have not... used it for many... years," Rowena choked out. The words seemed to catch and trip on her tongue, nothing like the smooth Berber words that seemed to flow out of her like water.

"With some practice I think you will speak just fine. Now, could you give me more insight on to why you want the job?"

"I want to go to England, but I have no family and no brother."

"You mean, chaperone?"

"Yes," Rowena said, grateful for the help. "No chaperone. Passage with you will be more respected."

"The word is 'respectable', and I dare say it would be, young lady! No, no, passage alone at sea for two weeks would not be proper! All right, well, I have seen you and I'm quite desperate. I hope that we can get along, but even if we don't, we will see each other but for a few weeks. After that, if we get along, I can leave you with a reference, at least. Now, I assume you have no real place to stay, so you can start immediately."

Rowena looked up.

"Will that be an issue? I need someone now. I need you trained and ready to go. If you cannot start now, I must look for someone else."

Rowena swallowed back her reluctance. She could not miss this opportunity to go home. This might be her last chance to leave Melilla for a long time.

While she was grateful to Sutton, he was never around. A week had passed since she'd awoken him in the middle of the night, and she had only seen him twice. She dreamed of seeing her father again and taking her rightful place as his daughter, no matter what it took. Whether or not it was wrong to leave Sutton without a word, she could not waste the opportunity to sail back with a respectable lady.

"Miss?" a maid called out.

Rowena set her jaw and walked forward. She had made her choice and she would not retreat now. This was her best way home.

"Come wi' me, then, and I'll show ye the way to a room. 'Ave a smile, miss. We're going 'ome—aren't ye happy?"

Rowena smiled, ignoring her cracked heart. She was going home. Home! To her father! This was the right decision. Sutton would forget her soon enough. She was just a former slave to him, after all, while a family awaited her in London.

Chapter Seven

LONDON, JULY, 1832

A LARGE, THREE-STORY VILLA loomed overhead as Rowena and Beatrix descended the carriage. Lady Merville chuckled at the sight.

"I remember now the gossip about this place being built. King George awarded him back his barony; your father won a bidding war on a shipping company, which, rumor has it, made him richer than most anyone else in England. Many among the peers tried to shun him and the baroness for not being good enough, even accusing them of being *nouveau riche*—clearly ignoring your stepmother's pedigree and the fact that she was a duchess from her first marriage. But no one said the peerage was driven by intellect... Anyhow, four seasons ago your father became popular for something in Parliament, and the men about town could no longer afford to ignore him. He donated more money to the charities than anyone else, built a children's hospital near the East Side for the lower class, brought in new doctors to work there, hosted the ball of the season that both Duke Beaumont and the Duke of Wellington attended, if but for a moment, and from then on no one has had the gall to speak badly of him. To his face, at least.

Some in the ton say this villa rivals that of the Duke of Cambridge, but I've never been inside either."

"Ton?" Rowena asked absently as she gazed up at the regal white walls and the high wrought-iron gate that wrapped around them.

"London society. The ton. Anyone who is anyone, child," Lady Merville chided her.

Somewhere beyond the house a child squealed with delight, pricking the hair on the back of Rowena's neck. Her stepmother had been pregnant when last she had seen her. It was possible the child was her brother or sister.

When cool fingers clasped her forearm, Rowena was jerked back to reality.

"Are you ready? The air is cooler than one would expect at the end of July, what with the sun being so bright. Of course, this is London, not Melilla. Ah, I miss the African sun already," the countess sighed, her eyes taking on a faraway look. "But enough of that. Straighten your bonnet. Gather your wits about you and come along."

Rowena thanked God again that she had found Countess Merville. Halfway through their voyage to England, the countess had abruptly demanded that Rowena tell what she was hiding. Unable to lie to a woman who had given her the chance to go home, she had spilled the entire story over tea. From that moment on, Beatrix, as she wished to be called in private, insisted on retraining Rowena how to act like a well-bred English gentlewoman. It was through Beatrix that Rowena had learned that her life in England might be a little more public than she had realized, with her father now a baron.

"Come along, Rowena," Beatrix said as she descended. Rowena obeyed immediately, turning her head carefully so as to not catch her large hat on the carriage door. She followed behind Beatrix, who marched to the gate without hesitation. Hurrying up the large, curved stone steps which led up to the entrance, Rowena hesitated only long enough to read the plaque on the wall: *Tajir Villa*. Merchant Villa.

When her father's longtime butler, Harrison, greeted them, Rowena almost forgot her plan to stay behind the countess. His protruding belly that had always seemed like a fortress when she was small now seemed slight. Rowena lowered her head, suppressing the desire to throw herself at him and cry. It saddened her to see that Harrison's eyes no longer twinkled with merriment. His thick hair was now snow white, and deep worry lines creased his face. Rowena stayed where she was, clutching and releasing her skirts to ease her nerves.

"We have come to see Baron and Baroness Brayemore," declared Beatrix.

"The baron is not available—" Harrison began.

"Then we will see his wife," Beatrix answered, waving her enormous fan about. She marched forward, giving Harrison no choice but to step aside.

Moments after being shown into a parlor decorated in green and gold, the door opened with a swooping gust of wind and Lady Brayemore stepped through. Rowena's stepmother was a bit older, but still a fair beauty at forty years of age.

"Countess Merville," Bernadette said, her voice slightly shrill as she gave a nervous curtsy. "What a lovely surprise. We were not expecting any visitors this afternoon."

"I have just come back from Melilla," the countess declared as her décolletage heaved with pride. "I went there on business, but came to like the place."

"Business?" Bernadette asked, her delicate face wrinkling in confusion.

Beatrix barreled headlong into describing her grandfather's business and real estate in Melilla, as though that were the reason for their visit. The Baroness listened politely to the tales of Countess Merville haggling with her dead brother's solicitor herself and dealing with the family business.

"That is very courageous of you, Lady Merville," Bernadette said, obviously still trying to cover her confusion at the surprise visit. "Are you not afraid to travel alone through those waters?"

"Afraid?" barked the countess. "Why would someone be afraid?"

"Why, pirates and rogue sailors. The French are waging a war against the Algerians, and just the other day my husband was speaking of a riot in Melilla. Were you there for that?"

"There are rarely pirates now, since the Americans made that treaty and are on the lookout. Besides that, Algeria is far enough from Melilla that French interference there does not concern me. As for the riot in Melilla, the Spanish army contained it in a matter of hours. I see nothing to fear, my dear."

While the countess looked the typical, docile English Dowager dressed in a cream muslin with pearl buttons and lace covering every inch of her shoulders, she was neither docile nor typical. The countess believed herself immortal, and so found herself to be just that – an idea Rowena found intriguing and somewhat inspiring. She understood her mortality too well to become as brave as Countess Merville.

Bernadette had finally turned to Rowena to change the subject of conversation when she was interrupted. This time the door burst open and in bounded a small boy with the largest smile on his lips, holding out a large, single rose. Seeing that his mother had guests brought the boy to a sudden halt. He stood like a surprised statue, scrutinizing each of the strangers intensely. When he turned his attention to Rowena, his eyes widened in shock. Without being prompted, the boy ran to her, then stopped just inches away, paling slightly when she knelt to his eye level.

"My," Rowena said, her voice hoarse with tears. "But you look just like your father. Does everyone tell you that?"

The boy pointed his fingers at her, slowly moving them towards her face until her forehead stopped them. "You are not a ghost," he whispered.

"Elliot!" Bernadette stood, trembling as she yelled out her son's name, but otherwise didn't move.

Rowena looked at her half-brother, shaking her head. "No, I'm not a ghost. And you're Elliot?"

Her bother nodded, still pale, his eyes wide. When she opened her arms for a hug, he threw himself into them.

"I do not understand what has come over you, Elliot! Where is Miss Evans?"

Rowena tensed. She eyed the countess, who shook her head when Rowena clutched Elliot closer, but she could not let go. Countess Merville smiled calmly with raised brows, a command for her to relax, all while Bernadette tittered on about Miss Evans neglecting her duty. The underlying edge to Bernadette's voice sent Rowena's heart racing at a furious pace, and she braced herself to face the nanny if need be. When Countess Merville turned her smile into a hard glare, clarity finally broke through Rowena's consciousness.

There was no need to protect Elliot. He was not a slave child. If he left her now, she could see him again.

Rowena breathed in, willing herself not to faint. Deliberately she looked at the English porcelain tea set, the English dresses, and the very English parlor.

She was in England.

"Elliot, I demand to know why you poked Lady Merville's companion between the eyes."

"I thought if I touched a ghost that my fingers would slide right through them," Elliot said, shrugging his shoulders. Rowena laughed, all of her energy threatening to spill out in hysteria. Elliot did not join in. He grunted in annoyance.

"That may be true, still," Rowena said, trying to appease him. "Because you see, I'm not a ghost. Which is why I cannot behave like one and allow your fingers to go through me. Someday, perhaps, we shall see a real ghost and try our luck at poking through it."

"You look just like the painting," he said suspiciously. "And you're supposed to be dead. So that would make you a ghost."

"Who told you that?"

Elliot shrugged. "No one ever said it, but they speak of you like they speak of my grandfather. How you used to do this or were like that. And sometimes Father gets sad and speaks to your painting."

"Elliot?" Bernadette whispered, her face now colorless.

"Mother? Do you feel unwell? She says she isn't a ghost," he said confidently, then suddenly faltered. "Don't you see her?"

Bernadette slowly turned her head. Her gaze lingered on Rowena, who fought the urge to squirm or look away. Finally, color seeped back into Bernadette's cheeks as a glittering of recognition filled her eyes.

"Rowena?"

Bernadette ran towards her, then pivoted to ring the bell for the butler first. She hesitated at the cord for a moment before rushing to grab Rowena into her thin arms.

A strangled sound between a squeal and a sob erupted from Bernadette as they embraced. Rowena found it almost too much to bear. Her emotions lingered between never wanting the hug to end and wishing to fling Bernadette far away from herself. She had not had such close contact with another person for years; it was stifling more than comforting.

The two women were still in a tight embrace when Rowena heard someone else enter the room. Her stomach twisted at the sound of heavy footsteps: the sound she used to stay awake to hear at night as a little girl.

Apparently annoyed by the display of emotion, Lady Merville pounded her cane upon the floor, and the room instantly stilled. Bernadette pulled away, dabbing at the tears in her eyes.

"What the devil is going on in here?" a strong male voice demanded from the doorway. It was a voice Rowena hadn't heard in over five years, but she knew exactly whom it belonged to.

"Sir, I have brought your daughter home to you," Lady Merville declared, over Elliot squealing out the tale in a rather haphazard way. "As you can see, your wife and son are quite overcome by the fact that she is, indeed, not a ghost."

The comment made Elliot puff in pride, which confused James Brayemore further. Rowena smiled as the crease in her father's forehead deepened. His skin was shockingly white instead of golden-brown as she remembered it, but his eyes were still piercing, and his hard face still held the faint smile lines. He stood as a giant among the confusion, filling her with reassurance. Rowena realized then that she *needed* him to be a giant to her still. She might be four and twenty, but more than ever she needed him to hold her up.

"Benti, my daughter!"

He caught her with ease and strength when she threw herself into his arms. Held by her father for the first time in five years, the flood of desperate tears she had once held back flowed without hindrance down her cheeks.

Lady Merville once again pounded her cane on the floor, clearing her throat. Both she and Bernadette spoke at the same time.

"Rowena, that is quite enough."

"John, we have guests."

Rowena let go of her father's coat and felt his arms reluctantly release her. A handkerchief held out by Countess Merville was helpful to dry her eyes as Bernadette bustled about serving tea, pouring hot water over the tension as much as into the cups.

"Whatever is going on in here today?"

Rowena turned to find her stepsister, Grace—now grown into a beautiful young lady—standing in the doorway. Her eyes were as sharp as they had always been.

Grace and Rowena hadn't got along especially well as children, though Rowena had always felt it wasn't entirely their fault. When her father had married Bernadette, they had given their respective children very little warning about the arrangement, throwing the girls together as though love would blossom automatically between them.

"Your sister—well, Rowena—I'm not sure you remember her. You were much younger the last time you saw each other—but you see, she's back." Bernadette twisted a small handkerchief between her fingers as she spoke.

Rowena stepped forward to greet her half-sister, who struggled for a moment to cover her surprise. But with the ease of many young women in society, Grace soon adjusted her features and smiled.

"It's nice to see you again, sister. You must have had quite the journey, being out there in the north of Africa for—how many years now? Five?"

"We were just about to have our tea," Countess Merville interjected. "Sit down, and we will tell you the story of how I came to find Miss Brayemore."

Grace seemed startled at the older woman's frown. Giving a respectful curtsey, she found a place for herself on the small couch next to her mother. Rowena sat next to Elliot near the piano, at the ready to answer any questions, but grateful Beatrix was already telling the tale they had concocted, her face radiant at the attention.

———— ⚶ ————

"What an extraordinary day," Bernadette declared from her dressing table, eyeing James across the room.

"That it was. I'm quite exhausted from all of it."

"Quite," Bernadette murmured, her mind drifting to the back of one of her drawers. "There is much to do now to solve her entrance into society. With it being the middle of the season and all."

"Yes," her husband replied, stifling a yawn. "We will speak of it tomorrow. Good night, my love."

The endearment hit Bernadette's heart like a bullet, but she smiled when James kissed her temple and murmured goodbye when he left the room.

Once he was gone, Bernadette could hardly sit still while Clarice undressed her and brushed out her hair. Her nerves were wound so tightly she might explode at any moment. Finally, Clarice also left.

When the door clicked shut behind the maid, Bernadette glared at her lovely ivory bureau. Her fingers burned to open the drawer and yet her heart pulsed too fast, causing her hands to shake. The letters from Madame Roussier were inside.

Bernadette had forgotten all about them until Rowena showed up. It had taken all her courage not to faint on the spot when their dark existence had entered her memory at tea.

With a fierce exhalation, Bernadette yanked the drawer so hard it came out completely, sending her to her backside. She waited, motionless, listening for footsteps running to investigate the noise, but silence answered her. With a staggered sigh of relief, she looked down at the contents of the drawer splayed upon the carpet. There were papers, a few drawings her daughters had painted when they were young, baby teeth, letters from her first husband and father before they had passed on, and a shell from her first time at the beach. Underneath the shell lay what she was looking for.

Moving quietly, Bernadette picked up the two envelopes with Madame Roussier's long, narrow writing on the outside. They were yellowed a bit, but still held perfect proof of the horrible thing she had done.

Methodically, Bernadette picked up the drawer and its contents and put them away. The letters were last, but instead of putting them back inside, she turned to her bed, clutching them in her fingers. Carefully, she slipped them underneath her pillow, hoping that one day she would gather enough courage to burn them.

With a shudder of horror, Bernadette fell into a nightmarish sleep.

"I cannot believe you have the insolence to come back here and not tell me you were in town."

Christophe looked up in surprise at the interruption.

"How'd you know I was home?" he demanded quietly.

Philip Daucer, the third son of the Marquess of Fillemore, tossed himself onto a leather chair, throwing his beaver hat to the settee.

"Hello to you, too, friend. How are you? I'm fine. Just dandy. Barely getting away with not getting married this season. Was thinking of going to Ravenwood for a week or two to do some hunting. Would you fancy going with me? Probably not, since I see you are brooding over something and prefer to think you aren't actually back in London."

"Sod off. I don't brood. How'd you find me?"

"Clement."

Christophe winced. A rookie mistake. His and Daucer's coachmen were cousins.

"Looks like you've been here a few weeks. Good God, man, have you been sleeping here? I didn't know you wanted to avoid your title that much. Cheer up, old man, it isn't the worst thing in the world to be next in line. Besides, don't you think you should go see your mother? Mourning is almost over, but I know she'd like to know you are well and back in town."

The pen poised in Christophe's fingers fell to his mahogany desk with a thud. "My mother is in town?"

"Your mother hasn't left London since, you know... Russell."

Christophe stopped, his mouth still open as his friend's words rushed through his ears again.

"What about Russell?" he asked quietly.

All color drained from Daucer's face. He stood suddenly and jammed his fingers through his hair. "I thought you knew. Isn't that why you're back?"

"Knew what? I was planning to come home around now. I was finishing here to make a start for Ravenwood this afternoon. I thought she would be there with Emily."

"Your mother didn't send you a letter telling you of Russell?"

A chilled silence swept between them.

"What did Russell do this time?" Christophe rose from the chair, but before his friend could even speak, he knew exactly what he was going to say. Still, he tried another route first. "He's in debt again?"

Daucer shook his head.

Christophe struggled to breathe. The air was suddenly as heavy as lead. His friend, who never cowered at anything, looked as though he wished to disappear.

"Russell is dead, Cinch."

Daucer's use of his childhood nickname, the one given to him by Russell, brought a bombardment of sudden memories of his brother as a child. No matter that they hadn't gotten along very well as adults; hearing that Russell was dead stole every word from his tongue.

"There was a fight at the docks, and he was stabbed. They found the blighter who did it. Wasn't in much better shape himself. I had no idea Russell could do such damage. He always seemed a bit soft to me. Anyway, it happened just after you left."

Christophe said nothing. Daucer blinked at him, looking as though he wished he could run away before finally continuing.

"You are the next in line, Cinch. You understand that, right? Your family has been waiting almost nine months for you to come back and claim the title." His friend stopped to flick a speck of lint off his jacket.

The delay was dramatic, allowing the reality of the words to sink deep into Christophe's head. As though aware that the shock was making it hard for Christophe to fully understand the implications, Daucer looked up and said, with careful enunciation:

"You are now the tenth Marquess of Candor."

Chapter Eight

CHRISTOPHE KNOCKED LOUDLY BEFORE entering the Earl of Glenville's library. Falcon, as his friends knew him, sat at an enormous desk. It was a relic from the first earl's conquest of some part of Scotland, or so the legend at Eton went. Christophe had never paid much attention to the story's details. Seeing the mammoth object for the first time, he wondered if perhaps the first earl had conquered Scandinavia instead of Scotland. It dwarfed Falcon, who stood over six feet tall.

"First time seeing the library?" Falcon boomed. "Or are you frightened of what we might do to you for having hidden yourself away for six weeks since coming home?"

Christophe let out a low whistle as the two shook hands, nodding towards the desk. "It looks like the thing is eating you alive. I wouldn't be surprised if it breathed."

Falcon laughed. "When I was a boy, it used to be the dragon that I would slay over and over again, but I was never brave enough to actually touch it. Only my sword could touch it. Once, I remember, my father called me down here at night to discipline me about letting a frog loose in the nursery, but I never heard a word he said. The fire made the desk appear alive, and I was so scared I agreed to the punishment of a month of polishing my father's boots."

"A rather unusual punishment for the future earl."

Falcon laughed again. "My father believed in getting his hands dirty. He watched my grandfather almost ruin the estate with his lack of true knowledge about working the land or mines. Early on he decided that the only way to truly be successful was to learn the work. Against my grandfather's wishes, he worked for a year among the farmers and miners. My grandfather apparently spent that year in a constant state of fear that his only son was going to die by way of a pitchfork, and never forgave him, claiming he had taken years away from his life by worrying him so much."

Christophe raised his brow as he took the preferred tumbler of whiskey.

"His hair turned completely white," Falcon explained. "His coal-black hair was a streak of vanity, apparently."

Christophe chuckled, relaxing for the first time in weeks into the easy atmosphere.

"How are you finding your estates? I've heard you've taken the way of my father a bit, learning to repair fences and herd sheep. Will you be there in two weeks for the yearly autumn festivities?"

"I don't tend the sheep, but I'm sure I'll be there in the autumn. I'll be between there and London for the rest of my life," grunted Christophe. "Russell left everything a mess. The lead mines are in dangerous need of repairs, as well as many of the houses. The worst of it is that a few new tunnels need to be dug which will end closer to some tenants' houses than is deemed safe. It's a delicate subject that we've discussed in circles for the past four weeks. Beside that, we have drainage problems and land that will no longer yield crops, as well as Ravenwood crumbling apart."

Falcon shrugged his jacket off and loosed his cravat while taking stock of the story. Most other landowners would have advised Christophe to stop negotiating with tenants, tell them they could move or go to the devil and be done with it—which was why Christophe would not discuss such a thing with most other landowners. Having been brought up by a compassionate, reasonable father who did not believe himself to be better than the working man simply because of the house he happened to be born in, Falcon was also a compassionate and reasonable man. And while Christophe could be ruthless in dealing with businessmen, he tended to always side with the little man on matters that greatly altered their lives.

"Have you found a plan that pleases everyone?"

"No," Christophe answered, staring into the fire. "But we'll find one. Digging cannot commence until every family is safely away. I am confident Daucer will find a way to make them see how getting a brand-new house with no leaks or cracks anywhere is better than living in an old house with a patched roof. Anyway, enough business. I'm here to meet my very first niece. How is my sister?"

"Perfect," the earl sighed.

Christophe chuckled away his urge to groan. "Still as smitten as ever? I'm glad to hear that, though I do not particularly wish to hear you wax poetically about my baby sister. When do I get to see everyone?"

"They return today from my mother's house. I had to come back early to greet you, though I don't mind very much. Your sister gets along better with my mother than I do, and since her grandchildren have been born, I take the fifth seat amongst them all. It could be altogether irritating if I didn't relish the fact that my mother has finally finished nagging me about everything. For once, I've done something right: giving her a beautiful, delightful daughter-in-law and three adorable grandchildren."

"To doing something right," Christophe declared, holding up his whiskey.

Falcon raised his with a smile and a grimace. "You will stay in England now, won't you?"

Christophe's smile waned.

"Cinch," Falcon warned. "If you leave again, your mother and sister will be heartbroken."

It wasn't that he didn't wish to spend time with his family. He loved them, especially the little broods that tended to call him Uncle Inch. Honestly, the obligations of being the new Marquess of Candor brought with them a strong desire to leave England altogether, though he didn't dare.

But that didn't mean he wasn't planning a short trip to Melilla one last time to search for her again.

Fatia. Her name was whispered in his heart, fainter than before, but still there.

"I know," he answered. "There is something I should go back for, but I can't bring myself to tell them that I'm leaving. I've spent weeks now convincing myself I must stay put."

"It must be something important," Falcon said. "Is it not something your man there in Melilla can take care of?"

The words sparked the glimmer of an idea, but he shook it away. "I will probably stay here. At least for a while."

Falcon laughed, thumping his somber friend on the back. "Well, I do have some advice for you, Cinch: stay far away from your sister."

"Why? What do you mean?"

"I mean that she intends to find you a bride as soon as possible. She is determined to find a way to keep you in England, and believes a beautiful young wench would be just the thing to make you stay."

Christophe cleared his throat, hoping it would clear his mind. Each time marriage came up, Fatia's face appeared in his mind. An inappropriate indulgence if ever he knew one.

"Don't worry, Cinch, I'm sure she will find you an excellent wife."

Falcon chuckled and Christophe sighed. Once his sister got hold of an idea, she never let go. She had teased him before about being unmarried, knowing nothing about Dolores and how he had tried to woo her, but it seemed now she was determined to marry him off.

Before he could reply, the front door opened with a loud commotion. There were shrieks and laughter, as well as stern reprimands and the low, gravelly voices of footmen. Falcon wiped the tears from his eyes and ran towards the door, his eagerness unmatched by anyone else in England.

"Emily has arrived with the children," he announced, holding the door open just as a familiar female voice rose above the chaos to calmly tell a child to stop sucking on her ribbons.

"Claire is here too," Christophe murmured to himself.

"Yes."

"How is she?"

Falcon shrugged, his demeanor more serious now. "You know Claire—the epitome of English nobility. She is in mourning for Russell, though she will probably stop at the year mark. Honestly, she seems to be almost... well, happier, if I dare say it. But these arranged marriages just for appearances must truly weigh on the people who are in them. It would be difficult to be married to someone you didn't love. Even if it was Russell."

Christophe grunted, not fully understanding his friend's wisdom, as he had never had the pleasure of being married. Not that he hadn't tried. In fact, he had tried twice.

"Russell was never too preoccupied with her happiness, only his own. I'm quite certain Russell escorting ladies of the demi-monde about London had its effects."

The visual Falcon provided was ugly. While Christophe had always held a sense of pity for Claire, he limited it to a glimmer. She was such a strong woman, always doing and saying the proper thing. She was well-educated, intelligent, and could be witty if she liked. Christophe always told himself she had married Russell knowing full well what was in store for her. But now, as he and Falcon walked towards the bustle in the hallway, he wondered just how much a girl of twenty could really know about marriage. Even one as intelligent as Claire.

Paul, the eldest nephew at age six, ran suddenly at full speed into Christophe's open arms. The two of them fell onto the marble floor with a gale of laughter. A small navy jacket blinded Christophe temporarily as his nephew hugged his head.

"I missed you, Uncle Inch!" he exclaimed, blasting Christophe's eardrum.

"I miss Inch, too!" cried Ryan to his right.

Ignoring the squeezing of his head that might cause serious damage, Christophe swiftly captured Ryan's legs in his free arm, bringing him tumbling down. Joyous squeals and giggles ensued. Paul finally tired of hugging him and let go, panting from the effort of his love. Christophe sat up, grabbed both boys in his arms, and brought them up to everyone else's eye level.

"Well, it seems as though they missed you," Emily declared, trying to make herself sound disapproving, despite the wide grin spreading across her face. "And the exercise of Africa seems to have made you robust enough to survive a six-year-old and a three-year-old. Bravo!"

"Sir!" exclaimed the governess, her voice somewhere between a hiss and a pant. "I cannot allow the children to—"

"You may take the afternoon off," Christophe said, pleased by his very noble hand wave.

"Yes, sir." The governess scowled, clearly unhappy with her authority being swept aside.

Certainly, her hurt feelings would be aided by her afternoon off to do whatever it was that governesses did when left on their own. There was no time for Christophe to care much about the woman walking stiffly away from them. He had children to spoil and a dragon in the library to slay.

<hr />

The back of his neck pinched as Christophe removed his glasses and tossed them to the desk. A blinding pain shot up behind his eyes, momentarily turning his vision black.

So much had happened while he was gone that he found little time to sleep. Although he preferred to be with his sister at Falcon Manor in the outskirts of London, it also meant that he had less time to work during the day. That he did at night, which led to less time for sleeping. It was a cycle he couldn't quite seem to break. Perhaps if Daucer came with good news on the weekend, he would be able to leave things be for a few days.

In the hallway a large German clock struck the hour of midnight, the clanging echoing through his temples as he placed the glasses back on the bridge of his nose. While he wasn't one to shirk any responsibility, Christophe now realized that being the second son had allowed him to do whatever he wanted in life. Now that he was the titled son, he was responsible for the entire family. It was no longer just his business he had to take care of. Now he had the title and dues to England. Hogwash and debt, mostly.

Christophe picked up the balance sheet and tried to focus on the numbers, but his mind had other plans. For the hundredth time since sailing home, Fatia's face appeared before him along with the unanswered question of what had happened to her. She had simply vanished. Though he had delayed his trip an extra week looking for her, he had met with no success. She was gone.

He blew out air loudly, trying to massage away the pain and her image.

"Sir? Is everything all right?"

Rudolf, his sister's butler, appeared out of the shadows. Christophe swallowed his irritation down. He hated having servants lingering everywhere, but he would have to get used to it.

"Migraine, sir? I don't doubt you're not sleeping enough. It is rather a lot of stress to handle right off the ship. Shall I have Cook mix up a tonic?"

The very idea brought relief to the backs of his eyes. "Yes, please. Bring it to the sitting room along with some fresh tea. Thank you, Rudolf."

The sincere thanks made the butler's ears turn red, but Christophe didn't care. He wasn't his brother or any other marquess strolling around England. He would not change the way he treated his staff just because the rest of society looked down on theirs.

With the relief of the magic tonic coming soon, Christophe squared back his shoulders and picked up his balance sheets again.

"There you are, dear brother," Emily said softly as she slipped into the library. "Why are you still awake?"

"I could ask you the same," he mumbled, his energy almost entirely gone.

"I have the baby to keep me awake," Emily said, picking up a novel she had left on the table the night before. "Besides, I sleep late into the morning. You though, dear brother, have been here for two weeks and you rarely sleep. It will catch up with you, you know."

"I know, but there is so much to get done. Russell made a bit of a mess with almost everything. I have letters here from Mrs. Watters at Candor Manor asking me if she should let the staff go or if I will be finally paying them. They haven't had a salary in almost a year!" Christophe sighed into his hands just as Rudolf appeared with a tea tray along with a headache tonic. Christophe downed it quickly and thrust the glass back to Rudolf. While its color was pleasing, the taste was close to what sweaty boots must taste like.

"I didn't know you were suffering a migraine, Cinch. Thank you, Rudolf, for the tea. You can retire to bed," Emily said as Christophe battled with his stomach to keep down the medicine. "Come here, Cinch, and sit down."

Christophe moved to the couch and let his body sink heavily into the cushions. The blood slowly stopped rushing deafeningly through his ears until finally he could take a teacup without his hands trembling.

"Are your migraines very bad these days?"

Christophe waved the question away. "How long will Claire stay with you?" he asked Emily, wishing to have a productive conversation.

"As long as she wants. If you go to London, she can't go. It would be entirely improper for you and her to stay together in Candor House. Unless you plan to marry her?"

Christophe snorted as his sister convulsed into giggles.

"Why, Cinch. I was only teasing, but the idea certainly doesn't deserve such a violent shudder either," Emily cried out. "I might just have to tell her how revolting you find her."

"Don't you dare," Christophe warned, savoring the black tea rolling down into his empty stomach. "You do, and I will just have to find a way to tell the story of how you managed to run into the freshly painted fence with your new dress."

"An innocent mistake!" Emily protested.

"Not at sixteen, dear sister, not at sixteen. I'm sure Falcon would like to hear about how you preferred to take in the vicar's son rather than watch where you were going."

"It is because of that story that I don't set foot in Cookston anymore," Emily said with a sigh. "It was quite embarrassing."

Christophe smiled as his sister giggled again. Ever since she was small he had found the sound of her giggle to be endearing.

"So, tell me about your latest adventure. I want to hear all the details about the shrunken heads and the terrible pirates. Were you captured by desert bandits? Did a princess find you and threaten to hold you hostage for all your perfume? Did the French bribe you out of most of your money?"

"No," Christophe murmured, unable to keep his thoughts straight.

"Christophe Pierce Sutton!" Emily exclaimed. "What has you so dreamy-eyed?"

"I am not dreamy-eyed," he growled defensively. "And I believe I would challenge you to a sword fight for those words, were I not so tired."

"Ah! Our fights were the most fun. Of course, the only time I won was when you let me. And that time the new young maid wore that rather revealing dress, causing you to stumble."

"Yes, I have the scar."

"So, if you are not dreamy-eyed, tell me about the desert. Anything exciting happen?"

Fatia's face floated before Christophe, her smile causing her face to glow.

"Do you know that each time you leave we place bets on whether or not you will come home with a dark-haired Spanish or Greek goddess hanging from your arm? I am quite tired of losing my money to Claire on it."

The statement made his blood turn cold. There had been a time just a few years before when he had indeed tried to bring home a Spanish goddess. Or rather, not a goddess but a woman he had managed to get pregnant before killing her husband off in a duel.

Not killed, his conscience tried to convince him once again, but he didn't listen. That was not the type of conversation his sister expected to hear right now, though. Or ever.

"Why didn't you bring her back?"

"Who?" he asked.

"The Spanish goddess that has you in a tizzy."

He instantly recalled the last images of Dolores, surrounded by bloodied sheets with a ghostly face that would never return to her natural dark color. The image distracted him from his sister's question until he physically shook it away.

"I c-can't," he stuttered. "There is no Spanish goddess."

"So, a French one? Or Moroccan? I find it hard to believe that my brother has no important woman in his life. You are too old not to have some inkling of settling down."

"Emily, I know you are taking this marriage thing quite seriously, and I promise you that I will, as well. Someday. By the way, where is Mother?"

"She is in Bath. Since Russell passed on she has become more and more serious about her work with the Quakers. There is a woman there in Bath having a difficult time. When last Mother wrote, she observed that those who are freed from of slavery alone seem to have a much harder time adjusting to normal society than those who come out of it with someone."

Christophe couldn't help sitting up suddenly at the idea of a single woman out of slavery living in Bath. Could it be her? It would have been very difficult for her to have come to England alone, without him knowing, but it would not have been impossible.

Extreme exhaustion suddenly filled him, bringing him to the brink of collapse. Perhaps it was the same feeling a woman had when suddenly bursting into tears.

"You should cut that back," Emily teased, gesturing to his hair, falling out of its pomade. "It is no longer fashionable for a man to have hair near his jawline. You've been gone a long time."

"I suppose I should," Christophe conceded. "Well, little sister, I believe it's time for bed. The clock is striking an ungodly hour."

"You won't be leaving any more to Africa, will you?" Emily asked as they left the room behind. "You will stay here now?"

The expectation and hopefulness in her voice prevented him from telling her of his desire to go back and search for Fatia. But no. He would not even allow himself to be so hopeful.

"I am here for good now, Emily. You will tire of me though, I daresay," he answered with a laugh.

Chapter Nine

OCTOBER, 1832

ROWENA AND ELLIOT SAT on a fallen log, watching their white breath swirl through the air—a rather mundane act that became amusing after having spent the last three hours in a carriage stuffed between Grace and her friend, Lady Alice Ellison. They had spent the carriage ride disparaging nearly every member of the London peerage. "But I'm not looking for manners, Cinch. I'm looking for your wife."

After such drivel, conversation with Elliot seemed far broader and much more interesting to Rowena. With him, she could giggle and point out snow bunnies or squirrels. And he never disparaged her choice of dress or books to read. Quite the opposite—he liked to listen to her read to him.

They had stopped on the side of the road to let the horses rest for a while and allow the servants and family to eat their lunch. Rowena stood when her father came trotting back to join the family. He and Mr. Holden, a friend of his who had decided to accompany them on the trip, had ridden ahead to see if the roads were clear of vagabonds. While that was their excuse, Rowena speculated that their ride had more to do with wanting to avoid the topic of conversation in the carriage.

"Someday you must start teaching me to ride, Father," she said, petting the horse as he dismounted.

"It takes a lot of effort for a lady to learn how to be elegant on a horse." Alice's nasal voice rang out from inside the carriage. She had refused to eat her lunch outdoors. "I believe there are a great many other things you must learn before you go traipsing about on a horse."

"Learning to ride in the heart of London would be difficult for anyone your age," Mr. Holden said. His voice was sincere, though his smile mocked her. "You must come back to Beeker Hall in the spring and learn there."

"Yes," Grace called out, laughter already in the back of her throat. "At least there when you get thrown off only the groom will laugh instead of all of London."

Rowena bore the brunt of the joke calmly.

"I will teach you, Rowena. If you can ride a camel, I am certain you can ride a horse," Elliot said stoutly, his small fists balled against his thighs.

"Camels?" snorted Alice. "Lord above!"

"Would you like to take a walkabout, Benti?" James Brayemore asked, holding out his arm. "My legs would very much like to stretch a bit."

"But how much longer are we going to be stopped here like a traveling caravan of gypsies?" Grace asked, glaring at Rowena in a warning to refuse the invitation.

With a smile of defiance, Rowena took her father's arm. Together they ignored the protests still coming from Alice and Grace as they moved down the wooded path.

"It's beautiful around here," Rowena sighed, snuggled into her father's warmth.

"This is where the Candor land begins," James told her.

"Lord Candor?" asked Elliot, trailing idly behind them. "The marquess?"

James turned sharply to look at his son.

"What?" the boy asked. "Grace says he is on her list."

"Your sister talks entirely too much around you," James clucked with a laugh. "If she only knew how intently you were listening."

Elliot blushed. Rowen patted his head, then sighed in contentment at the beauty and peace around her as they continued. The tall trees clustered about, the crisp leaves that covered the ground, the exhilaratingly cold English air as well as walking with her father all worked together to make her feel like shouting in gladness.

"I am exceedingly happy, Baba," she told her father, who kissed her on the forehead in response. "All I wanted all these years was to come home. My greatest hope was that you would still be here when I got back. It has not been without its challenges. Sometimes I still forget the words in English. Just yesterday I couldn't remember the word for 'spoon'. But it is all coming back."

"Why wouldn't he be here when you got back?" asked Elliot, absently swishing a stick about like a sword.

"Your sister dares to refer to my age," the baron replied teasingly, effectively changing the subject as he always did when her absence was brought up.

"Only because you are so gray about the temples," Rowena teased in return, squeezing her father's arm.

"Yes, soon you'll think I should have a cane to walk about with —or perhaps I should just stay home, as I am too feeble to be out,"

James grumbled good-naturedly.

"I did beat you in our race the other day," Elliot pointed out, laughing.

As James challenged Elliot to a sword fight to see who was stronger, Rowena looked out from the road to the slope of a hill stretching up beyond a clearing that held a pond and some farming land. Far behind the pond rose another sloping hill where a large, primeval manor stood. The far westward corner was beginning to crumble, though the sun gleamed against new windows on the north and east sides. With the rolling clouds behind it, the setting was quite enchanting. England had seemed a cold, unfeeling place when she had seen it as a twelve-year-old girl. Now she looked about her and drank in the beautiful country where she was quite certain she could live forever if given the chance.

"That is Duncan Manor, the Marquess of Candor's estate," James said, breathing hard as he battled his fervent son. "Apparently, it is in dire need of repair. The last marquess tried to get the courts to relinquish the entailment on it so he could sell it, but he never got anywhere before showing up dead one day down at the docks."

"How can one show up dead at the docks?" asked Elliot, aiming a victorious jab at his father, who had stumbled over a tree root.

"He, ah—well, he fell while down at the docks and hit his head awfully hard, son," was all James answered, looking ashamed for speaking of such things in front of a young boy.

Elliot didn't seem to mind as he lifted his arms in triumph. "I believe I need a shilling or two for my victory," he said with a smile, running away when James swiped at him with his stick sword.

"Do you know him?" Rowena asked. "The marquess, I mean."

Her father shook his head, though his eyes looked beyond her into the past.

"I believe it was the former marquess' brother that inherited, though I could be mixing him up with someone else. I knew the eighth marquess, the late marquess' father, who inherited the title from his second uncle. He was a doctor, but became the next in line when his uncle lost both of his sons. One to the war in France and the other in a horse accident, I believe. The man who inherited was a good man, who used his title to work against slavery and to promote the poor man's struggle within the parliament walls. It was he, actually, who built that small clinic on the East End. I bought it when it came up for sale by the ninth marquess. The man mismanaged his finances and estate, they say. His younger brother bailed him out of scrapes many times. Seems he made a fortune."

"Where did the brother make his money?"

"He's in trade, or something that makes Grace wrinkle her nose as though smelling something sour. She says he will give it up once they are married, if he knows what is good for him," recounted Elliot.

The pounding of hooves cut their conversation short against the ground. Two large stallions burst from the woods near the pond at an impossible speed. Each rider yelled encouragements to their respective horses, their greatcoats blowing wildly in the wind as they taunted one another. A tall, gleaming hat flew off one fellow and into the frozen lake, but he did not bother to slow down. No longer under the confines of the hat, the man's hair flew every which way, and Rowena wondered just how he would see where he was going. The path they were on was clear of obstacles now, but it seemed they were headed straight towards the other patch of woods, where the path disappeared into the darkness after just a few feet.

"Oh, Papa, look! Really, you must teach me to ride. It seems like the most freeing thing in the world," she exclaimed, feeling the spark of tension that the air held as the riders flew by.

Her father grunted in disapproval. "I do not plan on losing you, just as I have got you back. When you ride, you must promise me to be careful," he admonished.

Rowena paid no attention. She kept watch on the woods until the two men emerged at a slow trot now, both in high spirits. Rowena could imagine each one claiming victory by the gestures and shouts of incredulities that rose to her and her father. One dismounted, laughing and shaking his head in protest at what the other said, as he looked about for something – probably the hat, which had slid across the ice with the wind and was now stuck in a bush. The wind blew loose strands of sand-colored hair across his face. The way he laughed pierced her heart, reminding her distinctly of Mr. Sutton.

"Are you alright, Benti?"

"She looks ill," Elliot declared. "Are you going to flay the fox? 'Cause if you are, I would rather go back now and not watch."

"Flay the fox?"

"Vomit."

"Elliot, I do not believe your mother would be proud of that phrase."

"Sorry, Papa. Still, Rowena looks sick."

Rowena smiled at her little brother. "No, Elliot. I was simply reminded of someone."

Her father nodded. "There are times I believe I see your mother simply from the color of a dress or the way a woman walks. She was the most graceful woman I had ever seen," he said wistfully. He was holding back a low-hanging branch, and paused for a moment longer before passing through.

Taking his arm in her hands once more, Rowena kept them from walking back to the carriage.

"Do you think that one of those men was the marquess?" she asked, looking down the hill, only to find the riders no longer there.

"If so, I recommend you find another nobleman. That one will make a woman a widow all too early, judging by his horsemanship."

"Pray, do not tell Grace that we even suspect it is true," Rowena pleaded with a smile. "Otherwise she will demand we encroach upon his home to introduce ourselves."

They walked for a time in silence after their laughter passed. The last time she had walked this way with her father they had been in Madrid, wandering through the narrow streets during the siesta when all the city seemed asleep.

"We know that Grace is determined to be titled," her father said slowly. "But what about you, my dear Benti? Who will you marry?"

"I don't know, Baba. I'm sure I do not wish to marry a man simply because he is a duke or earl or some other part of the ton. Although I have calmly sat through Grace's lesson on the latest edition of Burke's Peerage and I now have a firmer grasp on the current English peerage, I have seen too much of the world to believe that love comes more easily with a title. Sharing the rest of my life with someone makes the decision quite important. It is a wonder the girls here do not take more time in thinking it over. They only look at the outside of the man—the shell, you could say

—and never stop to think whether they will be happy with what's inside until they die."

"Many do not have the luxury of time. And more still do not truly have the luxury to choose. Their parents choose the man."

"And the parents think more about land, wealth, power or politics more than they think of their own daughter," Rowena said ruefully.

"Still, there are those who are happily married to the person their parents chose. Even those in nobility."

"Is that the most important to you, Baba? That I marry a nobleman?"

Her father shook his head with a laugh. "I only wish you to marry a man worthy of you."

"I think you should marry a pirate," Elliot said, winning his fight against the willow tree ahead.

"We will see who we can come up with, Baba. For now, I am content to be on your arm."

"You just find a man who treats you well, Benti, and the rest will follow in its place."

⚓

Christophe entered the study, expecting to find his family setting up the card table or already playing some rousing game of Falcon's invention. Instead, they sat around the fireplace, reading the gossip sheets. He was also surprised to find neighbors among them and was exceedingly glad his new valet had made sure to dress him properly for guests. Had he been left to his own devices, he would have made a fool of himself.

"Cinch! Nice to see you join us!" Claire exclaimed from the settee.

Introductions were made. The neighbors turned out to be Lord and Lady Carlisle and two spinster sisters who called each other Miss Partson.

"Are you recovered from your trip?" Claire asked. "It's the first day you don't look ghastly, I must admit. Which saves us from calling the doctor, as we were just debating."

"No." Christophe grimaced, heading to the bar and Falcon's whiskey. "I do not need a doctor. Where is Mother?"

"She decided to go on to London," Emily said, without looking up from the paper. "She has a new girl working with her and the former slaves. Says she had to help raise donations for their clothing drive. It helps to have her influential face asking people to give their best donations, you know."

"I could have taken her tomorrow."

"She left yesterday, Cinch. You would know that if you had come down to dinner," Claire said, her rebuke tempered by her smile. "After a few days in London, she plans to go directly to Lady Arlington's. She is on the abolitionist committee, and Jacqueline said there was something they had to speak about before the other guests arrive."

His family was suspicious, which was to be expected. He had left inexplicably one morning in August, had been gone for four weeks, and then returned in the night as though he had never left. Upon his return, he had once again slept in his office until Daucer had come and physically dragged him out. Daucer had forced Christophe to bathe and sleep at his own house before again obliging him to present himself to his mother, who had nearly fainted at the sight of him. The family had made quick work of making him feel guilty enough to go to Falcon Manor for harvest, even though he had piles of work to be done on his desk.

In the end, the trip had been both for naught and good for business. The orange orchard deal was working splendidly; he had had to hire another clipper to bring back all of the imports he had been able to procure. But he had not found any news of Fatia or her whereabouts. She had vanished; disappeared as though she had never existed. Most troubling of all was that he now realized just how much he had fallen for her. Without her, it was as though he had never existed. It was worse than after Catherine had betrayed him.

"Well, I think it's a perfectly lovely story of resilience and family bonds," the blonde Miss Partson declared loudly enough to bring Christophe forward to look as though he was participating.

"As do I," agreed Emily.

"I find the story a bit—odd. I'm not certain what to think of the whole tale. You are always willing to think the best of people, which is an admirable quality that I strive to emulate, but I can't help noticing that the story feels like it is missing pieces," Claire said.

"You don't believe her?"

"I suppose there isn't any reason not to believe her. If one is cut off from finances and trapped in a war, the years could pass without the person being able to get home. It is lucky she found Countess Merville. That kind of luck seems the most unusual of all."

"Why do you think she might have run away?" Emily asked.

"There have been a few rumors," Claire said simply.

"Rumors from whom?" asked Lady Carlisle. Her eyes narrowed slightly, sharpening her features to those of a bird.

"Lady Alice Ellison, who heard it from Lady Grace Hastling herself."

"Who is Lady Grace?" asked the Miss Partson with the mousy brown hair, parted severely down the middle and pulled to the back.

"Her stepsister."

"The Duke of Auster's daughter is her stepsister? My, her homecoming might not have been everything she expected then," Emily said. She then turned to Christophe, who readied himself for an explanation he had not asked for. "Grace came out this last season and was the belle of society. She is very much the model of English ton, and is expected to make a superb match. She and Lady Alice, Claire's cousin, have become fast friends – probably due to their general disregard for anyone else. Grace has a beauty that muddles men's brains and manners that would impress the dragons. I know of quite a few bids going for her at White's."

"I do not wish to find out how you know about what goes on at White's," Falcon declared. "Please, do not go into detail."

"Really, Falcon. I have not tried to go behind enemy lines since my coming out," Emily said, smiling coquettishly at her husband. Falcon rolled his eyes and threw up his hands.

"You snuck into White's?" Christophe sputtered, choking back the strong liquor as best he could. "You—Emily—I do not know —How did you do that?"

"It was a very long time ago, and I did not actually get in," Emily said. "Anabel's brother works there."

"You shouldn't listen to the gossip your maid gives you," Claire said, before turning her full attention to Christophe, who was still struggling to control his cough. "Are you quite well, Cinch? Perhaps some tea would help you swallow that down."

"I'm sorry, I don't seem to follow who, or what, we are talking about," he wheezed, clearing his throat again for good measure.

"What started this path of confessions that I would rather not know anything about?"

His question resulted in gasps from everyone, including Falcon, who covered his with a smirk.

"Haven't you read the papers, Lord Candor?"

"Really, I don't know how he's missed it."

Christophe cleared his throat again.

"Dearest Cinch—"

"Claire, do not call me that."

"Candor."

"Nor that either."

Falcon laughed and soon everyone joined him, highlighting the difference the title made in his life.

"Ah, you will not get away with not using your title," Claire said. "You can't be rid of it. Except by dying."

"Ha. Very amusing, Claire. I will try my best, then, to get used to it."

"Now that you're in England, Candor," Falcon said, pausing to get a giggle from the Partson sisters, "you must focus on what is truly important: the gossip sheets."

"Darling, it isn't that we feel it is so very important," protested Emily. "The problem is this weather. One can only play so much vingt-et-un."

"Or crochet so many bonnets," Claire added.

"Or embroider so many kerchiefs."

"I agree the rain has made things a bit dull this last week," agreed both of the Miss Partsons. Christophe moved farther away. The way they smiled without ceasing unnerved him.

"Besides, Falcon, you seem to know more about the story than anyone," Claire pointed out.

Falcon gave a bow, then flashed them all a smile. Though his average looks tended not to distinguish him from the crowd, Falcon could garner quite a bit of attention thanks to his charm and innocent smile.

"I concede that the weather has made these days dull. I also concede that I have read the gossip pages word for word."

"Would someone mind telling me what we are talking about?" Christophe asked again. "Since it is apparently vital I know these things before the season starts."

"Oh, darling! It is vital that you know these things before the Arlington Ball next week!" exclaimed Emily with a teasing grin.

Lady Carlisle nodded vigorously. "She will be there with her father and stepmother."

"I do not understand what warrants this to be so interesting. And since when have I agreed to go to a ball?"

"Oh, Cinch! She is the daughter of Baron Brayemore. Though some do not believe he deserves the title, he has the devotion of King George. It was he who helped the king earn money, or a treaty, or some such thing. At any rate, his daughter has returned, though she was thought dead for five years!" Emily said, ignoring his comment about the ball altogether. Falcon shot him a look that revealed Christophe would have no choice.

The Partson sisters took up the story of how the girl had been separated from her father during the French invasion and rescued by English missionaries in north Africa. The blonde one clenched Christophe's forearm tightly, keeping him in place next to her. But it wasn't long before Emily interrupted the sisters, sweeping her arms about as she told a fanciful tale of a young girl lost on the docks while her family sailed away from Algeria at the beginning of the French siege. The performance was met with claps and sighs by the end.

"So, Cinch. What do you think? Could her story be true?" Emily asked, now serious.

"A girl trapped in Algiers? Of course. Once the fighting began, it would be quite difficult to get out, especially being female. What I don't understand is why a young English girl was there in the first place."

"She practically grew up there, only coming to England for a short time, during which her father met the new baroness and married her. They went back to Algeria for him to finish some business. A friend of mine, Chastity Fallbright, knew her back then."

"I remember a story of an English businessman in Tangier. He was respected in the area," Christophe said. "He was known for traveling with the nomads when he was younger, and was both feared and adored by the native people. I heard a legend that the only man who ever tried to steal from the Englishman was found with his head severed, which some say he displayed on a post in front of his house as a warning. I do doubt that part was true, though."

"Cinch!" Emily gasped, her face turning a strange shade of green, all romanticism gone from her face. Claire set her tea down slowly, along with the cake she had almost brought to her mouth. The two Miss Partsons sat ghostly pale, trembling in their chairs. Only Lady Carlisle seemed eager to hear more.

"Blast," Christophe muttered, shoving his hair behind his ear.

"Using that language isn't going to help your cause right now," Emily chastised him, her face slightly recovered. "Go on. *Without* any more stories of heads on sticks."

Claire groaned in protest, but Emily gave her brother an eager nod.

"The Algerians respected him because he took care of more than his share. There were stories of him riding into remote villages with food and barrels full of water. There were other stories still of him paying debts for men, of buying slaves only to set them free, and of being an adoring father to a beautiful little girl. The girl earned her own fame with her voice. Some legends claim she performed for a few magistrates, the English ambassador and several sultans."

"What happened to them?" asked the Miss Partsons.

Christophe shrugged. "There are several endings. One story says the Englishman went back to England just as the French blockaded Tangiers, leaving behind his large estate outside the city. Some say he left because the girl died. Others still say she became a singer in Europe or hypnotized a rich sultan and persuaded him to marry her."

Emily sighed with contentment.

"Why would an English girl want to marry a sultan?" Claire asked, one brow raised in surprise.

"It would be like marrying a duke or prince here," Christophe tried to explain.

"Do you think it is the same girl?" Lord Arlington asked.

Christophe laughed. "I have no idea. I've never bothered to think about the story as being true."

"A beautiful English girl who is suddenly thrust into working with missionaries..." Claire mused. "I can't imagine her being the same girl."

Christophe shook his head.

"At the moment, life in Algeria is harder than before, although things are better in some places. If she was in an area where the French had taken over, then perhaps she didn't have as many difficulties. Living where the French are not yet in control would be harder for a European girl all alone."

Christophe fell silent as his family discussed the new information, his mind wandering to Fatia. As her face appeared in his mind's eye, blurry lines started to connect to something he couldn't quite yet understand.

"Are you alright, Cinch?" Falcon asked in a low voice.

He pushed Fatia's image away. "Fine. Bit of a headache," he lied.

"Well, I want to get to know this young woman, and I believe you are the next best person to make her feel welcomed," exclaimed Emily suddenly, breaking the threat of a heavy mood.

"Yes, of course!" exclaimed the mousy-haired Miss Partson. "You have been to Algeria. You are the best positioned to help her acclimate to England again."

"I beg your pardon?" Christophe asked.

"Emily! You cannot match her and your brother together before you've even met the girl."

"Emily," Christophe warned. His tone did nothing to stop the gleam in his sister's eyes. "I can be perfectly receptive to our neighbors without your meddling hand."

"But I'm not looking for manners, Cinch. I'm looking for your wife."

Chapter Ten

CHERSHIRE MANOR

ROWENA TRIED TO QUIET her breath as she walked into the glowing dining room of Cheshire Manor.

Before-dinner gossip was something she did not yet grasp well; she always found herself standing alone, wishing she could hide. At her father's suggestion, she had taken a bath to calm her nerves. She had felt much better until she'd realized that she would now have to walk into the dining room late, which might start gossip about her not knowing the proper traditions—or, worse, that she refused to adhere to them.

Young, gleeful laughter floating from the parlor almost caused Rowena to run back up to her room. After four weeks of visiting different aunts and uncles within her father's family, meeting with younger people had been both exciting and intimidating. The best way to fit in with a crowd who knew nothing of anything she had lived and with whose habits she had little in common was silence, she had found. Silence followed by a smile or two was the easiest, but she was to attend her first ball in her life in just two more nights and she wasn't quite certain silence would work there.

While she had practiced dancing with her maid a few times, the very idea of dancing in public filled her with horror.

"There you are, Miss Brayemore," Lady Arlington said, taking her hands. "We thought perhaps you weren't feeling well enough to join us for dinner."

"I'm sorry for being late—"

"Do not worry so," the duchess interrupted, handing her off to a footman. "Please, Matthew will take you to your seat."

Rowena followed the footman dutifully, pressing her hands together to stop them from shaking.

"Miss Brayemore, it is such a pleasure to meet you," said a short, slender woman as Rowena sat down. The woman's eyes sparkled with genuine pleasure, which settled her nerves almost instantly.

"My dear Lady Glenville!" exclaimed Lady Bonneville, one of her father's friends. "Let me introduce you to the Honorable Miss Brayemore. Miss Brayemore, the Earl and Countess Glenville. And to your left, you have Lady Candor, Lady Glenville's sister-in-law. I convinced Lady Arlington to forgo the formalities of table seating tonight."

"Amelia, darling! What a saint you are! We so wished to meet Miss Brayemore that we would have incited a round of musical chairs to change the seating."

"Do not think for a moment she is joking," Lady Candor added with a small smile. "Emily has a way of getting hers when possible."

Rowena felt a pang of homesickness at Lady Bonneville's hearty laughter, the sound reminding her of the large windchime outside the female baignoires at Saed's mansion. A strange, aching pain shot through her heart. For a moment, she was overcome with the strange desire to run back to the mountains of Algeria. She shook her head slightly with disgust. There was nothing in Algeria for her and everything for her here in England.

"Are you alright, my dear?" Emily asked quietly.

"It's very—hot, isn't it?" Rowena asked, trying to shake away the feeling.

Lady Glenville squeezed her hand as Lady Candor handed her a glass of wine.

"Take a sip of wine and it will pass," Lady Candor said. Rowena wondered if she was the wife of the new marquess or the widow of the former. "You may call me Claire. Sometimes I feel the same way when I attend these things. But we're a small party, and I will stay by your side the entire night if you wish. We won't even have to converse if you get tired."

"This is a small party? There are almost forty people!" Rowena said in a hushed voice.

Lady Glenville giggled. "All right, not so very small. But not so very large either. There will be more at the ball. You will be attending, won't you?"

Her blood ran cold, but Rowena forced herself to smile.

"Emily, dear, where is that brother of yours? You said he would be here. I told you I expected him to come," Lady Bonneville barked before Rowena could answer Emily.

Lady Glenville sighed dramatically. "Oh, darling. He may have ascended to the title now, but he refuses to let go of his work. Quite improper, considering his title and all that, but he won't let anyone say it to his face. Except our Claire."

"England would fall if not for our new marquess!" Lady Candor declared. "Or so he would have us believe."

Rowena giggled, the wine relaxing her nerves. In the midst of acceptance, she suddenly felt young for the first time in a long time.

"Better?" Lady Glenville asked, her attention back on Rowena.

"Much," Rowena answered with a smile.

"Good! I have so very many questions for you, I don't even know where to start!"

"My dear, please don't fatigue Miss Braymore during dinner. You have all weekend and the rest of the season to make her acquaintance," Lord Glenville said sternly, his eyes twinkling in contrast.

"Oh, posh! She doesn't look like she fatigues easily! Besides, I'm the most enjoyable company at this table—"

"I will have to disagree with you," Lady Candor interrupted, giving her sister-in-law a wink.

Lady Glenville giggled before continuing. "You see, Miss Braymore, I'm so intrigued by your tale. I have never left England before, even to go to Wales or Scotland. My husband's family has a crumbling castle there, in Scotland I mean, but he has yet to take me."

"Darling, crumbling is the word to focus on there. Since it is, in fact, crumbling, there is not much reason to go and no place to stay."

The lady ignored her husband, who didn't seem the least bit concerned. Instead, he looked adoringly at his wife as she chatted on. Rowena noticed that many near them expressed their disapproval of his open sentiment by sighing loudly or coughing into their wine.

"You have seen so much of the world," Lady Glenville was saying. "I'm quite jealous. Here we are, about the same age, and all I have done is produce some children. I think it's time I went on a trip or two, since the pirates are as good as abolished and there is no war on the continent to impede me. Do you recommend traveling?"

"Very much," Rowena said, pushing away her alarm at the revelation that Emily had more than one child already. "My travels only extend to the North of Africa, one trip to Berlin, though I was quite young and do not remember it very well, and a small bit of Spain. I do intend to travel more in my life, though. At one time, I had small drawings hung on my wall of all the places I wanted to visit one day: Rome, Berlin, Paris, Moscow, Prague. I used to sit and dream of the places that seemed to hold the mystery of another people and language."

"How many languages do you speak? I should think I would like to see Africa as well, though not just in the North. I would very much like to see how differently people live, and since I do believe everyone on the continent lives almost the same as we do here, I should think Africa would give me that taste of difference. India, too. And then there are the Americas. Do you have any desire to see America, Rowena? I can call you by your Christian name, can I not? And you call me Emily, for we are practically friends already."

"I would like to go to America one day—"

"If Rowena were to go to the Americas, she would be soon arrested and hanged," Grace interrupted, commanding the attention of at least half the table. "She believes the black man is equal to her, you see—though no doubt that idea started from her own skin becoming so dark from the African sun, one could barely say she was English at all. Apparently, when she worked in the mission, she ate next to the black children and shared a room with a black maid."

There were audible gasps from several women as Grace sat back, looking smug. Rowena frowned, but Grace pointedly looked away.

"Lady Grace, you are in the presence of many abolitionists. My mother also works very hard towards the new Slavery Abolition Act. She is well-acquainted with some of the Quakers there and is desperately trying to convince my brother to take his seat for the vote," Lady Glenville declared. "The Dowager of Candor would very much agree with your views, Miss Brayemore, and not with those of others at this table."

Rowena couldn't help feeling victorious at the sight of Grace blushing, though her victory was squashed when she saw her stepmother nervously biting her lip and whispering to her father.

It was nearing nine in the morning when Christophe finally rode up the curved drive to Chershire Manor. After handing his horse over to a young stable boy, Christophe took a deep breath and strolled to the front. The butler had no time to announce his presence before Emily cried out and Claire greeted him with her wry smile.

"You aren't even dressed, Cinch!" Emily shook her head, stopping herself from hugging him when she saw the dust on his coat.

"How could I be, if I came here on horseback?"

"Is the horse also to blame for you no longer shaving your face?" Claire asked, tapping her own cheeks.

"Well, have some coffee, for you look half-frozen, and try not to scowl so much as you scan the room. The other guests will think the countess invited a ghoul to entertain them," his mother admonished.

Christophe tried to smooth his expression into one of passive interest as he glanced around the room.

"Are you very tired, dear?"

"Overly so. For the last five days, I've been on horseback for over twenty-four hours between London and Duncan Manor. I have slept little, as there always seems to be more to do. The mines are in shambles, the tenants' houses are crumbling; everything needs a solution."

"I thought you had found some solutions?" Lady Candor asked.

"For some of the problems," he answered, then turned to his sister-in-law. "Emily, must you bounce around me as though you were still twelve years old?"

He received a playful swat in reply.

"Careful, Cinch, she has learned to punch as well," Falcon called from a wing-backed chair to Christophe's right.

"My dear sister, you are being awfully overbearing. What is it you desire? You prowl all the more when you have something to say and can't quite find the right moment."

"Emily thinks she has a wife lined up for you. All you have to do is say yes," Claire said. "But Emily, he does not wish to speak about the subject."

Emily huffed. "Why must you take the conversation from me? He must marry, and soon—so he must start to listen."

Christophe looked at the two women, his fatigue starting to overwhelm his senses. "You are relentless. Why the sudden interest in my marital status?"

"A way to keep you in England," Emily answered. "And the fact that the next heir is our cousin, who is quite a horrible human being."

"True. Very well, then. Give me your list of women so that I may point out all the reasons I do not wish to marry them."

"Not so easy, Cinch. When teased too much, she gets worse," his brother-in-law warned. "You might as well allow her to tell you the gory details of your imminent match and not say a word. You must take the woman out for a walk through the park before you can come up with a suitable reason as to why you cannot marry her. It's a very long process, denying a suit; much easier to just marry the lass. It's what I had to do."

Emily gave her husband a round punch to the shoulder, which didn't stop him from chuckling harder. Two young women who had been quietly taking their tea on the other side of the room rose to leave. Christophe assumed his family's domination of the space had a little something to do with that, as well as their inability to speak in hushed tones.

"All right, dear sister, do tell me all. I hope you don't have the lady who was sitting over there in mind. While she's pretty, she's too young."

"Grace?" gasped Emily. "Certainly not. I'm sure she will try her best to seduce you, since you are a marquess, but she does not suit you. Not at all. Though I will acknowledge that she is pretty."

Claire snorted, and Falcon choked on his tea.

"Come now, you cannot deny she is pretty."

"Perhaps. That is, when she smiles and tries to be pleasant. The problem is that she seems to be in a perpetual state of pouting. I've begun to think she believes it makes her looks perhaps more—"

"Seductive?" Claire suggested.

Falcon grimaced openly. "If she thinks that, then someone should point out to her that, in fact, the opposite is true. It makes her look most unbecoming."

"Enough of Lady Grace. Back to what is important," Emily commanded.

"Oh, no. I know that look. You are quite determined in this."

"Very."

"How many girls are on this list?" Christophe asked with a sigh.

"Only one."

Falcon snickered as Christophe choked on his tea, leaving him coughing and wheezing out a reply. Emily gleefully watched him struggle with the statement. Were they children again, he would have pushed her directly into the mud for her self-assured look. He wheezed again and was finally capable of answering his haughty little sister.

"You are putting quite a bit of weight into one prospective wife. Why?"

"She is perfect for you."

"How can you possibly know this?"

"Because she has been in North Africa for years and she has a look about her that says she has seen more of the world than most of we ladies—just the woman for you. She will listen to and understand your stories, and perhaps she has a few of her own."

"Who is this woman?" he demanded.

"Remember the lady the Partson sisters were asking you about?" Claire put in.

"Miss Brayemore. She's here!" Emily clasped her hands at her heart, looking as though she might burst from happiness. Her smile widened as Falcon's chuckling became all-out laughter. Even Claire joined in to confirm Christophe's defeat. With exhaustion and cold seeping into his bones, he finally threw his arms in the air. A hot bath and rest before the ball were out of reach unless he stopped this argument of wills with his sister.

"I will dance with whomever you wish me to dance with. I will smile, and I will make nice. But I will not offer marriage."

"Yet," Emily said, her eyes twinkling. "You will not offer yet."

Chapter Eleven

ROWENA PULLED THE HOOD of her cloak closer to find some warmth. The wind had picked up as the afternoon settled in, bringing a cool mist with it. She dreamed of a hot bath as she forced her feet to march along. A long, hot bath before the ball would be just the thing to settle her nerves, since her walk hadn't.

Coming around the corner of the garden path, she stopped in her tracks. Two men covered in stood on the covered terrace, the smoke trails of their pipes following the way of the setting sun. One looked to be the Earl of Glenville, who was a kind man and one she feared nothing from, but the other had his back to her. He was tall with broad, strong shoulders and had a low voice that carried well with the wind. His entire physique reminded her of Sutton, but if she was honest with herself, Rowena would admit that there was not a day during which something did not remind her of him. Some mornings she awoke desperate to see him.

The London season was approaching, something she had looked forward to before realizing that she and Sutton might run into each other at a ball or social event. Society in London seemed quite large from the outside, but it was not large enough for them to never pass near each other. While it was possible that Mr. Sutton did not frequent society, the idea offered little comfort. Worse still was the idea that if their paths *were* to cross, he probably wouldn't recognize her. Everything, from her name to her face, had changed. Even her skin and her figure were different. Her hair was clean, always up, and her hips no longer jutted out but curved smoothly under her many skirts of silk or gauze. The person in the mirror seemed entirely foreign to her some days.

Cold tension coiled around her. Irrationally, she didn't wish to pass by the two strange gentlemen. She turned on her heels towards the stables. The smell of hay and horses would comfort her while she waited for the men to enter the house.

"Relax," Rowena murmured to herself. "There is nothing strange about men on the terrace. This is England. A woman can pass by men on her way to a dinner party without being molested."

The cold wind took the role of disciplinarian, whipping hard across her face as though to make her believe her own words. Many times since coming home she had needed to chide herself, soothe away the strange breathless desire to run. Sometimes it was from tea with Grace's friends, other times dinner with her father's associates. Sometimes it was simply entering a room where Bernadette was. The instinct to run and hide, to never come back, she could usually tame while in the house. It was in unfamiliar environments that it caused her to go mute and impeded her from hearing what was being spoken around her. Many times she would lie in bed at night, unable to remember the dinner party she had just attended.

This time neither her lecture nor the wind's cold whipping could convince her to turn around, however. Instead, Rowena continued into the warm stables. At least Fatia had known what she wanted: to get home to freedom, to see her father, to eat enough and to wear silk slippers again. While becoming Rowena had satisfied all the things Fatia had longed for, the change required Rowena to question what she now wanted. Unfortunately, there seemed no reasonable desire within her other than to see Sutton again. It was as though seeing him would stabilize her somehow, remind her of who she was, and tell her who she might become.

A whistling sound pulled her from her thoughts as she entered the stables. It could have been the wind, but when a piercing scream followed, Rowena froze. She knew exactly what it was. For a moment, fear threatened to send her to the floor. It wasn't until a tiny voice cried for help that her fear broke.

This was England, her mind seemed to scream. England. Not Algeria.

A man grunted with effort. Something fell to the floor with a dull thud, a whimper following. Rowena flew down the length of the stables as the whip drew back again, just beyond the last stall. Without thinking further, she threw herself around the corner, twirling her cloak to envelop the small heap on the floor.

A long, sharp pain sliced across her back, but the only thing Rowena concerned herself with was the trembling under her chest. Brown hair smelling of dust and hay tickled her throat. The boy, not much older than ten, shook without ceasing, his thin arms clutching at her. The whip came down twice more before she heard curses spill over her. The third strike cut through her dress and corset, but Rowena kept her mind on the trembling soul under her woolen cloak and hood.

"What the devil!" screamed a man before an iron grip pulled her away from the boy by her shoulder. Rowena whirled around, sending the man stumbling backward, nearly falling over.

"You are sacked, sir."

The stable master at Chershire was bulky, greasy, and smelled of cheap liquor. There were days of growth on his cheeks, and his hands were shaking in rage. Rowena could not help her lips curling at the sight of him.

"Damnation, woman! Get out! 'Tis none of your blasted business!" the man roared, suddenly finding his bearings.

"I pray you stop using such language, sir. And it is you who must leave. You are dismissed."

Rowena stood firm, not moving an inch as the stout man stepped in closer to her, his jowls shaking. He made to grab the boy from behind her, but Rowena moved quicker than he, pressing the boy against her side. She brought her head closer to the man's and narrowed her eyes.

"You do not want to add molesting a baron's daughter to your grievances, sir."

The man's eyes widened. His already red face turned purple. His mouth opened and closed, but no sound dared to come out. Another stable hand came in through the back door and stopped in his tracks at the sight before him.

"Go to the house and fetch Baron Brayemore and Lord Arlington. Now!" Rowena demanded, not moving her gaze from the head stableman.

"It doesn't matter what you tell 'im. I've been in the duke's service for over twenty years. This *boy*," he said, sneering at the trembling body against Rowena's hip, "needs to learn 'is place and his job. I can't 'ave 'im dropping saddles that cost more than 'is life on the floor. This is the best way for 'im to learn to never do it again."

Rowena's rage boiled higher, but she kept her peace as the stable master continued to bellow. There would be time enough to say what she wished. Right now, she was more concerned about wrapping the boy in her arms to stop his trembling.

"Rowena! What is going on?" her father's voice finally boomed from the front of the stables. Behind him came Lord Arlington, looking rather grim.

"Mr. Dermont! What is this about?" the duke demanded.

Mr. Dermont pointed to Rowena with a fat, shaking finger, his voice no longer filled with as much confidence.

"She came flying in 'ere, throwing 'erself onto the floor, and I couldn't stop the whip in time, your grace."

The pain searing through her back suddenly became more pronounced as Mr. Dermont reminded her about the wound.

"You whipped my daughter?" The baron's voice was low, barely audible.

Mr. Dermont stammered, throwing spittle about as he searched for an explanation, but Rowena wasn't about to let him speak.

"I came into the stables after hearing this boy being hit by a whip. His offense seems to have been dropping a saddle on the floor. If it is that one that remains there, I would dare to say it is too great a burden for this small boy to lift above his head. Perhaps if Mr. Dermont would feed his hands better or give them jobs more adept to their age and weight, fewer offenses would be committed. I also must comment that perhaps Mr. Dermont would have more patience with his charges if he didn't indulge in the bottle before finishing his work."

Mr. Dermont again turned a mottled purple, but Rowena pressed on.

"I have discharged Mr. Dermont."

"Rowena—"

But she did not give her father time to make his statement. "I realize that he is your man, your grace. Please forgive me for overstepping my bounds. You have the last word, but I will not be leaving this boy behind in this man's care. He will not see Mr. Dermont again, even if he must become my charge," she said, feeling her hands shake under Lord Arlington's narrowed gaze. "You, take this boy to the kitchen and tell Mrs. O'Riley to give him some warm milk. Then send him to the nursery to be washed and spend the night. I will be there in a moment to tend to his wounds."

"Your grace," began the baron. "Please, forgive my daughter. She has overstepped your authority—"

"Brayemore! You do not mean to defend him?" demanded Lord Arlington. "Look at your daughter! Her dress is ruined. And she's bleeding!"

At that moment Bernadette flew into the stables and shrieked in horror. Unconscious of the agony she would cause, she placed her hand on Rowena's back.

Sharp, burning pain burst in a shock through her body. Bile rose in her throat, and memories of the first time she had been whipped threatened to overtake her senses. With a deep breath, Rowena pushed those memories away and moved to lean against her father, out of reach from her stepmother's hand.

"I'm the man your father hired to train his racers when 'e was alive, your grace," Mr. Dermont was saying, pleading with Lord Arlington.

"Go and sleep off your drunkenness," the duke commanded. "My secretary will see to you tomorrow. This is your last night here."

Mr. Dermont's curses echoed through the stable. Bernadette gasped in horror, but the man only seemed proud of bruising her ears.

"I suggest you do as you were told, Mr. Dermont," Lord Arlington warned. "Go and sleep off your drinking. Come, Miss Brayemore, you must get that cleaned and bandaged."

James took hold of her hand, careful not to touch her back, but the fabric of her dress pulled painfully against the drying blood, opening the wound again. Trying to force herself not to faint, Rowena bent towards the ground as they came up to the terrace.

"May I be of service, Brayemore?"

"Thank you, but my daughter will be fine once she can lie down a bit."

"She is hurt. Shall I call for the doctor?"

Rowena shook her head, still looking at the floor.

"I am qu-quite fine," she stuttered, nausea flowing over her in waves.

"Nonsense. Falcon, run and see that the doctor is summoned and that a bath is prepared for the lady in her rooms. I will carry her there."

The demands were called out quickly and with authority. Her father explained that she did not wish to be carried, but the man paid no heed. Even as she feebly protested, the stranger gathered her gently into his arms, somehow managing not to pull on the wound.

"You will be all right," he murmured.

Cradled against his chest, Rowena dared to relax and breathed in a strangely familiar musky smell. The last time she had been whipped, the man had left her to crawl back by herself to where

Selma waited for her with the salve they had used to heal the wounds.

"Almost there now. Are you in pain?" the man asked.

Suddenly, the voice seemed to burst through her memory, stopping her heart.

It was Sutton.

She jerked her head up, only to find her vision filled with stars at the pain. She gasped for breath, but it was too late. For the first time in her life, she fainted like a swooning debutante... directly in the arms of the man she had dreamed of seeing again.

※

"You are an ass," Christophe mumbled to himself.

They were but a few feet from the house now, but instead of hurrying Christophe slowed his pace slightly. He was alone outside with her, the baron and his wife having passed by him in a hurry to meet the doctor at the door, and suddenly he had a very strong urge to see the woman in his arms. It occurred to him that he knew of no man who would sacrifice themselves under a whip in place of a boy, much less a woman.

Light from inside the house streamed down on them, revealing brown, reddish hair swept across her face, the color reminding him of Fatia.

Fatia. Just like that, his attention turned to the woman who had plagued him since the day she had vanished. The ache in his heart was just as strong as it had been five months ago, but he shook it away yet again. He had promised himself to let go of Fatia and move on. Christophe looked down again and forced himself to be reasonable.

Yes, both women had brown hair with red flecks through it. Both were about the same height. But, of course, she was not Fatia. Just as the other three women whom he'd mistaken for Fatia had turned out not to be her.

"Thank you, my lord," Bernadette said as Christophe handed the girl over to the footman. He bowed to the baroness, who paid him no attention as she smoothed back her stepdaughter's hair just as the girl's eyes fluttered open.

Christophe knew he should turn and go in the other direction; the entire situation no longer involved him—but he couldn't leave. Against his own advice, he dawdled behind the footman and baroness as they made their way to the stairs. He hoped to settle his disappointment, but the girl's face remained obscured by the baroness all the way up the stairs. At the girl's room, the view opened, and Christophe found himself looking into eyes that seemed once again familiar before the doctor bustled through and the door was soundly closed.

"My God," he moaned to himself. "I find her everywhere."

Christophe entered his room, heavy with the certainty that he needed some rest to remove this obsession with Fatia from his brain—and that he was a fool.

Chapter Twelve

"TIME TO GO," EMILY crooned, her voice suspiciously sweet as she walked into Falcon's room, where Christophe and his family were having a glass of wine.

"What have you done?" he asked. She looked entirely too gleeful.

"I have done nothing!"

"I don't believe you," Christophe answered, folding his arms in front of the door to impede anyone's passing. "You are starting to giggle, which means you're lying."

"I'm not," Emily protested, her eyes darting to Claire as her giggles turned to full laughter.

"Out with it," Claire demanded.

Emily gasped for breath. "Sir Randal has been invited."

Claire groaned loudly while Emily tried to control her snickering.

"Who is Sir Randal?" asked Christophe, hoping the man had nothing to do with him.

Claire sent Emily a stern look, but it was too late. Even Daucer and Falcon were snickering into their cups.

"You will know him as the one who pursues Claire all evening," Daucer said.

"As I'm sure some others will as well," Christophe said with a shrug.

"Yes," Emily gasped, trying to control her merriment. "But he is hard to miss. He reaches only to Claire's shoulders, has a protruding belly that looks as though he has swallowed a boulder, usually wears a pink or garish green waistcoat, and within a moment of arriving will be seen wiping his brow repeatedly. Crowds make him nervous."

"But he braves them to see our dear sister-in-law," Falcon said, flashing Claire a wide smile.

Claire looked as though she were ready to light hot coals under all of them. "I'm glad you both find it so very amusing. I will be sure to let Sir Randal know that you wish to dance the dinner waltz with him so the two of you can discuss fashion, Emily."

"Don't you dare! Oh, this terrible gown makes it rather difficult to laugh."

"Perhaps it was meant for a proper lady of the ton who doesn't burst into a fit of giggles over a man's pink waistcoat," said Claire.

"If he is here, you must be kind to him, but not lead him on," Lady Candor said firmly as she adjusted her gloves. "Now, come along or we will be late. Falcon, you owe me the first dance."

"I would be delighted," Falcon answered before the family descended the stairs.

They greeted their hostess, who was already looking annoyed with the receiving line, and entered the ballroom. Everything about it pricked Christophe's nerves. The heat, the crowd, the smell; it was all insufferable. Looking about, he noticed some young ladies trying to make eyes at him and frowned. Of course. For young ladies, a ball was all about finding a husband.

"Lord Candor," boomed a voice from not far enough away.

Christophe turned to greet the man, but found himself amid a sea of lacy frocks and giggles. Claire took a step back with a grin. He could expect no help from her.

"Nice to see you again, Candor," the voice boomed again – a voice Christophe was certain he should know. Before he could place it with a face, the cluster of young women parted just enough to let through a thin, tall man with sunken eyes and a nervous smile.

"Lord Rathford," Christophe said, uneasy at the surge of giggles his bow seemed to cause. Being away so long from balls and parties had put him out of practice with the odd ways of younger females.

"Allow me to introduce you to my daughters," the man said proudly, with a hint of desperation in his voice. "This is Lady Jessamine and Lady Hester. And these are my daughters Lady Frances and Lady Winnifred."

Now Christophe remembered why the man had a right to be desperate; he had two sets of female twins—all of which were apparently looking for husbands.

Politely, Christophe bowed over each of their hands as they giggled self-consciously and whispered behind their fans. Since each had to whisper above the other while Lord Rathford and he exchanged niceties about Parliament, their words were easily heard. When the niceties ran out, Lord Rathford looked at him, then at his daughters, and waited. Claire stood to the side, looking very entertained. Christophe wished he could ignore his societal responsibilities just to spite her.

"Lady Jessamine, would you do me the honor of the next dance?" he asked, holding his hand out for her card. It was a wonder the girl managed to give it to him with all the giggling she was doing. After two very long minutes, he had his name on each girl's card.

"Debutante's mistake," chided Claire as the giggling twins walked away. "You will end up dancing all night—and making more than one girl think she has a chance with you, if you are not careful."

"I have lost my touch, it seems," Christophe mused. "Or perhaps I never had one. *Perhaps* I used to have friends who would stand by me and help me instead of hinder me."

"Why, whatever are you saying, Cinch?" Claire asked with innocence, her fan spread out over her chest. "I would have helped you, really, but I thought you wanted to dance with them."

"Hmm. You helped me, and now I will help you. Sir Randolph, I presume?" Christophe grinned as Claire turned with trepidation to face the short man already mopping sweat from his brow.

"Why, yes, Lord Candor. I didn't think you would remember me, as we met only once five years ago. You were with your brother at Parliament. 'Twas shortly after the death of your father. Quite a loss for England, he was." The man puffed, his chest heaving with a wheeze.

"I recognized you instantly," Christophe said with a smile, as he shook the man's hand. "Do you know my sister-in-law?"

"Of course! My lady," Sir Randal muttered, bowing over Claire's hand long enough for her to shoot Christophe a death glare. His smile broadened. "May I have this dance?"

"Of course you may, sir!" Christophe exclaimed. "I must go and find my own eager partner. Have a lovely time, dear sister."

Christophe laughed as Claire mouthed words of hatred at him before taking Sir Randal's age-spotted hand. His grin sobered when he found Miss Jessamine nervously fanning herself at the edge of the dance floor.

"Oh!" Her hands fluttered as he bowed over them, the fingers still trembling when he gathered them in his to direct her to the dance floor.

"You do not think so ill of me as to suppose that I would forget?" he asked, smiling. "Come, Lady Jessamine. Let's dance."

With neither partner gifted in the art of small talk, the dance passed in relative silence. Christophe was happy to note that he still moved just as gracefully as he used to, but that was hardly the thing to say to a lady. When the dance ended, Lady Jessamine left with a pout.

The next dance was with Lady Winnifred, who constantly tripped over imaginary obstacles. Lady Hester laughed each time they touched hands during the quadrille, ending each laugh in a snort, and Lady Frances made up for all her sisters' silence by talking incessantly through the entire dance, even when they stepped apart from one another. She simply included everyone down the line in their conversation.

Once he had deposited the last Rathford with her family, Christophe swiftly took Claire to the dance floor for a good scolding. Waltzes worked well for those.

"Let me tell you a little about the last four dances and how I passed them," he began, dropping his voice to tell his tale of woe.

"I do not think you suffered as much as I. Do you see my glove? It is ruined from his sweat." Claire held up her hand. "This is after one dance, Cinch."

Christophe laughed aloud as they waltzed together.

"I still don't understand how Russell ever strayed from your side," he murmured.

"Alright. I forgive you. How can I not when you say such pretty words? But this is my last dance now; I am retreating to the card room. Sir Randolph disapproves of cards."

"I will join you," Christophe said, but a small hand on his shoulder dashed his hopes of a quiet card game. He turned to find himself accosted by his sister.

"Do you see her?" Emily asked, clutching his arm as she craned her small neck. She stood on her toes as though it would help her see over the people in front of her, but being so small she barely rose to the level of everyone's shoulders. "You aren't even trying to look."

"No. I don't see the point. You forget that I have not met this young woman, and wouldn't know what to look for."

Emily exhaled in a puff of frustration. "You would recognize her as the woman you ought to marry."

"Emily," Christophe warned, though he knew it did no good.

"Very well, then. We will split up. I will go that way and you go over there," his sister said. Even as a child she had always assumed everyone would do as she told them.

"No, I was going to play cards."

Emily glared daggers at him.

"Fine; I will go to the terrace for a smoke. When you find her, you will signal to me and I will come running just as our lapdog used to do," Christophe drawled, already pulling the cigarillo from his silver case. He preferred to get his emotions under control before meeting the girl who was not Fatia. It was unfair to compare the two, but his mind had already done it. Since she wouldn't be Fatia, but Miss Rowena Brayemore, he wanted to be able to control his disappointment when he finally had to bow over her hand.

His sister rolled her eyes, but didn't discredit the plan. "Perhaps she has gone to freshen up. I could look for her there and come back to find you. It would seem a little more natural that way, at any rate. Very well. Yes. I will come find you."

With the inevitable pushed back, Emily sauntered off, and Christophe couldn't help breathing a sigh of relief. The cool air on the terrace helped push away his anxiety, though a low hum continued in his belly. Light burst in front of him with the lit match, soon leaving only the burning ember at the end of the cigarillo.

He slumped against the terrace wall. Suddenly, the last memory he had of his brother appeared in his mind. They had been leaning against the walls in Duncan Manor, on a night much like this one.

Christophe blew out his smoke in frustration. Every time he thought of Russell now, he had to quell the anger that squeezed his lungs. He had been his brother, and Christophe had loved him, but he had also been an idiot. To pay off some gambling debts, Russell had sold their estate in the north at half the price it was worth—and told no one. Then Christophe had found out the hard way that Russell had dismissed the workers at the factory in Cookston instead of paying them when he had again mismanaged the money. For that, Christophe wished to stomp on his very grave. It was going to take quite a bit of coin to get the family estates and money back in order, but it would take even more to get back the respect of the people in Cookston.

Throwing the cigarillo aside, Christophe exhaled the white smoke, then lit another. The housekeeper at Duncan Manor needed an increase in salary for keeping the house standing unpaid for so long; he needed to find another groundskeeper and someone to repair the stones falling from the house walls. And the list didn't end there.

Christophe rubbed his temples. Perhaps if he managed to stop mulling over what was already done, an idea would come to him from somewhere of what he could do.

Lady Camille Roussier stifled a yawn as she looked around the ballroom. Already she had been plagued by several men desiring to dance with her, but it was too early to accept anything yet. She smiled to herself at the overly eager English women in the ballroom, swooning and flirting each time any lord came to ask them for a dance. They were too... eager. She had no energy to think of more varied vocabulary. Truthfully, she had none. She had no plan to expand her use of her father's language beyond getting along in society. Coming to England had at least brought fluidity back to her English, and a large vocabulary was for bluestockings —something she was most certainly not. She was too beautiful to stay behind closed doors, reading or advocating or whatever it was that bluestockings did.

Camille shuddered, smoothing the iridescent satin of her skirts.

"Are you cold, dear?" asked Aunt Prudence, the sister of her mother's recent husband, the Viscount of Kent. "We could move further in. Or you could try dancing. It would warm you."

"No, dearest aunt," Camille said. "I am exactly where I want to be. Lady Alice and Lady Grace know to come and find me here."

Remembering the vision of herself in the mirror before leaving that evening, Camille smiled. With her dark blonde hair gathered loosely about her head, her heart-shaped mouth plumped by her own teeth and her slim figure made so by abstaining from too many cakes, Camille knew that she was quite probably the most beautiful woman here. Of course, compared to the drab English ladies, she would have stood out even in a governess's dress.

Camille almost laughed aloud at her own wit.

She was able to stifle the giggle, but her smile was caught by a man walking by who looked to be in his thirties. He bowed before her, taking her fingertips almost to his mouth as he introduced himself as Lord Newsbury. Camille was familiar enough with Burke's Peerage to know that the man was in direct line to inherit the title of Earl of... well, something or other. More importantly, the man had quite a bit of money. He was known to have invested well, though some said it was in the slave trade that was doing so well in the Americas. Camille couldn't care less.

Lord Newsbury's eyes seemed to bore straight into her; his presence suddenly made her body tingle with emotions that baffled her. Lady Camille decided she liked it.

"Lady Camille, I'm sure you are parched. Might you join me for a glass of champagne and then the next dance?" asked Lord Newsbury, already offering the glass to her. She took her time in taking it from his gloved hand, perusing his body coolly.

He was fashionably dressed and would do nicely to garner the jealous attention of the men she had decided were acceptable to marry. Lord Newsbury might make the list as well, but somewhere down the line. She did, after all, wish to have a husband who would be enjoyable in the marriage bed. Camille knew much about the goings-on that happened after the vows and took her mother's advice of finding a virile man seriously. She could hardly think that a man was virile after thirty. That was so... old.

"What excellent champagne," she lied, setting the subpar drink on the next tray. "I would love to dance, my lord."

"Mademoiselle," Lord Newsbury said with a bow. The next set would be a waltz. She usually saved the waltzes for the younger lords, but the elegant way Lord Newsbury carried himself made her wonder how it would feel to be in his arms.

From the moment the first notes struck, it was clear she had made the right choice. There was something curious about Lord Newsbury's black eyes and the small crinkles at the corners. And the way he looked at her. It was absolutely... *fascinant*. She bit her lip, trying to come up with a better word than 'curious' again. The English language was so limiting.

As Lord Newsbury whirled her about the room, a familiar face in the crowd of dancers made her look twice. Then again. It was a young woman she was certain she knew. If she remembered the face, it was because the woman must be important in ton society. Those were the only faces that she bothered to remember.

But the woman didn't look important, although Lord Glenville stood next to her, and he was an earl. Or, rather, she was fairly certain he was. *Dieu*, but she needed to review that peerage book again if she was ever going to know who was who. As boring as it was.

The woman was familiar, but Camille was certain she had seen her in worse conditions. Possibly war conditions back in Algeria? That could pose a slight problem, since Camille's stories from Algeria never included the fact that they had gone for days without clean water to bathe in or how she had gone an entire year without a new dress. It had really been quite a traumatic experience.

"What is it, my dear?" murmured Newsbury. "I find myself intrigued as to why your eyes have wandered from mine. Do I no longer hold your interest?"

"No, no, my lord," Camille blurted. "I thought I saw someone – a girl – I think I know her. Who is that woman dancing with Lord Glenville?"

Lord Newsbury looked across the room so gracefully that no one would ever realize he was searching another out.

"That is Miss Rowena Brayemore, my lady," he answered.

Shock burst from her as an indelicate cough and stumbling of feet. Thankfully, it was the end of the waltz and no one noticed except for Lord Newsbury.

"Are you upset?" he asked. "I will retrieve you some lemonade."

When he left her, Camille almost ran to her sister, who was entertaining a small group of friends nearby. She pulled up next to her and pointed in Rowena's direction, watching her sister's beautiful eyes narrow until they widened in surprise and recognition.

"She could upset our reputations," murmured Camille, so low she wasn't sure she was actually talking. But Marine heard her. After a few moments' pause, Camille sighed when a smile appeared on Marine's lips. That meant she had a plan and Camille wouldn't have to come up with one. Not that she couldn't, she told herself, it was just that plans took so much effort.

"My, but I thought this ball would be a bit more exclusive," Marine announced. Camille grimaced at the abrupt change in conversation but was pleased to notice that Lady Alice and the other girls perked up.

"What makes you say such a thing?" asked Lady Meredith, a girl well on her way to being a worse gossip than her mother.

"That girl, if one can call her that, has somehow made her way in here." Marine waved her hand towards the other side of the room with a snort.

"She's Baron Brayemore's daughter. Mama says he is rather common because he still dabbles in trade. Even without her father's title, she is technically part of our society. Her grandfather was the second son of an earl. And her mother was the granddaughter of a Spanish viscount," recounted Lady Mary. A woman who knew everything was always such a bore.

"She is not a noblewoman, I can tell you that," drawled Marine. "Lord Brayemore is a coward. The French blocked the port because Algeria was ingrate. You know? A sultan cannot hit a French ambassador with his fly fan. *Non!* Lady Alice, you know this story? No? You English think there is nothing outside of England. But this girl, here, this Miss Brayemore, she is a scandal. In the chaos of this time in Algeria, she lived with us. To be a sister to us. I was young, very young at the time, but I remember the day she tried to run away to be with her lover. Very foolish. Very ungrateful."

"But the paper says that she worked with missionaries there. She says nothing about living with you," protested Miss Elizabeth, a red-headed girl with more freckles than there were stars in the sky.

No one turned to look at her.

"I heard Mama tell Mrs. Paxton that the nephew of the missionaries is saying she never worked for them. He says they never mentioned her once in their letters to his mother. And besides, they were murdered in the desert on their way back home. She would have been left alone in the desert with those savages for months!" explained Lady Alice in a hushed voice.

"And who can say what they made her do?" exclaimed Miss Elizabeth.

"Perhaps she is married to a heathen and wishes no one to know!" giggled Lady Meredith.

"Then she has no right to claim any of our proper gentlemen," Lady Alice protested with a pout.

"Baron Brayemore has accepted his daughter since her return," interjected Miss Elizabeth.

Marine scoffed. "If he were to know the truth about his *fille,* he would send her away. She is no good. And no good for Lady Grace."

She smiled smugly while the girls around them gasped in shock. Marine took great satisfaction in shocking people.

Two gentlemen standing at the edge of the group, hoping to find a dancing partner, chided Marine, but were only too willing to escort as many ladies to the terrace as they could. Soon afterward, a roguish-looking gentleman whisked Marine away for the next dance, leaving Camille alone with Lord Newsbury.

"Do you actually know Miss Brayemore?" asked Lord Newsbury as he handed Camille her lemonade.

She tried to avoid a response altogether, but he was not to be ignored, so she tried the approach of defense. She was unwilling to allow some lord to take Rowena's side. If anyone had to suffer, it should be Miss Brayemore, not herself and Marine. They were young, after all, and they had suffered so many years without silk dresses and all the finery they should have had. Now that they had it again, Rowena Brayemore should not be allowed to take it away from them.

"Certainly I do. Her father betrayed my mother."

"Well, then, I think I may get to know this Miss Brayemore," he said, smiling across the room before leaving Camille alone.

She had little time to understand the anger and hurt that gathered in her stomach before she was interrupted by Miss Elizabeth, who looked at her with wide green eyes.

"You know starting a rumor such as that could ruin Miss Brayemore."

"It is not a rumor. It is the truth," Camille said, pleased to see that the guests were already buzzing with the story. "She did not think about her reputation when she ran away with her lover!"

Miss Elizabeth said no more, slipping away into the crowd. Camille was grateful to be alone. She didn't know who was right and who was wrong in the story of Rowena and her mother, but she did know that she was young and deserved a rich husband. And she wasn't about to allow a strange woman to ruin any of that.

Chapter Thirteen

CHRISTOPHE STAYED OUTSIDE, AWAY from any
debutantes and their salivating parents. He was about to make an
escape to the card room when a swish of lavender skirts caught his
attention. Instead of going inside, Christophe poked his head
around the corner to find a young lady in lavender silk standing
with his old classmate, Mr. Highston. Something familiar about
the young woman kept him outside a little longer. She stood
straight with her back to him. Her head was high, her chin tilted to
look up at her companion.

Christophe fell into the shadows to watch them. It was rude and
unforgiving, and he would be the talk of the party if caught
spying, but he could not move away. There was a soothing
familiarity about the girl; something that reminded him of the
mountains of Algeria. Perhaps it was her hair, curled up on the
sides, the hair underneath separated into large ringlets with ribbons
woven through them. Or perhaps it was the lavender dress—a
color Saed's wife, Nadira, wore often.

The last possibility was that he was madly obsessed with
anything that might draw him back to Fatia, which meant he either

needed sleep or to be locked up. Christophe scrubbed his face with his hands and hoped beyond reason that Highston and the girl would be gone when he looked up again.

No such luck. Mr. Highston held the girl's hand in his and kept it a moment too long before finally letting go. The girl said something and Highston looked annoyed for a second, but soon straightened his spine and followed after her.

Feeling like a cad, Christophe moved to return to the ballroom.

"Miss Brayemore, I insist you take my jacket," Highston said, snapping Christophe's attention back to him.

So this was Miss Rowena Brayemore, the girl who got the accidental whipping. The girl whom he had carried into the manor, who had eyes that reminded him of Fatia.

She turned towards the garden, towards him, fully ignoring Highston and his jacket. For a moment, she seemed lost in the moonlight, and Christophe had a second to look at her eyes.

They were the same eyes he remembered peeking out from under a hijab as she sang to a camel.

Eyes that stared at him nightly in his dreams as the light of the fire gloried around them. He could see them framed by her hair, pulled down around her face and gathered at the nape of her neck, with a gold chain woven through it as she sang near Saed's dinner table.

"Fatia," he whispered, the spoken words awakening him from his stupor. He pushed himself against the terrace wall, trying to open his eyes to his own idiocy. It was not her. The lady in front of him was a baron's daughter, not a slave given to him by one of his business partners.

Miss Brayemore turned slightly as she spoke to Highston. Everything, from her animated movements to her frequent smile to the eyes that never fell to the ground, told him she was not Fatia.

But something didn't add up.

Fatia. Melilla. The lost girl. Rowena Braymore in Melilla. Countess Merville. Countess Merville had brought Rowena Braymore back from Melilla. Miss Braymore had worked with missionaries.

Christophe rubbed his temples. The only missionaries he had heard of the entire journey from Algeria through Morocco were the missionaries that had been found dead just outside of Melilla. Killed by common thieves.

Thieves. They were in his nightmares, taking Fatia away, back into slavery.

How could she have disappeared so fully? In Melilla he had checked ship rosters that had left the port at the time of her disappearance. There had been nothing strange about them— nothing but one blank spot on the roster of one ship for an additional lady's maid. For the Countess of Merville.

The pounding in his head blocked out everything as the truth swam before his eyes.

It was a lie. This Miss Braymore was Fatia. Or rather, Fatia had been her, Rowena. An English girl enslaved in Algeria. That was why she had asked him to take her to England.

He had said no to protect her. Bringing a foreign woman from Algeria, a former slave, back to England would have complicated everything. He wouldn't have been able to marry her, even before he knew he was a marquess. England was not yet suited for marriage between an Englishman and a former slave. But had she told him she was English, had she told him she was Lord Braymore's daughter, he never would have said no.

He shook himself awake. Surely not. Fatia had not looked English. She had not carried herself as this English woman did. The girl moved her head as she spoke with Emily and Newsbury. Emily said something, and Miss Brayemore responded with a wide smile.

It was her. And yet he doubted. Not once had she spoken English to him. Never had she told him who she was.

When she laughed again, the fire within him turned as cold as the North Sea. Highston held out his arm and Fatia, no, Rowena, took it. Fatia. Rowena. He was no longer certain. What he was sure of was the sharp pain that seemed to be piercing his heart. He stepped into the dim light as Emily passed by.

"Is all well, Emily?" he called out when she was close to him.

She started at his voice. "I thought you were inside. Lady Grace is straining her neck trying to look for you. The more the twins talk about their dances with you, the redder she gets."

Christophe grimaced. He had no desire to dance with Lady Grace. He had no desire to do anything. But he knew what his sister was going to make him do. She was going to make him meet Rowena. His Fatia.

"Are you coming, Cinch? You promised me you would meet Miss Brayemore and be on your best behavior, although maybe we should put it off for another day. You look rather... defeated," Emily pronounced, her eyes narrowing. "Are you well?"

Christophe swatted his sister's hand away from his forehead. He refused to look anything but uninterested. The very idea a woman could affect him so made the fight rise within him, damming the drain of blood from his face.

"Shall we go and meet your friend? I think I deserve a thank you from her," he drawled.

"Yes, let's go meet her. But only if you behave."

"I always behave," he said, bowing over his sister's hand.

"Stop it. You are being strange, and I don't like it. Start acting more like a marquess."

"Like Russell, perhaps?"

Emily scrunched her nose. "No, please. Nothing like Russell. He would flirt with every single woman in this place, and I don't want you to do that. Just have a glass of champagne and relax. You work too much, you know," she added as he drained the contents of the glass she handed him, squinting at the brightness of the ballroom. "It is rearranging your head, I think."

Christophe ignored his sister, looking for lavender skirts instead. He found them near the chairs, speaking to Claire. Giving a glance around the ballroom, Christophe found there was a strange, nervous energy in the air.

"There she is," Emily said, waving Claire down.

"Yes," Christophe whispered, clenching his teeth against the arrow of pain that sliced through him. Suddenly his hands were cold and clammy, and a faint thud was starting at the back of his head. "There she is. Shall we?"

His heart beat loudly, his blood rushed through his ears as they approached. Fatia. She had run away from him, and now she pretended to be this Rowena, who had thrown herself between a boy and a whip. He couldn't take it. He didn't wish to see her. But his feet kept walking.

Damned propriety.

Just as they took their last steps towards them, both Claire and Miss Brayemore turned, and Christophe found himself staring into wide brown eyes rimmed with green.

"Miss Brayemore, may I present to you my brother," Emily announced. "The Marquess of Candor."

Rowena turned, dread already descending upon her. She had known that Emily wished for her to meet her brother, and that her brother had turned out to be the man who had carried her into the house. The man who smelled of Sutton. Who had the same voice as Sutton.

With a deep inhalation, she turned and found familiar eyes staring at her with a mixture of mirth and detachment. Mr. Sutton. In the flesh.

She gasped, trying quickly to cover the sound with a cough. When he bowed to her, she curtsied, and suddenly her stays seemed too tight. And yet she could not tear her eyes away from his stormy blue ones.

"Miss Brayemore," he said in a deep voice that sent waves of warmth through her, threatening to topple her.

His face held no surprise within it, which she found very odd indeed—quite the opposite of how she must appear as she resisted the strong urge to wipe the sheen of nervousness from her brow. She wondered if it were possible that another man in England looked exactly like Mr. Sutton.

"I believe we have met under other circumstances, but have never been formally introduced," he said.

She looked at him in horror, her body turning cold as she waited for him to announce that she had been his slave. But he only smiled. His eyes shifted to the windows, where the stables were.

"Yes, of course," she stuttered. "Thank you very much for coming to my rescue."

It did not matter that his eyes remained distant; the smile still shot bolts of lightning through her. When he took her hand, energy radiated from that spot up her arm until finally exploding in her chest. It wasn't until he released her hand that Rowena could finally expand her lungs and swallow. Unfortunately, her humiliation was not at an end yet, for her gulp of air came so forcefully that all those around her heard it.

"Are you hurting, Miss Brayemore?" Claire asked with concern.

"Shall I escort you to your father?" Sutton, no, Lord Candor, asked, his voice still low and sultry. His eyes wandered over her face as though investigating it.

"I-I am fine, truly. Please, do not fuss," Rowena stammered.

"There you are," a voice called out, invading their group. "Shall we, my lady?"

Claire rolled her eyes, but managed to make introductions. "Miss Brayemore, this is our friend, Lord Daucer. You might have to get used to him hanging around. He has a habit of intruding upon our group."

"I'll have you know that Lady Candor personally asks me to come each time. It is she who cannot have enough of me," Lord Daucer said, kissing Rowena's hand with a twinkling eye.

Rowena was grateful for the interruption, but too quickly Lord Daucer was leading Claire to the dance floor. Lord Falcon had already taken his wife to dance, which left Rowena and Sutton— no, Lord Candor—alone.

"I believe we are to dance together then," Lord Candor murmured, holding out his hand.

"I-I don't believe that would be a good idea." Panic flooded her belly. "I'm not very good at dancing, m-my lord."

But he chose not to heed her words. He took her hand, pulled her close, and waltzed her towards the other couples. Bergamot floated around her, daring her to lean into his warmth and safety, but she ignored it and kept her spine straight.

"Too late, Fatia," he whispered against her ear as they swept across the floor together. Thrills shot through her. He really was Sutton. The realization caused her to stumble, stepping on his foot.

"Do not stop," he murmured, holding her firmly and turning her at the corner again. "Relax. Allow me to guide you. If you leave the dance floor now, you will cause a scene."

Pure, unadulterated joy drowned Rowena's soul. Her heart beat so loudly she was sure he could hear it. A sense of complete and utter safety flowed through her when she looked at their entwined hands near his broad shoulders. These were the same hands that had once caressed the marks on her back as though they made her precious.

They turned about the floor almost gracefully, until on one turn his hand twisted, pulling the bandage on her back. All night she had ignored the throbbing, but the tug from his large hand against her wounds sent fire through her. It was impossible not to whimper.

"Forgive me," he whispered. His eyes were wide with concern for her, all detachment erased.

"No, do not worry," Rowena exclaimed, trying to keep hold of his touch, but his hand hovered over her now, the weight and heat gone. Swallowing against the loss, Rowena dared to look up. But her eyes got only to his mouth before her right foot stomped on top of his boot.

"I am—so sorry," she stammered, looking at his chest again while measuring the steps silently. "I hope I did not hurt you."

"Miss Brayemore," he said in a low voice that hid laughter, "I seem to recall holding your foot in my hand. I do not believe such a tiny thing could hurt me."

"I am not so tiny," she replied, finally looking at him. His blue eyes were like the night sky at dusk. A smile tugged at his lips for a moment, threatening to spread further. She waited, watching, hoping to catch his smile as a drunkard must hope to catch drops of gin. He was so very handsome when he smiled.

Candor leaned into her ear, causing her to panic inexplicably.

"Try to relax, Miss Brayemore, and enjoy the dance. You look as though I am slowly killing you," he said.

Heat flooded her. She tried to paste on a smile, though her efforts were more like a grimace. Her hands began to shake, and she once again stumbled.

"Did you think of me, Fatia?" he asked softly. She looked up to find his eyes haunted by emotions she didn't recognize. "Do you think of me as Rowena, too?"

She blinked at him just as the music ended. Before she could answer, Grace assailed her.

"Rowena," she said, her voice dripping in false sweetness.

"Lord Candor, this is my sister, Lady Grace."

"Good evening, my lord," Grace said, pushing her way closer to Lord Candor. Rowena looked at him as Grace gave her deepest curtsy.

"It was a pleasure, Miss Brayemore," he said with a bow before turning and leaving. Rowena stared, unable to believe that her moment with him was over.

"Come along, Rowena, your father wants to see you," Grace said, grabbing her arm and pulling hard. "Besides, did you really expect the Marquess of Candor to ask you for another dance after that disastrous one? Yes, sister. I saw you fumbling about. I'm certain you won't be getting any more offers to dance at this ball. How you manage to embarrass me at every turn, I will never know. Your disastrous dance embarrassed James as well, I'm sure. What other reason would he have for calling you to retire before the bells ring?"

Chapter Fourteen

CHRISTOPHE SLEPT RESTLESSLY FOR only a few hours. A beautiful woman illuminated by firelight who seemed always just out of his reach filled his dreams. He followed her through trees, then through deserted streets, but each time he thought he was close the woman retreated further away.

When he finally wrenched himself free of the dream, he found that night still surrounded the manor. He rubbed his face with his hands and closed his eyes again, but to no avail.

Pulling on a pair of loose trousers, boots and wool jacket, Christophe set about trying to sort through some correspondence, but his mind kept wandering. There were four letters, and each held worse news until the final one. The investments in the canals in Egypt were going better than expected. That, at least, was a relief. He needed the money from them if he was going to set about implementing the wage increases at the factories in Cookston.

He looked at the clock and grimaced. Not yet six in the morning. A walk might invigorate him, perhaps get rid of his nervous energy.

The house was deathly quiet. No one was about, not even the scullery maid, as he twisted through the hallway to the empty ballroom, where he supposed the doors to the garden would still be unlocked from the ball. The empty ballroom magnified the clicking of his boots against the floor. His spine tingled in disgust at the foreign scratching noise his shoes made as he stepped in spilled lemonade and ratafia crumbs. A mixture of sweat, perfume, and smoke still clung to the air.

The ballroom held the look of a successful evening, and yet Christophe's shoulders slumped at the sight. For him, it had been a failure. He had expected too much, apparently.

"I expected nothing," he protested to himself, closing his eyes in frustration.

It was a lie. Firstly, he had expected to find out that the girl who had been whipped only reminded him of Fatia. Secondly, he had expected to call himself a fool for thinking she was Fatia. Thirdly, he had expected to enjoy himself by dancing with the look-alike while finding out that she was completely different from Fatia. And finally, he had expected to then travel to Duncan Manor, where he would use physical labor to put Fatia behind him once and for all, before admitting to his family that he was going to take the step of procuring a wife seriously.

He had expected his sister to go through with finding him one. There is only one on the list, she had said. It was amusing, really, that she had chosen Fatia. How very ironic. But then, she hadn't really chosen Fatia; she had chosen Rowena Brayemore.

Which brought him to what he had *not* expected.

He had not expected the girl to be Fatia. He had not expected his mind to become a befuddled mess when faced with her. He had not expected the woman he had traveled through the desert with to have lied to him. He had not expected to still feel that strange connection to her, regardless of her holding back the truth.

Disgusted with himself, he yanked open the terrace doors and breathed in the cool, early morning air. To his right still stood the refreshment table, from which he grabbed a glass of flat champagne and drank, wincing at the flavor. The first rays of sunlight peeked over the horizon. They were still too weak to cast any great light on anything, but they were strong enough to draw his eyes through his glass to a figure moving in the garden. The obvious answer was that it was a servant coming in to work, but the figure rounded the fountain, only to start the circle again. He peered closer.

"For the love of all that is holy," he muttered, walking down the terrace steps. The woman must be drunk. Or insane. She wore only a simple cotton dress with a small woolen shawl.

He ambled towards the woman, wondering how he would convince a drunk woman into the house; then he heard the singing.

It was a lullaby. In Arabic.

The throbbing at his temples lessened a bit as he leaned against a tree and closed his eyes. It was Fatia.

Fatia.

Miss Brayemore.

Taking the steps carefully, Christophe made his way towards the woods, then changed his direction towards the fountain before stopping dead in his steps.

"What the devil am I doing?" he asked aloud. Catching sight of Rowena's long braid trailing down her back, Christophe knew exactly what his subconscious was thinking and chided himself. She was alone, as she probably wanted to be. He should leave.

Rowena's lips started to move again, but all he could think of was how they had felt against his in Melilla, sun-dried and cracked, yet warm and full of life. Now they would be smooth and soft. It was the champagne thinking for him, yet as his feet started again in her direction, heat pooled within him.

Christophe whistled quietly as he approached, not wishing for her to be frightened. Rowena rose slowly from her perch on the fountain rim to meet him.

"*Salam,* Master Sutton," she whispered, her voice betraying some happiness. A queer sort of happiness that seemed out of place. Perhaps due to an excess of champagne.

"Hello—Miss Brayemore."

Although his hands itched to touch her silken hair, he did not have the right. Not here in England at Chershire. There would have to be some move on her part before he could gather her against him.

"Did you come here looking for me?" she asked, her voice barely audible.

"No," he said, then hesitated. "I could not sleep. Though I do not mind running into you."

"You should be careful who you run into on your morning walks. If word gets out, you will find yourself in compromising positions with debutantes who wish to marry a title," she said, trying with difficulty to suppress a smile.

"You are not that sort of woman. Or have these cold customs changed you?"

He dared to take another step.

"No, I am not," Rowena said. "But my stepsister is. She is quite determined that the two of you have much in common and that she would make you the perfect wife."

"What is it that we have in common?" he asked.

Rowena shrugged, biting back a smile. "She says that about each man she meets under forty who holds a title."

She slowly turned around, stepping again into her worn path encircling the fountain. He couldn't help laughing under his breath. When she came around again, she was smiling as well.

"And what do you think, Rowena? You say your sister is looking for a title, but what is it that you are looking for?" he asked softly, blocking her path.

Her gaze moved out over the horizon for a moment as pink crept over her cheeks. "There is a man who seems to live within my very being. I cannot forget him."

Christophe stilled.

"I'm sorry, Lord Candor. I am in a rather strange mood this morning. I have not been sleeping well."

He tried to keep himself from touching her, but in an instant his finger was on her chin, tracing the indentation. Inside, he groaned at the fire that shocked his finger, half unaware that he was now tracing her lips.

"Sutton?" she asked, her voice low.

"*Na'am,*" he whispered in Arabic. Yes.

He wanted to be inside her, but it was not the intimacy of the bedroom he was thinking of. No, he wanted to step inside her and bury himself there. Never leave her being. She would never go where he could not.

"What do you desire, Fatia?" he asked again.

At that her face froze and paled.

"Anything for your slave, Master Sutton?" she spat mockingly, her eyes glittering with anger.

The effect of the accusation was akin to falling into an icy river. Never could he have imagined she would say that. His heart slowed until it stopped altogether. He stepped away, wanting to be far away from the words and the woman who had spoken them. Within a second, she had gone from the most desirable woman in the world to someone he no longer knew.

"I do not, nor will I ever, own a slave, Fatia," he said in a low, dark voice. "From the beginning, I told you I would not take you as a slave. I took you to Melilla; I helped you. After all that, you disappeared. I never hid myself from you—but now, here, you accuse me of seeing you as a slave, Fatia?"

"My name is Rowena. Not Fatia. Fatia was a slave. I am the Honorable Rowena, daughter of an English baron," she said with a shaky voice.

"And why didn't you tell me before?" he demanded, barely able to hold his anger at bay.

Her face drained to ghostly white. As she lifted her fingers to her own cheeks they trembled, but he did nothing to soothe her. He wanted answers.

"After all I did for you, you disappeared, never to come back. Why didn't you just tell me who you were?"

She said nothing. Long minutes passed in silence.

"I'm sorry I insulted you. I know you as Fatia," Christophe finally said. "But now, as I see it, I do not know you at all. For you did not trust me enough to tell me who you were. I would have brought you home. I would have done anything for Fatia. I searched for her—for you. I thought perhaps someone had taken you, for I could not fathom Fatia simply... leaving. Without saying goodbye."

They stood, staring at each other, Christophe willing her to speak. He wished she would say something, anything, to excuse her behavior, but she stood silently by. Finally, his shoulders sagged in exhaustion. The sun was rising and they should not, under any circumstances, be seen together in the morning fog.

Rowena moved to take her leave, but Christophe wouldn't give her the satisfaction of leaving first. He quickly clicked his heels, gave the Honorable Miss Brayemore a bow, then turned and walked away.

Rowena stared at herself in the mirror. Griffin waited to finish dressing her, but she couldn't seem to make herself care. All she wanted to do was go over her morning encounter with Lord Candor again and again, the shame threatening to make her retch each time. It culminated in her memory of watching him walk away from her and her inability to say anything to ease the pain she had caused him.

She had stood still, watching him. Even after he was gone, she had continued to stare after him, wondering why she had said what she had. As the sun came up over a brilliant pink and orange sky, she had spent another quarter of an hour slumped against the edge of the fountain, feeling dark and burdened – exactly the opposite of how she had felt upon waking.

He had been the first subject on her mind this morning. Her mind had whirled with images of seeing him again and her acting like an elegant lady of the aristocracy.

Her reflection winced at the horrible truth. Her behavior had been anything but that. In the garden, her desire for him to kiss her had been so strong she could hardly breathe. But he hadn't kissed her, and all because she couldn't control the strange anger that had come over her. All these months back in England, and she had held her tongue each time that restless anger had invaded her body. Each time until now.

Rowena picked up her brush again, the wooden handle suddenly heavy in her hand, just as Grace burst through her door.

"Is my sister here, Griffin?"

"Get on with you," was Griffin's reply. "She's just out of her bath. Don't you be botherin' her none."

Rowena couldn't help smiling at her maid. From the first day she employed her, Griffin had shown fierce loyalty – something that seemed to annoy Grace greatly.

"You have no right to tell me anything, Griffin. If I had my way, you'd be sacked for speaking to me like that. Unfortunately, my sister doesn't seem to care whether I feel insulted in my own home or not."

"'Tisn't your home, m'lady," Griffin said with a sniff. Grace huffed and stomped about the room, making Rowena wish she could hide all day.

"Hello, Grace," she said instead, coming out of the dressing room in half-dress. "I didn't think we would see you so early this morning. Didn't you stay out late?"

Grace narrowed her eyes, her hands fisted at her hips as Rowena lifted her arms for Griffin to place the dress over her. The way her sister stared made her heart flutter, but she forced her face to stay neutral. She knew every mark on her body was covered. It always was; Griffin made certain of it. Still, she couldn't help lightly touching her shoulders as Griffin cinched up the back of her dress. The moment she touched the edge of the bodice, Griffin swatted her fingers away.

Rowena smiled. Grace's eyes narrowed even more.

"There are rumors going around about you," she said finally. "Why do you always wear dresses that are worn by Quakers? The neckline is much too high. It isn't even fashionable."

"What rumors?" Rowena asked, choosing to ignore the usual statements about her dress.

"That you ran away with your lover and that some lady came to your rescue when the man kicked you out."

Rowena dropped into the nearest chair. Her skin developed a cold layer of sweat under all of her garments. She could hardly concentrate on the words Grace was saying. Simply trying to breathe with her corset on was word enough.

"Who is saying this?" she asked, finally able to breathe enough to get out the words.

"Lady Marine and Lady Camille Collins."

"I do not know anyone of those names!"

"Their mother married a German count, Lord Kent, who lives in England half the time."

"I do not understand why they think they know such a story about me," Rowena said, her head pulling back at a particularly difficult knot in her hair. She was grateful to be facing the ceiling when Grace informed her of the next bit of information.

"They say you knew them when their mother lived in Algeria. Her name before was Madame Roussier. So, is it true?"

Rowena lowered her head, fighting against the twisting in her chest. She thought of her time with Saed, how she had learned to control her panic and ignore the pain. She thought of Selma, who had taught her to breathe deeply without moving her body too much so as to not let the master see her emotions. She thought of every tool she had learned in slavery to resist fainting from the terror of what might come of this predicament.

"They do not know what they're talking about," she said faintly.

"Lady Marine says that you worked for her mother. As some sort of servant."

"Worked?" Rowena asked, forcing herself to laugh lightly. "Grace, my father was not titled until he came here a few years ago, but we lived quite well in Algeria. I grew up with two personal maids, my own opera singing teacher, my own tutor, an orchard around my house and almost any dress or item I could have dreamed of. Why would I work for those two girls?"

Grace studied her face for a moment before shrugging. She turned to leave, but paused and turned around slightly.

"I hope you aren't lying to me, Rowena. You know you would ruin my chances at a good match if this rumor turns out to be true."

As Grace stomped out of the room, Rowena caught Griffin's eye.

"Yes, Griffin?"

"The truth has a mind of its own, mistress. Comes out with or without permission."

"Thank you for your concern, Griffin," Rowena said stiffly, unwilling to entertain the truth of her words. "I will see you after dinner."

___

"My dear Miss Brayemore," a voice drawled from behind her as Rowena left her room.

Mr. Holden, another guest—and one both Lady Candor and Lady Glenville had spoken of with distaste—stood watching her from an enclave in the hall. The smoke from his pipe billowed about his face, his cold eyes fixed heavily on her.

"Good evening, Mr. Holden," she said calmly, resisting the urge to glance behind her. He would know she was thinking of retreating if she did so. Timing was important when running from a predator.

"What a welcome surprise to have company," he drawled, still staring straight at her. Rowena stepped to the side of the column, but not forward. Neither could she step back just yet. "I am not the only one late for dinner. Tell me, did you know about the stairway just around the corner that leads up to the east wing of the house?"

Rowena kept her alarm deep below the surface, refusing to look to where he pointed. "I did not," she told him, lifting her chin. "I will see you at dinner then?"

Mr. Holden laughed as he crept closer.

"How is your wife, sir?"

He stopped short, his eyebrows raised. "She and your sister are in the library, making plans for the season. My wife seems to think she will be out of confinement and ready to take on London only a month after giving birth to my son."

"Or daughter," Rowena said lightly, stepping to the side again, this time angling herself slightly backward.

"I certainly hope it is a boy; I could then put my duty behind me. You have no idea what it is like to bed her," Mr. Holden said with a shudder. "There is always so much talk about the greatness of a match in terms of money, power, and status, but no one ever talks about whether the woman will be a terror to live with and bed."

For a moment, a strange twinge of pity tempted Rowena. He had quite a long life ahead of him with his wife, a woman quick to point out every flaw in everyone she saw. She could not imagine being married to such a person.

"Perhaps motherhood will soften her."

Mr. Holden laughed. Quicker than a mountain lion on its prey, he was at her side grasping her arm.

"Where are you going?" he asked breathlessly. "The stairs at the other way. Don't you remember?"

"Mr. Holden," she demanded. "Kindly let go of me."

"Ah," he said, breathing in her scent. "But you are a woman of the world. With five years away, it is impossible that you are without experience in the ways of pleasing a man. And I need some pleasing. I will not tell anyone. Upon my word, it will be our secret."

Nausea rose in her chest. She planted her feet firmly and leaned away as he trailed his nose about her neck. There would be a moment when he would loosen his grip, if only she waited for it.

She was right. Just as Mr. Holden lowered his lips to her neck, his hand loosened. Rowena jerked away and fled down the hall, with Mr. Holden directly on her heels.

"How dare you," he growled, not daring to shout.

Just as she reached the main staircase, someone stepped up behind her. Panic seized her. How he could have got to her so swiftly, she could not understand. In her fright, her foot slipped upon the carpet and she went down, almost falling headfirst down the stairs, were it not for a strong hand grabbing her waist.

"Let go," she hissed.

"Are you all right?" a deep voice asked her. One that was not Mr. Holden's.

Rowena turned to find Lord Candor releasing her waist and Mr. Holden staring at them in white anger.

"How dare you molest her, sir?" Mr. Holden sneered, stepping towards Rowena. "Come, dear, I will escort you to your rooms."

"You will do no such thing," Rowena snapped, stepping away from him.

"You will leave her alone," Lord Candor said, directly blocking Mr. Holden's way.

"Holden! What are you doing up there? I've been waiting for you to escort me to dinner," a female voice called from the bottom of the stairs.

Mr. Holden's face hardened for a moment before he bestowed a smile on Rowena and graced her with a bow.

"I must go. I hope I leave you in good hands, Miss Brayemore. Until we meet again," he said, then was gone.

The only person left to hear Rowena snort her response was Lord Candor, who seemed surprised, then agitated. Without another word, he bowed and turned to go.

"Lord Candor," she called softly.

He stopped, but did not turn back to her. It was more than she could have hoped for.

"I wish to apologize to you," she said. "I have tried to come up with words that are sufficient to express my regret at how I treated you. You told me from the beginning that I was not your slave, and it's true you treated me always with respect. Many other men would not have treated me so well. I'm sorry for insulting you this morning."

Somehow her speech ended with her hand floating up to his shoulder and landing there, as though it had permission to do so. It wasn't until he stiffened that she noticed it and quickly dropped it back to her side.

Lord Candor stood still for a long moment before finally turning his head over his shoulder.

"I accept your apology, Miss Brayemore," he said coolly. "I forgive you. Now, I must bid you good day. They have readied my horse, and my valet awaits. Perhaps we shall see each other again."

She watched him walk away with nothing more said. He did not look back, and she understood that it was not so much anger he radiated, but loss. It traveled through the air, hitting her squarely in the chest. It was her fault they had lost each other, lost their chance. First for leaving Melilla so quickly, for not telling him the truth about who she was, and now for spitting in his face when she should have worshiped at his feet.

Chapter Fifteen

NOVEMBER, 1832

BERNADETTE USED EVERY OUNCE of energy she had to walk to breakfast. She had only just awoken from a deep sleep an hour before, and yet already she wished for her bed. From the bottom of the stairs, she could hear Rowena and Grace exchanging clipped remarks, bringing her energy to a new low. The idea of sitting through breakfast threatened to bring on one of her headaches, but she couldn't stay away. John was here to meet Rowena, to whom James had all but betrothed Rowena five years before.Christophe donned his hat again and headed to Brooks's. He rarely indulged his misery, but this was one time he deserved to.

"My lady, this just came for Miss Brayemore," Johnson, the young footman with spots all about his face, said, handing her a missive.

"Thank you," Bernadette murmured, swallowing her horror upon seeing the Candor seal. The footman would already be spreading some sort of gossip about the letter; he didn't need to also tell the other servants about her reaction. "I will take it to her."

The young footman walked away, unaware of Bernadette's shaking anger. Everyone knew the new marquess was somewhat unconventional, but even with his common upbringing before the title befell his father, he should know it was beyond the pale to send Rowena private messages after only one dance. He had not even bothered to call on her in person yet! Perhaps Bernadette had been right in suspecting that something more inappropriate was going on. As Rowena's stepmother, it was her duty to open the missive and find out what was happening before a scandal brought down the entire family.

Finding herself alone in the foyer, Bernadette scurried past the parlor and into the front sitting room. There she slipped a letter opener under the missive's seal and held it up.

Dear Miss Brayemore,
Several weeks have passed since we last
saw each other at the Arlington Ball. I
am in London and was hoping that I
might find you at home today to receive
visitors.
Yours,
Lord Candor

Bernadette crumpled the paper in her fist upon reading the signature. Yours. A rather intimate way to sign. Rowena must have done something to invoke such intimacy. What was worse was that Grace had set her cap for Lord Candor already before the Arlington ball. He was young and rich and now had a title; he was exactly what Grace had always looked for. It was vastly unfair of

Rowena to flirt in such a way with the man her sister wished to marry.

Bernadette slipped the wrinkled note into her skirts and walked with clipped steps into breakfast. Her plan to be rid of Rowena was about to be put into place with John's arrival. Knowing he was looking to marry again, Bernadette had written to him about Rowena's return. If she could just convince Rowena to spend some time with John, and show James what a promising and convenient arrangement marriage between the two of them was! She would have to do everything in her power to convince Rowena to spend time with him. After a few weeks, Rowena would surely understand the benefit of marrying such a man and leaving London. Indeed, she must see what a lucky match it would be for her. No one else would be interested in a woman who had been gone for five years with no proof of where she had been or what she had been doing.

Bernadette would set the plan in motion that very morning by convincing John to go shopping with Rowena so as to leave Grace at home for a fateful visit with Lord Candor. John was better for Rowena anyway, just as Lord Candor was better for Grace. All would turn out well, thanks to her.

"Good morning," Bernadette greeted her daughters cheerily, hiding her nerves. "Are you darlings getting along this beautiful morning? Grace, dear, I do think that dress is lovely on you. Rowena, what a lovely dress you have too. Are you going shopping for another ball gown today? And to get fitted for a new winter coat? You will need it."

It was quite obvious that Grace was just as surprised as Rowena to see Bernadette taking breakfast with the rest of the family. She would have tried to share a joke with her sister, but was too afraid of being misunderstood. Still, it was quite amusing to watch Bernadette prattling on about the fine morning just as Grace's face hit every emotion between surprise and exasperation. Rowena decided she would stay quiet and simply watch the entertainment.

"What are you going on about, Mother?" Grace asked, her eyes narrowed. "Why should I stay in to wait around for visitors that won't be coming? London is practically empty now."

"Lady Harrow is still in town with her daughters, and you know Alice and her mother won't leave for another week. Those of us who stay in London must stick together!" Bernadette said with false enthusiasm.

"Good morning," a strange, low voice boomed from the doorway, clearing the air immediately.

Rowena turned to find a large man walking towards her. His shoulders spanned almost the entire doorway, and he was so tall she had to crane her neck as he came closer. The handsome coat he wore stretched across his broad chest, curving inward at the waist to show off his trim shape. He either padded his jackets or was a very strong man, Rowena decided, hiding her awe and fear. His attire was different, and he was much taller, but the face was almost just as it had been when she was twelve. It was John, her father's second cousin.

"John! I thought you would stay in bed longer today. You arrived so late last night," Bernadette declared loudly as she offered him a cheek to kiss. He obliged her before turning to Grace and planting a kiss on her as well.

"Good morning, Lady Grace. How are you?"

"Very well, John," Grace answered, her voice filled with mirth and her face transforming from fatigue to youthful beauty. Jealousy struck Rowena upon seeing the quick alteration.

It wouldn't do for her to be jealous of Grace's beauty. The harsh Algerian sun and years of hard work were revealed in thin wrinkles at her own eyes and lips. Certainly, they had to take their toll somewhere. It would be impossible to have creamy, pale, smooth skin after the life she had lived for five years.

"You have come just in time," Grace was saying. "My new dress is arriving tomorrow, and I simply must find a new hat. Will you come with us? John has simply the best eye for matching things, as you can see by how well-attired he is. His late wife, Margaret, was the best-dressed woman London or Bath had ever seen. It was such a shame to lose her so young. When she was presented, she caused a sensation in London. It is rumored that the queen herself commented on her beauty."

John winced visibly, but turned a broad smile to Rowena.

"Hello, Miss Brayemore," he said in a husky voice that surely caused a stir among ladies. It actually produced a slight ripple in Rowena's own nerves. "I doubt that you remember me. You were but a babe the last we saw each other."

"I was twelve years old. You pulled my braids and said I sang like a rooster."

John roared with laughter. Bernadette fell into nervous giggles, and Grace laughed much harder than a lady should.

"Oh, Rowena, I do believe you are still offended by the remark after all these years," she teased in an inhumanly high pitch.

"I do not think so. It's just that I do not find the humor in his remarks."

Grace shrugged her shoulders with a smirk. "I do not remember how you used to sing—whether it was like a rooster or a songbird."

"It was neither," Rowena said defensively, but the rest of her comment was lost when her father entered the room.

"Hello, John," James boomed after kissing each of the women on the cheeks. "If I had known you were coming last night, I would have waited at home for you. I do apologize that no one was here to receive you."

"Rowena was here," Grace pointed out, looking at her with raised brows. "She refused to come and play cards with us. Where would you have gone to?"

Rowena sipped her coffee as she spoke. "I retired early. I told you I would when I declined the invitation to the dinner party at Sir Henry's. I haven't been sleeping well and needed some rest."

The room went quiet as the footmen served the men their breakfast. It was painfully clear she should have come out of her room last night when John's arrival was announced, but she hadn't been able to drum up the courage. Once again, she had not lived up to London etiquette.

The silent rebuke finally ended with John and James beginning a discussion about the upcoming Parliament session. Rowena tried to listen while simultaneously trying to finish reading the newspaper. Grace took the society pages from her and could not help making a remark about leaving the 'real' newspaper to the men. When Rowena lifted her head to reply, John reached for the item in question, forcing Rowena to let go or make a scene. While she hadn't understood all of what she had read about politics and investments anyway, John ripping the paper away infuriated her.

She said nothing though. Instead, she turned to listen to her father talk, hoping she could at least gain some insight.

Within seconds, the famous Duke of Wellington took center stage. From the solemnity of her family, Rowena realized that the man still inspired awe and respect in England since his victory at Waterloo almost twenty years before. It was the new railway system that brought the great duke to center stage today, though; he opposed the railways coming to London from every which way in England, fearing they would bring too many undesirables to London. His excuse sounded rather cantankerous. It seemed to Rowena that modernization and progress couldn't be prevented simply because one man did not wish to be surrounded by those who were poorer than he, but when she started to say so, Grace spoke more loudly.

"I must side with the duke. Can you imagine this city filling up with even more people who cannot take care of themselves? The entire city would become a slum!"

"The duke is very intelligent," affirmed Bernadette, though it was clear she didn't really understand what the conversation was truly about.

"The railways would allow us to travel so much easier through England. Besides, fresh produce would come to the city at a fairer price," James said, steepling his fingers as he looked upon the family.

"But along with it will come beggars. The city will be in ruins within a few years if the railways really do connect London with just any place in England," complained Grace.

"They would come looking for jobs because there are none in the countryside," Rowena said, her voice clipped.

"It would be nicer to ride instead of a carriage, I would think. It would make the trip shorter. Surely you agree with that, John?" asked Bernadette, eyeing Grace and Rowena nervously.

"There are drawbacks to the railways," John said thoughtfully. "But I do agree it will make travel more palatable. That is why I have invested in the new line being put together to connect Birmingham with London. I don't disagree with the Duke of Wellington, but I think it would be quite easy to keep the cost at a minimum so as to make the undesirables stay where they are. It will, on the other hand, allow farmers to get their produce farther and faster than now. It will also allow for the transportation of textiles and coal, as well as people who are willing to pay, at a much faster rate. In the end, it will not only increase work but also better the lives of all of us."

Rowena watched her cousin's large hand delicately grip the family porcelain teacup with ease. Clearly, he was familiar with riches and luxury, though his link to nobility was through his mother's brother. His burliness was to be expected, as he had already been quite tall and strong at the age of fifteen, but his fine dress and manners came as a surprise.

When Grace entangled John into turning the conversation to ties and cravats, Rowena took the opportunity to speak with her father.

"Baba," she said in a low voice. "May I meet you at the Parliament when you are finished today? I would like to speak with you—"

"James?" Bernadette called out. "How about you meet John today for lunch? Oh, goodness. Excuse me, Rowena. Were you saying something to your father? I just remembered that he and

John were to eat lunch together, you see, and felt I should remind him."

"I do not require reminding," James said matter-of-factly. "I remember perfectly." He took out his pocket watch, mumbling to himself about tables and hours. "John, I can meet you outside my offices at one o'clock."

"Rowena, you should go with him. John, don't you think she should go with you? You don't mind, do you, dear? It's just that today is our day to receive callers, and Rowena never really likes to stay. I'm afraid the callers tend to bore her. So, you will go and have lunch with John and your father?"

"Of course," Rowena answered tightly before pushing her chair back to stand.

Instead of the chair moving back smoothly, its legs stuck in a small break in the floor and stopped suddenly. It was prevented from falling over by John's sturdy hand. His quick reflex saved Rowena from falling straight onto her derriere, but nothing could save her dignity. Still, she knew she should thank him audibly or be shamed for her lack of manners. Unfortunately, just before she could open her mouth, his fingers started stroking her sides.

Rowena found John smiling innocently at her when she snapped her head around to glare. Had it not been for Grace looking on with raised brows and a strange smile on Bernadette's lips, Rowena would have slapped him roundly across the face.

"Thank you, John," she muttered instead, choking on her cowardice.

"At your service," John said with a low bow. Before Rowena could leave, he grabbed her hand and brought her naked palm to his lips. "I wish only to serve."

Rowena ripped her hand away. John straightened, smiling as though he had not noticed.

"I will meet you here in one hour," he said. "I have a desire to see the museum beforehand, and I thought you could accompany me there as well."

"I look forward to it," Rowena answered, leaving the dining room as quickly as she could.

• • •

"Good afternoon, my lord," a butler said gravely, with a curt bow, before allowing access into Tinja House.

The foyer awed Christophe when he stepped in. He had had no idea the baron was so wealthy. The trouble with legends was that one never knew what in the story was true and what was made up —and the story of Mr. Brayemore becoming a baron was a legend.

Christophe could now see for himself that the part about the man's wealth was no exaggeration. It was said that Baron Brayemore had helped King George acquire some coveted piece of artwork, which in turn had kept England from getting into quite a mess in Morocco. A mess that could have led to war between the two countries. The idea made Christophe shudder in the middle of Baron Brayemore's foyer. While he had no doubt the English army was stronger, he also knew that a war with Morocco would have been long and bloody and was best avoided.

"Lord Candor!" exclaimed Baroness Brayemore as she glided into the entryway. Turning, Christophe noticed the fountain built into the wall behind her, decorated in colored stones and pouring into a small pool. It was something he had seen many times in North Africa as a place to wash one's feet before entering the house. Here in London, he assumed it was more decorative than functional.

"I am so very pleased to see you here. What brings you out today?" the baroness asked. She smiled, showing straight white teeth as she lifted her hand. It was almost shocking how young the lady was. Having wed the Duke of Auster at barely seventeen, Christophe realized that Lady Brayemore might not yet be even forty.

"I came to call upon Miss Brayemore. I sent a note ahead," Christophe said.

With a flick of her wrist, Lady Brayemore summoned the rotund butler to step forward with the silver platter holding his card. Lady Brayemore took it, turning it around in her delicate fingers as she regarded him.

"So you did. I received your note this morning, but I am afraid my stepdaughter decided to go out for the day. Her cousin came into town, and she greatly wishes to become reacquainted with him. Would you like to have some tea with Lady Grace and me? The wait might prove fruitful."

Christophe bowed his head in acceptance, wishing he could decline and run after Rowena wherever she might be. Propriety, with all its strings and rules, demanded that he accept the offer for at least twenty minutes—and how well Lady Brayemore knew it.

Reluctantly, he entered the parlor, to the obvious delight of Lady Grace and her friend Lady Alice. He was instructed to take the seat between the girls by Lady Brayemore, which he did before bracing himself to pass a miserable tea-time.

Christophe stood to take his leave for the sixth time and was finally allowed to go. Every time he had stood up before now, someone had begged him to stay longer and he had done so, always hoping that perhaps Rowena would walk in after a few more minutes. But she had not.

Stepping into the sunlight, Christophe sighed with relief. The two-hour tea had felt more like two days, particularly when Lady Harrow and her two daughters had joined them. Lady Alice, Lady Diana, and Lady Mary had spoken only in monosyllables, Lady Harrow and Lady Grace had exchanged a constant stream of sweetly coated, poisonous quips, and Lady Brayemore seemed to have forgotten how to speak altogether. The only fruitful thing about the afternoon was that he could say with authority that Claire was correct in her assessment of Lady Grace.

Down the street, his carriage was already being turned around to pick him up, but he didn't much feel like sitting anymore. A long stroll through Hyde Park would do him good. The hope that by walking he would run into a woman who sang lullabies to camels may have also been a reason to walk.

Once in the park, Christophe lowered his hat and his gaze, making himself look as uninviting as possible. There was only one person he wanted to see. If she wasn't in the park, he preferred to get to the other side and on to his office without being noticed.

When he had almost walked the entirety of the park's length, a small commotion near the pond caught his attention. A woman in a striped walking dress and a large matching hat stood in the middle of several parcels scattered on the ground. When the large man near her picked up one of the parcels, he said something that made the woman laugh.

It was Rowena. He was almost certain.

Jealousy rose within him as he watched the very muscular man hold out a bulging bicep for her as she stepped over a knot of roots. Apparently content with picking up one parcel, the large man, almost certainly the cousin Lady Brayemore had mentioned, signaled to a footman nearby, who approached and quickly took everything else away.

Again Rowena laughed. The wide-rimmed bonnet moved just enough when she looked up at the tall man to show Christophe her lovely face. They were at the entrance now, debating something. When Rowena pulled away, the man held her hand to his arm a little longer than a polite gentleman should. It was a trick to show he wished her to stay – a trick so many men used. The fact that it usually worked on women made Christophe grind his teeth in jealousy.

He wished he could approach the cousin and plant him a facer, but that kind of behavior would only land him in the gossip columns the next morning. The chances of it impressing Rowena were slim; besides, judging by the looks of the opponent, Christophe wasn't even sure he would come out a winner. Of course, if the cousin didn't let Rowena enter her carriage, Christophe would find out soon enough.

Fortunately for his physical health, the cousin finally let go. Rowena seemed to say her farewells quickly, before motioning to the footman to shut the door. Once the carriage was out of sight, the large man didn't seem too forlorn. He tipped his hat to various ladies on his way out of the park, grinning at everyone he encountered.

With disgust for the cousin and his own badly spent afternoon, Christophe headed straight home with every intention of working until his mind succumbed to his desire to think on something other than Rowena. But once he arrived home, Miss Brayemore invaded his thoughts in the form of a note written in gentle, looping handwriting.

> *Lord Candor,*
>
> *I am informed that you visited my father's house today. I regret that I was out with my cousin John and did not have the opportunity to speak with you in person, but perhaps that is for the best. I believe it would be better for you and I not to see each other anymore. I hear you are rather occupied, having inherited the family title, and I am still trying to settle quietly into life back in England. It would be best for us to stay on separate paths.*
>
> *I wish you luck in your future.*
>
> *Sincerely,*
>
> *Miss Brayemore*

Chapter Sixteen

"GOOD DAY, CINCH," DAUCER said, bursting through the doors with an evil glint in his eye as he threw his cape and hat onto the table next to him. "Honestly, you should hire a better butler. One who will let me in without having to run around the man."

"I told my staff I did not wish to be disturbed, yet you seemed to have managed to get in here just fine, Daucer," Christophe said irritably, though he found he was grateful for the distraction. He lit a small cigarette before throwing another to his friend. "Have you come to work?"

Daucer's brow rose incredulously as he exhaled smoke.

"I don't find that at all funny," he said, throwing himself onto the settee in a pout.

For the first time in their lives, it was Daucer who appeared tired. Exhausted, really. Rubbing his hands over his face and through his black hair, he appeared like any other businessman during negotiations. It was impressive how quickly he had changed from his noble, sedentary lifestyle to working as a merchant. Being the fourth son of a family on the edge of financial ruin had been just the right motivation for Daucer to come and work with Christophe. Discreetly, of course, so as not to upset his mother.

"How was yesterday?"

Smoke billowed out in large rings as Daucer hesitated.

"One ship came in from the Indies. At first it surprised me not to see you on the docks. But when I remembered how absolutely smashed you were three nights ago, it seemed to me that an extralong hangover was very likely. I made your very gracious excuses to the crew. You may thank me in a moment," Daucer said with a smile.

Christophe grimaced at the reminder of his behavior a few nights before. Seeing Rowena with her cousin had sent him straight to the bottle, and it had indeed taken two days for his head to recover.

"Not that they care one iota for the flowery words," Daucer went on. "They just wanted their pay. The captain said they had a run-in with a bad storm, and some cargo rotted before getting into port. I checked it. It wasn't enough to make a dent in your profits, but it was enough to run the cook off. Apparently not having any salt or sugar or something was the last straw for him. So you need to hire a new one. Except that I already did. And I found a new valet for the captain of the *Dolores*."

Daucer paused and waited. Christophe tipped an imaginary hat with a smile. With a dramatic sigh, his friend and employee continued.

"Coming back to land, I spoke to Lord Newsbury, and he is willing to join with us in the mining plan. He also believes he can convince Lord St. Cloud and perhaps his cousin, Mr. Foxhorn. But we will still have quite a problem with Baron Rothstad. He is of the ancient idea that if the people did not wish to be poor, they would have found a different place to be born in the world. The man's an ass. Hopefully, he'll drop dead soon enough. Lord Newsbury is friends with his grandson, Mr. Worth, and has already been coaxing him into our way of thinking."

"Thank you, Philip," Christophe said, purposefully using his friend's Christian name. His friend eyed him sharply. "I appreciate it."

"Are you about to drop off?" he asked. "Why are you calling me 'Philip'?"

"I just want to thank you," Christophe said. "What news do you have from Cookston?"

"It's only been two weeks since you've been back." Daucer kept a straight face, but his eyes twitched subtly.

"You haven't got into trouble, have you?"

Daucer balked. "Me? I haven't got into trouble for nearly two years."

"Yes, but that was quite a bit of trouble, as I recall," Christophe said with a knowing smile.

"You cannot expect me to keep track of the marital status of every lady in London," Daucer muttered. "And I have more brains than to get into trouble in the countryside. The men out there are far more prone to shoot first, or worse, break my nose, and ask questions later."

"Perhaps if you married, as your mother wishes, you would find yourself properly restrained," Christophe said, biting against a smile.

"I get enough from my mother and the earl, Cinch. I don't need more pressure to marry," Daucer finally replied, before becoming exceptionally thoughtful. "Speaking of women, how are the women in your household? Making your life impossible as usual?"

"Yes. Last week I had to sit through two very tedious teas, all because some ladies wanted to get a glimpse of the new Marquess of Candor. I am like an exhibit at the museum. Thankfully, they believed me when I said I was indisposed yesterday and did not drag me off to another. But they did not leave without threatening to be back tomorrow."

"Whyever would a lady want you to call?" Daucer asked, a large smile spreading across his lips. "You are rumored to bite."

"Apparently, they don't mind if a marquess bites their virginal daughters. Everyone wants a title for them."

"Whose tea did you attend?"

Christophe shot his friend an annoyed look. "Do I look like someone who pays attention to their names?"

"So, while I've been out traveling all of England to track down the men your brother threw away without pay, you've been having tea with beautiful women?"

"Hardly," Christophe said, rather exasperated now. He knew Daucer was teasing and yet, as always, he couldn't help but bite at his friend's quips.

As expected, Daucer laughed. "Did you call on her?"

"Yes. And she was not there."

Christophe narrowed his eyes when Daucer laughed harder.

"Why, you no-good brute," Christophe accused, rising from his chair. "How much do you already know, and to whom have you been speaking about it?"

"I only needed to speak to *you*. Do you not remember how much you talk when soaked?" his friend asked, still laughing. "You are smitten, Christophe Maximilian. More so than with that trollop Catherine."

"I am not that transparent," Christophe protested, his voice cracking against his will.

"When you're drunk you are," Daucer chuckled, wiping tears from his eyes.

"Perhaps her beauty overcomes me."

Daucer wasn't believing any of his mockery. "No, you care for her. And far too deeply to have just met her at Chershire a few weeks ago. Between deciphering your babble the other night and remembering that Miss Brayemore left Melilla with the Dowager Lady Merville, I have concluded that it is she you were brooding about this past summer. How's that for putting two and two together? I didn't get my degree in mathematics and law for nothing, you know. I can still count to four."

"I did not—she is not—" Christophe started, and then gave up, slouching in his chair. "I do not know what to do about her."

"Marry her."

"She is being courted by her cousin. I saw them the other day. He made her... he made her laugh."

"That is grave indeed. I take it you witnessed this the other day before going to White's and drinking two bottles of scotch?"

"It sounds ridiculous when spoken aloud, but ever since I watched him make her laugh, I have not been able to get up the courage to call on her again. Besides, the prospect of having to pass another tea with her sister, in the event that Rowena is not present, nauseates me."

Daucer went to the small table where Christophe kept the best whisky and poured two glasses.

"That stuff cost me a fortune!" Christophe cried out. "It is hardly one o'clock in the afternoon."

"Perhaps it will set your head right. Besides, I think I will need it when you tell me how you actually met this girl."

He wasn't about to get any work done now. With a sigh of resignation, Christophe took the glass of scotch while giving Daucer an abbreviated version of how he met Rowena. His friend watched him walk a hole into his carpet but said nothing, letting Christophe do all the talking. At the end of the story, Christophe threw himself back into his chair and glared at his desk.

"Well, that was very entertaining, though I still fail to see why you cannot offer for her hand. Your guilt for not having seen who she was?" Daucer said.

The hair on Christophe's neck stood up, but he only had time to shoot Daucer a scathing look in his own defense before a footman entered the library.

"A Mr. Rousch, my lord," a footman announced.

"Mr. Rousch?" Daucer asked. "The investigator you hired to look into Catherine all those years ago?"

Christophe waved the questions away.

"I don't have your natural abilities with women, Daucer. I need some context to what is happening with Miss Brayemore," he hissed. Daucer smiled and snuggled further into his chair. Christophe rolled his eyes, wishing he could remove the smug look from his face.

"Lord Candor," Mr. Rousch said with an exaggerated bow.

"Come in, Mr. Rousch, Lord Daucer was just leaving."

"Me?" Daucer asked, his face a blanket of innocence. "No, no, I have nowhere to go. Do enlighten us, Mr. Rousch, of your news of Miss Brayemore. You see, I know whom you've been investigating. So, then, you may speak freely in front of me."

Christophe shot his friend a look that would have turned most men to stone, but Daucer refused to meet his gaze altogether. He instead focused all of his attention on Mr. Rousch, even thrusting a glass of whisky into the investigator's hands before settling back in keen silence for the man to speak.

Mr. Rousch shifted uncomfortably, and Christophe followed suit.

"If you would like the man to speak, perhaps you should stop glaring at him," Daucer advised Christophe, who almost jumped from his skin, so focused was he on staring at Mr. Rousch. "I do believe you are making him nervous, Cinch."

"Yes. Pardon me. Please, Mr. Rousch. Do go on," Christophe said, clearing his throat to calm his nerves.

"Yes, sir. Of course, sir," the small, sweaty man said, nervously playing with the hem of his jacket. "I have only watched her for a small bit of time and so have little to report. She leaves around this time every day."

"At the social hour?"

Mr. Rousch turned to Daucer. His Adam's apple bobbed with a nervous swallow. "Yes, my lord. She goes shopping, to the bookstore, or to her father's clinic to read to the elderly patients. But today she will probably go towards the East End. Kipper Street. She visits a church there and a building there filled with, ah, with people from America. Former slaves."

"What does she do there?" Christophe asked, as Mr. Rousch wiped his forehead with a dingy handkerchief.

"I spoke to one of the neighbors and it seems that one day, a while ago, Miss Brayemore assisted a woman as a, well, midwife, of sorts."

"Truly?" asked Daucer.

"The story goes that there was no midwife about who would help the woman. The Vicar went to find a Quaker woman he knew wouldn't have a problem with helping, you know, sir, a colored woman. Miss Brayemore stayed with her. The neighbor also says that Miss Brayemore sent in a Quaker girl to teach the children to read and write. She says the schools won't let them in on account of their skin color."

"So you believe she is going to visit this place today?"

Mr. Rousch nodded.

Christophe rose. If Rowena was leaving the house, he wished to use that information to his advantage. It was the reason he had employed Mr. Rousch in the first place. But he also did not want to give the man any more gossip to run with, so he rose deliberately slow, and languidly put his coat on.

"I must be off. Mr. Rousch, thank you for your work. Lord Daucer here will set you up with my secretary for your payment."

With that, he strode out of the study and called for his carriage to be brought around.

"Mr. Rousch," Daucer said, turning to the man with a smile. "Would you like a drink?"

⚓

"Where are you going, Rowena?" John's deep voice boomed as he opened the library door. He stood with a glass of port in one hand and a book in another. "Out and about by yourself in London again? Aren't you afraid the wolves will devour you?"

"No," she said, taking her hat and parasol from the footman. "Thank you, Dirkle. I'm taking Alfred. Do you have any more questions?"

John smiled as he leaned against the door frame, which seemed too small to hold him in. His eyes darkened, though his pose was casual.

"I know you are in the habit of leaving the house unchaperoned. I simply wondered where you might go when you do it."

Rowena held his gaze, her own devoid of any emotion. "I do not believe it is any of your business, John."

Without waiting for an answer, she turned slightly and walked towards the door. She did not move any faster than she would have if John hadn't stopped her. She kept her face blank and her demeanor slow and insouciant as she instructed Neeves to remind her father about her wish to see him before he left for his club that night. It was imperative that she moved with ease. Fear was the easiest way to control someone, and she was quite certain that John liked to be in control.

Now ready, she turned to take her leave, hoping that John had lost interest in her. It was disappointing, but not surprising when she found him taking hold of her parasol instead of taking his leave. Rowena slowly turned around to face him. Neeves stayed with his feet planted to the floor just a few feet away, despite John having waved him off. Rowena smiled inwardly at the footman's loyalty to her. It was no small feat. All the other servants below were more loyal to John than to her.

"Rowena," he said in a low, sensual tone. "I did not wish to offend you."

"You didn't offend me," Rowena said evenly, daring to look him straight in the eyes. "You were simply asking questions. Though why you feel free to ask such personal questions, I do not understand."

She wished John would just admit that he had come to see if she would marry him. Only when he admitted it could she refuse him. But he never said anything of the kind. Strange flickers of emotion lit up his eyes each time they spoke, as they did now, but the flickers would leave almost as quickly as they came, leaving Rowena with no real evidence of his feelings for her.

"I must return to Manchester for a few weeks. When I come back, I would like very much to escort you to the opera and discover what you find so fascinating about it," he murmured, pressing closer.

Her desire to squirm overpowered her. "We will have to see what ppera is playing and whether my stepmother can chaperone."

"Perhaps there will be no need for a chaperone, dear Rowena," John said, shrugging. For a man so bulky, his movements were surprisingly graceful.

"What does that mean?" Rowena asked, taking advantage of his movement to take a step away.

John smiled. He had an admirable beauty, that she would be a fool to deny, but there was something so disingenuous about the way he paid attention to her. The strange gleam in his eye convinced her that marriage was more of a plot than anything else. Though he was the typically amicable Englishman, he was not right for her.

"There is a contract of marriage that our fathers drew up years ago. It was done verbally, but most would see it as legal and binding," John said.

The admission shocked her. John slid his index finger against her jawline.

"I will not treat you unkindly, cousin. I'm not an unkind man. As long as you stick to your vows of a proper English wife, we shall rub along just fine."

John lowered his head to kiss her, but Rowena stepped out of his reach. She almost laughed when he sighed in exasperation, as though dealing with a child.

"I do not see myself as your wife, John. I'm sorry. I simply do not see you in that way."

"But Rowena, what other choice do you have? To wait around for love? You would have to go quite far to find that. Have you not heard the many rumors of how you really spent the last few years? No one even speaks of the little story you concocted to pass yourself off as virtuous. If you receive another offer, you can be sure it will have more to do with his wealth and power than..." John paused to rake his eyes over her: "...you."

Rowena drew herself up, fighting her emotions at the harsh words. She yanked her parasol free, but John caught her wrist instead. With the strength of an ox, he kept her a prisoner as he stepped up behind her and pressed his hips slowly against her bottom while his other hand caressed her cheek. When she didn't respond, he relaxed his grip.

"You know nothing about me, John," she said, angry that his words were causing tears to pool in her eyes. "My virtue is as intact as Grace's." She yanked her gloves up so hard it pained her hands.

John laughed, the sound so loud she was certain it reached the streets.

"You were no missionary there, Miss Brayemore. And I have proof. I know where you were and how you got there. The rest I fill in with my imagination, though it doesn't take much to understand what you were doing all these years. A beautiful woman with a figure like that would only have been useful for one thing."

Dread rose within her, but she replaced it with anger and forced herself to stomp through the door. She had no idea what proof he might have, but either he was bluffing well, or he was threatening to ruin her and anyone else involved with her. At least the blinding fury kept away the tears.

She was already at the top of the stone steps when John came out to finish his speech in his thundering voice. Thankfully, they did not live in a neighborhood where people took to promenading.

"I will see you soon, Rowena. Perhaps we can make a public beginning to our short courtship. There is no reason to make it a long one," he called out. "Of course, there is always the option of no courtship at all—just a quick elopement."

Rowena fought to control herself, rolling her shoulders back and biting her tongue against the scathing remarks she wished to make. Once she felt her legs were sturdy, she stepped out and marched across the pavement, holding her head high to convince John she was in control.

He stood still at the door as she walked to the gate and into the street. Though he had done nothing to indicate he would follow her, she moved quickly, battling her desire to run. It wasn't until she was quite far away that she realized she had left the carriage behind, but that was really no matter. Her emotions were running too high to be caged up in a carriage at the moment. Hopefully she could calm the swirl of anger and fear inside her before getting to her friend's house through some exercise.

But even walking could not erase what John had said. While Rowena's heart now beat slower than before, each step only drummed into her further the fact that if she married John, she would be as trapped as she had been in slavery.

Too preoccupied with the devastating thought to notice where she was going, Rowena quickened her pace around the corner and ran straight into a brick wall of gray wool.

Chapter Seventeen

CHRISTOPHE HAD NEVER IMAGINED that a woman could achieve much force when running into a man, but this one had. When he grasped her arms to balance her, it surprised him that there was little to grasp.

Then there was some strange gibberish, sounding much like a muttered apology in Berber. His heart quickened.

"Rowena?"

"My-my lord," she sputtered as Christophe stepped back. He was quite certain the surprise on her face mirrored his own. Underneath the surprise, though, she looked as though she might burst into sobs.

"Miss Brayemore, is something wrong?" he asked. It was a foolish gesture to make in public, but Christophe couldn't help gently touching his fingers to her cheek. She jumped back as though touched by hot coals.

"Nothing, my lord. I'm quite fine. What brings you to the vicinity?"

Christophe did not believe her, but dropped his hand. "I came looking for you."

Her eyes flashed at his comment. Like a haughty child, she placed her hands on her hips and stared him down.

"Might I walk with you?" He did not wait for an answer before taking her hand and placing it firmly under his arm.

"No, my lord. I'm sorry, but you cannot come with me."

Christophe stepped back in astonishment.

"Where are you going without a maid to chaperone?" he asked, his eyes narrowing.

She pursed her lips into a fine line. "It's no one's business where I'm going." Anger filled her eyes. Her chest heaved with it; her eyes burned with it. In fact, she rather looked ready to slap him. "I am quite tired of men in this country thinking they can control every single step I take. It's a wonder women trust themselves to men here at all. You are not any better than those in Algeria! You are not my master. *No one* is my master. I struggled to be free, only to find that every man around here thinks he can control me!"

Christophe kept his face blank. He was glad she had the sense to hiss and not scream her words, as many women would with this much anger running through them. Still, already a couple across the street were slowing their pace. With her rant seemingly at an end, he did the only thing he could to publicly smooth the situation; he bowed gracefully over her hand and stepped back.

"I did not mean to offend, Miss Brayemore," he said in a low voice, and her features softened considerably. "I simply wished to call on you and thought perhaps I could join you in your walk."

Miss Brayemore shifted her feet. Eyeing the couple across the way, Christophe saw with relief that they were moving on, their interest somewhere else.

"If I were merely walking, I would gladly have your company, my lord," she said, now calm. "But I am making a private call."

She turned away from him slowly and hailed a hack coming down the road. It was strange that she wouldn't take her father's carriage, but he had little time to reflect on that.

Before entering the hired hack, she turned to him. "It was good to see you again. I didn't know you were back in town. Perhaps we will see each other again soon."

There was no time to respond before the hack drove away, leaving him on the deserted street.

"Miss Brayemore is here!"

The cry went up as Rowena stepped out of the hack. She instantly recognized little Bill's voice and prepared herself for the force of his hug.

"Miss Brayemore!" This time, her skirts muffled his cries as he hugged her about the legs.

When he had squeezed as much as his arms could, little Bill lifted his head to look up at her, and once again her heart melted. To her he embodied the image of one of the slave boys who had drowned in the river just a few weeks before she had left Algeria. She and Selma had both thrown themselves into the water after him, but the strong current had carried the boy away within seconds. They had almost drowned themselves because of the current, struggling out only because there were two of them to work together.

"Hello, Bill. Is your mother home?"

"Yes'm. And Pop, too! He got three days off from da railway."

"Has Miss Mindy come to give lessons yet?"

Bill suddenly found his shoes very interesting. Rowena looked too, and noticed the laces were missing to fit his feet better. She made a mental note to send shoes with the second-hand cart the next time. If Bill's mother would accept them, she would have gone right then to buy new ones, but she knew the shoes would be refused.

"Miss Mindy said I did good at the math'matics, but dat my writin's not up to par."

Rowena laughed at Bill's attempt to recreate Miss Mindy's very proper accent. With her hair pulled back tightly and always dressed in black, Miss Mindy seemed a severe lady for her twenty-one years, but inside she had a heart of gold. She worked hard to educate the children who couldn't afford to go to school, and those not welcome there. When they had first met, Rowena had been so happy to find someone willing to teach the children that she had offered Miss Mindy a high salary, only to be talked down by the woman herself. It had been Rowena's first experience with Quakers. She had found the whole experience quite amusing.

"Very well, little Bill. You just keep doing what Miss Mindy says, and I'm sure your handwriting will improve."

Bill grumbled something about never needing handwriting when he was going to work on trains, but several other children bursting from the building covered his words. Most of the families in the building were former slaves, either escaped or freed. Of the five families, two women were widows and three had husbands who worked the railways.

The clamor of little voices filled Rowena's ears as she slowly moved towards the building. Some asked if she had sweets, others asked if she had brought ribbons or books or toys. Always prepared, Rowena held up the baskets. She turned a full circle so they all could see and noticed a carriage with the Candor seal at the corner, partially hidden by a tree.

Lady Candor worked tirelessly as an abolitionist—most of the housing, clothing and work the former slaves received was all due to her and the efforts of the Abolitionist Society—but she rarely came to the neighborhoods in her finest carriage. And she never came unless there was a scheduled event where other people would also be present; it set the other women ill at ease.

If Dowager Candor was in the neighborhood, it would be a perfect opportunity to speak to her about a few things. Rowena made a mental note to find what building the Dowager was visiting, then turned her attention to Mr. Grant, Bill's father, who was walking towards her.

Rowena had met Cordy's husband only once before and was once again struck by how gracefully he moved his large frame about. With wide, muscular shoulders and a chest that even sailors would be envious of, she often wondered what his job had used to be, but never found the courage to ask. None of the people here wanted to speak about their past. At least, not with her. She knew they found her to be kind, but she was still an outsider in their eyes. As far as they knew, she had grown up privileged and with everything at her fingertips. Which wasn't entirely unfair—at least until she was seventeen.

"Miss Brayemore," Bill's father said, taking his hat off with a nod.

"Mr. Grant. It is so nice to see you again."

Christophe watched the scene from across the street, hidden in an abandoned doorway. Behind the crowd of children came a large gentleman, black as night. The man hesitated a moment in front of Rowena before bowing, as though reminding himself to do so.

While the two of them spoke, he turned his worn hat around and around in his fingers. That, along with his unpleasant habit of looking down constantly, bespoke the man's past as a former slave. Recently freed or escaped, Christophe would venture.

After exchanging a few words, the man took the baskets from Rowena and went back inside, giving her thanks while every part of his body seemed to want to reject the gifts. Christophe understood the man's pride, but had more admiration for him in taking the basket than rejecting it. Too often he had seen men keep their pride at the expense of their children's empty stomachs.

A few minutes later, a very matronly young woman came from the side of the squat building. Everything about the woman indicated she was a Quaker, from her drab dress to her ugly bonnet to the scrubbed face and tightly coiled hair. Christophe's father had used to work with them in the crusade to outlaw the slave trade, and his mother still worked closely with them in her mission to free slaves from America. The Quakers seemed to be some of the hardest-working people in all of England, which earned them his admiration.

Shame washed over Christophe. His mother's admonishments to take up his seat in Parliament, where he could make a difference, ran through his head again. Her belief in his ability to create any change was flattering, but he was convinced there was more he could do from outside the government than inside.

Kicking a stone away, he growled at his country's politicians. Next year the Anti-Slavery Act would be voted on in Parliament. If it passed, it would make slavery illegal in all places the Crown was recognized. It was a better law than one that only served England, but as always, there were exceptions. Territories held by the East India Company would be exempt, as well as the Island of Saint

Helena and the Island of Ceylon. Christophe had no idea how that had been negotiated, but knew someone high up had worked their magic. Or perhaps someone rich. What irked him most was that emancipation for the territories where slavery would be abolished would only be immediate for the children. The adults would have to work for another six years before receiving their freedom. So much for abolishing slavery.

And yet the lords all patted themselves on the back over it. It was enough to want to throttle the lot of them. But then at least England itself was slave-free, unlike America, and the Royal Navy roamed the coast of Africa, stopping any slave ship trying to get by. Those two facts kept him proud to be English, despite the idiots who surrounded him.

"M'lord," a man in a well-worn green coat said from the street. He moved with a great limp, and the removal of his hat revealed a large bald spot on the top of his greasy head. It shone as though polished to impress, while dirty brown hair grew out the sides and hung down to his shoulders. The jacket was smeared with three different colors of God-knew-what. His pantaloons were no longer a distinguishable color. Any movement from him turned the air stale.

Christophe stiffened, then returned his focus to the building where Rowena had disappeared.

"What do you want?" he asked. The last thing he wished was to be interrupted. Or worse yet, have Rowena see him.

"You the owner 'ere, m'lord?" the man asked, his foul breath saturating the air. "You gonna do somethin' about these people? That woman there says she's gonna bring more of them in 'ere. We've been tryin' to reach you, m'lord, to appeal to yer good senses. The good English boys and gels can't right play an' live 'ere with these people comin' in."

Christophe responded with a grunt, which seemed to embolden the man to sidle up to him and peer at the building as though the two of them were partners in spying. The urge to push the man away rose up strongly within him, but Christophe deemed himself slightly more mature than a five-year-old and ignored the impulse.

"I know you was thinkin' about destroyin' the buildin' there. Might be the easiest way, m'lord. To git rid of 'em, I mean."

At that moment, Rowena came out one door with a baby in her arms, and Christophe's knees almost buckled under. The baby had skin the color of cream and coffee, with wide eyes that looked about while she calmly sucked on her fists. A strange tingle started to quiver in his middle at the sight.

Without another word to the foul-smelling man, Christophe swung himself into his carriage and left to find Daucer. If he couldn't give Rowena babies, he could at least make certain the real owner of that building didn't demolish it.

Chapter Eighteen

DECEMBER 21, 1832

ROWENA TRIED TO WALK as gracefully as the other women through the crowd at yet another ball her family had insisted she attend with them, but it was no use. The fashionable puffed sleeves worked nicely to block anyone from going anywhere they wished to go. After trying again and again to get through the crowd, only to walk in one large circle, Rowena took to the outside wall and made her way behind the women already seated.

She had left the house quite confident in her choice of dress. It was a simply cut gown in emerald silk that came high enough to cover the markings on her back. At the neckline, it curved along her collarbone and dipped slightly at the front, where her breasts were pulled together so tightly they almost touched. Along the waist of her bodice, thin threads of gold looped around, teasing one another as they continued down to the hem. Her sleeves were not puffy, but lay almost flat against the tops of her arms, the rest covered by very long gloves. It was beautiful—but now in the middle of all the other women, she was beginning to regret her staunch refusal to go along with the ridiculous fashion of puffed sleeves. Without them, she was clearly out of place.

Her sleeves were probably not the only bad choice she had made. There was also her hair, which was adorned with several gold chains that held tiny pearls. Only half of it was gathered into an intricate weave, with the rest cascading down her back in perfect curls.

She should have realized that ignoring Grace's stares and comments did not mean she could withstand the same from strangers in the ton. Already she was receiving glares and raised brows, signaling obvious disapproval.

"So, she finally dares to step into a London ballroom," croaked a lady with three large peacock feathers in her hair, glaring straight at Rowena. "I have to admit that she is pretty, in a foreign way. I rather expected her to look like she'd been dragged across the Atlantic."

"Hmph," replied a woman in a garish pink dress, her double chin bulging against her neck. "She looks every bit the sultan's mistress to me. I am more inclined to believe the stories of her being in a harem. Just look at what she is wearing! Not at all English-looking."

With her last remaining willpower, Rowena turned to face them fully, only to find them undaunted. They not only refused to divert their gaze, but glared back at her. Movement, Rowena decided, was the order of the day.

"Good evening, Miss Brayemore."

"Good evening, Lady Candor," Rowena replied, keenly aware she had almost knocked into Lady Claire as she had turned around.

Taking her elbow, Claire led her through the crowd, the masses parting at just the right time.

"How do you do it?" Rowena asked. "I couldn't get through."

Claire laughed as they approached Lord and Lady Glenville. "Years of practice, Miss Brayemore. This is a small crowd compared to the crushes during the season. You'll get used to it. Do not look so horrified!" she added with amusement.

"Miss Brayemore," Lord Daucer greeted her, looking very dapper in his dark grey jacket. "How lovely you are tonight. I dare say I haven't seen anything lovelier in a very long time—don't you agree, Falcon?"

"You are daft if you think I will fall for your games again," Falcon said with a laugh. "My wife is always the most beautiful in my eyes; though I do agree that emerald suits you, Miss Brayemore. Don't you think, love?"

"I certainly do," his wife agreed.

Lord and Lady Glenville took to the floor, but not before Emily sent a pointed look back over her shoulder. Immediately, Lord Daucer stepped up.

"May I ask for this dance, Miss Brayemore?" he asked, flashing Emily a smile before turning his full attention to Rowena.

"I do not think you truly wish to dance with me," Rowena laughed. "You need only to look at the bruising I inflicted upon Lord Candor. It is still present on his toes."

"I have no desire to look upon Cinch's large, probably oaf-like feet, Miss Brayemore," Lord Daucer replied, his eyes twinkling as he took her hand.

"Cinch?"

"Christophe. It's a family nickname I've picked up on. Come, time to dance."

Across the way, she spotted Lord Candor himself dancing with his mother, who seemed to glide across the floor. Rowena tried to concentrate on her feet instead of on Lord Candor and how handsome he looked in his navy coat.

"Do not think so hard about the steps," Lord Daucer told her. "Pretend you are a child again, being forced to dance with your nanny, and you will quickly find your feet complying."

Rowena laughed. "Was it terrible, then? Dancing with your nanny?"

"Torture," Daucer answered, his eyes sparkling as he took his bow. "She must have weighed at least twenty stone, and always stank of cabbage."

Laughter caused her to stumble, but Lord Daucer brought her back into step within seconds, as though it had never happened. He could not, however, help her when she missed her cue to follow the women down the line. Hew shoes pinched painfully as she ran to catch up. Lord Daucer sent her an encouraging wink and smile, but Rowena knew she was making a fool of herself.

When the music finally ended, she could have hugged the musicians for their mercy.

"You truly were not so terrible, Miss Brayemore," Lord Daucer said, kissing her hand gallantly as they rejoined their group. "But perhaps our next dance will be a waltz? Then I could lead you better as we glide across the floor."

"Well," Rowena said, "if you wish to torture yourself, who am I to refuse your wish?"

"Should we get a drink?" he asked her, guiding her slowly to the refreshment table. "I wanted to ask you if you received the note from Dowager Candor."

Rowena looked at him, startled he would know about such a thing.

"I had it delivered for her. Our families go back a long way, you know. Candor and I have been friends for decades."

"Yes," Rowena answered, mulling over that information. "It seems Lady Dowager Candor has placed me on a committee for their newest building on Kipper Street."

Lord Daucer came to a stop. Cautiously, he lifted two glasses of champagne from a nearby footman before speaking.

"Does that please you?" he asked.

Rowena bit her lip.

"I'm confused by what they mean..." she began. "I was told at the bank that Lord Candor had bought the building."

"And you do not like the idea?"

"How did he know about it?" Rowena asked. "I didn't realize his mother's work interested him—"

"He bought the building, Miss Brayemore," Lord Daucer interrupted. "But he placed it in the Society's hands, with your name as the first trustee."

"Mine?"

"He followed you," Lord Daucer explained as he sipped his champagne. Rowena followed his lead, allowing the bubbles to slip down her throat and calm her nerves.

"I still don't understand," she finally said.

Lord Daucer sighed before turning fully to face her, searching her eyes before speaking again. "If you don't understand that he cares for you, I am not sure there is anything that I can do but speak plainly. If you care nothing for him, I pray you leave him be."

With that, he bowed and slowly walked away. Rowena looked around, but everyone was much too occupied with the dance to notice her confusion. Near the doors, she glimpsed a navy coat covering broad shoulders standing with Lord Arlington and Mr. Nall.

When Lord Candor gave the two men a short bow and disappeared into the crowd, Rowena quietly slipped from the ballroom and followed him.

⸱⸱⸱ ♨ ⸱⸱⸱

Lord Bellevue's library was packed with books that looked as though no one ever touched them. The fire cast a low glow over the middle of the room, leaving the sides in deep shadows. Christophe crept forward, making certain no one was present, before throwing himself onto one of the chairs and slowly exhaling. As much as he would enjoy blaming his sister's incessant chatter in the carriage for his restlessness, he knew the real culprit was another woman entirely.

The library door creaked open, and Christophe held his breath, wishing he could hide.

"Lord Candor?" came a whisper as a woman in an emerald dress slipped through. The firelight caught on her hair, giving off a red glow. "Lord Candor, there you are."

"You shouldn't be here. You can't be seen alone with another man, Rowena," he said, rising slowly.

"*Yallah*. Sit down," she said.

Her Arabic exclamation caused a smile to tug on his lips, but sparks of light shot through his eyes when he turned his head. A string of curse words soon followed.

In front of him was the tinkling sound of a muffled giggle.

"I am sorry," Rowena said. "I should not laugh at you. I see you are getting a headache. Sit down and I will help you."

"As you did in the desert?" he asked, cautiously taking his seat again.

"Yes, my lord. Only two things have changed since then," Rowena said as she walked to stand behind him. "One is that you know who I truly am, and the second is that I have to both apologize and offer my thanks. Maybe that makes three things?"

"Those are the only changes?" he asked, breathing into the gentle pressure her fingers measured out over his scalp. "You should not be here. You should not be touching me."

The sounds of the orchestra drifted into the room. The door was slightly ajar, but it would not be enough to keep them from a scandal if someone were to find them. He could not seem to force himself up though. If he was made to marry her, he was not so certain he would mind.

"I will leave you soon, my lord," she whispered. "I do not wish to get you into trouble, but I do want to thank you. Lord Daucer told me about the building on Kipper Street when we danced this evening. Yesterday's letter confused me."

"But did it please you? I'm glad you received the letter. I was afraid you would not, just as you never received my note."

"Your note? When did you send a note?"

"Just last week. I came into town to apologize for my behavior at Chershire Manor. I was too prideful to do it in the moment, something I finally realized while working at my family estate. When I had the opportunity, I came back to town. The note I sent ahead of my visit."

"I did not receive a note," she said, her voice carrying a tinge of suspicion.

"I also left my card when I came to call."

"I didn't receive that either."

"I didn't think so," he drawled. "I saw your stepmother place it underneath a tea saucer."

"You had tea with my stepmother? Ah, then it was you! You were the visitor they were so excited about. It seemed strange to me that they would not say who you were, but they do many things I find strange. My sister is quite excited at the prospect of you courting her."

"I do not wish to court Lady Grace, Miss Brayemore."

"Do you not?" she asked. "Grace will be disappointed."

Christophe chose to settle into her massaging fingers instead of answering.

"Lord Daucer told me you followed me yesterday. I thought I saw your family carriage and wondered if your mother was there. I never thought you would follow me."

"You refused to allow me to escort you and entered into a hired hack. Unchaperoned."

"Do men so often molest unchaperoned women in London, for it to be such a dangerous place?"

"There is quite a bit of crime, actually." Christophe turned to look straight at her. "Especially in the areas which you seem to want to frequent. While you do not flaunt your wealth, it is clear to everyone there that you have some."

"Why did you buy that building?" she asked.

Again, he stepped closer before answering. The glowing embers highlighted the red in her hair, and he couldn't help the smile that spread across his lips at the sight.

"I bought it for you," he answered. "A single woman cannot own the title, so I placed it in the Society's hands, naming you as the primary trustee."

"I-I am quite speechless," she confessed. "The last time we spoke, I said some very unforgivable things. I don't understand why you are being so kind after what I said."

"Do you not?" he asked.

Even as he spoke, she shook her head. He wished he could touch her, smooth back her hair, caress her face. But he couldn't. He wouldn't.

"The former owner was a fool," he said, leaning against the couch. "I know you will treat the people well. Already you've done exceptional things, my mother tells me. It's very noble work."

"Not so noble," she protested. "I'm idle most of my time. Visiting Kipper Street does more for me than for the people there, I am sure."

"You are unhappy?" he asked, clasping his hands together to stop them from touching her. It should not have been such a struggle.

"I have no reason to be unhappy," she said, breathlessly.

Her voice nearly made him forget what he wished to say. With all his words gone, he almost lowered his lips to hers. Thankfully, something made him step back and think. He recognized that his aching head, and the firelight, was making him soft. He should not wish to kiss the same woman who had vanished from him without reason.

"I should get back," she said, her voice also a whisper.

"Who are you?" he asked, stopping her mid-turn. "I have walked with you through the desert as Fatia, watching you closely, listening to you sing to camels. I saw you start to blossom and relax a little in Melilla. Remember how you trusted me with your nightmares and stories of your past? Yet you did not tell me who you were. You ran from me. And now here, you are teasing one minute, distant another."

Silence fell heavily upon them. With each tick of the clock, his agitation grew. He had brought her through the desert; he deserved to know who she was.

A sharp pain shot like a bullet behind his eyes, from one temple to another. When Christophe jerked his hand up towards his head, he heard Rowena whimper in fear and saw her cower from him. Another jab of pain stabbed through his head at her cry, jerking his body slightly forward and making her shrink further back.

Christophe steadied himself, balancing his head with little movement until the pain subsided. Seeing Rowena still hunched away from him drained him of niceties.

"Did you think I would hit you? You know who I am! I never once raised a finger against you!"

"I'm sorry!" she said in a strangled whisper.

Her face was awash with heat. Tears rolled silently down her cheeks, washing his anger away instantly. He approached her slowly, breathing steadily, but wavering between wanting answers and wishing to hold her. Gently, he brushed her hair back and wiped away her tears.

"Why are you so nervous?" he asked softly. "Never tell me that your father hits you."

"No. He would never hit me. I'm sorry to insult you again. You have only ever been kind."

"A grave injustice has been done to you, Miss Brayemore," he said, wiping her tears with his knuckles. His need for answers was slowly fading. There was not always a clear reason for one's actions. Perhaps her reasons simply boiled down to fear. Fear of what men before him had done to her.

Slowly, he leaned forward, cupping his hand behind her neck. He ran his tongue along her bottom lip before capturing fully her mouth. It was the same as and yet more than he remembered in his dreams. She tasted of champagne and exotic woman. When she opened her mouth, he took the opportunity to taste her with his tongue. She placed her hands lightly on his chest, and Christophe stepped forward, pressing his entire body against hers. His legs trembled as her curves melted into his frame.

Their passion mounted, every nerve in his body tingling with anticipation, though he was too rational about where they were to take it further than a simple kiss. Still, they had a few more moments before they would be forced to separate. Her fingernails dragged through his hair as he held her waist and pushed her gently against the wood-paneled wall.

Christophe wondered momentarily if she might push him away or slap him, but she did not. It did not take long for his hands to find their own way up towards her hair, stopping when he remembered her coiffure.

Her lips left small, buttery kisses on his mouth as his fingers dared to explore down her neck and along the sides of her breast. She groaned slightly, awakening him more fully to the moment. She desired him as he desired her. Greedily he pressed her breasts, the silk straining but refusing to release them further.

"Rowena Brayemore," he whispered against her neck.

"Yes," she breathed.

In the next moment, she froze. The fog in his head cleared, and he heard it, too. Drunken male laughter.

She pushed him away just as he stepped back. Hastily looking her over, Christophe was glad that his fingers had never run through her hair as they had wished to. Except for her heightened color and her slightly slanted bodice, she looked the same.

Beautiful.

"Sutton," she pleaded, looking at the doors as she smoothed down her dress.

"Yes, of course," Christophe said. Ignoring how he must look, he marched to the library back doors and yanked them open. "Go through here for about five paces, then turn right. I will send Claire to get you, and the two of you will enter the ball together. But you owe me a dance."

Rowena laughed nervously. "A dance? Are you well healed from the last time?"

"I can bear the bruising," he whispered before pushing her gently through the doors. Once she left, he leaned against the doorpost, lit a cigarillo, and waited.

"Candor!" boomed a voice as two men entered the library. "You aren't thinking of escaping, are you?"

Christophe languidly inhaled the smoke before turning to Lord Roberts and the Earl of Romney himself, Lord Bellevue.

"I had thought of it," he said as the other two laughed. Lord Bellevue refused his offer of cigarettes, stumbling instead to his box of cigars.

"What kept you from doing it?" asked Lord Roberts with a guffaw. "You've no wife to complain to you back home."

"No, but my sister would certainly cut out my heart if I dared to escape. I was just about to go back in now to dance with Lady Candor."

"Yes, Lady Candor. What a beauty she is," Lord Roberts said, waving his cigar about in the air. "Your brother was a fool to leave her bed. They say she is chilly, but mark my words, you can make any woman warm-blooded with a little time. Just takes some patience. The fault is with the mothers: they are raising their girls to be like wooden dolls, saying a true husband prefers them to be like that. Just takes a bit of time to light a small kindling under them, but soon enough they can be burning for you!"

The man's laughter echoed through the library. Christophe cringed, but had to agree that the fact most English girls had no personality was through no fault of their own. That did not mean he wished to marry any of them. He would rather take his chances with a girl who sang to camels.

The men made their way through the hallway back to the ballroom, the smoke from their cigars billowing about them. Just before they entered, a footman approached and offered a letter on a silver platter to Lord Bellevue, who sighed before ripping it open.

"For all your blubbering about women, Roberts, you never are able to give me advice on how to get my wife to speak to me instead of sending me missives through the staff."

"Perhaps that has more to do with a Mrs. Green than anything else?" Roberts answered with a chuckle. "You see? You're heating the wrong kindling!"

"Well, now, tell me what to do. According to this, the woman Lady Bellevue hired to sing tonight with some young Italian buck seems to have been waylaid in Portugal. She says she will be most embarrassed if I do not do something to fix it. I! It is not I who arranged for an Australian singer to come here to sing! But now that there is a problem, it will be all my fault if I do not fix it."

"I could fix it."

The earl looked at Christophe in disbelief. "You? Do you sing like an Australian woman, Candor?"

"No, my lord, I do not. But I know someone who does, and she would be delighted to help you out in your moment of need. The best part is that she is already here."

Chapter Nineteen

"AND NOW, LADIES AND gentlemen," Mr. Vitelli called out, his voice as fluid as silk, "as my friend, the beautiful and talented Ms. Clearwell, could not make it tonight it is my pleasure to perform a duet with another, equally beautiful lady."

The announcement made several people in the crowd sit up straighter, including Christophe. This was the moment he had stayed for. After two exasperatingly long solos by Mr. Vitelli, he was going to bring out Rowena and awe all of London society. If all went well, the paper tomorrow would praise her performance—and the rumors the Roussier sisters were spreading might finally cease.

Mr. Vitelli gave a theatrical turn as Rowena appeared from behind the musicians, and a very satisfying gasp went up from the crowd. Lady Bellevue raised a brow at her husband, who shifted to throw Christophe a threatening glance. Christophe tipped his chin, but Lord Bellevue did not seem mollified. That was all the attention Christophe planned on giving the man, however. This was Rowena's moment to impress a good portion of London, and he wanted to remember it for all of eternity.

She was beautiful in her emerald silk dress, the gold thread at her hips shimmering in the gaslight. Compared to any other woman in the room, she was the most beautiful.

Rowena began to sing, her voice filled with sheer exuberance, the sound pulsing through him. He was an idiot to wait before entreating her father for her hand. He ached to make her his.

When Vitelli joined her, their two voices mesmerized the audience. The two of them gazed at each other as they sang the duet from Romeo and Juliet. Like well-trained actors, their eyes glittered when they looked at each other, their faces torn as they sang of their fate.

Christophe's heart skipped a beat when Rowena's hand reached out towards Vitelli. He was too far away to touch her, but acting his part, he ran towards her, then knelt. His eyes adored her as Romeo, and she looked back at him lovingly as Shakespeare must have envisioned Juliet.

The song stabbed at the core of most of the crowd, especially the women, who were pulling handkerchiefs from their purses. Christophe eyed Vitelli, trying to relax his jaw as the short Italian hovered his palm over Rowena's lower back, never touching her, but giving the impression of such. He had always thought opera to be a sophisticated form of entertainment, but felt now that he would never let any woman he loved enter into such a profession.

As the parlor erupted into applause, a presence sidled up to him. A female presence.

"Pray tell, what is it that you find so alluring about her? A proper woman of our class would not show off so very much."

He lowered his eyes to find Lady Grace, her perfect blonde curls bouncing, standing just a little too close to him.

The audience, now warmed to the entertainment, shouted for another song. Rowena blushed as Mr. Vitelli took her hand in his and whispered something in her ear. His body was far enough away from hers, but the very act of his lips being so near to her skin made Christophe's stomach roll.

As they started a new song, something between a snort and a disgusted sigh to his left reminded him that he was not alone.

"You see it, too, don't you? The way the two of them interact together. I have a theory about it—one I believe you should hear. There are rumors that a lady once deceived you, trying to gain you as a husband. I would not like to see you hurt like that again."

"Lady Grace, I am trying to enjoy the concert."

She smiled sympathetically at him and waved his greeting away. Were he not well-educated, he would have turned his back to her then; but his manners and education instinctively gathered his emotions and put them away.

Her teeth sank into her bottom lip as she forced her eyes towards the singers.

"It is said that she was a slave. Can you imagine? I knew these things happened a hundred years ago, but I did not think it still happened. I mean, not with English ladies." Lady Grace took a dramatic pause. "You, of all of us, know what men in the Orient do with white women as their slaves, do you not?"

"I believed she was in Africa, Lady Grace."

Lady Grace smiled demurely at him, ignoring the correction. He noticed how she tilted her head up and pressed her lips together in a perfect pout. Falcon was right; it made her somehow ugly.

"Whether she ran away—which I am coming to believe—or not, that does not account for what she did during her years away. If she lied upon her return about working with the missionaries, she will fall from any status she might have had. No lady in the haut-ton will tarnish their reputation by allowing her in their circle. And no *real* gentleman should waste his time with her. She would only tarnish his title."

Lady Grace paused. Christophe hoped she was finished with her tirade. Unfortunately, she was not. She dared to draw her index finger down the length of his bicep, arching her brows at him.

"You deserve to be with a woman who does not lie about her past, my lord," she purred, beginning to trace her low décolletage with the same finger.

"Good night, Lady Grace."

She halted his retreat. "There is a contract between my stepfather and his first wife's brother," she whispered. "It states my sister is to wed her cousin, John. The marriage did not occur, due to Rowena's disappearance. Now that Rowena is back and John is a widower, the family is happy they can find their destiny again as a match. Do you not think it is interesting how fate has brought them back together?"

Much to his dismay, the comment caught Christophe off guard. He stayed silent, opting to pretend to be above anything as base as jealousy. Lady Grace smiled before gliding away towards a group of malicious debutantes with a triumphant air.

The concert concluded a few minutes later with the grand finale of Mr. Vitelli and Rowena singing a duet from Verdi's *Otello*. When Mr. Vitelli leaned so closely to Rowena to sing "un bacio... un bacio... ancora un bacio," nausea washed over Christophe. Mr. Vitelli would never have a kiss from Rowena, if he could help it.

The audience erupted into applause when the song ended, which was rather unlike the ton. Mr. Vitelli took his bows again and again, but Rowena seemed suddenly uneasy, as though just then noticing how many people were watching her. When Vitelli pulled her forward, the audience clapped almost as loudly as they had for Vitelli and she finally smiled, looking directly at him as she did.

☙ ❧

"I cannot believe she is here. She does not deserve to be among decent people," sniffed Marine Roussier. "I feel vile with such a woman here."

"She sang beautifully," Miss Elizabeth said.

"Hmph. Why are you always on her side, Miss Elizabeth? Are you friends with such a scandalous girl?" Marine demanded.

Camille watched as Miss Elizabeth shrank back at the accusation. Marine was back in control of the conversation. "Mama told me all the details of Miss Rowena Brayemore just yesterday. You will not think anything about her is beautiful after you hear what kind of woman she is."

At that, all the girls leaned closer to listen.

"*Alors,* I was a child when first I saw Rowena, but I remember how terrible she was the first few weeks. Do you remember, Camille, how rude she was during the first weeks?"

Camille nodded her dainty head. She clouded her eyes with tears, trying her best to play her part.

"*Mon Dieu,* she was so ungrateful. Mother took her in after her lover dumped her on the streets. She said we were to treat her like a sister, because she was the daughter of a friend. She was nothing like an older sister! *Non!* My mother thought to do right by her and gave her many chances. It was only after the ungrateful girl ran away the second time that my mother changed her mind."

"Ran away?" asked Miss Elizabeth. "Why would she need to escape if she was your guest?"

"She wished to be reunited with her lover. My mother was trying to save her from herself."

The girls gasped behind their fans, drawing narrowed eyes from the group of women in front of them. Marine dropped her voice lower as the girls leaned in closer.

"Mama kept her at our house, but told her she had to work and earn her keep. So many people had fled by then, even some of our servants!" she said.

"She forced Miss Brayemore to work?" asked Lady Katherine.

"Mama was trying her best to keep that ungrateful girl from becoming a common whore. It seemed to be the only solution."

"Did it work? Or is that when your mother sent her to the missionaries?" asked Alice, leaning in so closely that Camille's nose was overcome by her potent perfume, which smelled like a mixture of flowers and lemons. Such a terrible combination.

"*Non*, Alice! *Ce n'est pas vrai!* It is not true! Mama never sent her to the missionaries," Marine said, rolling her eyes as Alice moved back with a huff. "Rowena was never with missionaries. *Jamais.* She did behave for a little bit, but soon Mama was forced to choose between who she could afford to feed and clothe, and she had to keep those, ah, servants who were loyal to us. The day Rowena screamed at Mama in the most ungrateful manner, Mama decided to let her go."

"Into the streets?" shrieked Elizabeth, with her gloved hand over her mouth.

"*Mais non,*" Camille answered, forgetting Marine's admonishment to keep quiet. "She sold her to someone as a wife."

"She *sold* her? Like a slave?" gasped Lady Mary.

Mary. They hadn't noticed the girl before now. No one ever did; she had the most terrible habit of whispering everything.

"Her father never came for her. What else was Mama to do?" Marine said, shooting Camille a look that promised a good tongue-lashing once they returned home.

"But she sold her as a slave? Just because her father did not come?" Miss Elizabeth whispered, her delicate face dangerously pale.

"Miss Elizabeth, she sold her to a man as a wife. Not very different from our dowries here. She simply went about it as their customs dictate."

Marine waited for the comparison to sink in. Color returned to the girls' faces quickly enough for the story to continue.

"So she is married, then?" Lady Alice asked.

"I would assume that she is not," Marine said with disappointment. "She never would have been able to leave if she was. He must have tired of her and either sold her or pushed her out to the streets."

"I'm not sure I believe you," Lady Mary said, her voice louder than at any other time in her life. Miss Elizabeth nodded along with her.

Camille looked nervously at her sister, but Marine was calm, with an evil glint in her eye.

"I will prove it to you," she said calmly.

"How?" demanded Lady Mary, her nervous breath reducing her voice back to its normal volume.

Marine shrugged lightly. "She has a birthmark on her arm in the shape of a crescent moon. Do you remember the mark, Camille?"

Camille nodded.

"Well, then," Marine said. "Let's all give our congratulations to Miss Brayemore on her singing."

"What are you doing?" hissed Camille, trying to keep up with her sister as they crossed the room. Marine snuck a peek behind them at the other girls following and only shook her head once.

"Miss Brayemore!" she exclaimed, her voice dripping with sugar. The group of girls practically fell over each other when Marine stopped so suddenly. "How lovely it was to hear you sing! Never say you don't remember me! And my sister?"

"Of course, Marine Roussier, I remember you," Miss Brayemore answered, her voice trembling slightly. And rightly so. Camille knew her sister could be cruel, and she was beginning to think the behavior came from her mother. Still, Camille couldn't find any sympathy within her for Miss Brayemore. It was their turn for society, not hers.

"It was nice to see you. Please excuse me. My stepmother is waiting."

"But Miss Brayemore!" Marine gushed, throwing her arms around the other woman. "It is so nice to see you. Oh, dear! My bracelet!"

"Let me help you," Miss Elizabeth offered, but Marine had no intention of accepting help for a bracelet she was pretending was stuck.

Camille smiled at the ingenuity of Marine as her fingers pulled the fabric on Miss Brayemore's sleeve. Miss Elizabeth continued to fuss loudly about the bracelet, which brought more of a crowd around them. Marine rebuked Miss Elizabeth loudly when Miss Brayemore requested that they allow her to look. When a sizeable crowd drew around them, Marine winked at Camille before giving one great yank. The air filled with the sound of ripping fabric.

All eyes focused on Miss Brayemore's hand, where the entire sleeve of her dress hung limply around her wrist.

"My, what a darling birthmark you have, Rowena," Marine said, breaking the silence.

Even Camille leaned in. There, just as Marine had said, was the crescent-moon-shaped birthmark on Miss Brayemore's upper arm.

"It's true!" shrieked Miss Elizabeth, her anger at Marine not allowing her to help now transformed into intrigue and horror.

Lady Candor made her way through the cluster of young women to help pick Rowena up from the floor.

"You should be ashamed of yourself, Miss Marine," she admonished. "You have ruined Miss Brayemore's dress."

"It is more shameful that a woman of your rank would lower herself to friendship with a common *salope*," Marine contested, before turning her back on the marchioness with a victorious smile.

In all the ensuing commotion and conversation, Camille never saw where Miss Brayemore disappeared to. She pushed the small bit of conscience that fought to bring Miss Brayemore's ashen face to her remembrance brutally aside. As she had told herself before, it was their turn to be in society, not hers.

Bernadette sought her daughter the next afternoon when the stillness of the house started rattling her nerves. Gossip could smooth things over and help the time pass by quicker.

Miss Marine's behavior after Rowena's splendid performance had been appalling, but Bernadette was more nervous about Miss Marine's last name than the girl's behavior. After speaking with a few friends, she had found that Lady Kent, a woman married to a

German count, was the girl's mother, and she was coming into town the next week. Lady Arlington had told her that Lady Kent was a French woman named Josephine Roussier who had lived in Algeria for several years. After that bit of news, Bernadette had required a carriage home.

Once Lady Kent came to town, it would be only a matter of days before James saw her. Bernadette knew that at one point Madame Roussier had expected James to marry her. If she was still as vindictive as she used to be, she would not wait long to tell James she had sent letters informing him of Rowena.

It had been a well-played plan, really; Bernadette had to give Madame Roussier that. Pick up the weakest object still beloved by James, write to make sure he knew it was in her possession, then get the love, respect and money she felt she deserved. It was what Bernadette would have done. James would have gone back for his daughter in an instant, giving Madame Roussier another chance to seduce him.

Once James knew about the letters, he would ask Bernadette about them. And she was never able to lie to James.

The truth of the matter made her knees buckle. Soon she might be thrown from her house by her own husband. She loved James fiercely, but she could not believe he would continue living with her once he found out the truth. And he would keep Elliot with him. She would lose them both in one fell swoop.

With shaking fingers, Bernadette turned the doorknob to her daughter's room. Grace was angrily pacing in front of the fireplace, which sent agitated chills down her spine. Bernadette tried to leave without Grace noticing her, but it was too late.

"Listen to this nonsense!" Grace cried out. "'Had she not been born of noble blood, she surely would have had a brilliant career on the stage.' How infuriating!" She stomped her feet like a child. "I was born a duke's daughter, not her!"

Bernadette sat down with shaking limbs.

"I do remember now that it was her dream as a little girl to be an opera singer," she said quietly. "Her father always indulged her, though I'm certain he never dreamed of allowing her to take to the stage. That would have been too vulgar, even before James was a baron. After all, her maternal grandfather was the son of an earl."

"I'm sure she did much entertaining for her sultan, or whomever."

Bernadette shot her a warning glance, but Grace refused to cower.

"The rumors from the Bellevue ball are more than just rumors, Mama. Marine proved she was speaking the truth. Today they speak about her voice, but by tomorrow they will be talking about her past. She put herself in the spotlight last night, and now the damage of her past choices will come back to hurt me. Had she not come home—"

Bernadette brought her shaking hand down heavily on the table. The sound resonated so vociferously that Grace jumped in shock, and Bernadette immediately regretted the action. Sleepless nights were taking a toll on her reflexes.

"That sounds an awful lot like jealousy, dear daughter. While you may be right in your concerns about your sister's return making your season a bit more difficult, jealousy on your part will make it downright unbearable. She is back, whether or not you like the timing. At nineteen it is sometimes difficult to understand what is important in the long run of life and what passes by like water in the Thames, but it's certainly old enough to care for your sister and be happy that she is indeed alive and well. While some invitations have been long in coming, there is no indication that your reputation is suffering because of her."

Grace stiffened. "This will cause me more trouble. I'm certain of it."

"You received the earnest affections of many fine gentlemen last season, many of whom I am certain will make you an offer before the end of next year," Bernadette said quietly. "If you choose one of them, you will be set quite well for life. James has made sure each of them has money in their own right."

"None of them are good enough."

"They are all good enough."

"I am a duke's daughter!" Grace shrieked.

Bernadette bit against the unladylike words that threatened to pour out of her. "Not every daughter of a duke marries another duke. There are only two on the market this season. Both are far too old, and neither one has shown any interest in you," she finally said, much calmer outside than inside.

"As I said, perhaps if Rowena hadn't come back—"

"Enough!" Bernadette commanded, her shame and anger getting the best of her. She couldn't believe it possible that Grace lacked so much heart. It was all too much to bear at that moment. "I came upstairs to tell you that John is coming back to town."

"John?" Grace asked, a smile spreading across her face when Bernadette nodded. "Good. Then we have hope that Rowena will still do the right thing by us before the season fully starts. When will he arrive?"

"In two days."

"Well, it doesn't matter much. We are all invited to the Glenvilles' next week for their hunting party. I assume Rowena will come."

Bernadette was suddenly weary.

"I must go lie down, my dear," she said, kissing her daughter on the cheek. "But, one minor question."

"Yes?"

Bernadette paused at the door, wrestling with her question.

"Did Miss Marine or Miss Camille ever mention their mother sending James a letter about Rowena? To tell us where she was?" she finally asked, purposefully keeping her voice soft.

"Letters? No, I never heard them say anything."

Bernadette smiled, but stopped herself from sighing with relief.

"Good night, darling."

"Good night, Mama."

Chapter Twenty

"CINCH, WHAT A LOVELY surprise," Claire said as she entered the parlor of the Candor Dowager house. "What brings you here?"

"Just a visit," he answered, kissing Claire's cheek.

"I haven't seen you in a week. Not since the ball," Claire said, watching him as she took her seat. "Did you stay to hear Miss Brayemore sing? It was quite lovely."

"I did," Christophe said, glad to keep the conversation less than personal. "But I had to leave immediately afterwards. A footman delivered rather distressing news from Cookston. Vandalism at the mines."

"Oh, dear. No one was hurt, I hope?"

"No. No one was hurt, but mine thirteen is out of commission until we can fix the tunnel. That won't happen until the spring."

Claire poured tea as she listened dutifully. "Will that affect the workers at all?"

"Not on my watch," Christophe answered, watching relief flit across Claire's face. When she met his eye with a full teacup, she actually blushed. It was the first time he had ever seen Claire blush, and the sight of it quite took him off guard.

"I don't mean to pry," Claire explained, taking a sip from her own cup. "Russell always became angry with my prying. It's just that sometimes I wonder if I could have done something to keep Ravenwood and Cookston from becoming as dilapidated as they are."

"Ah," he said, his questions of whether had she known now answered. "In reality, there is nothing you could have done as the marchioness if my brother would not approve payments. I do not blame you for any of it, Claire."

"That is kind, but probably not true," she said. "A better person than me could have done more. All I could think of was to use my pin money to at least pay the servants at Ravenwood. I thought that would hold things in place, at least until I could speak with you. But then you left, and Russell died, and my pin money was not enough to make up for all the debts that he left."

"You used your pin money? To pay the servants?" he asked, his hot tea dangerously close to spilling.

Claire nodded, waving her hand to brush away his anger.

"It was not such a hardship. I had enough dresses and hats and all such things. Plus, we had to eat while Russell was gallivanting about London. I was one person with a staff of twenty. And it was just a temporary fix; I meant to address you directly and lay out all that I knew about Russell. Leave it in your hands, so to speak. But you left before I made it to London. And, well, now it really is all in your hands. I am sorry about the mess."

Christophe abandoned his tea on the round table to pace the floor. It took longer than expected for him to walk out his anger at Russell this time.

"I will pay you back every cent," he breathed.

"I did not tell you this for you to pay me back. I am quite well taken care of. In fact, I was going to offer to pay for some of the expenses that you are having to deal with."

Christophe shot her a look of disdain, but she merely waved it away. "Do not be so chauvinistic. The debts were my husband's —"

"And my brother's."

"Even so, I am responsible for them."

"I will not take your money."

They stared at each other for a time. Christophe could see the wheels in Claire's head turning, and was ready to go head-to-head with her if need be. She must have seen that in his face, for she smiled.

"No need to argue, Cinch. If you won't take my money, then I will not take yours."

"I will pay you back."

"No," she said firmly. Christophe drew back in surprise. "You will let my conscience be soothed by not paying me back. You will not take my money and I will not take yours. Quid pro quo."

Christophe tried to think of a convincing argument to counter Claire's, but finally gave up. He stuck out his hand in resignation. The way her face lit up upon taking his hand made it well worthwhile.

"Now, have you come for our outing?"

Christophe turned to her in surprise. "Outing? Isn't it too cold?"

Claire laughed. "When we heard you came back last night, your mother and I decided to plan an outing with the boys. The sun is shining—and besides, we are going to the Cox's Museum. Afterward, we promised them chocolate."

"Who will count the frogs?" asked a small voice as Christophe and Claire walked into the foyer. "I can count my own correctly, but Ryan doesn't know how to count."

"I do!" shouted little Ryan. "One, two, fwee, fibe, seben, eight, ten!"

"Darlings, we are not going to the park unless the sun is still out after we see the museum," Claire was saying as she approached the boys, but they paid little attention. Ryan was already looking towards the other end of the foyer, where a figure was moving. Christophe followed his nephew's gaze, unable to keep himself from smiling in amusement at Claire's mischief.

"There's Miss Ro-rena!" shouted Ryan, who, though only three, was quite stocky and could plow an adult down with his hugs. Rowena's attention immediately turned to the boy as he threw his full weight into her arms.

"Lord Ryan," the governess complained, trying to pull the little boy away.

"I will give you a chocolate if you stop trying to pull off Miss Brayemore's arm," Christophe said, trying to sound stern. Falcon chuckled as his son immediately dropped to the floor and ran to his uncle.

"Apologize for plowing into Miss Brayemore," Emily admonished Ryan as he stuffed his chocolates into his small mouth.

"No harm done," Rowena protested.

"Might I suggest, then, that you stay away from him now?" Claire said, indicating Ryan's now very chocolaty fingers.

Rowena laughed. Christophe found himself leaning closer to her. When she turned to look at him, he had no choice but to speak, though he wasn't sure he had any voice.

"Good afternoon, Miss Brayemore," he said, his tone strangled with the emotion he was trying to hide.

"It is nice to see you again, Lord Candor," Rowena answered with a smile as she took his offered arm. "When did you get back?"

"Yesterday," he said, pulling her gaze to his.

"Right," Claire said, swinging her parasol. "I'll sacrifice my dress at the hands of a three-year-old. The two of you will have to follow behind."

Christophe snapped his focus away in time to see the rest of his family pulling away in their phaetons. Ryan waved at them with chocolate-covered fingers.

"They left," Rowena said, staring dumbfounded after the retreating phaetons.

"Please forgive my family. It seems they're having a bit of a joke at our expense. We can take my phaeton," Christophe said. "If you would like."

"Indeed, my lord," Rowena said, turning her attention to the only phaeton left. "It would be lovely to take a ride with you."

"It is not a camel," he acknowledged, opening the door and holding out his hand. "But I would not object to you singing to it. The horses may well love to listen to you as much as that beast did."

"Tessie?" she asked, her eyes again meeting his.

Her smile spread wider when he cursed under his breath.

"You named the camel who ate most of your food and snorted into your hair?"

"She was a good camel. A keen listener," Rowena explained while inserting her gloved hand into his. Rowena then hoisted herself up into the curricle without more help from him before flashing him a smug smile. In response, Christophe grabbed the side and jumped directly into the seat. Rowena shrieked in laughter as the phaeton rocked violently, lurching her to one side and almost over the edge. When she slammed into his solid form, his hand grabbed her waist to keep her inside.

"That was almost worth pulling my back," he said.

Rowena laughed. "Where shall we go?"

"I wish to show you something."

With a snap of the reins, the horses started off down the busy streets of London. With an open phaeton they had to keep their proper London distance, though Christophe couldn't help but recall how close their bodies had been at times along their journey.

"We are going to St. James' Park. Have you been?" he asked.

Rowena shook her head but said nothing else. Her face lit up at every scene they moved past, whether it be flower vendors, fish vendors, ladies moving to and from shops, or a stray dog trotting down the road. Each time he caught a glimpse of her she seemed absorbed, as though memorizing everything around her.

"It was the first place my father ever took me in London," he explained, no longer needing to shout above the traffic. "It's adjacent to the famous leper hospital, which he said was the greatest example of English civic duty. Until his dying day, he gave a monthly donation to the hospital and to the gardens. St. James is not as fashionable as Hyde, but it boasts fantastic views of the city."

"Is that why you like it? Or does it have more to do with memories?" Rowena asked.

The question caught Christophe off guard. Memories of the place overwhelmed him for a moment. The first time his cousin had visited him in London, they had gone there to play and see the pelicans. He and Albert had made it a favorite spot for themselves, along with Daucer and Falcon. A decade ago, the four of them could spend an entire afternoon on the garden lawns, acting as young males do. There was a peace there, far away from the public crowds of the other parks.

It also had a few more alcoves than Hyde Park, where one could steal a kiss or two. An unpleasant memory of spending a rather dishonorable afternoon with Catherine dared to resurface in his head. This was not the moment to remember that.

Slowing the horses to a walk, Christophe turned to Rowena. She looked about her with a wide smile on her face, her hand on top of her hat as though the great thing might blow away. When she felt. his gaze upon her she turned, a beautiful blush creeping up over her face and what he could see of her neck.

"Would you like to see the pelicans? They are great, monstrous birds with beaks bigger than King William himself," Christophe told her, delighted to find her smile brighten more.

"Yes, please!" she said, not waiting to be helped down from the curricle. Another chance to touch her wasted.

They made their way through the paths to the metal barrier that surrounded the pond where the giant creatures bathed. The enormous birds never ceased to amaze Christophe with their strange habit of entertaining those who watched them. As one bird turned about in circles and performed what looked like a bow, a giggle, like chimes being lightly struck, caught his attention. Rowena covered her mouth, and the sound disappeared behind kid gloves.

"Your laugh is one of the most beautiful sounds. I thought so from the very first time I knew of it."

Rowena ducked her red face at the confession.

"Why have I never heard of this entertainment before?" she asked, laughing again at a pelican trying hard to keep their attention.

Christophe laughed now. "I doubt it is the sort of place Lady Grace would take you."

"Most certainly not," Rowena said, grinning widely. "My father told me that the pelicans came in 1664 as a gift from the Russian Ambassador."

"That was a long time ago. It's a wonder they've stayed here so long."

"Much to my delight, they have," Christophe said, unable to tear his gaze away from her. Pushing off the railing, he offered Rowena his arm and guided her towards the Blue Bridge. There they would be graced with a grand view of Big Ben and Buckingham Palace. "I suppose you would have come here at some point during your life, perhaps to glimpse the coronation procession, but I'm glad that you have seen it for the first time with me, Miss Brayemore."

"It's breathtaking," she answered, turning from east to west to soak in the majestic views of royal London. "Is it all right that we're alone?"

Christophe motioned to the footman, a good sixty paces away.

"We have a chaperone," he said. Everything within him wished to kiss her. To feel her soft lips against his – but he didn't yet dare.

"Thank you for bringing me here. The trip has brightened my spirits greatly."

"Did they need brightening?" he asked, closing the gap between them.

Rowena lifted her eyes with a sigh.

"Miss Brayemore, Tessie is not the only animal who can be a good listener. If something is troubling you, I wish you would tell me. Perhaps I can give you advice, having been raised here in England and knowing all the ways of the ton. It wouldn't be rumors or gossip, would it?"

Rowena shook her head with a weary smile. "Rumors and gossip seem to be a part of every problem, so yes, in a way they are part of this one as well."

"I am sorry I wasn't there to help you. At the end of the ball, I mean."

"There is nothing you could have done."

"Nothing honorable, anyway," he said. "Is your family pressuring you?"

She looked at him, her expression puzzled.

"To marry," he clarified.

"Not yet," she answered. "But it seems there is some understanding I should marry my cousin. John will be back in London any day now, and I expect the pressure to increase."

He searched her eyes, and she did the same, each of them looking for answers to questions that couldn't seem to put into words. Rowena was the first to look away.

"Pardon me, Lord Candor. I should not tell you these things."

"Why?" he asked, pressing his leg to hers. "I believe I have known you longer than any other person in London."

"You forget my father," she said.

The scent of jasmine filled the air when she moved. He leaned his head in and breathed deeply.

"Jasmine. It suits you well," he said.

"A bit better than the camel scent I wore in the desert," she said.

He laughed, a comfortable warmth settling in his middle.

"You cut your hair," she said, her hand raising on its own before she schooled it back to her side. Christophe swallowed in disappointment when she did not touch him.

"Yes."

It was too tempting to resist one second more. At her next exhalation, he pressed his lips closer and found hers ready. A small sigh escaped her mouth as he covered it with his. Not until that moment had he realize that he missed her to the point of sickness. Her presence near him, touching him, awakening him again to the world he had not realized he had become dead to. She had become everything that embodied life, and for that reason he had spent the last eight months in a kind of sick melancholy.

Reluctantly, he pulled away. Breathing in the brisk air, Christophe smiled. He could have shouted his happiness to all the city. He finally had her alone. Now was the time to persuade her to court him.

But before that he had one question.

"Why did you leave me in Melilla, Miss Brayemore?"

Rowena froze. Her brain was slow, muddled by his intoxicating smell and the way he looked at her. It seemed that every time the man kissed her, her brain went to fluff. And now he wished to know about the past.

"I admit I did not pay as much attention to you during the day as I should have, but never did I expect you to run away," Lord Candor said, pressing his shoulders back as he surveyed the park. "What did I do, Miss Brayemore? The doubt has followed me from Melilla. Did you feel—I mean, perhaps you felt I took liberties I should not have?"

"No!" she cried out, a flock of birds taking flight at the sudden noise. She lowered her voice. "No. I did not feel that."

"Then why?"

"I asked you to take me to England, and you said no," Rowena replied, her throat trembling.

"I said no to a woman I believed was half Algerian, who would be shunned in London society. I would not have said no to an English woman," he said, his voice betraying his emotions.

"An opportunity for me to go home came. I could not take the chance that you would refuse me again."

"You did not even give me a chance! You did not trust me to tell me who you really were. After all that time, did you not know me enough? Did you truly think I would leave you behind in Melilla to fend for yourself when all you wanted was to go home and find your family?"

"I-I do not know," Rowena said, her head feeling too light. "I had to take my chances with Countess Merville, for I did not know when another one would present itself. Besides, you are an English nobleman. You could not go back with a former slave at your side."

For a long moment, they looked at each other in silence.

"I cannot blame you for leaving, for coming back home," he said. "But had you told me who you were..."

His voice trailed off, and Rowena looked away. Perhaps it was too late to ponder what could have happened if she had told him the truth.

"Forgive me, Rowena. My pride has got in the way."

"I should have told you," she admitted. "My only excuse is that I didn't have the courage."

Lord Candor rubbed his forehead before smiling at her.

"Let us forget it, then. At any rate, I should simply be happy you found your way safely and contentedly," he said quietly.

Rowena laughed bitterly.

"Are you not happy?"

"I am a woman walking in circles," she said. "Truthfully, I cannot place what or who I am. Between Fatia and Rowena... well, perhaps I have metamorphosed into someone else. I don't feel like I belong here in England. Even so, I have not yet worked up the courage to leave these shores. Perhaps one day I shall."

The air shifted as Christophe stepped closer.

"You are Miss Rowena Brayemore, daughter of Baron Brayemore," he quoted with a smile. "You have come a long way, and you should not allow others to push you out of your home."

"I don't know if I'm brave enough to stay."

"You are the bravest woman I know."

She tried to smile, but found no energy to keep it. If she was brave, she would stand up and tell her family once and for all that she would not marry John. But she hadn't. There was a small chance that if she did, she would disappoint her father, and she did not wish to disappoint him.

Lord Candor folded his arms across his broad chest and leaned back against the railing of the bridge.

"If you try to run from the past, it will catch up with you, Rowena. It is better to allow it to find a place as part of you and be the whole person. You were a slave and now are not. You can choose what will come next. But don't try to hide who you were. Secrets just add to misery."

"Are you saying I should tell all of London the truth about my past?" she asked, turning now fully towards him.

"You have nothing to be ashamed of," he said, his eyes gazing directly into her soul.

"You say that because it would not affect you, but it will affect me and my family greatly. I have seen enough of the ton to know they would very much accuse me of wrongdoing, with or without evidence."

"You are wrong when you say that it would not affect me," he said, gazing straight into her eyes. "I care too deeply for you not to be affected."

Rowena frowned at his admission.

"Had you just told me in the beginning, even in the middle, of our journey, I would have figured out a way," he said, regret entering his voice. "You didn't give me a chance."

"I'm sorry I did not tell you, but if you listen, I will tell you now anything that you wish to know."

"You don't have to explain anything. I think I understand much of what I wanted to know before. You found Countess Merville and left Melilla. With her at your side, you had a sort of alibi. At least in part."

"Yes, that was part of my thinking, but what I wish for you to hear is the beginning. If you want to listen, I will tell you how I ended up in the mountains of Algeria as a slave. I do not wish for you, or your family, to think the rumors are true."

"I don't believe the rumors," he said, crossing his arms and leaning comfortably against the bridge railing. "But I would like to listen to your story."

"I was born here in Evenshire, England. We moved to Algeria when I was just two. My mother died from a fever when I was seven and took my brother with her. Contrary to my grandfather's wishes for me to return to England, my father kept me in Algeria. I do not believe he could bear the thought of going back without my mother, and I like to believe he couldn't live without me. Besides, he was very successful in Algeria and I was very happy. I only ever remember being happy. Being spoiled."

She looked out into the horizon, soaking in the view of London beyond the park, before continuing.

"I was thirteen when we traveled back to England so that my father could marry Bernadette. He thought it best for me to have a mother, and I believe now that he was lonely. In England, I began schooling with a governess whose goal it was to raise me as a good, English lady. I didn't take too kindly to the idea. I wished to be a great opera singer, not someone's wife. After less than two miserable years, I had had enough of England, the governess, and my new little sister. My father had enough as well. He needed to go through Spain on his way back to Algeria, and I convinced him to take me along. Since he was never a father to say no, he gave in. Bernadette came later, claiming she wished to spend time with me and see this country that I loved so much. Much to my contentment, we were there for two years before it came time to leave again. I can't say I was happy to go back to England, but I was older and looked at the idea with different eyes."

"Coming home for a debut would be different to moving to England," Lord Candor acknowledged.

Rowena shrugged with a smile. "Undoubtedly, the dreams of a seventeen-year-old are different from those of a thirteen-year-old," she said. "But I had the idea of making my debut as a singer, not as a debutante."

"Did your father know of that particular dream?"

"He did, though now I doubt he had plans to indulge me. At any rate, with the threat of the French blockade, I understood we had to leave Algeria. Leaving my childhood home was difficult, but necessary."

"You meant to leave before the blockade."

"Yes. My father had everything planned, but he was called to Spain just a few days before our ship was to leave. He wanted to take us on the clipper to Spain, but Bernadette was uncomfortable with the idea. I was left in charge of closing up the house and getting Bernadette and the servants to the ship. It was not supposed to be difficult to do, and I remember feeling quite grown-up with the responsibility. We did not know, though, that our maid, Ana, had different plans."

"What plans?" Christophe asked darkly.

"She called me off the ship with the excuse that there was a problem. Once I stepped off the gangplank, I remember something hitting me hard on the head and a damp, stinking cloth pressed to my nose and mouth. When I awoke, Madame Roussier was there to tell me that she had just bought me from Ana."

She paused for a moment, but was too far into the story to stop now.

"I didn't believe her. It seemed like such a strange thing to do. I was someone she knew; I had grown up with a rich father and my own servants. I simply couldn't understand the motive behind it. When I demanded she take me back to the ship, I was drugged with opium. They kept doing it until I was too weak to fight back. That's when I realized she was speaking the truth."

Rowena tried to shrug the story away, but for reasons she could not understand, hot tears rolled down her cheeks.

"When they took me off the opium, miserable experience that it was, the cook told me almost two weeks had passed with me in the attic. When my father didn't come back, she said it was because he didn't want me. I didn't believe her. I knew about the blockade and assumed he was coming, just by a longer route. As time went by with no word, Madame Roussier lost any idea of my father coming for me and began to regret having stayed. By then the port was closed and she was stuck with me, a reminder of her poorly thought-out plan. So she treated me like a slave."

"You were seventeen?" Christophe asked quietly, tucking her hand into his elbow as they walked.

"Yes."

"I do not believe I would have taken it very well to find my life so changed at that age."

"I did not take it well. Twice I tried to escape Madame Roussier's, but the second time, when I finally managed it, I... went back on my own."

Christophe said nothing as they passed the pelicans and the curricle came into sight once more.

"Do you think me a coward?" she asked, peering up at him. "To have gone back?"

He closed his hands around her waist, but leaned in and whispered in her ear instead of lifting her. "I know what happens to unattended girls in Algeria. I do not blame you for going back."

Rowena did not have a chance to answer before he lifted her onto the seat.

The urge to place her head against his shoulders was so strong it was difficult to resist. As though sensing her need for touch, Lord Candor pressed his thigh against hers. Under her skirts, his fingers found her hand and gave them a gentle squeeze before commanding the horses forward to take her home.

Chapter Twenty-One

IN THE SANCTUARY OF his library, James Braymore poured himself a large brandy, looked intensely into the glass, then pushed it aside. Many claimed liquor to be the perfect way to calm nerves, but he knew from experience that it was a lie. The numbness only encouraged a man to drink more and more until his problems melted away in a haze. But those problems always came back in full force, along with a headache, the next day.

In deliberate contradiction with his mood, the sun shone brightly through the spotless window, spreading a golden sparkle across his lacquered desk. The gems of light taunted him to take just one sip. But he didn't.

He would need his control to deal with his wife over the next few weeks.

Thinking of Bernadette caused a new rush of anger and indignation to surge through him. The last time this kind of rage had enveloped him, he had ended up killing a man. True, that the same man had not only stolen from him but also killed one of his servants and tried to kidnap Rowena when she was just three years old. Some would say he had reason to be irrationally angry—but, being a respected man of business, he should have shown the community that law was above revenge. Unfortunately, he had given in to his anger. Even as his bare knuckles had cracked against the man's bleeding head again and again, he had known he should stop. When he finally had, the man was beyond mending, and he had been forced to finish the job with a bullet. To do any less would have been cruel.

That same uncontrollable anger threatened him now. He threw a book aside and tried to think of something, anything, other than his wife's betrayal. The dull thud of the book hitting the wall was not enough to dissipate the crushing horror of what he had learned that morning.

Bernadette had known Rowena was alive all along.

Giselle Roussier, as he had known her, had told him she sent not one, but two letters to him about Rowena. While he wished to think that Giselle was lying, there was no reason for her to. It was just like her to want to gloat about having 'saved' his lost daughter. Probably her idea had been that he would either pay a ransom in money or help Giselle get out of Algeria. That plan had fallen apart when he had never replied to her letters. And he had never replied because he had never seen them.

James ~~John~~ scrubbed his face with his palms. Bernadette was not a naturally unkind woman. She had always been genuinely fond of Rowena. She had only traveled to Algeria for his daughter, hoping to have time there to form a bond without the other girls about. Though she had cried at the idea of leaving Grace with her parents, she had been so determined to come to Algeria for a few years.

A burst of emotion rose within him: a toxic mix of love and betrayal that drove away the lingering amount of self-control. Before he could reign it back, James found his fist through the wood-paneled wall of the library. Pain radiated out from his knuckles and around his wrist, but it wasn't enough to take away his inner agony. It would never be enough to alleviate his guilt. He should never have taken Rowena back to Algeria. He should not have indulged her.

Tears blurred his vision as James remembered his little girl, only fourteen years old, begging him to take her home. Home, where she could smell her mother and see all the things she loved. Algeria was where she was free, a place she understood, he remembered her telling him. In England, she was practically a foreigner. And just like that, he had said yes.

When the *La Corona* had arrived in port in Seville and Rowena hadn't been on board, he had panicked. Only Harrison's reassurances that Rowena would have gone back to the house calmed him. He had meant to go back to Algeria on the next boat, but Bernadette took ill and almost lost the baby. Instead of going, he had sent a missive to his house in Algiers each day—until, two months later, a letter arrived saying that Rowena had not ever returned there.

After Elliot was born, he had again meant to go back, but Elliot came early and both he and Bernadette caught fever. Elliot fought through it within a few weeks, but Bernadette's recovery was slow and tedious. James hired a man in Algiers to investigate Rowena's disappearance, but heard nothing for another four months. The day that the dirty, ill-written note arrived at their house in London had been the darkest day of his life. It stated that a woman fitting Rowena's description had passed through the morgue four months after she disappeared. Helsi, his valet in Algeria, had identified it as Rowena, then buried the body. It was then that James had given up his search. There was nothing he could do.

His hand brushed against the small lump in his pocket where he had shoved Giselle's note that morning before running out the door to meet her. He took it out now and reread it, the softly coiled penmanship taunting him. Furious with himself, he threw the missive into the fire and watched the flames consume it.

"It was clever of me to use your daughter's tale as a warning to my own girls about what happens when a daughter runs away with a man. They are spirited, you see, and even then I could see they might one day think with their passions instead of with their heads," she had told him. "As I did with you."

"Rowena did not run away with a man. She never looked twice at a man at that age. Singing was her only passion," James had answered calmly, though inside he had been anything but.

"You are right about that," Giselle, now Lady Kent, replied. Her voice was as cool and smooth as a pond, glistening with pride and dispassion. "Your servant, Aurora, sold her to me. The entire thing was my idea, really. One of my maids that Aurora and her fiancée didn't wish to go to England with you. They wished to return to Spain. So I stepped in and gave them a way to earn their way to Spain. You really should be thanking me. You and I both know what would have happened to her if she had been taken to the slave market. I'm sure that's what they would have done, had I not been there to take Rowena."

Bile had risen in his throat as he listened to her smooth, purring voice. Instead of lashing out, he stayed silent, hoping she would continue.

"Ah, well, don't thank me then," she said with a sigh. "I have forgiven you, you know. I admit that I allowed my broken heart to dictate my actions against you in keeping Rowena as a slave, but I did write to you. The first one I wrote immediately, hoping to get you to come back. I wanted out of that city, too, you know."

"A letter? In the midst of a blockade, you thought of sending a letter? I never received a letter, Giselle. I never received any word from you. You're a liar. You always were."

The woman's beautiful face had contorted with fury, her cheeks pulling in further, her lips pursing until nothing was left of their fullness.

"How dare you accuse me of lying!" she screamed, twisting her body and lashing her arms out. "You come here to accuse me of lying? You dare to pretend you are better than me? After you accept her into your home and pretend that you love her? You are a hypocrite and a liar! I sent two letters in my benevolence to you, and you ignored them as though I was less than your daughter! Less than a dung beetle crawling on the street! How dare you come here to speak with me about helping her! How dare you ask anything of me! I was left with one more mouth to feed because you did not come! You left all of us to starve in the blockade!"

James had wished for something to punch at that moment, but he had risen slowly and given her a stiff departing bow. The action stirred her to calm herself, once again her body becoming poised, her voice lowering, her color cooling.

"Perhaps you should ask your wife. I sent two letters; I'm sure at least one of them reached you."

He had left her house then, with no more said. There was nothing left to say.

The sound of the front door closing startled James. Already the sun was dipping to the middle of the sky. As it was Tuesday, he knew that Bernadette would have left now to attend her meeting with the orphanage committee. He sighed in aggravation. She was a woman with a good heart, who would have kept something like this from him only because she was scared. The months after Elliot's birth had been difficult. If she had found the letters and kept them from him, she would have been sick and scared, knowing that he would have left immediately—despite the war between France and Algeria—to search for Rowena.

Another sigh from deep within his chest finally took the lump away. Rage and guilt were exhausting him, and foolish though it was, he couldn't let go. This was all conjecture. To allow his mind some rest he would need proof of Bernadette's role in this, if she had one.

Quietly, he left the library and crept up the stairs. Within a minute, he stood outside the closed door that led to his wife's private quarters. The cold from the metal knob shot through his hand and up his arm. A dark foreboding thickened the air, forcing his lungs to expand wider to catch his breath. He lifted his fingers in vacillation, knowing that moment might change his family life irreversibly – but then a vision of Rowena standing at that piano, her young face lit up with the excitement of conquering the melody of a song for the first time, flashed through his mind.

Before he knew it, he was standing in his wife's private sanctuary.

"You are a fool, John."

John raised his brows, a move that enhanced his chiseled, dark features. The man was being impossible. And yet with just that devastating gaze he could almost make her anger almost melt away.

Until he opened his mouth again.

"I'm telling you this out of charitable impulse. If conversation will lead you to insult me, we can sit instead in amiable silence."

"You should have confronted her," Grace seethed.

"You mean I should have intruded on her private conversation with Lord Candor? Why do you care so much about her walking with him? Is he on your list?"

"I'm concerned about her betraying you, John," Grace answered, sweetening her voice.

"I am certain Lord Candor was merely being nice to her. They were riding into Hyde Park, where his mother and Lady Candor were with two small boys. Don't be so jealous. I'm not."

"She is rumored to be a trollop and is now showing her true nature. She didn't tell Mother that she would be riding about London unchaperoned with a bachelor."

John's face hardened, and Grace was surprised to find herself reprimanded. She wasn't being charitable to her stepsister, that was certain, but she was hardly lying.

"Lady Worthington's husband is away, and she is in dire need of attention," John said, changing the subject. His eyes were on the glass of brandy in his hands, but Grace knew he was watching her somehow.

She clenched her teeth to keep from running across the room and scratching his eyes out. Nothing riled her more than John and his careless liaisons. Not even Rowena seeking out Lord Candor.

"Must you throw every sordid affair you have in my face?" she grumbled, irritated even more by the childish notes in her own voice. "You should spend more time with Rowena."

"We will all meet again at Falcon Manor for the hunting party. Until then I must keep myself entertained." A slow smile spread over John's face. "How will you manage your feelings when I take Rowena to my bed?" he asked in a dark, husky voice.

"Mother asked you to marry her, not take her to your bed!"

John laughed louder than was necessary. Grace sank her nails into her palms to keep from slapping him. Once married, she could find her own way to John's bed. There she hoped to find release for the whirlwind of feelings she had each time he came to visit. She was keen to experience that release, but until then she could hardly stand his taunting.

"You look piqued, Grace," John said, sauntering over to her. She tried to stand and run away, but her legs didn't seem to work. Trapped, she stayed seated, eying John's movements as he got closer. "Do you feel all right? You aren't coming down with a fever, are you?"

Grace shivered at the touch of John's naked hand on her forehead. He smiled, then ran his long fingers down her cheeks.

"You desire me so very much, don't you, my Grace?" he whispered. "When will you marry so that we may have each other?"

Grace whimpered at the way his fingers traced her lips. Horrified at her lack of control, she clamped her mouth shut, but it was too late. John laughed huskily.

"You are very conceited, John," she snapped.

John lowered his mouth close to hers. Her heartbeat in her throat as their breath mixed.

"I am not half as conceited as you, my Grace."

He kissed her in a long, lingering manner, and all her reasoning melted away. Had the clock not sounded, she might have given everything away to him at that moment.

"I must be going."

"You need to court Rowena, John. For Mama's sake," Grace demanded, though her voice was hoarse.

"A man has needs," he informed her. "You will soon know that when you marry. Do not worry; I will convince Rowena to marry me. Whether the marriage happens by choice or by pressure after a scandalous encounter, it will happen. I need the funds. You just focus on getting yourself married so we can reunite in a whole different way." John bowed low and left the room.

Grace stomped her foot in agitation. Focus on getting married, indeed. If Rowena would stop ruining her life, she could do just that.

Chapter Twenty-Two

JANUARY, 1833

"CINCH! YOU MADE IT!" exclaimed Emily, appearing in her own foyer out of nowhere. "Ryan told me that he saw you from his window." When she allowed herself to dream of the future, she did so with Christophe in it—but with the rumors of her time in Melilla circulating, perhaps the worst she could do to him and his family was to say yes.

"Nice of you to welcome me, sister," Christophe said, with a kiss to Emily's cheek. "Where is everyone?"

She slid him a mischievous gaze, but he was too tired to take much notice. His sister was always up to something. "If you are looking for the hunting party, you are much too late for that. Tomorrow they will go out again. You can join them then."

"Until they return, I believe I will catch up on some work in the library," he said, rubbing the cold from his hands.

"You will not!" Emily exclaimed. "There are a few people who did not go with the hunting party whom you can help me entertain."

The weight of English propriety settled between his temples as he struggled not to sigh out loud.

"I am about to have tea with Mother, Lady Bellevue, Claire, Miss Elizabeth Bellevue, Lady Arlington, Lady Ruth Arlington, and Lady Grace Brayemore. Would you like to join us?"

Christophe swallowed hard, wetting his tongue before trying to answer. "If you are giving me a choice—"

"I am," Emily interrupted. "You can join me, or see to Miss Brayemore, who is by herself outside. The other guests don't seem to wish to be around her, and she obliges them."

"You should not allow her to do so," he said, his voice sounding awfully low.

"I could not convince her to stay inside with us. She keeps saying she is sorry to cause me trouble with the guests, who could all go to the devil for their treatment of her."

Christophe pulled on his scarf and coat before yanking the front door open. A young footman appeared as cold air rushed into the foyer.

"She is outside in the back garden, Cinch," Emily said. She turned away with a large, playful smile on her lips.

With speed he hadn't known he possessed, Christophe found himself outside and on his way through the sodden garden. Rowena was in the back, on the rope swing that usually sat neglected. He watched her fly up to a breathtaking height, then swoosh backward, her head barely missing the overgrown branches. Sneaking up behind her, Christophe waited as she flew up again and came back towards him. Without thinking, he reached out and caught the ropes in his hands, his pride pushing aside the instinct to swear when the rope burned his skin.

Rowena gasped, twisting herself around to look at him.

"Lord Candor? I didn't know you were here," she said, her eyes wide with surprise.

Christophe clicked his tongue, fighting the urge to stare at her lips and will them to come to his own. "Can you not use my given name when it is just you and I, Rowena?"

Instead of answering, she slowly turned away, her fingers gripping the rope tighter, her shoulders stiffening.

Christophe moved to the other side of the swing. "My sister tells me you are having a hard time of it here. That the other guests are treating you badly?"

"It is not your fight," she said, glancing about as she spoke instead of looking at him.

Christophe smiled softly at the firm line drawn across her lips and her clenched jaws.

"Truly, Lord Candor, you need not concern yourself with me," Rowena said. "There are those who saw us the other day in London and have already made clear to me that I should stay away from you."

Her words cut through him. Memories of Dolores laughing at his proposal crept into his mind. Though he knew there was no comparison between the two, the memory always caused him to redden like a schoolboy. He could hear her laugh echoing while he begged her to reconsider from his knees. The moment that filled him with the most guilt and longing was when he had reached out to her belly, only for her to slap it away.

Right now, in front of him, Rowena was hurting—and she, unlike Dolores, was not trying to pain him. Had he not been so busy with all the problems his brother had left him, perhaps he could have given her more attention than just one afternoon.

"Please excuse me, my lord," she mumbled. "As I said, I should not be here with you. I won't keep you any longer."

"Rowena, please," Christophe said, trying to push away his exasperation. "Might we take a walk?"

"Alone? My sister has warned me not to be seen alone with you. There are those who think I am trying to seduce you."

"Is it not the other way around? Are they not afraid that I'm trying to seduce you?"

Rowena shook her head. "I'm the villain about town for the moment."

They turned down the lane lined by trees, but not fully blocked from view of the house.

"Is your family pressuring you to marry Howe?"

Rowena looked over at him with a sad smile. "Lord Candor, you need not vex yourself for me."

"Need I not?"

Rowena said nothing. Her eyes and body shifted, as though she longed to run away from him.

"*Enta habibi*," he said, stepping closer, only to have her step farther away. "I have been unreasonably busy with all the problems that my brother left to me, along with the problems of my own company. I admit I am in the habit of working too much. I also admit that I should have called on you more after the last time we spoke. The problem is, I don't trust myself around you. There is an intimacy I feel since our travels that makes me forget the rules of England."

Her forced smile sent his heart plummeting. "I don't expect anything from you, Christophe." His name on her lips sent pinpricks through him. "I will come up with a plan for my own life. You are not responsible for me."

"You do not understand me, Miss Brayemore," he said, taking her hands in his own. "I wish to be your plan. I wish to court you seriously but have allowed other things to take away my time. That and my fear of you rejecting me, as you are right now."

"I'm not rejecting you," she told him. "It's just that they've told me I will cause you too much harm as your wife."

Slowly, her eyes perused his face until they settled on his lips. Her tongue passed over her own, leaving them moist. They looked soft. Kissing them would prove it.

"What are you thinking?"

She shivered. "I shouldn't say," she whispered.

"Perhaps of me kissing you?"

She lowered her eyes, seeming to notice their intertwined fingers for the first time.

"Will you look at me, Rowena?"

His lips widened into a smile as she lifted her head. She was the most beautiful woman he had ever known.

"You are so handsome when you smile, Cinch."

⚜

Rowena closed her eyes to steady her breathing. Just as she had hoped, all the air was suddenly drawn away from her. Christophe's warm tongue intruded into her mouth, his hands pressing the small of her back towards his firm body, and she allowed it all to happen.

The kiss was gentle at first, but soon turned desperate. His lips moved roughly against hers, his tongue pressing, teasing, begging for more. Rowena placed her open hands against his strong chest to steady herself. She could no longer feel her legs, only the tingling running up and down her spine and the heat pooling in her belly.

Christophe's strong hands grasped her shoulders and gently pushed her away, his mouth tearing from hers with an unsteady breath. A whimper escaped her at the loss.

"I have not always been an honorable man," he said hoarsely. "I have done things I'm not proud of. But I would like to be honorable with you. You deserve for me to be honorable with you. And if I keep kissing you—"

He did not continue. It seemed that the delicious words on the tip of his tongue, if said, would be enough to push him over the edge.

The wind invaded their space, sending cool droplets of water raining down on them from the leaves above. Their heavy breathing calmed. His lips caught her fingers and kissed the tips before she moved them over his cheek and down his neck. Once at his chest, she couldn't help pressing her hands underneath his jacket to feel his heat and strength. Before she could touch more, he dipped his head and softly caught her lips with his again. His hands grazed over her back, cupping her bottom to press her closer into him. Their lips worked in unison to ease their mutual desire, mounting just as quickly as it had cooled. In the midst of it, he lifted her into his arms and moved them both farther away from the house.

When shadows replaced the weak sunlight, Rowena opened her eyes to find that they were deep in the wooded area of the garden path. Slowly, Christophe let her slide down him until her feet hit the ground.

He scrubbed his face with his hands before shaking his head and laughing.

"You cloud my judgment with your kisses," he accused her lightly. "The ground is much too cold to lay you down upon it and take advantage of you. Not that I would. Just that I wish to. But I would not. Especially if you did not wish the same."

Rowena laughed as she stepped forward.

"I never knew you to babble, my lord," she said, wrapping her arms around his chest. With her head laid against his heart, she closed her eyes and allowed herself a moment of pure safety. "Even with the ground being cold, I am not sure I would stop you from taking advantage of me."

He kissed the top of her head before burying his nose in her hair.

"My Fatia," he murmured. "My Rowena."

"Whom do you desire, Lord Candor?" she dared to ask, pulling away. "Fatia? Or Rowena?"

"I desire all of you," he answered, pulling her back to his chest. "I knew you as Fatia, the girl I watched learn to smile again, learn to become free again. The brave girl who walked for days through the desert and never complained, who learned to stand proudly, and who sang to brutish animals, including myself."

Rowena smiled into his chest, but said nothing.

"Now that I have met Rowena and seen her as the same strong girl, wandering in an unknown desert called London, I find she attracts my attention just as much as Fatia did. Rowena is just as strong and lovely. Just as desirable."

"I'm not sure I agree with your assessment of Rowena," she said, finally having the courage to tell someone the truth. "I believe Fatia was much braver than Rowena has shown herself to be."

"Did you not throw yourself in front of a horsewhip to save a small boy? That was certainly brave. Perhaps not in your experience in Algeria, but it was for England. I know of no other woman who would have done such a thing." He looked back at her, searching her eyes.

"And yet I am too cowardly to play Charades with the other guests. I came here to escape it," she admitted, unable to keep her smile from spreading.

"I would call that sound intelligence, rather than cowardice. Charades with Lady Bellevue would surely run me out of the house," Christophe told her. "I know a much better game we could play."

"And what is that? Please do not say Chuck-Farthing, because I lost miserably to Claire earlier."

"No, no. This game consists of a man watching a woman walk towards him. Then he takes her hand as a minister recites some legal rules. Once the man and woman repeat said rules, they are declared 'man and wife'. And do you know what games a man and his wife are allowed to play?"

The pleasure filling his face made her laugh aloud. He reached to pull her against him, but she hopped away with a squeal.

"If you wish to play games, Lord Candor, we can play Catch Me," she said, laughing at his bullish snort.

Bouncing away from him, her foot caught on a root. Her laughter weakened her ability to catch herself, but she needn't have worried. Christophe caught her easily and held on long after she was again stable.

"Marry me," he whispered. "I've been a fool to wait so long to ask. I thought to give you time to acclimate while I put my family affairs in order before I asked you, but that was a mistake. I cannot stop thinking of you—of the children we will make who will speak Arabic and Berber. I find that when I'm faced with myself, I cannot fathom a life without you."

The words took her by surprise.

"You must know that you are the only man I would ever marry. If I were certain it would cause you no pain, I would agree to it this very moment."

He laughed gently against her neck, pulling her closer. The vibrations slid up to her ears and down her spine in a shiver.

"Rowena," he whispered. "*Enta habibi.* You, all of you, everything about you, is what consumes me. And I won't let you go. Even with the rumors in London. I know of your scars, of your past. None of it bothers me."

"You must also think of your family. Of Emily and Claire and your mother."

"You are everything to me. I cannot allow you to go, and my family will not allow you to go. You are not the only one strong enough to ride the waves of London society. I will not stop chasing you. I will not allow you to be cut off by society. So, you see," he said, spreading his fingers, "we are at a deadlock."

Her heart pounded loudly in her chest, screaming at her to say yes, but the word was too slow in coming. Before she could answer, a loud gasp came from behind them.

Rowena turned to find Lady Bellevue and Lady Arlington staring at them with open mouths. Every bit of warmth in her body drained at the sight of the two older women. Lady Arlington murmured something behind her fan, causing Lady Bellevue to titter with laughter. With tremors running through her spine, Rowena found the strength to hold her head high as though to say she had done nothing wrong, but she felt that the act fooled no one.

Christophe pulled her hand into the crook of his arm before marching past the ladies as though nothing out of the ordinary had happened, but they refused to be ignored.

"One would think she would at least try to be respectable. For her father and the rest of her family."

"Once a fallen woman, always a fallen woman. It stays in the blood, Rachel."

Rowena grasped Christophe's arm tighter as the voices faded, sneaking a look at him. His profile was hard, his jaws clenched, his eyes straight forward. She took his silent advice and looked forward, breathing a sigh of relief when she could no longer hear the women insulting her.

Chapter Twenty-Three

"GOOD EVENING, CANDOR," A male voice called as Christophe turned down the corridor. Looking about, he found the very man he did not wish Rowena to marry standing smoking at an open window. There was no need to think rationally now. When he pulled her onto the bed and brought her against his chest, she was safe again. Sleep crept upon her while in the arms of the man who would dive into rivers to save a boy and travel with a slave across the desert.***

"What are you doing in the hall, Howe? Do you need something?"

"I was told by the footman that Lady Falcon does not like smoke in the rooms," Howe answered.

"She would never keep a guest from doing as they pleased," Christophe countered. When an amused smile spread across his rival's lips, Christophe hastily qualified his statement. "To an extent, of course."

"Of course." Howe shrugged. "But it is not a hardship for me not to smoke in the rooms."

"I'm sure she would have found it satisfactory that you used your room's balcony."

"Ah, but this window has a better view," Howe said. "Good night, Candor."

Christophe nodded curtly, then waited as Howe made his way to his rooms, just a few doors away from his own. Though he knew the man expected him to do it, Christophe couldn't resist looking out the window where Howe had stood. Rowena's window could be seen easily from the vantage point.

Summoning all his maturity, Christophe entered through his own door, and not John Howe's. Punching the man for peeping into Rowena's window would not feel unjustified, but raging emotions would get him nothing but trouble.

The fire was out, making the room so dark he could not see his own hand in front of his face. Slowly, he threw the waistcoat in the chair's direction and turned, the hairs on the back of his neck standing on end.

Something was amiss. Someone was in his rooms.

He couldn't believe that he had missed the feeling when he first stepped in. He fully blamed his lack of perception on his mind being occupied by one certain woman. A woman who sang to camels.

And wasn't that the way of most tragedies? By way of a woman?

Christophe bent down slowly and took the knife out of his right boot.

"Christophe?" came a whisper from the general direction of the fire. "Are you there?"

"Rowena," he breathed out, replacing the blade. "Where are you? Let me light a candle."

When light spilled over her, he was overcome again by her beauty. Her hair was let down, the dim light catching and releasing the flecks of red throughout it. Her lips were parted, and her eyes were wide, though she didn't seem particularly frightened. For a moment, neither one of them spoke. He watched as her breasts heaved slowly up, then down. Her silk dinner dress in a warm copper tone made her glow everywhere.

"I'm sorry," she said, her voice a low whisper which held the power of his undoing. "I should not have invaded your rooms. It is just that I felt rather lonely. It isn't very proper of me, I know. I just thought that if I saw you, I might feel better. Safer."

He brushed her lips with his, but the light touch was not enough. Keeping the intensity of his feelings in check, Christophe pulled her against him, reveling in the feel of her in his arms. Just a few more days and she would be his. He had only to convince her of it.

"If anyone sees you here, they will spread terrible rumors," he groaned against her neck. "And yet, now that you are here, I cannot think of letting you go."

She relaxed her body against his. Unfortunately, the humor did not reach her eyes. Vulnerability filled them, not laughter. She tried to hide it with a smile, but it came back in the form of tears that she tried to sniff away.

"What is it, love?" he whispered, brushing his fingers over her cheeks. "What has you trembling?"

"Oh, Christophe, I don't quite know," she whispered, a quiet laugh escaping her mouth. "There is a fear inside me and I do not know why. I just know that with you I am safe."

Her trust left him speechless. He was trying his best to live up to what she deserved, and while he certainly was not that man yet, he would do anything to make himself into that man. Anything.

Slowly he backed up, sinking onto the bed when his calves hit the soft mattress, pulling her with him. She sighed contently as he laid his head on her soft belly.

She wore no corset. He grinned up at her in delight while she squirmed away. It was useless for her to do so. He would not be letting her out of his sight.

"I was dressed for bed already, with my maid dismissed, when I decided to come here. I had to forgo the corset," she explained quietly. He answered by burying his face in her softness.

He laid there for a minute or longer, thinking on what to do.

She glided her fingers back and forth over his shoulders and up his neck into his hair. He focused on the lightning sensations running down his spine at her touch. He ached to touch her as well, wondering what sounds she might make when he did so. Lifting her skirts slowly, Christophe glided his hands under the hem of her dress until he found her legs underneath. They were bare.

He groaned in pleasure at the touch of her smooth, warm skin, and she gasped at the gentle caresses he gave them. Her fingers dug deeper into his shoulders, awaiting his next move. His head still against her soft belly, he let his fingers roam over her bare thighs until they moved their way up, brushing gently against her center.

She moaned.

He lost all breath.

"I must take you back to your rooms," he whispered hoarsely, brushing the wrinkles out of her skirts. "I do not wish to tarnish your reputation before you marry me."

"Lord Candor," she protested. "Christophe, please. I can move into my own house. And I can be with you. Society would understand it; they think me a courtesan anyway, and no one would blame Emily or Claire."

Christophe stood suddenly, placing her solidly on her feet. He rubbed his hands over her arms to keep their trembling from reaching the rest of her body. Then he stepped closer, his left leg caught between her skirts and limbs. When she lifted her head to look at him, he used the proximity to nuzzle her neck.

"I will not take you as a mistress. I have not had a mistress in years, and have vowed to never take one again. The only way for you to have me is for you to marry me."

"I've seen the paper. The newspaper believes the Roussier sisters and will make me the scandal of the season," she whispered. "An English marquess cannot marry a woman rumored to be a concubine."

"The rest of the world be damned, Rowena, I want you as my wife. Nothing less."

Rowena tried to pull away from him, but he held her arms fast.

"You cannot escape me," he said.

"No, I cannot," she whispered. "You chase me in my dreams."

Christophe answered by quietly bringing his lips to brush hers, insisting on pressing against them harder until her lips moved apart and his tongue could gain entrance.

"You must return to your rooms," he murmured, pulling away. "But before you go, can I have your promise that you will be mine?"

Rowena hesitated. She opened her mouth, then closed it.

"What is it, *enta habibi*?" he whispered as he caught her hand to kiss it. "Why won't you say yes?"

"My father. I think perhaps he expects me to marry John."

"And if I can convince your father to take me as his son-in-law, will you take me as your husband?"

"Then I will do as he advises," Rowena said with a smile which calmed him. They could be married as soon as her father gave his blessing.

The hallways were dark as they walked past the staircase and down the next hall to her room, and he took advantage of that, his fingers massaging her soft side unhindered by a corset. Before he was ready to part from her, they arrived at her door.

"Until tomorrow, Rowena," he said, kissing her on the mouth, but pulling back before his body convinced him to take her back to his rooms and let the rest of the world hang.

He opened the door for her, and there was nothing left for her to do but walk in, which she seemed to do reluctantly. When the door clicked shut, Christophe turned towards his rooms with a sigh. Another night in a bed that was entirely too large for just one person.

❧

Before Rowena took two steps into her room, a candle burst into flame. John held it up with a smile of triumph, as though he had caught her at something. He clicked his tongue in mock disapproval when Rowena grabbed the door handle again.

"There will be no leaving and no screaming," John chided. "If you scream, it would awake the entire house to this rather scandalous situation. They would call the banns before you know it."

"John, please, you must go to your room. We can speak tomorrow."

Rowena cringed at John's loud laughter. Lord and Lady Bellevue slept just next door, and Rowena wasn't unconvinced the rumor that the lady never slept for fear she might miss out on gossip was untrue.

"Are you worried about Lady Bellevue and your reputation, Rowena?" John asked, clicking his tongue. "Really, you should have thought of that when you decided to sneak to Lord Candor's chambers. I had to do some naughty things with Lady Bellevue to keep her from seeing you. I didn't want her thinking my future wife is a trollop. Thankfully, Lord Bellevue was downstairs, playing cards. He's there now, though, in case you were thinking of screaming. He might come see what the fuss is, but I assure you he would assume the worst. In *you*."

"I am not a trollop," Rowena hissed. "You know nothing about me, John."

Immediately he was upon her, pulling her head back by her hair.

"I know enough, Rowena," he said in a low, cool voice. "On Tuesdays and Thursdays you go to Kipper Street to spend your time with people less fortunate than you. Perhaps that is why you consider yourself better than the rest of us? Do we not spend enough time with ex-slaves to be considered worthy of your attention?"

Rowena said nothing. She dared not look anywhere but his eyes. He wanted her full attention, and she wanted a way out, which would be easier to find if he was not fighting for her to look at him.

John chuckled. His hand let go of her hair, leaving a painful throbbing in the back of her head. Suddenly calmer, he threw himself once again into the chair.

"Would you like to know what else I know about you? I know that you go to the small church on Friar's Road almost every Monday, Wednesday and sometimes on Friday, though I suppose that depends on all the little social obligations of the weekend. I have also noticed that you try your best to get out of every social obligation, preferring to sit at home reading or, lately, trying your hand in the greenhouse. A very odd choice for a woman used to lying about until her master calls on her to pleasure him."

Her face heated instantly. John gave a low chuckle as he watched her.

"Ah, that was the answer I was looking for. You see, you say that you are not giving out favors to the marquess, that you are not a trollop, but I can quite plainly read on your face what your job was these last few years in Algeria. Did you have a good time of it? I hear they allow their harems to be a bit more open about their bodies; is that true? While the English woman is versed in believing she is not to take pleasure from her husband, they teach their concubines over there something very different, do they not?"

Rowena remained quiet. When John sighed heavily at the ceiling, she took the chance to take a few steps backward.

A very discreet knock on the door caused both her and John to jump from their places.

"Who is it?" John hissed. "How many more men are you going to entertain tonight?"

"I rather figured it was Grace, or your witness to this scandalous situation. Was that not your plan?"

John narrowed his eyes. "Not tonight it wasn't. I would much prefer you and I to go about this thing like civilized people."

"Rowena?" came a whisper through the door.

Rowena swallowed hard. The thoughts in her mind were chaotic. Before she could run to the door, John was behind her. He grabbed her by the arm hard, clamping another hand down hard on her mouth.

Only a minuscule squeak came out of her, but it was enough. Within a second, the door burst open and Christophe came through it.

John jumped, pulling her arm hard. The animalistic roar from Christophe smothered her own cries as he charged at John. Less emotional, John was ready for the movement. He swung his arm with perfect timing, clipping the side of Christophe's head. Rowena cried out as she watched Christophe's head swing to the side, the muscles and veins constricting in his throat.

John was as strong and solid as an ox, but somehow his punch wasn't enough to stop Christophe. Perhaps it was fury that made Christophe the stronger of the two men at the moment, for Rowena could not otherwise understand his ability to still charge at John with unrelenting energy. There was no other reason when it was Christophe who rose in triumph after a few more tumbles, with half of John's shirt in his fists.

"Outside, Howe," he demanded, breathing heavily through clenched teeth. "Now."

"In defense of my betrothed's honor, gladly," John sneered back, rising on his own as he jerked his shirt away from Christophe's grasp.

Christophe snorted. "She is not yours, nor is that any reason for you to fight me. You dishonor her and my sister."

John shrugged his hulking shoulders, eyeing Lord Candor as a prized fighter would. "We were just talking, Candor, about our wedding plans. I wouldn't touch her tonight. She probably still reeks of you."

The insult hit Rowena fully in the chest. She cried out as John swung, but Christophe easily ducked the movement, sending John off balance. Christophe took the opportunity to push him towards the door.

"We will do this outside. Like gentlemen," he growled.

Instead of following them, Rowena rushed to the balcony, her sore arm throbbing violently when she pulled the door open. Within a few minutes Christophe was lighting torches below. Then he turned towards his waiting opponent, his face like a warrior ready to call for war. Their growls rose to her balcony, but she couldn't understand distinct words. It wasn't long before other windows opened, and loud whispers joined the noises from the ground.

The fighting started again, with Christophe lunging forward and John easily moving away. Only a small punch landed against his shoulders, moving his less than a strong wind. On the comeback, John's fist connected squarely with Christophe's jaw. His head snapped back unnaturally to the side, but within a second he, too, was back in his fighting stance.

A door opened below, distracting Rowena's attention away from the crack of Christophe's fist against John's ribs. She watched Lord Daucer run across the terrace, his deep voice reverberating against the stone walls of the house.

"Stop. You are making fools of yourselves at this hour. You've awoken the entire house."

"He is trying to disgrace Rowena," snapped Christophe.

John laughed, blood dripping down his lip.

The Bellevues came out of their balcony with their daughter not far behind. The family exchanged distasteful looks towards her balcony.

"You may have had her first, but she is mine by contract."

"There is no contract. I've had it looked into."

John laughed again, undeterred. "I wish to make her my wife; you only wish to make her your mistress and defile our family name. I won't let you do it," he shouted, raising his voice for their audience. He gave a quick smile and a wink before Christophe slammed his fist into his gut. There was only the sound of knuckles cracking against bone after that.

Lady Bellevue turned cold eyes towards Rowena.

"This, my dear, is something I greatly regret you having to see," she said to her daughter, though there was no regret in the woman's voice.

"It seems the 'lady' in question finds this all amusing," the young Lady Daphne Bellevue said. "Perhaps she really was more involved in the demi-monde of Africa than she wishes to say. Surely a true lady would not find it amusing that two gentlemen are bleeding for her."

The two men crashed against the large stone fountain, cutting the monologue short. The noise brought everyone's attention back down below.

"Don't you dare break that fountain," called out Emily, which made both Christophe and John suddenly stop, their clenched fists in midair.

"I found him—" Christophe started to yell back, before stopping himself.

Rowena recognized that while John was bigger than Christophe, passion had given Christophe the advantage. John stood with a bloodied and bruised face, his hand now slipping towards the ground. Christophe, on the other hand, still had a strong hold on his opponent.

"Let him go," Lord Daucer said. Rowena noticed he wore his suit still, and looked as though he wished to punch something himself.

John wrenched himself away, spitting blood from his mouth. "She's mine to marry. It's what her family wishes of her."

"We will see," said Christophe, taking another step forward.

John backed up, wiping his mouth on his sleeve before shrugging his shoulders. "I should challenge you for taking advantage of her."

Daucer caught Christophe's arm as it moved with lightning speed. Rowena sighed with relief against her terrace door, her body starting to tremble.

"It isn't worth it," Daucer said.

"I should say she isn't worth it," Lady Bellevue muttered loudly, turning her hatred towards Rowena.

Feeling the eyes of the entire house on her, possibly including her friends, Rowena kept her focus on the men now walking into the house. John had claimed he did not wish for a scandal to bring them together, but now there was little but scandal surrounding her. And several witnesses. Even the servants upstairs had opened their windows. They would have the story up and down the streets of London before noon tomorrow.

She shrank back into the shadows as each window latched shut. With each click, her verdict was nailed into place. By tomorrow morning, the news would be all around London that John had been found in her bedroom, and Bernadette would insist they marry. The damage might be enough for her father to agree without argument.

Hopelessness threatened to cave in on her as she stepped back into her bedroom.

She listened for a while as doors opened and closed all along the hallway in the house. Someone shouted for another to go back to their room. Another growled about not being able to sleep properly and claimed they would be leaving in the morning. Unable to calm her nerves enough to sit, Rowena leaned against the bedpost. She listened to the various noises; the voices whispering and hissing, footsteps running, doors slamming.

"What are you doing with him?" Grace's voice down the hallway was near hysterical levels, though Rowena guessed she was trying to stay calm. "You are overreacting. John would not hurt a fly. Surely you can leave him to spend the night in a bed instead of in the carriage?"

As Rowena listened through the wall, her door opened. She jerked in fright, though it was only Griffin, her maid, who walked in.

"Did I scare you, miss?" Griffin whispered.

Rowena didn't answer.

"He was only protecting his betrothed," came the shrill voice. "I would expect better treatment from you, Lord Candor."

"Come, Miss," Griffin urged, saying nothing about Rowena being in the dress she had hung up hours before. "Let me see to you. I was told you were hurt in the scuffle. Sit here on the bed and let me look at you."

Rowena did as her maid instructed, breathing deliberately to keep herself from bursting into tears. When Griffin caught her eye and held her gaze, Rowena took strength in her maid's encouraging smile.

"I was worried about you when all the noise started."

"I'm all right. What are they saying upstairs?" Rowena asked quietly.

Griffin paused. Lord Bellevue shouted, commanding his wife to go to bed. His tone left no reason to doubt that Lady Bellevue would comply immediately.

"Don't you concern yourself with that."

"Will he make John leave?"

"I do not know. It is late, and there are many people advocating to allow him to leave in the morning. I hear that Lord Candor will leave as well. Probably to head off the scandal," Griffin replied, wiping the salve she had rubbed along Rowena's bruises off her hands with a towel.

Rowena sought her maid's eyes in the mirror. "He can do nothing about this rumor. There are too many witnesses. John was in my room, though I did not wish him here. No one will be able to stop Lady Bellevue from spreading this throughout the city. Before I am home, my father will have heard of it."

The hopelessness of her situation flooded her senses. Tears welled in her eyes, but she brushed them angrily away.

"He asked me to marry him," she whispered.

"Mr. Howe?"

"No, Lord Candor."

Griffin was quiet as she rubbed an oily substance on Rowena's shoulder that smelled of mint and lavender.

"I cannot marry him now."

Griffin thinned her lips as she brushed Rowena's hair. "I don't see why not."

"I am a neat, tidy package of scandal, and he will be the laughing stock of London for marrying me. Besides, my stepmother will try to persuade my father that I must marry John. I fear I will have little choice in the matter."

"Sleep, Miss Brayemore," Griffin said, gently pushing her into the bed pillows. "It will all sort itself out in the morning."

Rowena sighed. "I should leave here tomorrow."

"Hush now, and try to rest. You will leave when you are supposed to."

"I will try to stay in bed longer tomorrow, Griffin. If not to sleep, at least to avoid the other guests."

Griffin scoffed. "Good night then, Miss Brayemore. Sleep well."

"Good night, Griffin."

In the darkness, Rowena released her tears. At first relief filled her, but soon enough utter solitude and heartache replaced it. Though John had claimed he did not want to force her to wed him, he had done just that – or rather, Christophe had. Either way, tomorrow or the next day she would hear from her father. And soon after that she would have to marry John.

Curling up against the head of the bed, Rowena thought through the past years. Through all the times she had been afraid, all the times she had faced the unknown, and all the times she had somehow made it through. Tears fell by the hundreds along with her memories, each one passing until she came to the day Saed had given her to Christophe.

For the first time in her life, each moment of her past connected to the dot of another moment. If she hadn't been taken by Madame Roussier, then sold to Mohammad, then sold to Saed, she never would have seen Christophe that day. If she hadn't been beaten and abused and crushed, she wouldn't have taken to singing at night to the other women in an effort to calm them and herself into sleep. If she hadn't been singing one night as Saed had come home from a long journey, she would never have been used as dinner entertainment. If she hadn't sung so many times in the house, Nadira would not have thought her worthy to give as a present. If she hadn't seen the glimmer of hope in the way she had not felt afraid of Christophe, she would not have begged for him to take her. Had she not made a journey through a desert and mountain once before, she might have died trying to journey through it with Christophe.

She had endured five years of toil and suppression, and then she had found a man who saw her as worthy of protecting from others. And now those five years might come to naught, for if she married John she would fade away and die within herself. She was certain of it.

The only place she was safe was next to Christophe. He was the only man in years who had cared enough to stand up for her. Her lungs struggled for breath as she came to that realization. She had to see him. Run to his arms and stay there forever.

Without thinking she yanked open the door, the dark, cavernous hallway stretching before her. Rowena hesitated, listening for signs of someone awake. When she took a step forward into the darkness something moved, unfolding into the full height of a man before her. She gasped, extinguishing the noise with her own hand. She fumbled quickly for the doorknob, but two hands grabbed her gently by the waist and pushed her back into the room.

Just as she was about to faint, the smell of bergamot and cinnamon floated around her.

"What's wrong, Rowena?"

Rowena whimpered with relief, her body shaking from the tension in her muscles.

"I was coming to see you," she whispered.

"I heard you crying," Christophe admitted, brushing his lips against her cheek, down her jaw, and onto her neck.

"I was just thinking," she answered with a sigh. "Of my life, of you, of my future."

"Ah, my love."

His lips met hers in slow, raw kisses. She pulled away, skimming her fingers over his bruised face. In the moonlight, his skin looked blotchy and one eye was almost swollen shut.

"You should go downstairs and put something on that," she whispered, running her finger lightly over the inflamed skin.

"Tomorrow. Tonight I will stay with you. Please, let me stay with you tonight," he begged, walking her back towards the bed. "Just to sleep. I wish to hold you and make you feel safe. I feel as though that is the only thing I have ever wanted to do. I do not believe John will try anything more tonight, but still—"

There was no need to think rationally now. When he pulled her onto the bed and brought her against his chest, she was safe again. Sleep crept upon her while in the arms of the man who would dive into rivers to save a boy and travel with a slave across the desert.

Chapter Twenty-Four

THE SILENCE AT TINJA House was suffocating. Looking out at the busy street as Brayemore left Candor House, Christophe decided they would leave for Ravenwood that very night. The rumors in London were vicious and would only get worse. He had almost beaten two men to a bloodied pulp last night when he had entered Brooks's. Today's paper didn't help the situation. Rowena would be safer at Ravenwood until well into the season. With some luck and some planning, the gossips would soon find something else to talk about.

Bernadette looked through the window again and then back at the clock. Between those two places and her needlework, her eyes were boring a triangle into the parlor.

Three days had passed so slowly. The gossip was almost too much for a woman with her nerves to handle. The house lacked joy without John, who was staying with a friend, while Rowena said nothing in her own defense; rather, she had stayed quietly in one corner of the house since her return. Bernadette didn't know what to do with herself or her family. There were times she wished to throttle Rowena and John. And James. He was the reason Rowena and John hadn't yet been pushed to the altar, which was the only action that would stop the talk and her anxiety.

For the fifth time in ten minutes, Bernadette looked out the window for her husband. James was a very difficult man to read, but lately he was downright impossible. He refused to speak to her or to anyone, holing himself up in the library until dinner time, then setting out for his club or back to the library. All the mysterious meetings he had no interest in telling her about only increased her apprehension.

Just the day before, a strange card had arrived that Harrison had refused to give to her. Strangely enough, he had waited until he could give it to James directly. It all worried Bernadette. It had seemed to be the Candor seal, though she couldn't be certain. Lord Candor had come just two days before – though when he had asked to see Rowena, Bernadette had promptly told him that she was indisposed. Certainly he couldn't be thinking of marrying her, and so being seen with Rowena would only seal in other people's heads what the rumors said.

Bernadette gulped in air, working against the nerves that threatened to pull her into a faint. Rowena must marry, and soon. It was the only solution. And she must do so before James found out about everything. Bernadette could not afford an angry spinster stepdaughter.

A movement in the hallway made her jump up from her seat. Even when Elliot came in, she didn't relax. She couldn't.

"Hello, Mother! What's wrong? Did you forget you promised we could have tea together today? Are you unwell?"

Bernadette shook her head slowly while she reached out her arms to hold him. He was quite a caring boy, and despite being too old to hug in public, he never refused her when they were alone.

"I did forget, but it does not matter. Pull the cord and ask Harrison to have the tea brought in."

Elliot ran to the cord and pulled eagerly twice, looking guiltily at her, but Bernadette did not admonish him. She didn't have the energy to.

"Hello, Elliot! Have you been a good boy today? Did you go to the park?" Grace asked, coming into the parlor.

"Yes, and no. I was very good, but we went to the museum," he said, rolling his eyes.

Grace gave him a quick peck on the cheek, which he carelessly brushed off.

"What is it like out there?" asked Bernadette, twisting her handkerchief between her fingers.

Grace glanced at Elliot before speaking. Bernadette's fingers worked faster against her handkerchief.

"Multiple rumors are flying about with no sign of slowing down, unfortunately," Grace muttered, turning back to Bernadette. "Everyone in the park was cordial, but not overly warm. Lady Alice and the others ignored me, though that may be due slightly to my being on the arm of Lord Newsbury. They are a jealous group."

"Oh, Grace," Bernadette cried softly. "Did he ask to call on you again?"

"No, Mama," Grace hissed. "He did not. Still, I will not cry over Lord Newsbury or any other man."

"What else happened?" Bernadette asked, seeing hurt in her daughter's eyes.

"Lady Prudence and her sisters told me gravely that they had planned to extend an invitation to us for Lady Cecile's ball, but that it was going to be a crush and they had to 'make some cuts somewhere'," Grace said, mimicking Lady Prudence's nasal voice to perfection. "Not that it bothers me ever so much. I wouldn't have gone, anyway. But the Countess Riverston and Lady Seyemore deliberately turned their backs on me while pulling their daughters away. So I dare say I cannot expect an invitation to their balls next season."

"They are of the lower noble set, so do not allow their treatment of you to affect you greatly."

It wasn't entirely true that Lady Prudence was of lower nobility, but it was nice to say it. Certainly some rejection was to be expected, but Bernadette knew it would blow over once Rowena and John were married and living in Manchester. With that encouragement, Bernadette placed her cold hand on top of her daughter's. More tears ran down Grace's beautiful cheeks, despite her struggle to keep them back.

"Oh, Mother," she whispered. "It was awful to be treated like that. Even Lady Alice had some choice words for me about our familial ties. She suddenly feels quite superior, though we all know she is anything but."

"Lady Alice has long wanted you out of the way so she could take the spotlight. So let her take it and make an arse of herself."

"Mama!" gasped Grace, looking back at Elliot, who was too caught up in his drawing to hear.

Bernadette tried to straighten herself up, but it felt as though the weight of the world was pulling her down. "I am so overwhelmed with all of this. I do wish Rowena's return could have been a pleasant thing for everyone."

"We do not truly know the reason Rowena stayed behind in Algeria, but the truth is that she lied to us the very first day that she came here."

"Possibly, but if she did so it was with the intention of sparing our sensibilities."

They sipped their tea in silence, which caused the lump in Bernadette's stomach to grow larger. She was so twisted into knots she was unable to eat any of the yellow cake.

"Why don't you eat something, Mother?"

"I'm too nervous, Grace."

"You haven't eaten in three days," Grace insisted, trying to hand her a plate of cake which Bernadette refused to take.

"I'm worried about John. He hasn't come by. Have you spoken to him? Is he still willing to marry her? Marriage is the only way Rowena will get out of this alive. The best case would be to marry the man that she was found with during the weekend."

"Found with? Apparently, he intruded into her rooms," Grace said. Bernadette gasped. "Just to talk, Mother. He wished to convince her to marry him."

That was a small consolation. And it certainly made sense. Bernadette had noticed that when Rowena was around John at Tinja House, she was very good at never getting too close. Really, it was Rowena's fault for forcing him to have to find her in such a way to merely talk.

"I believe John would still marry her. He needs the dowry to buy that factory he wants," Bernadette said.

"He must marry her. It's the only way. Then she would be in Manchester and we would again be allowed to walk with our heads held high. Her past is not our fault, and I do not see why we should suffer for it. Nor should we suffer for what happened at Falcon House."

Bernadette wanted to scream. To cry. To faint. But she didn't. It took much effort, but she stayed strong and stoic. Unfortunately, staying strong wound her nerves so tight she was like a coiled spring. One more touch, one more rumor, and she might go flying into the unknown. To keep from bursting, Bernadette pretended she had nothing more to say. Once again, she turned to look out the window, hoping to see James coming home.

"Mother, stop," Grace whispered, placing her cold hand on top of Bernadette's. "We will sort this out, and soon."

Bernadette looked down to hide her nervous tears and found her silk handkerchief in tatters, the pieces falling through her fingers as Grace let go.

Christophe sat at his desk, facing a colorless Baron James Brayemore.

There was a long moment during which it seemed the man might cast up his accounts, so he looked about for something to throw in front of him, only finding a small ashtray. Since that wouldn't do any good at all, Christophe could only wait and hope that Brayemore would pull himself together. Just in case, though, he was ready to jump away. No sense in getting his new trousers soiled.

Finally, Brayemore opened his mouth, breathing in and out noisily as a bit of color seeped into his cheeks. It was enough for Christophe to relax his shoulders.

"My reason for telling you the details about this weekend is not to distress you. Quite the contrary. I wish to ask you for your daughter's hand in marriage."

"Marriage? To you?"

The question was met with silence.

Christophe struggled not to judge the baron before he knew what his qualms were. Or rather, who they were with. Whether Brayemore thought him not good enough for Rowena or Rowena not good enough for him, he did not yet understand.

"I already have a special license. I believe we should marry as soon as we can and announce it later."

"You wish to elope with my daughter? Without the banns being called?"

"I see no reason to wait."

"The custom is to ask for permission to court her. A rushed marriage suggests dishonor. You can be certain the rest of society will suspect her to have been dishonorable. First John, then you! It would be better for her to go away for a bit. I could take her on a trip."

Christophe clenched his jaws. The baron had a point. To dispel his frustration, Christophe focused on the heat the sunshine through the windows brought to his shoulders. He pinpointed the exact spot while his emotions settled.

"Perhaps, Baron Brayemore, I should tell you that my relationship with your daughter extends beyond this past week. Beyond the borders of England. I can see how, to you, it seems that I am coming out of nowhere to offer for her. Though we have not had a courtship within the normal bounds of English culture, we have, in fact, spent more time together than a normal English courtship normally permits."

Baron Brayemore raised his brows, but did not seem shocked. He sudddenly almost seemed eager.

"Speak, Lord Candor," he urged. "I believe you have the story I have been waiting to hear."

Compassion for Brayemore stilled Christophe. Having lived in Algeria for decades, the baron would not be innocent to the horrors that slavery caused. And yet he asked to hear about Rowena.

With a decisive flick of his wrists, Christophe began. Anxiety began to quiver beneath the surface of his confident façade, but there was no going back. He could not stop, finding no reason to leave out any of the story between him and Fatia, besides the stolen kisses.

Agony, failure, disappointment, and condemnation all passed over Brayemore's face while he listened. When the story ended, he said nothing. A slow rise of regret stole away Christophe's confidence in his choice. He couldn't help feeling instantly sorry.

When Christophe rose from his desk, Brayemore did not move. He stared straight ahead, stroking his beard with trembling hands, his face ghostly pale. Christophe crossed the room to the glass liquor tray, needing a strong drink to revive himself. He stayed there a long while to give Brayemore some time to recover.

After a full five minutes, Brayemore still had not moved an inch. The man's self-restraint was quite impressive. He would have expected a father to either be weeping or pounding holes into the wall, but Brayemore allowed the truth to sink in. Christophe poured a second drink and quietly returned to his guest. The baron seemed to have aged a decade in the last few minutes.

"You are correct that I should have made my intentions known to you, my lord," Christophe said quietly. "But now I have told you the story in its entirety, omitting nothing for sensitivity. You can see that I have been nothing but honorable with her. Between the various rumors going about, along with the gossip rags delighting in the rumors of her being a runaway, something must be done. The best thing would be for her to marry quickly, and to someone who is well-respected."

Baron Brayemore drew in a ragged sigh. He drank his brandy in one gulp, then turned to Christophe. His eyes held the look of a man who had failed; blank and distant. A feeling Christophe knew well. He was not proud of making Baron Brayemore feel that way.

"I do not wish for Rowena to know that you have told me. I am sure she decided not to tell me because she wished to not hurt me, and I would like her to think she has succeeded," Brayemore said.

Christophe sank back into his chair and scrubbed his hands over his face. He looked again at Baron Brayemore and winced. Rowena would know with one look at her father. His pain clearly stamped on his face.

"John will try to contest the marriage."

"He will not have time. We will have the ceremony this very evening. There is no written contract."

Brayemore raised his brows, but Christophe just shrugged. He would not apologize for investigating Rowena.

"True, but he could make a lot of noise. He is well loved by a few powerful noblemen and women," Brayemore said.

"How much money was he hoping to receive from Rowena's dowry?" Christophe asked. Lord Brayemore leaned back in his chair and eyed him. "I have no need for her dowry. Married to me, she would be allowed to keep it for herself. You may investigate me if you wish."

"I already have, my lord. Though I did it for Grace, not Rowena."

The admission made Christophe balk, then laugh. Brayemore's face softened into a smile as well.

"As for Rowena," Brayemore said, "when she was seventeen I set her dowry at fifteen thousand. I suppose he wished for that or more. It hasn't been on my mind since she returned, though I suppose I should have considered it. I know that she is five and twenty, but I still see her as a young girl just out of the schoolroom. And she has never even mentioned marriage." The baron rose abruptly. "I must go now."

Christophe pulled for a servant to be called. "I will be at Tinja House at five o'clock."

"I never thought it would come to this. I wished for her to make her own decision about John or any other gentleman. It was for that reason that I never pushed her either way. I never suspected that John would act in such an ungentlemanly fashion," he said, taking his hat from the footman.

Looking out at the busy street as Brayemore left Candor House, Christophe decided they would leave for Ravenwood that very night. The rumors in London were vicious and would only get worse. He had almost beaten two men to a bloodied pulp last night when he had entered Brooks's. Today's paper didn't help the situation. Rowena would be safer at Ravenwood until well into the season. With some luck and some planning, the gossips would soon find something else to talk about.

Chapter Twenty-Five

"ARE YOU ALL RIGHT, Benti?" Baron Brayemore asked, finding his daughter at the door of Tinja House. "Why are you out here?"

"I'm fine, Father," Rowena answered, shame still covering her from the encounter in the park with Lady Alice, who had loudly announced to anyone who could hear her that a common tramp was in their innocent midst. Rowena had practically run home. "Nothing I can't survive."

He narrowed his eyes but said nothing else.

"Come, my girl," he said, taking her hand and placing it on his elbow. She leaned into him and heaved a ragged sigh. "There, there, Rowena. If you are going to weather the storm, you can't make your own rain."

The old quote he had used so many times when she was young made her laugh. She lifted her head but held on to him tightly as they entered the parlor.

"James! You're back!" exclaimed Bernadette. "We must talk. This—this problem, it must be solved immediately! Poor Grace is being left out of dances and parties, and when Elliot goes back to school he must not carry this rumor with him. My nerves, James, cannot take another day of jumping each time the door is knocked on!"

"What rumor?" piped up Elliot from behind the desk.

The entire room jumped when his blond head popped up from behind the desk. The boy laughed with glee. James laughed along with his son, sending his wife a pointed look. She blushed like a disciplined school-girl. Rowena tried her best to smile as well, but Bernadette's nerves had obviously taken their toll on her.

"Elliot, do you not have to begin your work now?" Grace asked, just as the governess appeared at the door.

James looked down at his son and smiled. "Go on now, Elliot. Do your sums and tomorrow I will take you for ice cream. How does that sound?"

Before James could finish the promise, Elliot was up and running to the door. When his feet could no longer be heard running up the stairs, the tension in the room burst.

"Something must be done about this, James. We cannot continue to live in fear as we have the last few days."

"You must do something about all of this," Grace said at the same time. "Three days we've done nothing while the rumors only grow bigger."

"Grace was uninvited to a ball today. I cannot go out into London, and no one has come to visit me for three days, and we cannot keep this from Elliot much longer!"

"If it will help the family, then I will go," Rowena said quietly.

"Go where, Benti? Where would you go?" James asked.

"Perhaps to America. Just for a little while until all of this settles down."

"Going to the continent for a month or so won't make this die down. When you come back, you will still be ostracized," Grace hissed from her chair, her fingernails digging into its arms.

"I'm not guilty of anything, Grace. I did not run away from my father and Bernadette, nor did I ask John to come to my room. He caused that scandal."

"It doesn't matter," Grace answered, her voice dripping with unusual sweetness. James gripped the side of his chair in anger. "You lied from the beginning, and now no one will believe anything you say. Gossip only lasts as long as society is talking about it, and those Roussier girls have no problem embellishing to keep everyone doing just that. Their lack of imagination keeps the story from getting too salacious, but the scandal you caused at Falcon House added more fuel to that fire."

"Then I will leave permanently."

"I do not wish to be apart from you again, Benti," James said. He swallowed, unsure he could continue without shouting at half of his family that he was not about to allow them to separate him from his daughter, ever. "I have lived for a long time thinking you were dead. No, Benti, no. While I am not too gray yet, I am getting older, and I do not wish to send you away."

His words were met with silence. Bernadette turned from him abruptly. He braced himself to see her shoulders shaking with sobs, but suddenly she gave a screech and rushed to the window.

"Gracious! It's Mother! Whatever would bring her all the way here?"

James swore under his breath in Arabic—a particular expression that explained he had as much respect for his mother-in-law as he did for a dung beetle. Rowena giggled, but her amusement was short-lived.

"Lady Curtshaw," Harrison informed the family, with more formality than usual.

"Mama! Why have you come into town? You hate town. You always say you hate town. We were not ready for you, Mama. Harrison! Have the red room prepared for Lady Curtshaw and bring in more tea!" Bernadette's voice was so shrill it was difficult to distinguish each word.

Lady Curtshaw looked straight at Rowena, her eyes roving over every inch of her. "You are used to people looking you up and down, child? You didn't even blush like a well-bred lady. Instead, you looked directly back at me. I wouldn't even allow you in as a servant in my household."

"Quite so, Amanda, since she is my daughter," James put in.

Lady Curtshaw's eyebrows drew up to new heights while her pink lips pushed out in disdain. "I rue the day I gave you leave to use my Christian name, James. You make it sound filthy, like anything you say in those dirty, heathen languages you speak. *You* don't speak heathen languages, do you, child?"

"I'm not a child, Lady Curtshaw," Rowena answered.

"Don't mind Rowena, Grandmama," Grace interjected, throwing Rowena a glare. "She does not quite exercise the manners of a gently bred lady yet."

"I can see that," the elderly woman said in a huff.

Grace kissed her on the cheeks, which softened the lady considerably.

"Very well, let us talk of how to solve this scandal," she said, sitting down as though upon a throne.

Bernadette gulped in air before sinking into her usual chair to serve tea. Once sitting, though, she frowned at the teapot. Her hands were shaking far too violently to hold it up, which was all James' fault. He kept glaring at her – just like her father used to anytime she dared to speak. The heat from his scowl increased her anxiety tenfold.

Gathering her courage, she picked up a teacup, but it immediately fell from her hands and shattered. A maid appeared and cleaned it, making certain no trace was left, but Bernadette couldn't stop blushing. Now her fingers shook more, making her incapable of doing anything.

"My dear, get a hold of yourself. You never were good in a crisis. This is but a small crisis; nothing like what your sister got herself into. Nor your father once, when... well, we will not speak of the past. We have the present to deal with. We must simply make some arrangements. There is a very easy way to shift the direction of gossip around this time."

"What is that, Mother?" Bernadette asked, waving her smelling salts in front of her nose.

"She must marry."

"Exactly what I was thinking, Grandmama," Grace said with a triumphant smile. "She should marry John and move to Manchester. Everyone would forget about everything then."

"John? He's not even here," James said.

Bernadette glanced back quickly at Rowena, who was so quiet she was almost sure the young woman wasn't there anymore. Alas, she was, though shrunken back into the chair as though trying to make herself disappear. Bernadette quickly turned her attention back to James and her mother. She couldn't worry about Rowena. Right now was the time to straighten things out for Grace.

"He has been scared off. Have you bothered to inquire about him around London?" Grace snapped back. "Besides, who else will marry her?"

"Is John the only option?" Lady Curtshaw asked. "It would work better for the family, and that includes you, Grace, if she married someone with a title, even if it be small, and stayed in London. If she ran away she would still look guilty, which would bring problems to Grace and possibly Elliot. John is a nice man, but he is not titled."

"John has high contacts and does very well for himself," Grace interjected, her lips protruding into a pout.

"Rowena will not marry John," James shouted, slamming his fist on the table.

Bernadette noticed her poor daughter's lips tremble – something no one else ever seemed to notice. After all, Grace was Bernadette's darling baby, the one who had survived after two stillbirths. She was a strong girl, but not so strong to keep from being affected by James' shouting.

Tense, oppressive silence filled the parlor. The clock ticked loudly, which Bernadette found somehow soothed her heart into matching the rhythm. It was her mother who finally had the courage to break the silence.

"I heard that Lord Newsbury went riding with you, Grace. What about him?"

"Lord Newsbury?" asked Grace. "He is nice enough. I will give him up for you, Rowena."

Grace and Lady Curtshaw gave Rowena a brief look. Bernadette looked as well and noticed that her stepdaughter was turning a rather unbecoming shade of purple.

"But what should make him want to marry her?" asked Bernadette, bracing herself for a monumental outburst, if Rowena was anything like Grace.

"Newsbury is in need of money," Lady Curtshaw said, musing through her tea. "What say you, James?"

"Excuse me," Rowena said, standing so suddenly that Bernadette jumped. "I think it best that I leave."

"Well," huffed Lady Curtshaw. "I see you have little interest in your future and the future of your family."

"No, my lady. It is not I who have little interest in this family, but this family who has little interest in me. You speak as though I have no ears, no opinion, no thought on the matter, even though this is my future. You are no better than the masters who held me captive for years, dictating my every move."

Lady Curtshaw made an indistinct huff of indignation, but Rowena did not stop. Bernadette took up her fan and waved it about herself furiously, trying to drown out Rowena's words with the wind.

"If you care nothing of my opinion on whom I should marry or what I should do to relieve you of me, then I see little point in my being here at all. I will take Elliot outside and enjoy my last rays of sunshine before you all send me off to the guillotine."

"What a provoking girl, James," Lady Curtshaw said after Rowena had left.

Bernadette closed her eyes and willed herself to faint, but the only darkness she found was self-imposed. It could not keep her from hearing James' shouting back in what was certain to be a long discussion.

The sunshine would do her well. Rowena was certain of it.

She looked back at the house, the familiar stab of guilt hitting her, but again she pushed it aside. She would not apologize. Not when they were still planning her future for her as though she was a naughty puppy to be gotten rid of.

In order to curb her anger, she focused on looking for frogs with Elliot, whom she had rescued from doing sums with his governess. When they found none, they lay down against the large oak tree that shaded most of the garden, and she once again told him the story of the man who fought off mountain lions and saved a young prince from drowning. Her heart skipped a beat, the sound echoing in the emptiness that seemed to grow larger inside her. Lord Candor had not come again today. Out of sheer self-pity and longing, she inserted a princess into the story, surprised when Elliot kept any protest about it to himself.

Her brother focused his sights beyond the trees, his eyes locked on whatever he could see in his imagination, and Rowena looked with him. As the story spun, half of her mind planned her escape. It would hurt her father and her brother, but that seemed small compared to the prospect of her family selling her against her will to a man she didn't know, like Newsbury.

"Benti!" her father called from the back door that opened to the kitchen.

Elliot looked at her curiously as Rowena sat still, her spine stiff against the tree.

"Do you not hear him, Rowena?" he asked slowly.

"Yes, Elliot, I hear him."

"Then why do you not answer?"

"Because, Elliot, I no longer run when a man bellows out my name. Even if it is my father. He can come and find me."

Elliot's eyes grew large. Her tone was icy. Bitter. But she would not back down. When Lord Brayemore's large shadow was cast down upon them, Elliot stood up immediately and ran to the house. Rowena stayed still, her eyes focused beyond the world around her.

"Benti," her father said, wheezing slightly. He sat on the nearby bench and leaned towards her.

"I cannot believe you did not turn that ridiculous woman out of the house the instant she started dictating my future," Rowena said. She kept her rage tampered down as she had for years, but it boiled beneath the surface and she was certain her father could see it.

She met his eyes. For the first time in her life, she saw her father as an old man. His hair and beard were almost completely white now, and there were more wrinkles about his mouth and eyes.

"Benti, while Lady Curtshaw and I are not each other's favorite people, she came to help us. It is the way we do things here, Rowena. Had you been here instead of Algeria, you would already be married by this age. Women still marry men their family believes is better for them, many times without knowing the man very well."

"I will not, Baba, I'm sorry. I will take my dowry and be an old maid in the country first."

Her father blew out a puff of air that sounded suspiciously like a mocking laugh. "That will not make you happy. You must face up to this and your future. You are five-and-twenty, daughter."

Rowena paced the space between the tree and the bench.

"I will not do it," she said, without turning around to face the man she had dreamed of coming back to. Coming back, only to be sold off to a man she did not know, could not trust to treat her well – it was insulting.

"I wish for you to be safe and with a gentleman," her father answered quietly. "And I wish for you to be here, close to me."

"I see," Rowena murmured, surprised at how quickly her anger had turned to smoldering embers. The fire was not out, but it was no longer raging. It could not when her father looked so frail.

The sun continued lowering itself in the sky as her father's low voice rumbled around her. She looked towards the warm light, refusing to allow any of his words to reach her understanding.

"Rowena!"

She jumped at the sound of her father's sharp voice behind her.

"Yes, Father?"

"Do you agree?" her father asked. He no longer looked as weak, but he still looked tired, older. "Do you agree to marry? I will not force you, though I believe it is the best option. He has convinced me that you know each other sufficiently well enough to think this marriage will work out between you. In fact, he says he wanted to marry you before this incident with John."

"How could Lord Newsbury possibly know me well enough to want to marry me before this incident? He's playing you for a fool, Baba. I know nothing about the man."

"Benti," James sighed, taking her hand in his. "You've not listened to a word I said. It is not Newsbury who wishes to marry you, but Lord Candor."

Sheer surprise took away her ability to speak. Lord Candor still wished to marry her? But he had not visited her, nor sent a note since she had left Falcon Manor. With all the rumors going about London, he had not bothered to see how she was faring. For several nights now she had cried herself to sleep, thinking he had decided against pursuing a courtship with her.

"Lord Candor? Are you certain?"

Her father smiled widely for the first time in days. "Does it please you to know it is him? I dare say he is a much better option than Newsbury, even with his businesses and such that others disapprove of."

"I do not mind his business. I just—" Rowena stopped; the doubts on the tip of her tongue did not seem to want to form coherently.

"What is it, Benti? If you have doubts about your happiness with him, I wish to hear them before the ceremony. He desires to marry you, and quickly. No grand ceremony—just something small between the families. His mother is not best pleased, I believe, but it has all worked out. The ceremony will be in two weeks. Enough time for you to get a dress of some sort—and then he plans to take you to the country. Give some time for this to quiet down."

"The country? Perhaps that would be a nice change," Rowena mused, her tongue loosening. "But Baba, I don't know. What I mean is, how do you know when it is right? When it is worth the risk?"

"Marriage? It is difficult sometimes, but I can say that I have a good feeling about you and Lord Candor. He cares deeply for you."

"And I do care for him, which makes me wonder if I should not say no."

"You don't think you're good enough for him?" her father asked, a flash of anger in his eyes. "Let me tell you something: anyone who thinks your past makes you somehow lesser is not worth your time. Never question your value, Rowena, especially because of what other people do or did. Whatever you might have needed to do to survive does not tarnish you. We would all do anything to survive. Anyone who says differently is a hypocrite and a coward."

Rowena smiled away the tears her father's words had brought to her eyes and nodded.

"Now, are you willing to marry this man or not?"

"I am, Baba. I will make you proud."

James took her hand in his large, rough ones. "You need only know that you have already and always will make me proud."

Chapter Twenty-Six

SOMEONE TOUCHED THE PIANO keys as Rowena and her father appeared at the door of the parlor.

Two weeks had gone by in a blur of preparations and dress shopping. Grace—who had started taking meals in her room, claiming she had a sore throat—was rarely seen. It was Bernadette and Lady Glenville who took Rowena around to the shops to buy her dress and ribbons. Rowena was grateful for their help and had allowed them to make most of the decisions for her.

She looked down the short aisle to find Christophe waiting stiffly next to the minister. When their eyes met, his shoulders relaxed.

Each step towards Christophe highlighted each step in her past that had led to this very day. Moving to Algeria. Her maid, Aurora. Saed's mansion. Saed giving her to an Englishman. The journey through the desert. Then the journey to England. Their meeting again at Cumberland House.

It seemed surreal, and yet it had all led Rowena to this moment. Her smile stretched further as Christophe's eyes darkened with emotion, his gaze fixed on hers as she approached. She became so lost in them that she almost forgot they were not alone.

Grace, who had come to attend the small ceremony under threat from her mother, snorted when she tripped the last few steps, the ugly sound pulling her out of her reverie. Someone else giggled, joining Grace, but Rowena refused to look behind her. Defiantly, she took her future husband's hand. It was stained with ink and not half as soft as it should have been for an English marquess, but the touch was intimately familiar.

The sermon started and came to an end without Rowena hearing a word. Mindlessly, she had repeated the words told to her, all the while looking helplessly into Christophe's eyes. When the minister declared them man and wife, both fear and excitement zipped through her. She was well and truly married. There was no turning back.

"The blushing bride!" Lord Daucer exclaimed, twirling her by her elbows before pulling her against him into a sloppy, loud kiss on the mouth.

Lord Glenville gave her the same treatment before her new husband seemed to understand what was happening. Both men laughed when Christophe pulled her to him and gave her a long, deep kiss, though it wasn't long before their laughter turned to loud howls.

"Enough! Married couples should not kiss so much. It's bad for them. It makes their guests cast up their champagne," Daucer shouted.

Emily, Claire, and Lady Candor were much more refined in their congratulations. Everything whirled about her; the guests, the footmen, the food and champagne. For a moment, Rowena could not take in any more detail than the blur of happiness.

"Congratulations, my dear," said Lady Curtshaw, grabbing Rowena's wrist firmly with her age-speckled hand. "I'm glad your father made this right choice for you. You seem pleased about it, my dear. Of that I am exceedingly glad."

"Th-thank you, Lady Curtshaw," Rowena stammered.

"Don't be so surprised that I'm happy for you. What is good for you is good for Grace, though she seems to be pouting at the moment. Perhaps she thought she would marry first. But that is no matter. She is still much younger than you. Better that we get you sorted sooner."

"Yes, Lady Curtshaw," Rowena answered, the pleasantness of the conversation wearing thin. "I'm sure Grace will have a much easier time now that I will not be in London."

"Will you go to Ravenwood? I live just about an hour away from there to the north. You must come and visit me next year. Of course, I will be in London through the season now. I cannot abide traveling so much in so little time, you know. You may visit me in the summer. I dislike London in the summer. The heat is terrible."

The old woman patted Rowena's hand gently and gave her a genuine smile before letting go. Surprise kept Rowena from saying much, though she managed to murmur her thanks. Christophe appeared again at her side before she had more time to ponder what else to say.

"It was a lovely, *quick* wedding, Rowena," Grace said, gliding into view just as Christophe slipped his arm around her waist.

"It was lovely and quick, just as I wished it to be," Christophe countered. "You must thank your cousin for giving me the opportunity to wed my lovely Rowena so soon. And she is now Lady Candor. Please be so good to spread the good news about London while we are away."

"Of course," Grace answered icily. "I do thank you for taking her away for a while, Lord Candor. Perhaps now I will not be linked to so much scandal."

With that, she turned briskly away, her skirts sweeping across the heels of anyone nearby.

"She's jealous," Christophe whispered, pulling Rowena in close until his breath tickled her ear. "By the way, you're stunning in that dress. What do you say we be on our way? It's almost a three-hour ride, love."

They took a turn together about the room to thank their guests and say goodbye. Bernadette managed to stand to kiss her, though her hands trembled and tears streamed down her cheeks. Lady Curtshaw demanded they both bend down to kiss her, which they did. Grace merely waved from the corner.

"Benti," Rowena's father said, pulling her against his chest for a hug. He seemed unable to quit smiling long enough to speak. "I just want you to be happy and safe."

Tears welled up in her eyes as her father pushed her away. "Yes, Baba."

"Don't cry," he whispered, wiping away her tears with his palms. "This is the best for you. I truly believe that."

"I know, Baba."

"Go, then, and be happy. And delight me with a grandchild before I die."

Rowena laughed. "You are not so old to speak of dying, Baba. You will see Elliot's grandchildren before you die. I'm certain of it."

Her father patted her cheeks with a smile, then pulled her in for another hug.

Christophe's family crowded the door as Rowena turned and entered the unknown world of being a wife. She and Christophe settled into the carriage amongst the loud cries of farewell that slowly faded away as the family drew back to the house. Rowena smiled into the dusk as the whirlwind of the last few hours finally went still. She was married.

She looked out the window but found that little had changed on the darkened London streets other than her station. She turned to her husband. Even in the darkness, she knew he was watching her, smiling at her.

"Are you happy, Rowena?" His voice was quiet, though it still rumbled deep into her chest.

"I believe I am," she replied. "Though the carriage is making me too sleepy to think."

"Come, love," Christophe whispered as he pulled her into his arms. "Sleep now."

A lingering kiss on her temple was the last thing she remembered before falling into a deep, exhausted sleep.

<hr />

Christophe knocked on the door leading from his dressing room to his wife's bedroom.

His wife. A strange, nervous sensation washed over him at that word.

He inhaled deeply to calm his heart. Now she was his. *His.* Tonight he would show her just how beautiful she was, just how much he cared for her.

At the first murmured sound, he eagerly pushed the door open and looked around in the semi-darkness. Rowena was standing at the fireplace in front of the low-burning embers. Despite the dying fire bringing little warmth to the room, a fever spiked in his bones. Tonight, just as the first night at Saed's house, she stood in a gown so fine he needed little imagination. The sheer pink fabric traced a low neckline, dipping between her small yet perfect breasts. From there her curves swelled around her, smoother and fuller than last year. Instead of an underfed youth, she now looked like a grown woman.

Christophe swallowed hard, finally bringing his gaze up to her face, where her lips twisted in a coy smile.

"You torture me purposefully," he murmured, stepping further into the room.

She looked back in nervous silence. Her breath escaped her lungs in ragged wisps as his fingers lightly traced the contours of her face. Determined to calm her, Christophe dipped his lips to her and began light kisses along her jawline. Her body quivered in response; tiny groans escaped her throat.

"Why didn't you come to me?" she asked quietly. "After I returned to London, why didn't you call on me?"

"*Enta habibi*," he said gently. "You told me I should ask your father for permission, and so I did. Did you not already say yes?"

Her shoulders softened, but she drew her head away from his.

"Rowena," he whispered, slowly running his hands along her arms, smiling as her body softened.

"You left me alone with Grace and my stepmother. You did not come to see me," she said, gasping as his teeth bit gently at her flesh.

"I came twice. Once your stepmother turned me away, and the second time it was the butler. Instead of trying again, I sent for your father and planned the wedding with him. I'm sorry if you thought I abandoned you."

"You came to see me?" she asked between gasps of pleasure as Christopher rolled his tongue over her neck.

He nodded into her shoulders before blowing cool air where he had licked her flesh. Her hips tucked themselves under his, her breasts pressed just under his own chest. Christophe kissed her slowly, savoring her. His fingers explored the rim of her negligee, dipping into it, drawing another gasp from her. The animal instincts within him demanded that he rip the delicate fabric off, but reason reminded him what tonight was. He must be gentle. Slow. As much as she was relinquishing her passion again, still something held her back. England had nipped away at her confidence with its gossip and lies and rejection.

He left the rim of her negligee to caress down her curves. A slight amount of pressure from his lips coaxed her mouth open... and then her passion was fully unleashed. She pulled his head against her earnestly, opening her mouth over and over. When her back hit the wall and his hands possessively clamped her thigh up to his hip, he could feel her smiling into his mouth.

"My lord, you have a way with walls," she said with a giggle.

"I can show you many ways to use one," he groaned against her lips, his fingers running in circles over her creamy flesh. "But not tonight."

Again, he claimed her mouth, pressing his tongue around hers. The fire, the heat, the urgency, the desire; all the rising and flowing through him almost convinced him to take her up against the wall. The image shot a bolt of lightning through him, but what stopped him was the overpowering desire to be more for her. There could be passion without overstepping the bounds of a wedding night. There would be time enough in their life to teach her all the places passion could lead them.

His fingers wove through her hair, making pins fall with a jingling sound to the floor. She ran her palms down his shoulders and pressed them against his chest. Holding on to him for support, she lifted her leg to wrap around the small of his back as his hands gathered her up from under her hips. Then her fingers nimbly pulled on the buttons of his shirt until she had it free enough to tug it over his head.

Christophe pulled his head back when her fingers slid over his chin and down over his neck, making their way slowly downward. It was stimulating to watch her eyes become hooded at seeing him standing semi-naked before her. How magnificent to know their marriage would be a match of desire and passion. She traced his chest, his shoulders, running light fingertips down to his abdomen, awakening each nerve in her path. The nerves might be awake, but his head was becoming dumb with the desire to fulfill a need long neglected. It wasn't until her fingers stroked underneath his trousers that his mind returned.

"Not so fast, my love," he murmured in a pained voice. His body groaned in protest, but his heart and mind knew that his beautiful wife deserved restraint.

Rowena lifted her hands behind his head, bringing her body closer until her bosom was pressed up against his chest.

"Stay all night with me tonight, Christophe," she begged. "Don't leave me as other husbands do their wives."

"Tonight, and every night," he whispered, bringing his lips to her neck.

Swiftly, he scooped her into his arms and brought her next to the bed. With one tug, the lace bows at her shoulders released the lace negligee to the floor.

Like a starving man, he ran his fingers madly through her hair until it flowed down her shoulders and back. He pulled her close against him and ran those same hands up and down her body until she trembled and moaned. She turned her head to allow him access to her neck, to which he gladly made love with his lips while his fingers lightly traced every part of her body.

<hr />

Christophe lay with Rowena in his arms for hours as she slept. It was not discomfort that kept him from falling asleep, but the desire to watch her. The adrenaline of having finally gotten what he wished for, that everything had worked out well enough, pumped through his veins. Perhaps more than wishing to watch her sleep, that was what kept him awake. He could not help but wonder when his luck would run out. Life was never so easy. Difficulties would surely arise from somewhere.

Soon though, even with the dim threat of problems in the distance, Christophe drifted in and out of light sleep.

Rowena shifted to hover over him, her shadow calling him back from the dreams that had almost enveloped him. When her fingers touched his face, it required all his willpower not to smile. He forced his breath to steady as a trail of fire lingered on his skin where her feathery fingers touched. His lungs contracted sharply when the air between them closed in as she leaned closer.

When her mouth pressed against his he moaned in appreciation. There was no use in pretending to slowly wake up. Instead, he grabbed her arms and pulled her down hard against his chest. The suddenness of the movement gave her no time to pull away. When her mouth opened to squeal he possessed it, his tongue delving in, his hand pressing against the back of her neck to bring her closer.

"It is still dark yet, Rowena," he whispered, pulling her away before a surge of desire convinced him to make love to her again.

"I'm sorry. I always wake up before the English sun," she said. "Now that I am your wife you must learn that about me."

"You may always wake me before the English sun," he growled, dipping his head between her breasts.

She placed one thigh on either side of him and straightened her spine. His body immediately reacted. No man could keep from responding to seeing a beautiful woman sitting over him, her long hair flowing down her shoulders.

"You are either deep in thought or back asleep," she teased, her fingers caressing his chest. With even the slightest movement of her hips, she tortured him.

Taking her gently by the shoulders, he switched their positions, her back now on the bed, him hovering above her. She laughed in surprise. For the first time, he noticed that the skin at her temples crinkled slightly when she laughed and how genuinely her eyes sparkled. The clear, merry sound still made his heart stand still. Such a strange reaction. It was just laughter. And yet the very idea of never hearing that laughter again in all his life made his breath hitch.

"You don't regret this, do you?" she asked, reaching up to touch his fingers.

"Never," he murmured. "Why do you even ask? Why don't you see your own worth?"

"I'm worth the firstborn son of Saed Labdouni. That is quite a lot," she said with a teasing smile, but Christophe did not smile back.

"You're worth far more to me than that," he told her.

They stayed in silence for a moment. Rowena's eyes drifted over the contours of his face as though contemplating a painting. She stared so deeply at him that he almost wished to turn away.

"What are you thinking of?" she whispered.

"I was thinking about you," he admitted. "There has been too much cruelty in your life, and I intend to erase it all."

"That is impossible," Rowena murmured. "Besides, for better or worse, it has made me who I am today, I suppose."

"What do you mean?"

"I was much like Grace and Lady Alice and all the other young girls in London as a young woman. You never would have looked twice at me, had I come to London for my coming out."

"Well, in my defense, I would not have been in London when you were there for your coming out. I was in Spain," Christophe said.

"Building your empire?" she asked with a smile.

Christophe flinched. "I spent my time building my business, but I also caroused more than I would like to admit. My cousin and I spent many years living the life many young men live. Perhaps I wouldn't have noticed you, had I been in London at your coming out, but that would not have been your fault. It would have been entirely mine."

"Back then I was little different from my stepsister. I thought only of myself, my desire to sing on stage, and my dresses. Once I realized my father would not allow me to sing, I would have spent years pouting about it and generally snubbing any man that came my way."

"I am not sure I believe you," Christophe said with a laugh, his fingers dancing along her warm skin, smiling as a shiver overtook her. When his fingers reached her feet, he took them in his hands to massage through the knots of skin the bamboo beating had left her with. Her body instantly relaxed as though drugged.

"That feels lovely," she sighed.

"I wish I could have saved you from knowing Fellahi. I found a woman in an alley once, raped by him. She died in my arms before I made it to the doctor's house."

Rowena touched her husband's cheek, her eyes full of compassion.

"Mohammed Fellahi was a cruel man, and he was well known for it. When I realized Madame Roussier had sold me to him, I thought about killing myself, but I had nothing to do it with. I couldn't run away either, not with my hands tied behind me. When they left me at Fellahi's residence, the first thing his slaves did was tie me to a post and whip me. It's the introduction every new slave has there. Rose came out afterward and covered my wounds in salve before putting me to work. There was no time to rest or recover in Fellahi's house."

Christophe picked up the other foot and kissed it before beginning to massage it. Rowena sighed with contentment.

"Fellahi was known around the city for the perverse things he did with women," Christophe began. Just saying the truth aloud caused his heart to squeeze in pain. It was too hard to imagine what atrocities his own wife may have endured. "How long were you there?" he asked.

"A little over a year, I believe," she answered. "I was there exactly one year before things became more... intense. He did not notice me until his concubines started to die. Rumors abounded that he was in debt and could not buy more. Fellahi started acting strangely. He was tense, and always seemed to be just around the corner, watching. One night, screams came from the wing where his remaining concubine lived. I woke and ran to Rose, but she refused to say anything and told me to go back to bed.

"In the morning, I found out the girl had died in childbirth. Fellahi was so angry. She was his favorite. He marched through the house, ordering me and three other female house slaves to move to the harem the next day. He came to inspect us and give us his personal vote of approval. The fact that he approved of Dariah, whose right ear had been sliced off by a whip some years before and who had only six teeth remaining, told me he was more desperate than he wished to acknowledge."

Rowena shivered. Christophe pressed her closer to him.

"That same day, a midwife examined us while he watched. When she confirmed I was a virgin he—he—" Rowena's voice broke.

"What happened?" Christophe asked quietly into her hair.

"He pushed through me and broke the barrier with his hand," she said finally. Christophe squeezed her tighter to stop the shaking in her arms. "When the blood rushed out of me, I remember falling to the floor and vomiting in the corner."

"He never took you to his bed?" he asked painfully.

Rowena shook her head.

"He was found dead in the gutter the next day. A cousin took over the house and sold all of us off—thankfully, he saw me only as a dirty laundry slave when he sold me to Saed, so I didn't go to his harem. He never found me interesting at all. He never looked at me, in fact. Not until you came. God truly must have been with me."

"God? You thank Him for what happened to you?"

Rowena pulled away just enough to peer at him in the dark.

CHAPTER TWENTY-SIX   329
329

"Yes. It took me a long time, but yes. I thank Him because He saved me through you. I thank Him because Fellahi died before taking me to bed. I thank Him because at Saed's house I met Selma. And I thank Him for bringing me back to you. Had I not been a slave, I never would have found you."

Christophe went still at her words. Even his lungs stopped working. He ran his fingers lightly over her scars. Moving her hair aside, he traced the marks on her back that would forever remind her of the past. He lowered his head to brush the scars with his lips, an overwhelming desire to protect her slowly overtaking him.

When she looked over her shoulder, Christophe's heart melted at her beauty. Her hair flowed down her back; her eyes were sharp, and her full mouth was crooked into a seductive smile.

"No man will ever hurt you again," he murmured in her ear.

Chapter Twenty-Seven

"WILL THERE BE A sensational story in the paper, do you think?" Rowena asked a day later as she glided into the dining room. Christophe was already there, having his breakfast.

It was the first day they were out of the bedroom, having spent the entire day before locked away from the world in the east wing of Ravenwood. Unfortunately, the world had not stopped, and Christophe now found himself with a small mountain of letters requiring his attention. He stood when his bride entered, unable to stop himself from smiling, though he was certain he looked like a fool.

Her words slowly penetrated through his mind which was still focused on business negotiations. Returning to the present, he quickly discarded the idea of telling her the truth, which was that he had paid the papers not to run the full story. They had instead run a small article telling of the small ceremony and placed it just one page before the political columns, where most gossips rarely looked.

"There will be just enough said to quiet the other rumors and gossips, I imagine. If I'm willing to marry you and bring you into society, people will realize there must not be much behind the other rumors."

Her napkin stopped midair for a second before fluttering down to her lap.

"I see." Her voice was cool, a far cry from the murmurs and whispers she had uttered just hours before in bed.

"Don't sound so disappointed," he laughed, leaning down to kiss her on the forehead. "Would you rather more scandal?"

Rowena murmured something unintelligible and looked away. He watched as she took a scone and set it on her plate, then looked at it as though it were foreign to her. With great effort, she buttered it and brought it to her mouth. Everything within Christophe wished to ask her what was wrong, but he did not. Perhaps understanding a woman was more about waiting. And if that was not the wise choice, he would soon find out.

"So, because of your generosity in marrying me, the rest of London will now accept me to their tables?" Rowena asked bitterly, obviously chewing the scone without tasting it.

This was the time to answer, he assumed, though he did so with caution. "Partly," he said. "Mostly, actually."

"Is it my fault that John pushed his way into my room? Why is it that I must succumb to the whims of society? Why must I marry because the rest of society believes it is the only way to repair my reputation in their eyes?"

His fork hit his plate before Christophe realized he dropped it. The clatter made Rowena jump in her chair. He was instantly sorry he had scared her, but only because it made her snap her mouth shut. Not that she could say anything to stop the bleeding her previous words had caused. The room was too hot for him, the chair too hard. A deep, cold weight lay upon his chest, pressing so hard he thought he might burst.

"You did not wish to marry me?"

To his further distress, she said no more. She didn't look at him, didn't go to him, didn't see how much she had hurt him. With a sigh, he struggled to push the hurt off himself as he strode quietly to the window.

"You are right to think that perhaps it is a solution too often arrived at for far too many things a woman might not be responsible for, but it is also true that in this society, and this day and age, it is something that will clean a woman's tarnished reputation the quickest," he said, enunciated each word.

"Tarnished? You are calling me damaged goods?" she demanded.

"You are not damaged at all in my eyes, but in the eyes of society, you are more than damaged. There was little that could have brought you back into society at all, in fact, other than marriage to a man with a title, excellent reputation, and strong family ties."

"How dare you!" she spat, rising from her chair.

"How dare I? How dare I speak the truth? Wake up to what is around you, Rowena! This is not the promised land. I have told you, you are not damaged in my eyes. I've seen you at your lowest point, Rowena, and still I wished to marry you."

"Well! Perhaps you deserve a prize, my lord, for marrying me despite my past and where I was for five years. Surely more credit is due you," Rowena mocked, anger radiating from her in waves.

"I simply wish to have you understand me, Rowena. I asked for your hand before John entered your room. Your past does not matter to me. All that matters to me is you and our future together," he said.

His wife's face drained of all its color. Within another instant, his disappointment transformed into a wave of compassion. Rowena's shoulders shook uncontrollably. If he could just take a moment and try to understand her anger, he was certain they could find a way through this. Perhaps she was disoriented. Suddenly living in another house, having been married just two days ago. Perhaps this happened with all wives the first days after the wedding.

He should ask his mother—although sharing the fact that his bride was unhappy did not sit well with him. No, he would have to figure this out himself.

"My lord, Lord Daucer is here," a footman announced. "He says to forgive him for coming but it is an emergency."

Rowena turned around with alarm, her eyes wide and red.

"What emergency? Is someone ill? Does he need help?" she asked, moving towards the door with haste.

"I will see to it," Christophe said.

Rowena drew back, her haste now controlled. She gave him a defiant curtsy, then went back to the table.

"If I need your assistance I will call you," Christophe said, trying to be gentle even as he realized that he had somehow made a very important mistake.

Rowena waved him off as though he were a pesky fly. He turned and stalked out, still unable to place why, but knowing he needed to be away from her. Whatever problem Daucer had would be a welcome breath of air compared to his wife claiming she had married him against her will.

Christophe cursed for the fiftieth time in an hour. All the bad luck he had anticipated was now here, dumped on his desk. And it was much worse than he could have ever imagined.

"The ship is destroyed?" he asked again, this time only receiving a slight nod from Daucer. "Where is Moore?"

"Working out the losses. He said he would come here by tomorrow."

"Wouldn't it be easier if I went back to London?"

"Wait at least until Moore sends his report," Daucer said, accepting the arrival of the tea tray with relish. He attacked it as though starving.

"I placed your trunk in the green room, sir," the footman said before leaving the two men alone.

Christophe regarded his friend with humor. "So, you are planning to stay here, at Ravenwood, during my honeymoon?"

Daucer's hand stopped halfway to his mouth as he contemplated the question. Within a few seconds, his hand found his mouth, shoving the pastry in.

"I suppose I could stay at the inn," he said dramatically. Christophe rolled his eyes. Before he could tell Daucer to go to the devil, the door suddenly burst open and Rowena entered in a flurry.

"You will do no such thing!" she exclaimed. Again, Christophe noticed how beautiful she was with her hair swept up, revealing small pearls in her earlobes, her cheeks flushed. Desire swirled in him.

Rowena glided forward with an enthusiastic greeting, embracing Daucer as though he were a long-lost friend. She then looked at Christophe before sitting down in the chair, her face devoid of any emotion at all. Christophe chose to stay standing.

"I was merely jesting," he said. "He will stay in the green room."

Daucer, drat the man, grinned at Rowena with triumph and gave her a wink.

"Well, then, it's settled."

"Perhaps," Daucer said. "But there is still one more thing."

Setting down the teacup, he rummaged around in his jacket pocket with furrowed brows.

"Ah, here it is," he exclaimed after sorting through a small pile of papers. "There is to be a special opera near St. Valentine's Day. I know your husband is not in the know about such things, so I procured a few tickets myself. I thought someone who sings like you must like the opera."

"Lord Daucer!" Rowena squealed.

To Christophe's surprise, she leaped from the chair and enveloped him in a hug. Daucer reared back in surprise, but quickly regained his bearings. He wrapped his own arms around Rowena and purposely lingered there for a moment.

Christophe couldn't seem to break away from staring at the two of them. His best friend winked and shrugged his shoulders, to which Christophe held back a sigh. Once his wife's arms were back where they belonged, Christophe found himself able to break the spell his body was under and move away.

"We can go back to London for the opera, can we not?" Rowena asked him.

"Of course," he said. "I'm glad you're so pleased with the invitation."

"Very pleased," Rowena said, her eyes sparkling as she snatched up the tickets.

Christophe rounded his desk and sat down to start on the paperwork that Daucer had delivered earlier, pleasantly surprised when warm, buttery lips pressed into his cheek. She was halfway out of the room before he lifted his head.

A low whistle sounded as the door closed behind her. The sound came from the direction of his bothersome friend.

"It won't be easy working down here with her upstairs, will it?" he teased unmercifully.

"Shut up, Daucer. Isn't there some work for you to be doing?"

"I'm off to see about the new school you've ordered built," he answered, adjusting his coat and cravat. "Seems my mathematical skills are helpful somewhere. If only I could tell my father. Of course, he would probably die of shock if he found me working for a living. Such a terribly middle-class thing to do."

With one more smirk thrown in Christophe's direction, Daucer swaggered to the door and left.

"I'll be back in time for supper, but dining alone will not harm me so long as my loneliness can be drowned in a bottle of imported whiskey," he called out over his shoulder.

Christophe chuckled as he sat down to work.

Still, while it seemed that their argument had dissipated with the opera invitations, Christophe was not convinced Rowena was past her anger. Other men often spoke about their wives acting so charmingly with other people before turning into a—well, those words weren't really for his wife. He couldn't think of her in that way. She was simply disoriented. The wedding had come quickly, more than she had possibly realized it would come, and now she was a lady, a marchioness. She had responsibilities today that she hadn't had just two days before. Perhaps it was this pressure that had caused her to change so quickly from one humor to the next.

Time, that was what she needed. Which was convenient, as the news of the ship going down would give him enough work to fill the coming days. His honeymoon days.

But he couldn't think of that when some, if not all, of his men might be under the sea right now. He needed information as soon as possible to tell the families who were affected. But there was nothing to do but the work itself. The sooner he could get through ten hours of work, the sooner he could rest in his wife's arms upstairs.

If she would have him.

Chapter Twenty-Eight

LONDON, FEBRUARY, 1833

GRACE WATCHED JOHN ENTER the terrace with tense, narrowed eyes, his features lit by the dozens of lanterns illuminating the area. She hadn't seen him since the weekend with Lord and Lady Glenville, when he had run off and hidden like a coward. That had been almost three weeks ago. She seethed with anger again, her grip becoming too intense for the delicate wine glass it held.

"My dear cousin, you look as though you may break that," John said, sauntering up to her. He pried the glass from her fingers.

She made the mistake of looking up at him and found that he was looking straight into her eyes. Slowly, he slid his tongue around the rim of her glass. Just as slowly, he tipped it up for the last sip.

"Your cravat is crooked," Grace snapped, fanning herself with the useless feather fan that matched her dress. It did, at least, allow her to hide her blush from John.

Through the glass windows, Grace saw Lady Carson slipping into the parlor. She took a glass of wine from the footman before finding a table of men to flirt with.

"How can you entertain such a woman in your bed? Don't you see that she is probably entertaining all of those men in hers?" Grace asked maliciously. She cautiously looked through the corners of her eyes to see if John had followed her gaze.

Instead, he shrugged. Shrugged! The rumors were true, then. John always found some rich, bored lady to pay some of his debts while in London—but Lady Carson was so very old. Thirty, at least. And he didn't even seem to mind that she was flirting with other men in full view of him! It was enough to make Grace want to stomp both feet. Though she wouldn't. She refused to act like anything other than a lady.

Being a lady was very difficult when everything and everyone were perfectly detestable. First Rowena snagged a marquess whom she did not deserve. Now John was back to sleeping with rich widows and ignoring Grace. If Rowena had just done her duty, John would be unhappily wed right now, waiting impatiently for Grace. Then they would have entertained each other for the rest of their days and been quite happy. Perhaps she could even sneak in one of John's babies – a good reason to marry a fair-haired man instead of dark-haired. Such as Lord Trillman... his wife had been dead for some time now. He was older, but Grace was starting to wonder if that wasn't such a bad idea.

"You look ravishing tonight, Lady Grace," John whispered. "Care to take a walk through the gardens?"

"Are you mad?" she bit out. "They are poorly lit, and Lord Trillman is watching. Would you have me ruin my reputation and be a spinster?"

John chuckled, setting her nerves on edge.

"But then I could marry you," he murmured.

A thrill ran through her, up and down, before settling in her middle. Instinctively her body swayed forward, but instead of being greeted by his scent of smoke and musky male, she smelled vanilla and oranges. Lady Carson's smell. Grace always found the mixture nauseating, but tonight she was afraid she might not be able to control herself from truly vomiting. Perhaps she had drunk too much wine. Or hadn't eaten enough. Whatever it was, the thrill in her was gone, replaced by disgust, jealousy, and a strong sense of loss.

"Haven't you had enough for one evening?" she asked coldly, taking a step away from him. "Or are you so beastly that you need to bed several women in one day?"

John drew back, straightening to his full height, over a head taller than her. It was a movement that always frightened her, though she tried never to let him know.

"Are you jealous, Lady Grace, or simply in a despicable mood tonight? Remember, I am a free man, willing and able to do anything I wish. I need not have your permission to bed whomever I please, as many times as I please."

In spite of herself, a shiver of pleasure swept over Grace. She tried to think what it meant for John to take her as many times as he pleased, but the few images she could muster made her skin prick. She quickly pushed them aside. She had more important matters to set her eyes on.

"Who is that strange-looking man with Lord Carson and Lord Trillman? An Army captain recently back from India, perhaps? He's so very dark for an Englishman. He stands out like a black rose."

From the terrace, it was easy to gaze subtly through the French doors to the mansion, to the people roaming about inside. John swept his eyes over the crowd before settling on Lord Carson and his dark guest.

"Come, Grace. I see some people are dancing."

"You wish to dance with me?" she asked feebly, wishing she could slap her own face for showing such weakness with John.

But instead of laughing, John sighed. A deep, longing sigh that caused her heart to tear just a little.

"I will dance one dance with you, then let you be. Perhaps my dancing with you will catch Lord Trillman's eye," he murmured. "And if not, then he is a fool."

They entered together, walking at the safe distance that was required of cousins by marriage only. When they passed Lord Carson and Lord Trillman, Grace gave a nod and subtle smile but did not let her gaze linger too long. It would be better to keep Lord Trillman thinking she was a blushing, innocent debutante. That was what everyone said a man wanted, after all.

"Come, my Lady Grace. Let us dance."

Grace straightened her spine, her chin high as she curtsied with the other ladies in line. She knew her perfect posture made her look quite regal. When the music started, John twirled her about before switching partners. Back around again they went before meeting at the head of the line. She flashed her best smile to John, but when their hands met again her heart ripped in two. Tears dared to threaten her eyes, though she refused to let them fall. It wouldn't do to let her heart go to John. Or rather, it wouldn't do to admit it to herself. He was not titled, and she was determined to marry a titled man.

They pranced down the line again, then faced each other. Clap. Turn. Clap. She caught Lord Trillman's eye. He gazed boldly back.

The skin at the back of her neck prickled and Grace looked back to John. He also watched her intently.

The last note held out longer as they curtsied and bowed. Grace pasted a fresh, beautiful smile on her face as she straightened up. It was exactly the kind of smile that most men looked for when choosing their wife. Or their next wife, in Lord Trillman's case.

"My, Lady Grace, but you do dance beautifully," Lady Carson gushed, approaching her and John as they left the dance floor. "Please, come and meet a dear friend of mine, Lord Trillman. Lord Trillman, this is Lady Grace."

"I have had the pleasure of meeting her once before, my lady. And the memory lingers," Lord Trillman said, murmuring the last phrase into her hand as he kissed it. A strange thrill shot through Grace as his mustache tickled her palm. "Will you give me the honor of the next dance, Lady Grace?"

Panic, as well as excitement, ran through her.

"I would be honored, my lord," Grace murmured, allowing a small blush to tinge her cheeks.

"I will have her back to you soon," Lord Trillman said with all decorum to John, who seemed to be struggling to keep his face neutral.

"Do not worry so much about Mr. Howe. Lady Kent wishes to speak to him," Lady Carson said, dragging John away.

The night was going well. Better than Rowena had imagined it would. She had traveled to London with Griffin just yesterday to attend the London reopening of William Tell. Christophe had met her at Candor House, sweeping her into the great bedroom almost before she could even greet him. Since the day that Daucer had shown up at Ravenwood, Christophe had spent his time working out the problems of losing the ships and looking for the lost sailors. He had spent two weeks traveling to each man's family to personally deliver their pay, leaving Rowena alone at Ravenwood. While she had wished to go with him, the task was so solemn she had understood when he had said no. Her days passed by slowly. And now, for the first time in over a month, they found themselves alone together.

Rowena looked at her husband, who sat across from her in the large carriage as they rumbled down the streets. His face was gaunt from overworking, giving him the air of a much older man.

"I never told you how sorry I was for my behavior," she whispered, her courage gained with the darkness covering her blushes.

Christophe sat up straighter, his eyes glowing in the low lamplight. "What behavior?"

Rowena laughed nervously. "Was there more than one day? I should apologize for all of them, then."

Christophe said nothing in return, and neither did Rowena. She tried to think of something witty to say but she was too emotional for humor. She settled for being grateful.

"Thank you for taking me to the opera. I know that you are very busy."

"I am never too busy for you, Rowena," Christophe blurted. He quickly moved to sit next to her, holding her gloved hands in his. "I missed you, but I was not certain if you missed me. Everything has been moving so swiftly and I left you alone and—"

Rowena leaned in to kiss his cheek.

"We are new to this," she said. "At least I am. And I assume you have never been married?"

She meant it as a joke, but the strange look in his eyes made her wish she had said nothing. Christophe leaned away from her, his actions jerky and unnatural.

"You have another wife somewhere?" she asked, hoping it sounded teasing.

"No," he breathed out. "But I thought you knew that I was almost married once."

"Yes, I knew, Christophe. Lady Grace told me all about how she would heal your heart."

He squeezed her hand in the dark.

"I wish we could go home," he said, his voice low and sultry.

"Lady Sutherland invited us for dinner, and we told Claire we would come," Rowena reminded him, gulping when his hot lips found the place beneath her ear. "But—we could make a detour."

His deep chuckle vibrated through her.

"Or I could teach you something right here," he whispered, leaning forward to reach under her skirts.

The shudders running through Rowena kept her from saying anything intelligible in response.

The dining room at the Sutherland house was brighter than a summer's day in Spain. Innumerable candles and gas lamps were placed about the room, banishing all shadows to the outdoors. Christophe stood at one side, only half listening to Mr. Herring discussing the problem he was having with his factory workers forming a union. Christophe caught Rowena's eye at the other side of the room and gave her a wink. Her color was still heightened from their misdoings in the carriage, making her the most beautiful woman in the room.

Rowena stood next to Daucer, who said that brought the discipline of Claire's fan against his chest. How he wished he was over there, and not here listening about unions and miners; but of course, he had placed himself here purposefully.

The memory of the carriage brought forth the anxiety and guilt that had surfaced when she had teased him about being married. He was not, but that didn't mean she didn't deserve to know about his past.

Rowena deserved to hear the truth. She deserved to know about what he had done, what kind of man he had been. Or was, though he had spent the last three years trying to make up for his mistakes, trying to change himself for the better. He *had* changed, though he wasn't certain it was all for the better.

Mr. Herring droned on, heedless of Christophe's need to escape. Shifting restlessly from one foot to another brought attention to him from the others in his circle.

"You look rather pale, Candor. You shouldn't work so much. You should have taken a month's honeymoon to Paris or Istanbul."

"Madrid would get some color back into you," Mr. Bathom added, patting Christophe hard on the back.

"I'm fine, I assure you both," Christophe said blandly. "Please, excuse me."

He drifted about the room with his glass of port. More than anywhere else he wished to be at Rowena's side, but he couldn't go until the echo of Dolores's laughter departed from him. And the sight of her swollen belly bouncing with her laughter. The usual swirl of anger and failure engulfed him at the memory of the last day he had seen Dolores. The day she had told him he would never get to claim his child.

Caught up in his misery, Christophe didn't notice the small crowd gathering in the corner across the room until Daucer motioned him over.

"The problem is," Mrs. Pemmel was saying, a thin-lipped woman with a rather angular nose that made her sound as though she always had a cold, "the culture in the colonies is different. Forcing my brother to free all of his slaves right now and pay them as workers would ruin him. As it is, he houses them, feeds them, teaches them of God and in return asks that they work. They have every Sunday off and are brought up in much better circumstances than those of Africa, of that I'm certain."

"He would not be ruined, Mrs. Pemmel. They would have to adjust their way of living, certainly, but they would figure it out. The time of slavery is over for humanity. Those of us who are business owners, landowners and investors here in England manage to pay our workers and still make a wage. Your brother and the rest would simply have to do the same as we do," Daucer argued. "Fortunately for him, though not for his slaves, he has seven years of indentured servanthood to force upon them. Since he is so noble, I assume that he will take responsibility for the young ones amongst his slaves who will be set free immediately?"

The atmosphere tingled. Most people looked away, probably wishing to leave but not wanting to bring attention to themselves. A bold few looked to Mrs. Pemmel for her answer. Christophe rubbed his warm hands against his thighs, countering the desire to spell out every single argument against the seven years the slaves were forced to give to their masters through the Slavery Abolition Act, but he was not as charismatic as his father had been when speaking nor as on point as Daucer. He would be better off keeping his opinions to himself until the tightly coiled energy in his chest unraveled a bit. It would not do to raise his voice at another guest – ignorant half-wit though she may be.

He looked at Rowena and found her pale, her lips open slightly to breathe better. He placed his hand lightly against the small of her back, but she was too tense to lean into his comfort.

"Another problem with freeing so many of them all at once is that they aren't really civilized, and we cannot be sure what they will do. I'm certain they have no ability to think for themselves, not having the same capacity that we do for information."

This was said by a Mr. Abcott who, unluckily for England, aspired to become a judge. Rowena's lips trembled, her eyes cast down so low one might think she feeling faint. Just as Christophe hurried towards her to escort her away, Rowena's wine glass slipped to the floor and shattered, creating a startled silence around her. Everyone turned, and she faced them with wide, watery eyes.

"In my years away I had the misfortune of seeing slavery firsthand," she said, her voice strong and clear. "I can assure you that it is not a kind institution. *Any* institution based on believing that one kind of human is less than another—nay, less than even the horses or cattle that one owns—is a morally flawed institution that should be condemned. I have seen how those who find it morally correct to own another human 'house' and 'feed' them. Let me assure you that that is not all they do. Those who call themselves masters also beat them, kick them, ridicule them, and even force themselves upon them. The masters make their slaves feel less than human by forcing them to do what they would never do otherwise. They force men to beat other men; they force women to be concubines; they force children to leave their parents. I know of one man who loved another slave, only to be the one who had to give her away for the enjoyment of his master's friends."

Shudders ran through the crowd. Most of the ladies blushed and looked away. Rowena had no mercy, continuing before anyone could stop her.

"I was treated in ways you cannot imagine. My feet were beaten until there was little skin left on them, but still I was forced to work. My pleas for medical attention went unheeded, as did everyone else's. I was overworked and underfed and yet I know that I did not suffer half of what some did. I saw women and men beaten to death in front of me, children taken away or beaten in front of their parents. Slaves of all colors worked alongside me; all bled red blood, all were beaten down, left with only slivers of memories from their past life. Each man and woman went to sleep with demons dancing upon any hope that tried to infiltrate their minds."

Several women now looked green, and most of the men were swallowing hard in embarrassment. The room was quiet, uncomfortable, tense. The only one who dared to meet Rowena's eyes now was Mrs. Pemmel, who glared at Rowena as though she had no right to be there amongst them.

"But the people you were—associated with were not Christians," Mrs. Pemmel protested. "Our people in the colonies are. Surely you can see a difference?"

Rowena would not be put away in the corner, although Mrs. Pemmel turned away from her, clearly thinking the discussion was over.

"I do not believe that any man who believes it right to own another can truly call himself a Christian. Those who own slaves do so because they do not see them as equal humans. Slavery is an ancient practice, but it does not give us in modern times any right to continue it. People should not be seen as machines. Nor are they animals to do your hard labor while you sit around getting fat and rich. Do you know how the men under the Barbary Pirates suffered? I will give you one example. They were forced to stay chained together at the bottom of a ship for weeks and months at a time, most of them left there until they died. Or perhaps you prefer to hear how a slave market works? At a slave market, men and women are stripped of all their clothing and displayed for all to see. To say their dignity is also stripped away is an understatement. Women can be forced to prove they are virgins in front of men at the slave market before being taken as an addition to their harems. Men are shackled and beaten into submission. Both men and women are often drugged with opium to make sure they do not fight what their future holds. Once they are bought, and the opium is taken away, the withdrawal from the drug sometimes kills them. In North Africa there are many men of all races at these markets, as well as men of all different religions, including those who claim to be Christians. They are the ones who take their slaves to the New World."

Mrs. Pemmel finally looked ready to be sick. Christophe watched her turn pale before speaking again, though this time in a much quieter voice. "My brother is a good man."

No one dared to answer the woman. Where many women or men would have offered a rebuke or scoff at such words, Rowena offered silence. She gazed openly at Mrs. Pemmel, never faltering. The older woman's cheeks flushed red as she broke away from the crowd.

Slowly, everyone found an excuse to go to some other part of the room. Even Rowena found a reason to leave, Claire leading her by the arm.

"She really is quite something, Cinch," murmured Daucer.

Christophe watched his wife greet Lady Merville, seated on the other side of the room. He couldn't agree more.

Chapter Twenty-Nine

ROWENA DESCENDED FROM THE unmarked carriage onto the mud-caked street. The strange smell of poverty struck her immediately: rotting food, dirty streets, horse manure, and poor drainage. She told the driver to wait down the street, and he gladly complied. Once left alone, Rowena gulped in a breath and straightened her shoulders. Surely someone had seen her arrive by now, so it was too late to turn back. So many weeks had passed since she had visited. It was possible that Cordy and the other women would think she had forgotten them.

Her reasons for visiting were more selfish than honorable. After weeks of doing little more than learning how to run a household, Rowena felt a strong urge to be useful. On Kipper Street, there was always a need to fill, whether it be with Cordy and her family or with the neighbors. There was always a baby to hold, a child to help, or a woman to counsel. Being there gave Rowena a sense of purpose, a reason to feel good about herself.

But standing alone in the streets, dread started to creep over her. The street was too quiet. Neither Billy nor any other children came out. There was no greeting hollered from open windows nor crying babies. Two curtains were pulled back, then dropped again almost immediately without a word being said.

Usually Cordy's front door would burst open before she reached it but today it stayed shut, forcing Rowena to knock.

"Come in an' shut the door, missus. I mean, yer ladyship. I don't want none of them neighbors to start thinkin' I's too high and mighty. Folks 'round here already have problems wit us being colored darker than they is."

"They aren't making your life difficult, are they, Cordy?" Rowena asked, following her friend to the small living area, where she began to fold baby clothes while rocking the basket with her foot. Seeing the baby's peaceful, sleeping face melted Rowena's heart. Forgetting everything else, she dropped to the floor to gaze closer at the sleeping angel.

"Seems 'bout time you git yourself a babe, Lady Candor," Cordy muttered.

"What do you mean?"

Cordy sighed and set the clothes down. "I mean, I heard some rumors 'bout you. They sure do travel fast. That's what happens when you git up there in them high places. Best you be gittin' to the countryside 'n occupy your time wit a babe of your own."

"What rumors, Cordy?" Rowena asked, feigning ignorance.

"That you's the same as me; a runaway slave. But you didn't serve the fields like I did, did ya?" she asked. "No, yer skin's too pale."

"My skin is naturally pale, Cordy," Rowena answered quietly. "That doesn't make any difference in North Africa. First, I was a house slave, then I worked outdoors washing clothes. Female slaves don't work in the fields at Saed's house."

"Umph. Is it true you ran away from your papa? They all say you ran to a no-good man who sold you away."

"I was hit on the head, drugged and taken away from the port where a ship was set to take me back to England," Rowena admitted. "I don't want to talk about it."

Cordy stood and walked softly into the small kitchen. Rowena watched her friend pull the curtains back slightly with one finger before letting them drop again with a sigh.

"I'll serve ya tea one last time, yer ladyship, but after today youse can't come back here. It ain't good for us."

"But Cordy!" Rowena contested, passion building within her at the threat of being cut off. "I did nothing wrong. Just as you and Bill did nothing wrong. I don't see why you must cut me out of your life. Is this because of who I married? He's a good man."

"Ain't got nothin' to do wit' your new name, though maybe 'tis too fancy for someone like me to entertain, and it probably ain't safe for youse to come into dis neighborhood no more. But all dat aside, 'tis got nothin' to do wit you or me, and everythin' to do wit that little girl over there. 'Tis bad enough she got me as her mama, a former slave wit' no education. But she can't have no woman comin' round visitin' her with a suspicious reputation. Folks too quick to connect one to 'nother. Thay'll be judgin' her for her skin nuff as 'tis. She can't have no other reason for folks to think unkindly of her."

Rowena quietly accepted the cup of tea from her friend, the truth of her words hitting her hard.

"Dat girl there, she's born free, Miss Brayemore—I mean, yer ladyship—and I can't allow no one to git in her way for a good life. No one. Not even the woman who helped bring her into dis world."

The two women drank their tea in cold, sad silence, both of them holding back their tears. Cordy was right. With much regret, Rowena sipped the last of her tea and stood. She took another long look at the baby girl, who now stared back at her with wide, dark eyes.

"Sorry, yer ladyship," Cordy said as she held the door open. "I's sorry to lose you as a friend."

Rowena held her friend's cheek in her gloved hand for a moment, watching her dark brown eyes filling with tears.

"Best of luck, Cordy," she said in a strangled whisper, before the door shut with a firm click and Rowena turned to the eerily quiet street.

Christophe watched his wife slowly descend from the carriage. Her face told him everything before she even walked up to the house. Disappointment, anxiety, and abandonment surrounded her; the emotions weighed heavily on her shoulders. When she looked up towards the door, Christophe noticed the gleam on her wet cheeks. His heart crumbled as she rolled back her shoulders and lifted her head before entering her own house.

"Hello, love," Christophe greeted her silent entry. "What happened?"

"What do you mean?" Rowena asked, pasting her face with a fake smile.

Christophe smiled sadly as he pushed the stray curls away from her face. "You cannot fool me, *enta habibi*. I know when you are troubled. Since the sun is shining brightly outside, I can only assume that tears have made your cheeks wet."

He drew her against his chest, hoping she would throw herself into his arm and cry. He could hold her. He could soothe her. It would bring him the utmost pleasure if she would trust him with her troubles. But although Rowena leaned against him for a moment, she soon tried to pull away, never letting one tear drop. With a deep inhalation, she looked up at him with a weak smile.

"Come. Let's have tea upstairs. You look tired."

Rowena allowed him to guide her slowly up the stairs. Once in her room, Christophe dismissed Griffin, then set about loosening his wife's day dress and stays. She still said nothing as he pulled off her boots and stockings and sat her on the velvet settee. It wasn't until the tea tray arrived and Christophe handed her a cup of tea that Rowena finally spoke.

"It's very bad, isn't it? The rumors are not going away."

"Yes," Christophe said, knowing he couldn't keep the truth from her for long. "Lady Kent—known to you as Madame Roussier—has managed to amplify the rumors, and a man from Melilla. One of my servants, apparently, though I never met him. He is speaking of the marks on your back that he claims his sister saw."

He watched her pour tea, letting his fingers linger on hers when he took the teacup from her.

"Even knowing this, you allowed me to go out to see Cordy."

"Was there any stopping you?" he asked, his teasing producing a small smile from her. "If you prefer to stay indoors, then I will not force you outside, but I will also not force you to stay indoors if you wish to go out. You are free to visit your friends. I will not keep you from them, though I will insist from now on that Brody go with you. His punch is like solid steel."

Rowena tried to smile, but the attempt soon faded. "I wish you had prevented me. She does not wish me to visit her."

"But she has told you this and so you know it. It is different from assuming it yourself," Christophe said gently. "Why does she not wish to see you?"

"For the baby. She is a free person with two former slaves as parents. That background will not be easy for her. Cordy told me that she will need to have contact only with people who have an untarnished reputation," Rowena said, pausing to sigh in ecstasy at the way his fingers massaged away the aches from her feet. "So, they are saying that I ran away with a man?"

"Yes. Among other things," Christophe drawled, looking through the window instead of at his wife. "Some say Vitelli was your lover."

"What else?"

"They say that you ran away with a man who tired of you. In their version, Madame Roussier took you in until you became too much to bear with your constant running away. Then they say you were sold as a slave to be someone's wife, but that is where the rumors get messy. The timelines and such never seem to line up. Not that it matters much. Many are saying you tricked Countess Merville into bringing you here, though she is standing up for you."

"I must write to Countess Merville," Rowena murmured. News might reach even all the way to Melilla and where she was.

"I visited with the newspapers this morning and did my best to convince them to stop printing the story. I'm working on a scheme to convince the Roussier girls to stop talking about this nonsense, but they have caused a lot of damage already."

Rowena sighed, her shoulders sagging marginally. She still did not cry. Her resolve was just as strong as before.

"Cordy is right then," she said in a strong voice. "I should not be around her or her daughter. Not if I am going to be painted as a whore."

This time, when Christophe leaned forward to catch his wife by the waist and bring her to his lap, she did not struggle. To his surprise, she buried her face in his neck and sighed with weariness.

"You are not a whore," he said forcefully. "You are my wife, and you are worth more than any of these people put together."

"I could be a detriment to your business and your family. What if Emily is shunned from balls and events because of me?"

"My sister is much more likely to wish someone to the devil if that person spoke, or even thought, unkindly of you. You are her sister by marriage now. She is not one to be swayed by gossip."

"But it is the truth, Christophe. I cannot battle against the truth. The story the countess made up for me is not believed, which means I am not a very good storyteller, I suppose," Rowena said, a smile spreading across her face despite the serious predicament that she faced. "That, then, is good for you, is it not? That I am not good at telling lies?"

Unexpected laughter bubbled from his throat at her question as he kissed her lightly. They pressed into each other, smile against smile, their lips lingering until laughter turned into passion. It did not take long for that passion to churn up a deep desire to speak of more tender things, things said only between lovers. Christophe opened his mouth wide to cover hers, but Rowena pulled away with a sigh. Another indication that women were not beings willing to replace their thoughts with sex, which was unfortunate.

Or perhaps they were the shrewder, since after sex the problem would still be there.

Christophe put her down on the couch, then paced to the fireplace and back. She leaned against the velveteen back, her right arm thrown across her eyes to shield them from the sun, her lips pressed together pensively.

"It is only partly true, enta habibi. This rumor claims you ran away with a lover instead of being forced into slavery by a discontented maid. It claims you fooled your parents at the docks of Algiers to escape with your lover, and when he left you on the streets, you went begging to your father's friends to take you in," he said, kneeling before her. He kissed the creases that appeared between Rowena's eyebrows.

"I am not the only one with rumors about me."

"Oh?"

"Grace sent me a missive saying she saw you with Lady Carson at a ball last week."

Christophe pulled back as Rowena sat up straighter with a smile.

"You look like the cat that got the cream, my dear," he said with a laugh. "Yes, it is true that Lady Carson approached me at dinner last week."

"What did she want?"

Christophe grinned mischievously. "She wanted to let me know that if things didn't work out with you, she is now out of mourning."

"Oh? She believes she would be a better Lady Candor?"

"Without doubt," Christophe said with a sardonic chuckle.

He watched with amusement as his wife's eyes narrowed. It was nice to see her jealous; to know he was not the only envious fool in their marriage.

"Do you not think she would make me a good marchioness?" he teased innocently.

Rowena's eyes darkened, and her lips thinned. For a moment, he wondered if he had crossed a line. But instead of getting angry as he was afraid she might, Rowena suddenly relaxed and got up to walk towards him, her hips swaying invitingly against her skirts.

"No," she said in a low, sultry voice. "I do not think she would be perfect. Not for you."

Ah, and so *this* was how to distract a woman. Christophe smiled at the revelation. Rowena smiled at him too, before leaning in to kiss him slowly. She placed both hands on his shoulders before sitting on his lap, facing him. The position was more intimate than any he had ever experienced clothed, sending a delicious shockwave of desire through his body.

"And why is that?" he asked, trying to stay patient. His fingers itched to caress her sides, but his curiosity was piqued. What else would she do?

"She doesn't know how to sing to camels," Rowena said with a smile.

Roaring with laughter, Christophe placed his hand on each side of her hips and pulled them against his. Rowena yelped, but did not protest when Christophe claimed her open mouth with his.

"When will you sing for me?" he said in a low voice before nipping her ear, producing another shriek from her. Christophe couldn't help feeling triumphant in winning a change of topic as well as mood from his wife.

"Shall I invite Mr. Vitelli to come so I can sing a duet for you?" she teased, laughing at his disapproving growl.

"I do not wish for Mr. Vitelli to be anywhere near you when you give me my own private concert. In just your laces."

The primal noise that rose from her throat was enough to convince Christophe to pick her up and move to the bed, where he spent hours showing her that it mattered not what anyone else thought of her when he adored her already.

Once convinced, Rowena rewarded him by singing for him with nothing but the afternoon sunlight covering her.

Chapter Thirty

JAMES AMBLED UP THE stairs to Lord Candor's offices. The cool day outside did nothing to eradicate the smell of rotting fish from the building. His stomach rolled, but that was the least of his troubles. Each step up was harder to take than the last, as though his body resisted the idea of moving forward at all.

James stopped to lean against the wall before continuing. With shaking hands, he loosened his cravat to relieve his wheezing. His mood matched the dark stairway that led to Candor's offices. Why the man holed himself up at the docks, James could not understand.

A door creaked open above him, pushing James to climb the last few steps quickly. He had no desire for Candor or his secretary to find him leaning against the wall like a feeble old man. In less than a minute he was at the door, pounding on it with his cane, all the while trying to calm his breath.

"Good heavens, one could do without the dark stairs or that awful smell. When do you plan to move your offices to a district more befitting of your station?" James demanded as he finally burst into the office, delighting in the game of intimidating his son-in-law.

When Candor turned, he did not seem at all intimidated, his gaze distracted. Two large, glistening windows framed the marquess, opening the room to a magnificent view of large ships in the harbor. One very large vessel, in particular, stood out. Its lacquered masts gleamed in the sunlight, the snow-white sails strapped picturesquely to them. James joined his son-in-law at the window and openly admired the view. He had never found admiration to be a sign of weakness, as did many men in business. He preferred to conduct himself openly and honestly. Not being in any way invested in ships or ship races helped him show his feelings with no dent in his pride.

"That is a beautiful ship you have there, Candor. I heard she came in second. Do you plan to send her to race again?"

"No. Not for a while," he said matter-of-factly, turning to face his father-in-law with a look so serene that James felt a pang of jealousy. He would give half his fortune to have serenity again. "I am handing it over to the West Africa Squadron. There is a need for faster ships for them to catch slavers, and I'm interested in helping that endeavor however I can."

"You do so from the generosity of your heart?" James asked with raised brows.

Candor grimaced in a half-smile that disappeared with a shrug. "I would make more money if the clipper was racing, but lending it to the Royal Navy will not prove to be a bad business deal."

"No," James mulled. "And it gets you contacts that have rank, does it not?"

Candor laughed as he extended his hand to invite James to sit in the leather chairs. A tall young man entered the room with a tray of tea and a crystal brandy decanter. "We in business always welcome contacts. Don't you agree?"

"We do," James answered as he sank into the chair, surprised to find it luxuriously comfortable. He had expected an office that matched the neighborhood, but one could be fooled into thinking they were on Hyde Street. "You have done well for yourself, Candor."

Christophe waved away his secretary, opting to serve them personally. James raised no objections to the brandy, as there was no risk of overindulging with his son-in-law.

"I have done as well for myself as I believe you had done at my age. Not being afraid of hard work is the only secret. But now with the title comes quite a bit more responsibility and expense, unfortunately. I will need to stay in trade to restore Ravenwood and help Cookston, which is floundering from my brother's neglect."

"I heard something of the like. I respect your decision to keep with your business ventures. You are good at it, and every man should do what he is good at. Do you still own the paper factory?"

"No, I sold it. An American bought it. Do you still own the olive oil business in Spain?"

A bark of laughter escaped James. "How did you find out about that one? I thought I covered my tracks well."

Candor grinned and shrugged his broad shoulders. Strength rippled through him, the one thing that James resented losing with age.

"I have quite a few contacts in Spain," was all he said.

"Ah. And was there something else you wanted to discuss about my business there?"

Candor raised his brows at James' quick perception before launching into his proposition of merging his orange and spice importations with James' olive oil and chocolate importations. The two men discussed the venture for well over two hours.

A scuffling sound at the door stopped both men from starting their parting words. Both stood and slowly turned towards the noise.

"I told you that Lord Candor is busy." Candor's secretary had pitched his voice loudly, as though wanting his employer to hear him.

"And I told you, lad, that Lord Candor is certainly not too busy for this. Believe me, he will want to know. But don't take it from me. You could read about it in the paper."

There was a noncommittal grunt behind the door before the latch opened and the secretary burst into the room.

"My lord," Mr. Moore said, but before he could continue, a large man barreled in from behind, knocking Mr. Moore to the side. John stood in the middle of the room, tugging his jacket down and smoothing out any wrinkles the small scuffle might have caused.

"My lord," he said, his tone mocking. "Your secretary seems to think you are too busy for me. Ah, I see. You are with my uncle. That explains it."

"John," James said in a warning tone.

"I'm sorry, Uncle. Would you like to treat me again like a naughty schoolboy?" John asked, then directed a steely gaze at Christophe. "You can stop glaring at me like that. The family asked me to come here from Manchester because Rowena needed a husband. Since there was an agreement years ago and I was looking for a wife, some in the family thought it only natural for us to carry out the contract. No one said anything about you being interested. I do find it fascinating how you never bothered to court her. Secret courtships are never looked upon favorably, you know. Don't breathe so violently, Candor. I didn't force anything upon her that night. All I wanted was straight answers from her about where our relationship was heading."

Christophe snorted, his hands flexing and clenching.

"How can you even think of coming here after how you treated Rowena?" James asked. "Do you not see that Candor is willing to beat you to a pulp?"

John looked Lord Candor up and down with a smile. He leaned easily against the mantel and laughed like he had a secret. "You know, Candor, I believe it's time for you to drop the pretense."

"Pardon me, Howe?"

"As I said before, I came down from Manchester thinking everyone was on board for our marriage. I went to Rowena's room for a chat because no one would let me get near her—"

"Because she thought you would try to ruin her."

"Stop interrupting, Candor. I wanted to talk with Rowena and come to an agreement," John said before turning to James. "Did you ever wonder why Candor was out roaming the halls and just happened to hear us talking?"

"I didn't hear you. I went to the same window you used. When I saw you in her room, I went to teach you a lesson on respecting a lady."

"Tsk, tsk. You should be thanking me, Candor, instead of lashing out at me. I never told anyone that Rowena was in your room all evening. I never told anyone that the reason you found me in her room was because you had the very same idea, though probably yours was not as chaste as mine."

James' head moved like the ball in a tennis match. He almost dreaded Candor's response. He had wondered about the man's timing once, though since the wedding, it had been easy to forgive him. James stood with finality, gesturing to the two younger men to stay quiet.

"Alright. Let's move on. It seems both of you were rather lax in your propriety with my daughter, but she is married now."

"To the better man," seethed Candor, his fists still balled at his sides.

John gave a humble, mocking bow. He rose with a grin. "I agree. You will make her much happier than I. For me, she was simply a wife to keep me from being too lonely and a way to buy my factory in its entirety. An option I discovered you have taken away from me."

The wolfish smile on Candor's lips was so amusing that James couldn't help smiling himself. While it might seem childish to some, he understood exactly what Candor had been thinking and preparing for: exactly this moment. He knew John would not go away quietly.

"What are you here for, John?"

"It's interesting to find both of you here. In the same place," John drawled, circling the room until he came to the brandy decanter. "I needed to see both of you."

"About what?" Candor asked, his voice calm, his interest in John's matter barely perceivable.

"Lady Kent has... wooed me to act on her daughter's behalf. It was easy to get her to confess a great deal by pretending to be interested in her daughters. The woman seems to think it impossible not to worship the ground of those two ninnies," John said. "Really, Candor, calm down. Your temper seems uncontrollable. If I were actually willing to help the despicable Lady Kent, do you really think I would be here?"

"It is very possible that it was your plan all along," Candor said, his eyes so narrow James wondered how he saw through them.

"I have to defend my nephew on that point, Candor. He is neither deceitful nor disloyal to the family. If he is here, it is because he has chosen to help us."

Candor made a barely perceptible nod, and John went on.

"Lady Kent is quite put out about you demanding she leaves London. I have been told she is willing to do whatever it takes to stay here, even if it puts Lord Kent in the poorhouse. Though I am certain that is a slight exaggeration, her determination is not. She has a few more tricks up her sleeve," John said, lowering his overly muscular body gracefully onto the other chair. "Did you know she wooed a servant of yours in Melilla to come here?"

Candor whistled in surprise. "Yes, I was told in a letter that both Juan and his sister left the house one morning without a word. She told you that?"

"Boasted about it. The sister says she saw Rowena's scars. Both of them claim she lived in the same bedroom as you. Those rumors will run tomorrow in the paper."

"I think we can fight against the papers," Candor said with a grin.

"Mark my word, it will run," John said.

James stood to pace the back of the room.

"There is something else she claims to have knowledge about, too," John said, locking eyes with James, whose blood drained from his face. "The letters."

"What letters?" demanded Candor.

James knew it was his place to explain, but he found himself drained of energy. He waved to John, who in turn explained concisely what Bernadette had done.

Candor became very pale and very quiet. "We need to burn those letters."

"I have looked for them all over in Bernadette's room. Since I could not find them, I assume she has already burned them," James asked.

"Lady Kent believes them to be intact," John said. "She told me she employed two people to look for them."

"Thieves?" asked James.

John shrugged. "Perhaps. Perhaps not. Have you hired any new servants?"

James' body froze, his limbs feeling numb. His wife had hired a new scullery maid and a new footman.

"Brayemore, does Rowena know?" Candor asked.

"I can't believe so. Her behavior towards Bernadette is quite loving. How could she treat her as such if she knew?"

"She can't find out about the letters," Candor said. "It would hurt her too much."

James nodded. "I thought the same."

"It might surprise you that I did as well," John said, rising again from his chair to pace about the room. "We need to keep them out of the papers. Out of the gossip columns."

James nodded sharply. "To do that we will start with a small bit of bribery. Did you get the railway shares as well as the art?"

"Yes. I sent a notification to his solicitor today that I have the art he was looking for. The price I'm willing to sell it to him at might cause him a small apoplexy, but I put the price high to shock him into seeking me out. Let us hope he is easier to persuade than his wife, with the offer to reduce the sum liberally if he finds a way to take his stepdaughters elsewhere."

"Yes. Let us hope," James said.

"In the meantime, I will start packing Rowena to go to the countryside."

"She hasn't done anything wrong. Why should she have to go back to the countryside?"

"She should go to the country because she will be freer to go about her business, Uncle. London will be stifling, and she will not enjoy being the center of attention."

"Yes, perhaps," James said.

For a few seconds, all three men were silent. It was John who tired of the silence first. James had an inkling of what his nephew wanted even before he spoke.

"Well, did I make it worth your time?"

"Come along, John," James said briskly, ushering him towards the door. "Bernadette will be relieved we have somewhat made up our differences. Let's go back to Tinja House and dine together. Perhaps we can all go out to the opera later."

Christophe watched his father-in-law and Howe enter the Brayemore carriage from the window opposite the one that faced the harbor. The meeting had drained him of every ounce of energy.

"My lord," Moore said from the doorway.

Christophe turned in surprise at the severity in Moore's voice. "What is it?"

"A strange letter has arrived for you. It is rather weather-beaten and seems to have taken a long time to get here, my lord. I thought you would wish to see it immediately."

Moore handed over a yellowed envelope. Christophe turned it over to reveal a seal he hadn't seen in years. About four years, to be exact. The sight of it caused his blood to turn cold.

"Is something the matter, my lord?"

"No," Christophe answered sharply, ignorant of the surprised look on Moore's face. "That is all for today. You may go home."

"My lord, it is only now two o'clock. We were to dictate some letters."

"Go home!" Christophe said impatiently, appalled at his own lack of control, but unwilling to change his mind. He could not open the letter until Moore left. Whatever it contained, it could not be good news. "I will see you tomorrow."

Moore obeyed immediately, quietly leaving the main office to retrieve his things from his own small room. Only three silent minutes passed before the main door clicked closed and Moore's footsteps echoed down the stairs and out the door.

With shaking hands, Christophe turned his attention back to the envelope and, with a deep breath, broke Don Carlos' seal.

Chapter Thirty-One

ROWENA BIT HER LIP and tried to wiggle about in her corset behind a tree. She knew it wasn't proper behavior, which rubbed Claire the wrong way, but she couldn't help it. It was a warm March day, and she still had yet to become accustomed to wearing such things as garters and corsets and to have yards and yards of fabric on top of it all. Algeria was much warmer than England, but she couldn't remember being so uncomfortable there.

"The problem with that dress is the collar, not the corset," Claire said as Rowena rejoined her.

"You're right," Rowena groaned, trying to pull the lace off her skin for a moment. "Though I still dislike the corset."

"What does Cinch say about these dresses you wear?"

"He hasn't said anything."

"Well, then, I will say it. You look like a spinster in those high-necked dresses with all the lace about."

"Do spinsters always wear high-necked dresses? What a shame they cannot dress as they please because they are not someone's wife."

"Perhaps they choose not to be someone's wife and do not wish for the attention."

Rowena raised her brows, but Claire shrugged with a grin.

"Then I will keep the lace and high necks, for I do not want attention either."

"No!" Claire cried out, laughing. "That is not what I mean. We are going shopping."

Rowena sobered quickly. Surely Claire had read about her scars in the paper, but perhaps she didn't believe it. It would be hard for a lady in London to believe. A sudden desire to see Christophe rose within her. He had been so busy the last few days they had barely seen each other.

"I will go shopping with you," Rowena conceded.

"And buy what I pick for you?"

Rowena laughed. "That depends on what you choose. Shall we go this way?" she asked, turning to the right and bumping straight into Claire, who had decided to go left. The two of them locked eyes and fell into a fit of giggles.

Laughing too hard to stand up straight, Rowena's large hat tipped to the side, bringing her with it. Claire rushed to the rescue, snorting her laughter as she tried to straighten the hat and tuck back in the curls. So occupied were they that they didn't hear the four horses walking up the path.

When a horse neighed nearby, Rowena looked up to find herself looking straight at Madame Roussier—or rather, Lady Kent. Her blood turned to ice, ending her laughter immediately. Claire too looked up and stopped laughing, though a smile still lingered.

"Good morning, Lady Arlington, Mrs. Blight, Lady Wilson, and to you, madam," Claire said, her voice light with a hint of teasing.

"Lady Candor," Lady Arlington responded coolly, focusing her eyes directly on Claire while saying nothing to Rowena, the current Lady Candor in all rights.

Rowena curtsied curtly to the women, pronouncing each of their names quickly. Then she looked at Lady Kent. The urge to sneer at her, kick her, scream and pull her down was so strong she began to pant. But then she remembered what she had realized while alone at Ravenwood: she must let go of her hate before it consumed her.

Rallying against her intense feelings, she smiled politely, surprised to find her chest no longer restricted.

"I made it clear in my letter to you that you would not be welcomed in our circles if you socialized with less-than-acceptable people, Lady Candor," Lady Arlington said crisply.

Claire blinked at Lady Arlington as though she had said something entirely incomprehensible.

"At least Lady Falcon knows better than to join you," Mrs. Blight said, her lips so pursed it seemed they might be sucked permanently into her face.

"Lady Falcon is meeting us later at Foster's for ice cream," Claire said. "Tomorrow we will all attend the opera together."

Lady Kent snorted in disdain as she took a long drag on her cigarette. An English lady would never smoke in public, but a French woman married to a German duke could do as she pleased and still be accepted everywhere. The continentals were eccentric by nature.

"How is it, Lady Arlington, that a woman like that may roam freely while some threaten me to leave the city with my daughters?" Lady Kent asked, glaring at Rowena.

"The opera is for ladies," Lady Wilson said snidely, her pert nose stuck in the air as though she couldn't stand the thought of even looking towards Rowena. "I will make certain the opera house does not allow her to attend tomorrow night."

Something hit Rowena's hat as the others chimed in with their own sinister promises. She kept her hands at her side, not wanting to bring attention to herself by taking off her hat. With so many voices swirling around her, it was difficult to stay calm—especially when Lady Kent continued to stare at her with an evil smile.

"Claire," Rowena said, before stopping short. A strange smell filled the air, and her hat was beginning to feel hot.

"Rowena! Your hat! It's on fire!" Claire screamed.

All eyes landed on Rowena, but not one of them moved a muscle. Her fingers burned the instant she reached towards her hat. Claire helplessly threw her wrap onto the flames, but it instantly caught fire, causing squeals from the other ladies as well as their horses. While Claire screamed for help, Rowena struggled with the ribbon below her chin, but her fingers pulsed painfully. The heat on her head intensified by the second, sending her into a frenzy of nerves. To her vexation, the ribbon tied itself into a tight knot.

Sweltering waves of heat encased her head. When Claire slapped her hands away from the ribbons, Rowena dropped them with an anxious cry. In one brutal yank, Claire ripped the fiery hat from her head and threw it to the ground. The two of them stared at it in shock as the blackened fur melted into its middle, vaguely aware of horses bolting away. The cooling relief the breeze brought her caught Rowena's attention.

Tentatively, she touched her hair, a large part of the bun immediately falling off. Violent shivers of shock rolled through her body, but she refused to cry. Claire pulled Rowena's shawl over her head as they walked to the exit.

"Lady Candor, Lady Candor," a man called behind them. "Is something wrong? Rowena, what happened?"

Rowena looked to her left to find John standing on the sidewalk, his large frame blocking the afternoon sunlight.

"There's been a mishap," Claire started to say, before she cursed under her breath. "We didn't bring the carriage."

"No, we walked," Rowena said automatically, her nerves now numb, her stomach a block of stone. "There was a fire. My hat caught fire."

"What? Come. The family carriage is right over there, Rowena. Come with me. I'll escort you back to Candor House."

Claire stood back, measuring John. When Rowena moved to follow him, Claire held onto her arm tighter.

"I wish to get home, and he is the way to do that," she told Claire, who finally released her grip. "He is my cousin, and you are with me."

Her father must have forgiven John. She looked at John, who smiled back, perhaps almost apologetically. Surely, he was still the man who would do anything to get his way. She couldn't imagine he had changed too much. And yet it was as though a strange, darker edge to his character was gone.

John held out his hand to help her in. No strings attached, it seemed. With reluctance and some misgivings, Rowena gave him her hand and climbed into the carriage. Merited or not, it seemed she must also forgive this man. Forgiveness haunted her daily now, surprising her almost every time. Though, as it was, Rowena knew she could forgive John much sooner than Lady Kent.

"Would you like to go to Candor House or to Tinja House, Rowena?" John asked, his voice gentle and honest.

"Candor House," she replied immediately. Then she smiled back at him, hoping he understood their tentative truce.

John called through the window to the driver. Relief flooded over her. She was a mere ten-minute ride away from safety. She only hoped Christophe might come home early enough to hold her and soak up her tears with his shirt.

* * *

Three days had gone by since reading the letter from Don Carlos. Three horrible days during which Christophe had avoided his wife, speaking to her only when needed, all the while wishing he could throw himself into her arms and tell her everything. More than anything he wished for her forgiveness, but he couldn't receive that without telling her the story in its entirety. Telling her that could very well lead to him losing her altogether, and he wasn't ready for that.

Not wanting to lose his wife's love had brought him to his mother, though now all he seemed able to do was pace the floor as his mother continued watching him patiently. Down to his shirtsleeves, with his cravat and waistcoat long tossed aside, Christophe was still constrained. He knew the pressure in his chest, the anxiety and fear, would not leave him until he unloaded the entire truth to someone. He knew this, and yet it refused it come out.

Instead of a tonic, Christophe tossed back his second glass of whiskey and paced back towards his mother again. She, always calm, sipped her glass of wine and waited for him to speak.

Finally he began, the words coming out in halting sentences but soon moving into a free-flowing confession. He started with Catherine, then admitted his reason for going to Spain, moving into his freefall from honor while beginning his business there until he finally came to Dolores. The true reason he was here today, in front of his mother.

"Dolores was already married, but I started an affair with her anyway," he admitted.

His mother waited silently, with no judgment in her eyes. There was nothing but patience, and calm.

"I did it to spite her husband. It was a juvenile, shameful thing to do, but he tricked me out of some business that should have been mine and I... took it personally. After I seduced her, I told Dolores about my scheme, expecting her to leave angrily. She laughed and said she knew. As you may guess, there was little love between her and her husband, who tended to flaunt his affairs publicly. She was willing to use me to get back at him, and I foolishly thought I was above consequences. The longer the affair went on the more reckless she and I became. One night, while inebriated, I decided to publicly humiliate him. Even though he had tried to destroy my business ventures, they had, in fact, been thriving. His business was failing. I had the success and the man's wife, and I wanted everyone to know it."

His mother said nothing, though a weak flash of disapproval flittered across her face. And yet he had not confessed the worst.

"Don Pablo confronted me in the middle of a dinner one night, accusing me of corrupting his wife. He told the other men there that if I was willing to shame their women, my business dealings could not be trusted either. Then he called me to a duel."

"A duel?" his mother asked in horror. "What did you do?"

"I went," he admitted. "I met him at dawn, finally sober. At first, I boasted to all that I had no fear of the man. I was reckless with my life in Spain, as if it didn't matter at all. Albert and I both were. I will spare you the details, but suffice it to say that there were a few nights in which pistols or swords were involved, and we began to think it was rather funny."

"So you went because you really didn't think you would die? Were you willing to shoot him?"

"I went determined to shoot past him and show him for being the fool that he actually was. I was not about to spend time in a Spanish prison for dueling."

"You are still alive, so I can only assume that you killed Don Pablo."

"I shot past him," Christophe answered. "Quite a bit past, actually, but his gun backfired, which killed him instantly. Some accused me of having touched his gun, though most knew where I had been all night. Still, the rumors started to slowly hurt my business. A few weeks later, Dolores approached me and told me she was pregnant. In a sort of panic, I fled to North Africa. It was there, in the desert, that I realized what a fool I had been. It seems idiotic that it took me so very long to see how I was destroying everyone around me. I concluded my business in Africa, then I went back to Spain to convince Dolores to marry me. I had thought little of the child when I fled Spain, but as the business in Africa came to an end, I dreamed of them each night. By the time I arrived at Dolores' door, thoughts of my child consumed me. I wanted Dolores to marry me. So we could be a family."

"Did you love her?"

"No!" he admitted, plowing his fingers through his hair. "No, I didn't love her, but I was willing to marry her. She did not love me, either, though that does not excuse my behavior." Christophe paused before rising to pace again.

"What did she say to your proposal?"

"She laughed."

Christophe could still see Dolores under the large tree with her black hair piled loosely on her head, her belly swollen with child. Her lips had spread in an intelligent, joyous grin before bursting into her sensual, feminine giggle. She had been a rather breathtaking woman.

"She told me I was ridiculous. She said that she didn't wish to marry a man who didn't love her. She told me she would never marry me—that she would go to her grave telling everyone the child was Don Pablo's and that I was his killer."

The sun was waning now. Shadows darkened the parlor with no gaslights or candles to lighten the room. The darkness fit his mood. He would rather his mother not see so much of his face anymore, anyway.

"Despite her commanding me to stay away from her for the rest of eternity, I called on her when it was time for the child's birth. Her father tried to have me hauled away, but he wrongly assumed I wouldn't fight back. The child she was about to give birth to was my flesh and blood, and I was not going to allow anyone to keep me away. After boxing with a few of the footmen, I was left alone. For hours, all I thought of was holding the baby."

His heart was pounding so violently in his chest that he could barely breathe. To calm himself, he sank into a chair. Though his heartbeat stilled, his mind did not. He could still see the details of that day as clearly as though he was reliving them again.

"I could hear her screams," he said. "I was so nervous; no matter how much I knocked no one let me in. Then, like the calm in a storm, everything became quiet. The servants that were bustling about filtered away, then the footmen also scattered. I waited for the cries of the baby, but there was only silence.

"When I entered the house, I knew immediately that Dolores was dead. The air was as somber as a tomb. I ran about the house looking for her and came across the room where she lay. The stench of blood was everywhere. Her father came into the room weeping. When I tried to speak to him, he struck me, shouting that I had killed his daughter. When I asked for my babe, he said the child had found the same fate as the mother."

The nerves in his legs tingled from staying in one place for too long. He jumped up to pace again.

"Albert died a few days later. I was too deep in my despair to keep him from destroying himself," he whispered in a strangled voice. "When I came back it was with the deaths of four people on my conscience."

His mother grabbed his arm and pulled him down to the sofa close to her, forcing him to rest his head on her shoulders, but he could not relax into her arms. He did not deserve to. Even as she ran her fingers through his hair and his gasps for breath calmed, the tension within him refused to ebb away.

"You were young," she crooned. "People, especially men, do foolish things when they are young. But you came through. You offered to marry Dolores. And I know you are always true to your word. It was not your fault she died in childbirth. Many women do not survive it."

"I should have been by her side."

"Most men are not by even their wife's side when they give birth, Cinch. There was nothing you could have done," she replied, taking in a deep breath. "And now it seems that the babe truly is alive?"

Christophe nodded. "It's almost too much to hope for, but the letter says she is. A girl."

"So she is, what? Four years old?"

He nodded again against her shoulder. "She will be four in September."

"And she is coming here?"

"I must go and fetch her. Then we will come back here."

"You will claim her as your own?"

He noted that there was no hostility still in his mother's voice. "Yes, she will be given my name."

"Good," she said, and his heart started beating again. "I do not see how I could condemn you for anything, Cinch. It seems to me that while perhaps you were reckless, you were willing to do the right thing as you are now. What will you tell Rowena?"

Christophe released himself from his mother's arms to again pace the floor. Thinking about Rowena brought on waves of heat through his body. "I do not think I should tell her. Not yet."

"Truly?"

Christophe shrugged. If it turned out to be true, he might skin Don Carlos alive for keeping it a secret for almost three years – if the old man wasn't actually dead.

"I will say I am going for a business trip and send her to Ravenwood until I return."

"I think you should tell her before you go, Cinch. Anything could happen before then. If there is any possibility of her finding out from the gossips—"

"There is no one else who knows, Mother. And what if the child is not alive? I will cause her undue worry over the situation.

The fewer people that know, the better. If the child is alive and comes back with me, Rowena and I will face the gossips together."

"You think she will accept the child?"

Without hesitation, Christophe nodded. "I know she will."

She sighed softly before rising from the settee to cup her son's face in her hands. "I will not say a word, Cinch. I will respect your wishes. Go, fetch the child and come home."

"Thank you, Mother," he said, kissing her palms.

"What is the child's name? Did the letter mention it?"

"Her name is Eleadora. It means 'gift of the sun'."

"Eleadora," she repeated, letting it sink in. "What a pretty name."

Chapter Thirty-Two

CANDOR HOUSE WAS DARK and quiet upon his return, but Christophe barely noticed. He took the stairs two at a time, calling for his valet to join him in his rooms.

"I am leaving tomorrow for Spain. Pack lightly, though I will need enough clothes for two weeks," Christophe commanded his valet. "Send this missive to Lord Daucer, then come back for another to give to Mr. Moore."

"Going somewhere?" a man's voice asked from the hall.

Christophe spun around so quickly he almost lost his balance.

"Howe," he muttered under his breath. Claire stepping out from behind John Howe filled him instantly with worry. "Where's Rowena?" he asked, running to his wife's door and wrenching it open.

Rowena lay on the couch, curled up under several blankets. Her body shivered and jerked involuntarily in her sleep, the movements almost sending her to the floor.

"Is she ill?" he asked, gently running down her cheeks to soothe her sleep. A strand of hair fell across her face. When he ran his fingers through her locks, he found the ends after only a few inches.

"The doctor gave her a sedative to help her sleep. He says she won't wake until the morning," Claire told him, standing right behind him.

"What happened?" Christophe demanded, his voice raspy with rage and confusion. "What happened to her hair?"

"She's all right, Candor," Howe said.

"Why are you here, Howe? Why are you in my house, standing in my wife's room?"

"Come out so we can talk, Cinch," Claire whispered, and Christophe reluctantly complied.

Claire told him about the events of the afternoon in a whisper, her eyes darting to Rowena's room often. Listening to the story, Christophe's anger rose to previously unknown proportions.

"I will take care of this," he growled. "Tomorrow, I want you to take her to Ravenwood."

Claire looked at him in surprise. "Where will you be?"

"I'm leaving for Spain in the morning."

"Spain? She needs you."

"Take her with you," Howe suggested.

"I cannot take her. The business is not for women. Please, Claire, take her to Ravenwood and stay with her until I return. Howe and I will take care of this business with Lady Kent tonight."

Claire quite obviously did not agree, but she did not argue more. She left his room quietly, her disappointment showing in her posture. After sending Howe out, Christophe went to find his wife again. She still slept, though fitfully, looking so much more like the thin, fragile Fatia than his brave Rowena.

He stared at her for a long moment, whispering promises that he hoped he wouldn't regret, wishing he could push away all of his other responsibilities and lie down next to her. He wished he could hold her until the morning and have her wake in his arms, knowing she was safe. The truth was that she would wake alone, and the hurt she would feel would be enormous.

But he had to leave on the morning ship. Don Pablo had arranged even that. The will said that if Christophe did not claim the child within two months, they would send her to an undisclosed convent. He was still uncertain that the entire thing was not a set-up to lure him back to Spain and kill him, but Christophe could not take the risk. If his child truly was alive and waiting for him, then he must go. Too much time had already passed, and the next boat would be next week. A week would give him enough time to clean things up with Rowena and to make certain that Lord Kent understood he needed to control his wife, but it might make it too late for him to find his daughter.

A jolt of adrenaline woke him up as he entered his rooms. With rapid efficiency, Christophe checked his trunks, then dressed to make a visit to Lord Kent.

"Are you ready?" came a quiet, low voice from the doorway.

Christophe donned his hat with a quick jerk of his head.

"On we go then," Howe answered, leading the way to the door.

As he passed his wife's room, Christophe hoped to God she would forgive him for leaving her in this state and accept him once more when he returned.

John sipped his coffee slowly. He hadn't spent an entire night awake in years.

386	STEPPING ACROSS THE DESERT

Morning now dawned. Candor, who had just slipped away
again half an hour before, had done so with darkened circles under
his eyes but otherwise seemed no worse for wear. John, though,
felt like a team of horses had ridden over him. Evidently, if he was
serious about working and earning at least as much money as the
marquess, he would have to get used to the idea of not sleeping
much.

The idea did not sit well at first, but as he sipped his coffee and
looked around the richly furnished dining room that smelled of
new curtains and new upholstery, he decided he was willing to
exchange money for sleep. In any case, he was not willing to fall
back to the thin line that separated the higher middle class from the
lower.

The front door of Candor House opened. Low voices floated
through the partially closed parlor door, one sounding curt and
disapproving. John picked up the teapot and helped himself to
steady his nerves before facing his uncle. After the impromptu
meeting at Candor's office, John had assumed his uncle would
warm up to him, but regaining his love was proving to be more
difficult than he had thought.

To John's surprise, which he hid by downing his tea in one gulp,
a tall, thin man with onyx hair and suspicious eyes entered. Mr.
Moore, Candor's secretary. Come to babysit him, he supposed.

"Good morning," Mr. Moore greeted him, his low voice still
resonating with the same degree of disapproval he had on the first
day John insisted on entering Candor's office. "Here is all the
paperwork for you to present to Lord Kent. Your uncle, Lord
Brayemore, will accompany you."

"Do you think he is enough to watch me? Wouldn't you rather
come along?" John stretched his long legs out and flexed his

shoulders. He could crush this little Mr. Moore in less than two minutes.

"I am needed at the docks. We have two shipments coming in today," Mr. Moore said, his black eyes gleaming as he looked straight back at John. Strangely enough, the man did not seem in the least impressed by John's size. "Here is something for you, sir. Lord Candor had me draw it up. He is trusting you will do as you discussed with him last night, I presume."

John stood to take the papers just as his uncle graced them with his presence. After a short exchange, Mr. Moore left, claiming he had more work to attend to, which John doubted. He merely wished to be away, looking as though he were more important than a secretary truly was.

"What is that?" James asked after reviewing what they were to give to Lord Kent.

"The title to the metal factory," John said flatly, squinting to read it over again in case his eyesight was failing. "Candor bought it out from under me and is now giving it back."

"With the assumption that you come through today, mind you," James said, pouring himself a cup of tea.

"Why does anyone think I will not come through? I always come through when given a task. I dislike taking orders from the likes of Candor, but for what they did to Rowena yesterday I will do anything."

John decided to stay standing while his uncle had a piece of toast, reassuring him that Rowena was still sleeping and probably would be until late that morning.

"At which point, hopefully, we will be able to tell her that Lord and Lady Kent are booking their travel to the continent."

John noticed tears gathering in his uncle's eyes but said nothing. He rang for the footman and pretended to look over the factory documents again in order to give his uncle a moment to gather his composure.

"It's amazing what Candor had at the ready," John mused as his uncle finally stood to his feet. "Do you think he knew what kind of woman he was marrying?"

Silence answered him. John looked up to find James staring straight ahead, as though figuring out a puzzle suspended midair. When he caught John's eye, James moved forward again, a great exhalation leaving his lungs.

"I am not sure any man ever truly knows who they are marrying, John. And that is the best advice I can give you."

Chapter Thirty-Three

COOKSTON, MARCH, 1833

"WE WERE JUST WONDERING amongst ourselves whether you would return to London in time to go to the ball at Lord and Lady Wellington's," Mrs. Paxton was saying to Rowena. They were both in the garden of Lady Gailes, a neighbor Claire had insisted they could not refuse when the invitation had come for tea. She had been out of her confinement two months now, but did not find it in herself to attend the festivities of the London season that year. She found it much more to her liking to invite people to her garden, where she would serve them tea on pastel-colored plates.

Rowena smiled at Mrs. Paxton to keep from striking her in the face. Or perhaps dumping her tea on her head. Had she known Lady Gailes and Mrs. Paxton were friends, she never would have agreed to attend this small luncheon.

"We are uncertain as to when we will go back. Rowena adores Ravenwood and Cookston," Claire said.

"I would prefer to go to a ball with my husband. Perhaps if his business brings him back in time we will go," Rowena answered, immediately regretting referencing Christophe.

"Where is Lord Candor?" asked Lady Gailes' elderly aunt, leaning in with intense curiosity.

"Spain," Rowena answered loudly enough for her to hear. "On business."

"Lady Carson came back from Spain just two days ago. She said she had a marvelous time, though I can't imagine how. Spain alone must be a bore," Mrs. Paxton said. "Though perhaps she wasn't as alone as I thought."

Lady Hedgerow came closer, taking a deep interest in the little yellow cakes as she spoke.

"Are you speaking of Lord Candor? I was wondering when you were going to join him in London, Rowena. If you are leaving in the next week, we could travel together. When my husband wrote to tell me that Lord Candor was back, I immediately traveled this way, in case you wished to join me. I do not see why you should not. Especially since you are not yet of the condition to go into confinement."

Every pair of eyes traveled to Rowena's stomach for a moment. The unwanted attention caused a flush of heat to roll over her. No, she was not yet of any condition. If that was not humiliating enough, finding out from Lady Hedgerow, who claimed to be her friend now that Lady Kent was considered 'quite irrational', that her husband was in England brought a threatening lump to her throat. She needed time to process this tidbit of information, but Mrs. Paxton was giddy with the controversial news and could not let it rest. Rowena tried to catch Claire's eye, but she was looking straight at Mrs. Paxton, her lips pressed tightly together.

"We were speaking of Lady Carson's return to London from Spain," Mrs. Paxton said, barely able to contain her glee.

"Lady Carson? Oh, yes, she came to London about the same time as Lord Candor, I believe," Lady Hedgerow answered, oblivious to the pain she was causing Rowena.

"On the same boat?" shouted Lady Gailes' aunt, who seemed to have awoken with the gossip.

"Heavens, no!" said Lady Hedgerow after swallowing her third cake. "Lord Candor owns his own ship, does he not, Lady Candor? And Lady Carson only travels in the most luxurious of ships. At least, that is what I have heard. I do not know the woman personally."

Breathing was becoming difficult with each sentence said. No one seemed to notice Rowena's distress except for Claire, who handed her a plate of small cakes. She focused hard and took a tiny bite.

"Do you think Lady Carson is searching for another husband?" asked Mrs. Paxton suddenly, watching Rowena intensely.

"In my day, a woman did not go on the hunt for a husband so soon after losing one, even if she didn't find him attractive or love him. Even if she despised him! One followed the rules of society and waited," said Lady Gailes' aunt.

"I do not believe Lady Carson needs to get married again," Lady Hedgerow added. "She is financially secure and could easily live as a merry widow."

"But what about love and companionship?" asked young Lady Gailes innocently.

The older ladies turned towards her at such lightning speed that Rowena flinched. It was common knowledge that Lady Gailes had a loving match, something that caused others to be either jealous or skeptical of her.

"My dear, not all of us are able to find our love match. Why, look at Lady Candor!" said Lady Tollmister, the wife of a fearsome naval officer who had recently been knighted. Despite her husband's achievements, she held on to her title, being the daughter of an earl.

Both Rowena and Claire both looked up, but it was immediately clear it was Claire Lady Tollmister spoke of. Provocation gleamed in her eyes. Claire met her gaze willingly.

"Russell and I were a noble match," Claire said, meeting the woman's gaze steadily.

"Yes, a match meant for breeding, though there is no heir," Lady Tollmister said snidely.

Rowena's sister-in-law stiffened. It was all Rowena needed to be on her feet, her eyes blazing. With great detail, she envisioned pulling the lady down and pummeling her until she apologized. She had always slunk away from the violence that erupted frequently in the baignoires, but among the nasty women of London, she seemed to have developed a taste for it. At least in her head.

Before Rowena could move forward, Claire placed a hand on her arm.

"Thank you for offering to fill my plate, dear Rowena," she said sweetly, her eyes telling her to calm down immediately.

"Ah, well. Men are carnal creatures, always on the lookout for another beautiful woman. Even those who marry for love sometimes stray for a beautiful face or bosom," Lady Tollmister was saying with a tittering laugh, joined in by Lady Gailes' aunt and Mrs. Paxton. Young Lady Gailes didn't find humor in the comment at all. Her brows knitted together, her lips pursed into a thin line.

"The most we can hope for, as proper wives, is that a husband returns to our beds once the affair is over, for an affair or two is bound to happen with men," Lady Tollmister continued, encouraged by the roars of laughter from Mrs. Paxton. For the sake of young Lady Gailes, Rowena wished she might refute the harsh words, but she couldn't be certain her voice wouldn't reveal her desperation. She was no one to speak of a happy marriage. Already she and Christophe had spent more time apart than together. And she had not heard from him since the week he had left. Three weeks, to be exact.

The realization caused more anger to boil inside her. At that very moment, she would have gladly punched her own husband in the nose for leaving her in the country like a naughty child.

Lady Gailes, sitting rigidly in her discomfort, changed the subject quickly to the fashion of Johanna Fairhill. Though none of the upper-crust women could admit to liking her, they could envy and copy her fashion style without consequence. Everyone welcomed the change in conversation. A disagreement over laces and ruffles would not lead to outright war.

As the conversation continued, Rowena retreated into silence, sitting rather sullenly in her white metal chair. The Dowager Lady Gailes came to sit by her, placing a wrinkled, age-spotted hand on Rowena's arm affectionately to gain her attention.

"Do not worry about what Mrs. Paxton says, though it holds some truth," the old woman said, which did nothing to reassure Rowena in the least. "Your husband is young, and you are still pretty. He will be back by your side before you know it. The carnal woman cannot hold their attention long. Besides, it is his duty to have an heir."

Rowena's stomach revolted against the idea that Christophe would come back to her simply to create an heir. Deep down she knew it couldn't be true, for he had told her that he loved her not only with words but also in the way that he touched her, spoke with her, sought her out, protected her. He knew who she was and still he had married her. He would not do that to simply turn away from her only a few weeks later.

The words he had spoken, however, had been in Arabic, not English. She knew stories of the many men throughout the centuries and across cultures who had separated their love for their wife from love of their mistress. Perhaps to Christophe, love was different in English and Arabic—a separation that could fit two separate women, one for each.

I will never let another man hurt you again.

He must have included himself in that phrase as well. Surely.

"I do believe short hair may come into style," Lady Hedgerow said, too loudly.

"Yes, Lady Candor makes it look so charming that it may very well become the thing. You must show it off in London for it to make any impact, you know," Mrs. Paxton said, practically bubbling over with malicious happiness at the turn of the conversation.

Griffin had cut off the singed areas, then evened out the other side, resulting in more than half of Rowena's hair now being gone. With even the slightest breeze, it required several more pins than usual to keep it from falling about her face. Some tendrils had fallen around her eyes already since earlier that morning.

"Well, what say you ladies to a game of croquet?" Lady Gailes asked in a high voice, her eyes darting between Mrs. Paxton and Rowena rapidly.

Rowena smiled away her disgust. Not to be outdone, Mrs. Paxton gave an equally bright smile.

With croquet organized to keep the women from beating each other to a pulp with their biting words, the afternoon tea managed to drag on for an eternity. Claire glanced at Rowena with concern every so often, but didn't say a word. She did not have the knack for kind, reassuring words, as Emily always did.

"Mrs. Wright, is there any correspondence for me?" Rowena asked the housekeeper as they entered the manor. "Any letter?"

"No, my lady," she said in her slow drawl. "Shall I send up some tea to you?"

"No, thank you, Mrs. Wright," Rowena answered, feeling more weighed down with each step by the knowledge that Christophe was in London and had yet to inform her. She paced the hallway. Bit by bit, her emotions organized themselves into the fire of anger, try as she might to think on all possible explanations. There had to be some reason that his whispered promises had so quickly disappeared.

For another hour Rowena paced the space in front of her fireplace, ignoring the dinner and Griffin's pleas to eat until she suddenly came to one conclusion: she could be Fatia and wait, or she could be Rowena and demand an explanation on her terms.

Quickly, Rowena ran through the halls and down the stairs until she found Claire reading in the parlor.

"Pack your things, Claire, if you wish to come with me. I will leave for London tomorrow."

"What do you plan to do?" Claire asked with raised brows.

"Confront him. I want him to tell me the truth."

"And what happens if he is having an affair?" Claire asked gently. "Russell was his brother, after all. Though I know them to be different men, I know from experience that a man is capable of straying, even when he professes to loving his wife."

Rowena hesitated at the words. Claire's face was soft, but Rowena knew it was not easy for her to be so candid about her late husband. Still, though she could have sympathy for her sister-in-law and friend, she could not allow herself to be overly sympathetic to her husband. She rolled her shoulders back, her decision made.

"Then I will make my demands, and he must choose which path he prefers. But what I will not do is bide away my time waiting for him to grace me with his presence."

Grabbing Rowena by the shoulders, Claire looked deep into her eyes and gave a firm nod of agreement.

"Good for you, Rowena."

Chapter Thirty-Four

CHRISTOPHE WALKED INTO CANDOR House with his daughter beside him. Looking down, he absently wondered when he would cease to be amazed at that word: daughter.

"*Papá?*" the little girl asked, her eyes wide as she gazed up at him. Despite her mother's dark coloring, the child had his blue eyes, a queer thing to behold as her dark curls stuck out from under her cloak.

"*Sí, Eleadora?*" he said. Her English would come soon enough. In the meantime, he spoke to her in Spanish. "Did you have fun at the park?"

Eleadora nodded, her curls bouncing about her head as she slipped her tiny hand into his. It was strange, the love that had suddenly welled up in him at her touch. While crossing the channel to find her, he had nervously paced the deck of the boat, not knowing if he would be able to love the girl he was determined to adopt. In the end, he needn't have worried. Now that he had her, he couldn't fathom how he had lived before without her. His anger towards Don Carlos for keeping his daughter from him was not yet extinguished, but Christophe knew it would fade away. He might have lost Eleadora's baby years, but he had the entire future to spend with her. The only thing that made him nervous now was his wife and how to tell her of his new love.

There was the letter he had written two days ago, asking her to come to London. Before she found out from someone else that he was in town, he would have to gather his courage and send it. It was time she knew his past, just as he knew hers.

"*Vamos arriba?*" he asked his little girl. She nodded, gleefully swinging his hand up the stairs. Their playtime before her nap had become a special time for the two of them.

They mounted the steps together, Eleadora placing her small hand in his so as to jump from one step to another, at times her balance tipping too far back. He wondered at her courage and sense of play, and her faith that he would catch her if she were to fall. Eleadora's trust of him had been almost immediate – so much so that he wondered if she could see how alike they were, at least in the color of their eyes and the set of their jaws and mouth. Mercedes, the nurse, had taken more time to convince. Even after he had started speaking to her in fluent Spanish, she remained distant and untrusting. He couldn't help admiring her for it. Her job was to protect the child, and she was doing an excellent job.

The three of them entered the nursery and were just sitting down when the doors burst open. Eleadora jumped out of her tiny chair, looking ready to cry.

"What the hell are you doing?" Christophe growled, before realizing that his own tone of voice would push little Eleadora over into tears.

"Oh, my! I frightened you!" Emily exclaimed quietly, ignoring her brother's glare. "I'm so sorry. Come here, my little niece, and see what I have for you. Your father is being very naughty and grumpy, isn't he? Perhaps it's because he has something to tell his wife."

Duly chastised, Christophe mumbled that Eleadora didn't understand English, though barely loud enough to be heard. Emily ignored him and dropped to the floor, her skirts billowing out around her as Eleadora cried quietly. Slowly, Emily coaxed the small girl to come closer by producing a brand-new porcelain doll from a brown box. Immediately Eleadora stopped crying and looked at it in wonder as Emily pretended the doll was speaking. Slowly the little girl walked into Emily's arms, her eyes transfixed on the beautiful doll.

"Do you like her? I saw her in the store and just knew you had to have her. Cinch, ring for tea, will you, so that this lovely little angel can try the lemon cakes we bought for her? Oh, my, she is beautiful, isn't she? Even with your eyes and chin, dear Cinch."

"We?" Christophe asked cautiously as he rang the bell to the kitchen.

"The boys are here with me. I sent them to the garden on strict orders not to come here for an hour."

Emily laid her cheek against Eleadora's curls and breathed in. Having forgotten her fright, Eleadora allowed her aunt to snuggle her closer, finding her doll more interesting than anything else. She fingered the porcelain face with wide eyes while Mercedes looked on. Looking back to his sister, Christophe found her trying desperately to hold back tears as she ran her fingers gently over Eleadora's cheeks. "To be sure, Cinch, she is beautiful. I'm not sure how you did it."

"I'll have you know some ladies find me attractive," he protested, feeling the same comfort he had when he and Emily had still lived in the nursery. They had shared so many things back then.

Emily looked at him with feigned shock before bursting into a fit of giggles. Eleadora looked at them with wide eyes and burst into laughter as well.

"You see? She already knows who she should look up to!" teased Emily. "You will have very little respect to work with, Cinch!"

The two of them laughed again just as the tea came in. Eleadora's eyes lit up at the assortment of cakes and scones and jellies, much to the delight of her aunt.

"Come now, Eleadora. We must start taking our tea. Once your cousins are here, they will eat everything! Mama! There you are! How did you get lost?"

Christophe turned to the door to find his mother standing as immobile as a statue, staring at the little girl held in Emily's arms. Slowly she entered the nursery to kneel before Eleadora, who was busy nibbling a bright yellow cake.

"Good!" Eleadora declared, holding up the cake and spreading a smile across her lemon-smeared cheeks.

Christophe's chest swelled with pride at Eleadora's first English word. He also sighed in relief that she hadn't chosen to say one of the many curses he had found himself saying often during their trip home.

"Oh! My lovely child! Is it good? It's my favorite as well!" exclaimed his mother, taking a cake for herself, though it was obvious to Christophe that she ached to hold Eleadora rather than a lemon cake.

"That is your grandmother, Eleadora," Emily told her quietly, pointing at her mother with a smile. "Grandmother."

"Grenmuter," Eleadora repeated as Emily and Jacqueline shrieked with delight. Eleadora laughed out loud, beaming with pride.

Seeing they didn't need him, Christophe slipped from the nursery and head to the library. Now that he knew Eleadora was comfortable with his family, perhaps he could go out to Ravenwood instead of sending the letter for Rowena to come to him. That way she could spend a few days getting used to the idea of a sudden bastard daughter.

He hoped she would not leave him or demand an end to their marriage when she found another woman's child in the nursery. Christophe heaved a miserable sigh. He was uncertain whether he could raise a daughter if Rowena left him.

Christophe was so engrossed with his dilemma that he didn't notice the murmurings at the front door. When he stepped down and turned towards the hall, he came face to face with Claire.

"Cinch," she whispered, handing her parasol over to the footman. "You have less than a second."

Her warning barely registered before Rudolf moved away from the door and allowed Rowena to step through.

She looked directly at him, stopping his heart mid-beat. She was so beautiful. More so than in his dreams. Something within her had changed. Though she had been every inch a woman when he left, she seemed so much more confident, poised, elegant and ladylike than he had ever seen her before.

"Hello, Christophe," she said as she took off her gloves and handed them to Rudolf. "Might I speak with you in private?"

His heart filled with dread.

"Did you have a good trip?" Rowena asked.

Christophe flinched at her formality. His hands itched to gather her in his arms, but he was smart enough not to. He pressed his hands to his thighs.

"I missed you," he mumbled. She waved his admission away with her hand.

"When did you arrive, Christophe?" she asked, turning from the empty fireplace to face him squarely in the eyes.

"Six days ago," he admitted weakly, looking up to the ceiling as though he could see to Eleadora's well-being from the library. Claire had retreated up the stairs, and he wondered if she had found her way to the nursery. For her to go directly there would mean she had suspicions already. And if Claire had suspicions, then Rowena probably did as well. It was possible that Rowena's anger was directed at Eleadora.

Rowena walked to his desk and exhaled. He watched her pick up a piece of paper, realizing too late that it was the letter he had meant to send. Immediately he wished he could snatch it away, but he was half the library away and would never reach her in time. He would have to endure his shame at the cold fireplace.

Her lips pressed tightly together as she tilted the letter to the side and read it. It was the twentieth version and no good as far as letters went. He was terrible at conveying the warmth that overcame him just at the thought of his wife. He seemed unable to explain his ludicrous desire to see her every day, all day. Nervously, Christophe crossed his arms and leaned against the bookshelf.

"Hmm. Well, I'm here," Rowena said. "As you wanted, though clearly you did not want it so soon. Still, I will not bother to go back home and wait for that missive to arrive. It might take until next year, since it is already two days old. What I will do is ask for an explanation."

"To what?" he asked calmly, hoping to understand how much she knew before he spoke.

Anger flashed through her eyes, but she seemed calm otherwise. Quite the change from the woman he'd married. Admiration for her rose from deep within him. This woman was fully Rowena; a woman who knew where she was and what she wanted.

"How are we to do this, Christophe? Are you finished with this business that you were involved in?" she asked.

The question took him by surprise. "I am not, Rowena. I do not intend to give up my business."

"I see," she said, her shoulders drooping slightly. "Shall we attend the Wellington ball together? I see they invited us. Your threats must have got through to at least some of those in London."

"Wellington owes me money," Christophe replied, without thinking. The hurt in her eyes almost crushed him. He cursed himself silently. Inside, he ached to hold her against him, to kiss her, to make love to her. Instead, he found ways to hurt her unintentionally. "But Lady Wellington wrote you a personal note to make sure you understand she wants you there."

Rowena smiled wryly. "I suppose that is something. My husband is powerful enough to make Lady Wellington take extra measures to invite me. But you did not answer my question," she said. "Will we attend the ball together? Or would you prefer to go alone?"

The question was confusing. He could not imagine what made her think he wished to go alone. Unless it was a test—but to what end, he could not fathom. Hoping to break this strange, brittle atmosphere, he laid out his heart and waited for her answer.

"I would like to escort you if you wish to attend. I missed you."

Rowena looked at him, the hope in her eyes fleeting. "Very well. We will go together."

There was silence for a few minutes while Christophe struggled to stay put. Her new confidence slipped slightly, leaving her looking suddenly very small. He imagined himself pulling her to his chest, murmuring words of love into her ear, but he stopped himself when her hair caught his eye. He had forgotten about what had happened the night before he left. Even the letters he'd read upon arriving, which had disclosed every detail of Howe approaching Lord Kent, had not reminded him. He had been so wrapped up with Eleadora that he had forgotten about the suffering of his wife.

Lost in his feelings of abhorrence for himself, Christophe answered Rowena's next question automatically, without hearing her words.

"Did you arrive with her?"

"Yes. She's upstairs."

The tenuous atmosphere changed instantly. Rowena spun around to face him. Through the sharpness in her movement, Christophe realized that something in this very moment could alter the course of their lives irreparably.

"She's here? In Candor House?" Rowena cried.

He stepped forward in confusion, but then hurt and anger overwhelmed him. Any wife would need time to consider all the implications of accepting a bastard child, but she sounded as though she would throw the child out if she had the choice.

"Where would you like me to put her?" Christophe asked coldly, leveling Rowena with his gaze.

She stalked towards him, undeterred by his crisp voice or his stern look. "She has her own house. She can stay there."

"I don't understand what you mean to say, Rowena," Christophe answered, trying to hide just how perplexed her comments made him. "You want her to stay in Spain?"

But Rowena didn't stay to explain anything to him. She marched through the door and practically ran up the stairs. Christophe was late in reacting, but caught up with her by the time she reached the top of the stairs. She only hesitated for a second. With a huff of disgust, she turned left and ran faster to distance herself from him. The first door she threw open was a guest bedroom. She checked inside before she moved on to the next.

Christophe pulled the door closed, wondering at her searching so erratically. It was as though she wasn't looking for a child.

Rowena threw open another never-used guest room, stepping back when she found it empty and moving on to the next. He narrowed his eyes and watched, knowing he had missed a vital piece somewhere along the way.

When Rowena threw the door to Mercedes' room open, a loud shriek answered. His wife turned to him slowly, her face as white as snow.

And suddenly he understood. She thought he was playing her for a fool—with Mercedes, of all people! The woman must have been close to fifty and while she had the looks of someone who had been attractive when younger, she didn't tempt him from his marriage vows in the slightest.

"Rowena!" Christophe shouted, half in desperation and half in laughter. "I can explain."

Rowena closed her mouth tightly, struggling to hold back her tears.

"Well, I do find myself relieved that it is not Lady Carson," she said finally in a quiet, quaking voice.

"She is the nursemaid, Rowena," Christophe said, stopping three feet away from his pale, trembling wife.

"The—what?" Rowena asked, just as the nursery door burst open, with Emily, Claire, the boys and Christophe's mother, holding Eleadora, spilling into the hallway.

"What happened?" Emily asked breathlessly, her face knotted with worry.

"We heard shoutin'!" exclaimed Paul, his face covered in sticky crumbs. "Have you met my new cousin, Aunt Rowena?"

"Paul," admonished Claire quietly. "Come back and have another taste of the raspberry cake, will you?"

"Ok!" he shouted.

"Me, too!" his brother exclaimed.

Emily gave Christophe and Rowena worried glances before following her children back into the nursery, leaving her mother in the hallway with Eleadora in her arms.

"Cinch, this is why you should always tell your wife the truth as soon as possible," she said, kissing Eleadora on her pudgy cheeks. "She's tired, I believe."

Eleadora rubbed her eyes with chubby, tiny hands as Jacqueline handed her over to Mercedes. She fell into Mercedes' arms the moment she held them out. Christophe kept the nurse back long enough to plant a kiss on his daughter's head and sticky hands. He would never tire of marveling at how small her hands were. He couldn't wait to see what Rowena and his babe would look like just born, for it would be so much smaller and just as marvelous.

"The nursemaid? She is not your mistress?" Rowena asked, still in shock.

Christophe couldn't help the laughter that erupted from him, though he clamped his mouth shut when none of the women in the hall joined him. Mercedes quickened her step to pull Eleadora into her bedroom. Jacqueline shot him a look that warned he was only getting himself in deeper trouble before she entered the nursery again, leaving him and Rowena alone in the hall.

"She's not my mistress. Why did you assume so?"

"I asked you about Lady Carson downstairs. You answered that you came back with her."

"I admit I didn't hear the bit about Lady Carson," he admitted, taking advantage of her confusion to advance towards her. "I only heard 'her' and assumed you meant Eleadora."

"Eleadora," Rowena repeated. "She is yours? Yes, of course. She looks very much like you."

"I thought she died in childbirth with her mother."

"Catherine?" she asked, confused.

Christophe shook his head, stopping now just a few inches from her, forcing her to look up at him.

"Come, *enta habibi*, let me hold you. I have missed you so much. I will explain everything to you. Let's go to our rooms and I will tell you everything. I promise."

Much to his surprise and delight, Rowena leaned into his arms and was easily led back through the hallway to their rooms, where tea awaited them. As well as silence.

Walking through the doorway, she seemed to gain strength and immediately pulled away. He sat on the settee, his eyes never leaving her loveliness. Rowena stalked to the window and sat down, her body so tense it seemed like a statue. The sun's ray hit her profile, outlining her beauty, and Christophe realized just how much he ached for her. He just as quickly recognized how afraid he was that she might make him choose. He loved Rowena and wished for nothing to separate them, but he also loved Eleadora now and couldn't bear the thought of being without her.

And there it was. The thing he had been fighting all along and suddenly couldn't deny anymore. He loved her. He loved both of them. His heart thawed at the realization. And when she finally turned to him, he hoped it would be with a look of love as well as a look of forgiveness. A look that said they could get past this.

Her face, however, was devoid of any emotion, and her voice was hard.

"It seems you have a lot of things to tell me. So I suggest you get on with it."

Chapter Thirty-Five

ROWENA TRIED NOT TO give in to the lost, hurt look on Christophe's face. It was imperative he understand how deep her hurt ran.

It had not been right of him to keep so many things secret. He had left her alone in a moment of need because he hadn't trusted her enough to tell her about Eleadora. During the trip into London, Rowena realized that while her husband knew almost every intimate detail about her life, she knew little about his. It was even more disconcerting now that she found he was hiding a child in the nursery while all the other members of the family seemed to know.

As his wife, she should not have been the last to find out.

"I missed you," Christophe said again, his voice raspy and pain-filled. He seemed repentant, but she wasn't about to let him get by without an explanation.

Instead of talking, of explaining things as she had asked of him, he came closer. She forced her body to stay rigid as he touched her cheek. Two rough fingers grazed her smooth skin. She couldn't breathe while they were in contact with her. Thankfully, he soon dropped them to his side and cursed in frustration.

"Are you not going to look at me?"

His frustration with her was too much. Anger flitted through Rowena, growing larger each time it zig-zagged through her belly and up into her lungs. It caused her heart to race and her breath to become short, as though she had been running a long time. Waiting for explanations that he didn't want to give was exhausting. While she waited for clear instructions on where her place now was, he was spending his time being frustrated that she wouldn't respond to his touch.

"I believe I might look at you when you finally start talking," Rowena said, her voice so cold she barely recognized it.

He stepped back, the air filling with confusion.

"You are angry," he said finally.

"Did you not expect me to be?" she asked. "Did you truly expect to come back to London and hide and not upset me? Did you think that when I heard from Lady Tillmister that you were back I would not be angry? I was mortified, humiliated and ashamed not to know where my husband was while others knew perfectly well he was home! It only added to my humiliation that all of London is whispering about you and Lady Carson coming back from Spain at the same time. I am sure Mrs. Paxton could not wait to return to London to tell everyone she knew that I did not know you were there. Just this morning, before leaving Ravenwood, three notes arrived from women who gleefully informed me that they had spied you and a woman with raven-black hair entering several prominent tailors!" she exclaimed, hardly able to contain the volume of her voice. "What did you expect from me, Christophe? Did you expect that I would stay in

Cookston? Is that what you wanted? Or were you thinking of sending me further away?"

Her husband hung his head, as well he should, then sat down heavily on the velvet chair near the empty fire.

"I was going to send for you because I wanted you here. Well, no, actually, I believe I decided I would go to Cookston and explain things there."

"Explain now, Christophe."

She waited in stubborn silence until, finally, Christophe spoke. His voice was far away, his gaze even farther in the past.

First he spoke about Catherine, telling the story from the beginning. A stab of jealousy hit Rowena as he described his infatuation with Catherine and her charm. The jealousy turned to sympathy as Christophe recounted finding out about the child Catherine had abandoned in the countryside, her attempt to lure Daucer into having an affair, and her eventually betraying him by publicly accepting an engagement to another man the night before he had thought they were to announce their own engagement. Rowena found herself sitting on the edge of her seat, forcing her arms to stay by her side when they were desperate to reach out to him. It wasn't about punishing him by keeping her comfort from him, but rather her need to hear more. This child, Eleadora, was not Catherine's. There was more to the story. There had always been more to the story about why an Englishman traveled through North Africa, why he had planned to live there up until his brother died and left him with the responsibility of being the marquess. She had always known that. But she had been content with him keeping his secrets until he could share them.

Until now. Now she needed to have everything out in the open.

"There is talk that you and Lady Carson went to Spain together. You were seen arriving the same day."

Christophe appeared confused. "You believe those rumors?"

"I do not know what to believe, Christophe," she answered steadily. "You didn't wish me to be here in London. I feel I no longer have a place with you."

"That is not true!" he exclaimed, jumping from his chair. He rushed to her side and knelt in front of her. Taking her hands in his, he kissed them over the knuckles, then turned them to kiss her palms. "There is no one else taking your place. Your place is here, next to me. I've been a fool, Rowena."

Rowena hesitated enough to allow the heat in her middle to still into a calm pool instead of a raging sea. Still on his knees, Christophe looked up at her, the pain evident in his eyes.

Christophe raised her to her feet and lowered his lips slowly to hers. She allowed the kiss because she could no longer deny herself contact from him, but instead of a long, deep kiss as she needed, Christophe pulled away almost as soon as their lips met. Briefly, he leaned his forehead against hers before guiding her to sit down.

"Please, I cannot tell the story to a shadow staring at me from the window."

Christophe paced the small space between the floors and the empty fireplace as he began again. Rowena believed him when he said he left out no detail. Jealousy slashed her heart over and over again during the stories of his carousing with all kinds of women. Then he spoke of Dolores, and Rowena's jealousy surged. The way he spoke of her, Rowena knew it had been Dolores who had broken something within him.

There was a subtle change in his tone, as though the climax was coming. He had not mentioned any child with the other women.

Her heart skipped a beat. Perhaps it had been losing Dolores, the love of his life, that caused him so much pain.

When he described why he had started the affair, she almost wished to stop listening. Carousing with women was one thing, but to have a deliberate affair with a married woman was something unexpected. She struggled against the contrasting visions of who she knew him to be and who he had been before. She listened with nauseated anticipation for his declaration of undying love for the raven-haired Dolores, who became more and more beautiful in her mind. Callously, she felt he had got what he deserved when Don Pablo caught him with Dolores—until he mentioned the duel.

"I felt no real remorse," Christophe said. "But I could not blame him for his anger, nor deny him the satisfaction of meeting me for a duel. I decided I would shoot beyond him and wait for my punishment, whether it be death or injury."

"At least you understood his anger," Rowena asked quietly. "What happened?"

"His gun backfired and killed him." Christophe's face turned ashen with guilt.

"That is not your fault, Christophe," Rowena answered calmly, though her heart skipped several beats with anxiety. She rose partially from her chair to go to him, but immediately sat back down when he turned away from her. He did not wish for comfort, and while the idea pained her, she understood.

"No, it was not my fault the gun backfired, but it was my fault we were dueling in the first place. The rumors that I must have toyed with his guns eventually caused me to flee. I ran even after I knew Dolores was pregnant with my child."

"Eleadora."

414   STEPPING ACROSS THE DESERT

"Yes."

"But how did you know that it was your child?" Rowena asked.

Christophe turned to her with surprise in his eyes. "She and Don Pablo were not intimate."

"Is that what she told you?" Rowena asked. "I see you in Eleadora, Christophe, I don't doubt she's yours. But I wonder why you were so convinced of that at the time."

"Don Pablo was gone often, which allowed for Dolores and me to be together." Christophe hesitated, then continued with a grimace. "Almost every night."

"I see," Rowena said. She wished very much to say a few choice words in Berber, but refrained. "Did you love her?"

To her surprise, her husband laughed bitterly.

"I didn't love her. But in Africa I decided that I was honor-bound to offer her marriage. It was my fault she was a widow, now living with her father in shame, pregnant with my child. But when I went back and offered her marriage she laughed at me."

"She laughed?" Rowena asked in surprise.

"She laughed and said she told everyone the child was Don Pablo's and did not care if they believed her or not. She said she would stay in Spain and defend the child as Don Pablo's to her dying day before marrying me and moving to England," Christophe said. "She was a very proud woman. Marrying me and moving away would be admitting that she had lied. She would not back down."

Rowena stayed quiet while Christophe continued with his story. She tasted her husband's fear and misery at finding Dolores dead, along with his baby. His despair at being too lost in his dark melancholy to keep watch over his cousin Albert was palpable.

Albert had ended up dying in an opioid cave while Christophe was away in Africa.

"I had to bring his body back to England and admit to my family that I had not kept guard over my little cousin. I made up a lie about his death because I could not tell my aunt about his opium addiction and the strange parties he would attend. Instead, I told her he died of consumption. I came back to England hard and cold. I dived into my work to keep me from thinking of all my failures, but soon enough I felt caged. That was when I left again. This time I went straight to Morocco, where I found that house—where we stayed together, you and I—and decided I would live there. José convinced me to travel into Algeria to finish some business he couldn't get done through messages. I was up for another adventure into Algeria, not having been since Albert and I went, years before we settled in Spain."

"How old was Albert?"

Christophe narrowed his eyes. "When we left England together or when he died?"

"When you left."

"I was twenty-three, so that would make him two and twenty."

"And when he died?"

"I am one-and-thirty now, and it was four years ago, so six and twenty."

Rowena wrapped her arms around his waist, laying her head against his back. His back stiffened, but that did not deter her. If he wanted her by his side still, she wanted him to know that it was a place she wished to be.

"It seems he was old enough to understand he needed to look after himself, as you were. If you are going to take on the guilt of your actions at seven and twenty, why should he not take on the responsibility of his own at the same age?"

"Well, perhaps he could if he were not dead," Christophe said coldly, still rigid, as if daring her to let go of him.

"If you had died in the duel with Don Pablo, would you be more content in death if you thought Albert was taking on the guilt of your death as his own?"

"Of course not," he answered, trying to pull away from her, but she strengthened her hold on him.

"So why do you take his death on as your fault?"

"Even if I could let go of his, there is still Don Pablo and Dolores," he started to say.

"Both of which cannot be your fault. While your actions were rash and, dare I say it, surprising, you didn't force him to call you out. Dueling has been illegal for several decades now. While I can understand a man battling out his honor with his fists, I cannot condone duels. If Don Pablo and Dolores were not intimate, then their marriage was a pretence. I would be surprised to find that he was not doing the same with another woman."

"But I embarrassed him in the worst way," Christophe protested. "I would have called myself out, were the roles reversed."

"Perhaps he should have paid more attention to his wife instead of calling out the men who did," Rowena said with a smile she couldn't keep hidden. "The idea that men can go gallivanting about with other women while their poor wife stays at home and rots is not acceptable. Though I do not like the circumstances of her being married and being with you, nor is it very respectable of you to conduct business in such a way—and I do hope you do not make it a habit of being intimate with the wives of your business partners – I do not condone Don Pablo feeling justified in dueling away his shame while never thinking that perhaps his wife wished she had the same option."

Christophe slowly turned around, still held in her arms, and looked at her as though she were a peculiar creature he had never seen before.

"You are a strange woman," he murmured.

"I'm not," Rowena said with a shrug. "Most women feel as I do. They simply never say so."

Christophe cautiously wrapped his arms around her waist and took her lips in a chaste kiss.

"As for Dolores, many women die in childbirth. And while you feel guilty for her husband's death, it does not sound to me as though it would have upset her much."

At those words, Christophe pulled away.

"Perhaps you do not think it is fair of me to say so, but since I did not know the woman, I'm making certain conclusions. Since she did not take you up on the offer of marriage, I can only assume that she did not worry about her economic nor social future. If she was a woman used to the luxuries of life and thought that life would be threatened by having a child in her circumstances, then she would have taken you as a husband, despite her pride. The fact is that she did not feel the need to marry you. Since you did not love her, and she did not love you, she felt no need to attach herself yet again to a loveless marriage."

Rowena watched her husband think about her words, but it was hard to read whether he agreed with her or not.

"She was not laughing at you when she laughed at your proposal; she was laughing at your sex, who always seems to think that marriage to a man will make everything better for a woman.

She knew what a loveless marriage was and knew she did not want it again."

When Christophe did not answer, Rowena decided to move on to her final questions. Perhaps her husband would need time to mull over the differences between men and women, which he so clearly did not yet understand.

"How did you find out that Eleadora was still alive?"

Christophe's face hardened. "I received a weather-beaten, aged letter from Don Carlos. It was a letter that was to be released upon his death, explaining where I could find my daughter. I had only a few weeks to retrieve her before his instructions were to place her in a convent somewhere in Spain, where I would never find her again. Never know of her."

"You're angry at him," she said, speaking with disregard for how Christophe would react.

"He kept my daughter from me!" Christophe roared. "Do you expect me to be happy? Content that I lost her first years? I mourned her birth and death each year, always wondering if she had been born girl or boy. All I wished was to have one moment to hold the body of my babe before Don Carlos buried it. He took away my rights as a father away from me."

Rowena waited for him to say more, but instead he folded into his anger and despair. Sinking into the opposite chair from her, Christophe placed his head in his hands and breathed heavily to fight back his tears. The clock ticked away the seconds, then the minutes, as Rowena waited. She did not know if he wished for her to hold him; she did not know if he wished for her to leave. So she sat in her chair, enduring the silence until she could no longer.

"Where does this leave us now, Christophe?" she finally asked. "You are both angry and guilt-ridden. You have a daughter living in this house and you have me. Where do you wish to go from here?"

Christophe looked up into her eyes and swallowed hard.

"It seems to me you should take the last few years as your payment for the guilt against Dolores and Don Pablo. Then consider it paid for and be ready to move on. Let go of the guilt over Albert, for he was a grown man in control of his senses and able to make his own decisions. Stop feeling guilty about your baby dying, for she lives and is asleep just down the hall."

"And you?" he whispered.

"And me? That is your decision."

"I need your help. I need you by my side. I cannot live without you."

"You will give her your name?"

Christophe nodded. "I can't send her away. Even if she is a bastard, I will give her my name and hope to make her life easier in any way that I can."

"Good," Rowena said with a nod. "But if you call that beautiful child a bastard again, I will call you out myself."

That comment received a small smile from her husband. The smile that always caused her heart to speed and still did so, despite the weight of their discussion.

"I will have the staff told that if I hear anyone calling her a bastard or treating her as such they will be let go, with no references," Rowena announced firmly.

"Will you stay with me, then?"

"Christophe. There was never a question of whether I would stay, only whether you desired me to. I've made a place for myself in Cookston. I do not deny that I was hurt after you left me alone just hours after Lady Kent tried to cook my hat while still on my head, but I found I missed you terribly."

Christophe groaned at the mention of her hair, raising his eyes to her head as his fingers raked through it.

"I missed you, too," he confessed. "I wished every day that I had found the courage to ask you to come with me to Spain, though each time I convinced myself that it was better to leave you here in England, with Claire."

With that said, he lowered his lips to hers, this time raising her onto his lap. She soon found herself drowning in the passion that his kisses always brought her. When his hands left her neck to roam over her cloth-covered breasts, Rowena giggled at his groan of frustration.

"You must stop wearing these terrible dresses," he teased.

When she gave no reply, Christophe turned her around to undo it while kissing her neck. His left hand pulled at the long laces as his right hand smoothed her curves over and over, building up the heat within her. The loneliness that had plagued her while he was away seemed to burn up like a piece of tissue paper, replaced by the desire for him to never leave her side again.

With a cry of triumph, Christophe pushed down the bodice of her dress. She shrieked in surprise when he swooped her up into his arms and into the bedroom. Lowering her to the bed, Christophe hesitated as a cryptic look shadowed his eyes.

But just as her anxiety started to build, his look softened. Slowly, he lowered his lips to hers again, taking them in a deliberate kiss before pulling away only enough to whisper four strange words.

"I love you, Rowena."

Chapter Thirty-Six

RAVENWOOD, SEPTEMBER, 1833

CHRISTOPHE SLOWLY PLACED THE newspaper on the table and stared at it in confusion. The article was a complete surprise. Rowena had said nothing. Absolutely nothing.

He wasn't sure whether he should feel betrayed, proud, or sad. Her not telling him seemed significant. His mother had known; the article mentioned her too many times for him to believe she did not know. That fact made him wonder how many other people in the family knew.

Perhaps it was revenge on him for keeping so many secrets from her. But that didn't sound like Rowena.

He sat, staring at the paper while waiting for his wife to come back from her walk through the gardens at dawn. No matter how little she slept, she still awoke before the sun rose. The days he woke with her movements, he joined her, but she never purposely disturbed him. Today he had slept right through her waking. Perhaps she had been quieter on purpose, knowing that the article would come out.

Again, he turned his attention to what he had just read. The stillness in the room helped him process through the flurry within him. Pride: yes, he did feel that. Rowena was the bravest woman he knew. He was proud of her courage. The paragraph that mentioned her whipping jumped out again, bringing with it a wave of anguish. He wasn't sure if he would ever be able to not feel great sadness at how she had been treated.

Tapping his finger against the polished table, Christophe dug deeper and had to admit there was a small bit of betrayal as well. She hadn't warned him or asked for his opinion.

Noise in the hallway caught his attention just as the doors to the dining room burst open. Eleadora ran through them with Mercedes at her heel.

"*Papá!*" she cried with a smile, throwing herself into his arms. He laughed as her full force hit him.

"Good morning, Ms. Gonzales."

Mercedes answered in heavily accented English with a grin. She was finally finding comfort in her place with them and in England. Though it had not been easy, Rowena had eventually found an English governess willing to share the place of educating little Eleadora with Mercedes. They did not wish for Eleadora to lose her Spanish roots, nor did Mercedes wish to lose her position. The amount of work Rowena had done to merge everyone into place in the past few months amazed him. They had grown closer than ever before, with no secrets lingering between them.

Christophe frowned at the article.

"*Mamá!*" Eleadora exclaimed excitedly, wriggling around on Christophe's lap until she finally reached the newspaper on the table. "*Mamá!*"

Her second exclamation was directed towards the door, where Rowena now stood in a beautiful yellow dress. Besides the dress being fancier than she normally wore, more in the style that Claire would wear. There was something entirely different about his wife that morning that Christophe couldn't quite explain. She captivated his attention as she accepted Eleadora's vigorous hug, with one just as spirited. Though he had witnessed this embrace every day now for months, it still caused his heart to constrict in happiness. Before sailing to Spain to retrieve Eleadora, he never could have imagined how well they would all acclimate to each other.

"Good morning, love," Christophe murmured as Rowena approached him with Eleadora in her arms. She greeted him and Mercedes, kissing Christophe once Eleadora was settled in her own chair, a plate of eggs set in front of her.

Christophe watched his wife move to the sideboard and fill her plate, all the while trying to pinpoint what was different about her. A sudden stab of fear and joy jabbed him as he wondered if she were with child. Certainly, she wouldn't keep *that* from him.

"What do you think?" she asked, nodding towards the article.

Before he could answer, the doors burst open again and Claire came through in an unusually noisy manner. He scrambled to his feet again, exasperated with his family already.

"Rowena!" came a shriek from the doorway. Christophe straightened again before fully hitting his chair, knowing full well it was his sister who shrieked. Emily entered along with their mother, who was not shrieking but holding her granddaughter, who joyfully joined in the squealing. Everyone had come to Ravenwood for Eleadora's birthday, and no one had yet left. He would not be surprised if they all stayed until Christmas.

"You didn't say anything!" Emily exclaimed. "Did you know about this, Christophe?"

"It seems I did not merit being told either," Christophe said in a low voice.

His wife raised her eyebrows at him. "I kept it from everyone except for your mother. It was all her idea."

"Was it?" Emily asked, turning to their mother. "That doesn't surprise me."

"It surprises me a little that you agreed to it," Claire said, moving to fill a plate.

"You're right," Rowena admitted, taking her seat again.

Christophe took his cue from her and sat down again. Having finished her plate of eggs, Eleadora crawled onto his lap. The pressure of her curly head against his chest grounded him, steadying his heartbeat and bringing him to focus more clearly.

The gossip of what Rowena had admitted about her past at the dinner party in London had circulated through town, but many refused to believe it. Now that the gossips had moved on, he was surprised she had decided to be interviewed for the newspaper article. He saw nothing for her to be ashamed of, but had she asked him his opinion, he would have told her there was no need to bring up the past again.

Perhaps that was why she hadn't asked him.

"When did you do this? I have not seen a journalist come to Ravenwood," he said.

"While we were in London," Rowena admitted. "You were working long days."

"It's interesting to find that you can keep meetings with a strange man hidden from me," he said in a low voice that made Emily titter nervously about him not being such a bear.

"That is your mother's doing," Rowena answered, her eyes glittering with laughter. "She invited both Mr. Connelly and me to tea every day for a week."

"It is beautifully written," Claire said.

Eleadora abandoned her father for her aunt at the sight of the scones and jam on her plate.

"Do you think it is too much?" Rowena asked.

"I think it's perfect. Mr. Connelly writes very well," Christophe said as he went to stand behind her. She took his hand in hers when he laid it on her shoulder.

And that was when he realized what was different. It wasn't the glow of being with child; it was the dress she wore. Besides it being made of a beautifully spun linen the color of sunshine, it did not reach her neck with a barrage of buttons. Christophe looked at Claire, who had scrambled to her feet in surprise.

"Rowena!" she exclaimed. "Your dress!"

"Yes," Rowena said with a laugh. "Do you like it?"

"It's beautiful," Claire answered first, her eyes dropping to the pink lines that licked at Rowena's shoulders. "They are not half as bad as you had me believing with your dreadful, high-necked dresses."

"You're beautiful in it," Emily confirmed, Eleadora echoing the sentiment with a mouth full of jam and scones. "I find you to be very brave."

"Just as I have said before," Christophe said, pulling his wife to her feet. "You are beautiful exactly as you are. I approve wholeheartedly of the new dress."

He turned her around and kissed her on the lips as Emily and Claire cleared their throats uneasily.

"I have a feeling we might all see a new side of Cinch, thanks to the new dresses," Claire said with a roll of her eyes as he and Rowena pulled away from each other.

"At any rate, it's done. My story is out. Do you believe it will have repercussions?" Rowena asked.

"Any repercussions that may come we will face together," Christophe said. "With Lord and Lady Kent gone from London, though, it seems the gossips have found other things to talk about."

"Like Lady Grace eloping with Mr. John Howe?" Emily offered with a smile.

"It seems you are not the only scandalous one in your family," Claire teased. Rowena and Emily laughed.

Christophe leaned down to murmur into his wife's ear as the laughter and chatter continued. "You can always be the most scandalous in your family with me," he whispered. "We could start right now, even."

Rowena laughed and swatted him away from her. They sat down together at the table. The footman poured more coffee and tea into their cups, and the family continued with the gossip of the ton at that moment. Christophe held his wife's hand in his, occasionally kissing her knuckles and realizing what a strange series of events had brought him to this moment. This moment in which he had everything a man could ever want.

~~~

Sunshine gleamed through the tall, narrow windows that rose up in the hallways upstairs. Rowena stepped into the sunshine, then into the shade, then again into the sunshine as she made her way to the nursery. All the house was quiet, everyone in their separate corners to either rest or work. She had nothing else to do, having finished reading her novel and already settled some household disputes. Seeing that the afternoon was still warm, she decided to peek in on Eleadora.

The door's hinges creaked slightly as a curly head popped up instantly from her pillow. Eleadora stared at her with wide eyes, a silent smile spreading across her lips. Soft snoring drifted from Mercedes' room.

"Shhhh," Rowena said, stepping into the room. "Have you finished napping?"

Eleadora nodded.

"Would you like to go for a walk? Come."

Rowena held out her hand as the little girl quickly scrambled down from the high bed. All the covers fell to the floor with a dull thump, but neither paid them any mind. Eleadora picked up her doll and scurried out to the hallway, immediately holding up her arms for Rowena to carry her.

"*Arriba,*" she said.

"'Up,'" Rowena answered back. "'Please.'"

Before the little girl could fully repeat the words back, Rowena had her in her arms.

"Did you sleep at all, darling?" she asked, walking quickly down the hall with a twirl or two to make Eleadora laugh.

"I sleep lot," she answered in her giggles, though Rowena knew it wasn't true. Certainly, though, for a small child, sleeping and lying still in one's bed must seem like the same thing. It wasn't playing, and it wasn't eating; it was merely boring.

"Let's go and find beautiful birds then," she said as they stepped into the garden.

The two of them ran through the garden paths, around the flower beds, and over the small hill, stopping each time Eleadora found a butterfly, a brambling or a magpie anywhere nearby. She ran at them, laughing with outstretched arms. When they flew away, she pouted for a few seconds before being coaxed into chasing something else by Rowena or Finch, the gardener. By the time they reached the pond, Eleadora was tired enough to sit quietly and throw crumbs of dry bread to the resident ducks, who quacked in appreciation.

"Are you tired, precious?" Rowena asked quietly as Eleadora's small body dropped to the ground. The small girl didn't make a sound when Rowena took her in her arms and brought her against her chest. "Shall we go home?"

"No," Eleadora said firmly before popping her thumb into her mouth and snuggling closer to Rowena. "You will sing and I will listen, and the ducks, too."

"All right, darling," Rowena said, chuckling.

The breeze picked up, rustling the red and golden leaves until they toppled from the trees onto Rowena, Eleadora, and the ground around them. Eleadora picked one up from where it gently landed on her nose and studied it, peace and security measured on her face.

"*Yalla tnam Reema,*" Rowena sang softly, watching Eleadora closely. "*Yalla tnam Reema, yalla yijeeha elnoum.*"

Eleadora dropped the golden leaf with a sigh. She looked back at Rowena, fighting against her drooping eyelids with as much energy as she could muster.

"*Yalla tnam, yalla tnam,*" Rowena sang, quieter now than before. She couldn't help smiling at her adopted daughter, marveling at her smooth skin that gradually darkened at her hairline. There Eleadora's deep black curls shone like dark diamonds under the sunlight.

"*Yalla tnam Reema, yalla yijeeha elnoum.*"

She repeated the song again and again until sleep clung gently to the little girl, making her limp in Rowena's arms.

The last note rang out, fading out into the distance, calling out to Christophe as he approached. Rowena smiled as his broad shoulders blocked the sun, allowing her a good look at him. He seemed much the same as he had been the first day she saw him: strong, determined, in control. But the heaviness was gone. His posture was not so rigid, and his lips were turned up more often in a smile.

Just as they were at this moment.

"Shall I take her from you?" he whispered.

"I could carry her," Rowena teased. "I have not yet lost my strength."

Just to show off, she gripped the beautiful girl closer and stood up, unaided, with a triumphant smile. Christophe laughed gently, brushing back her fallen hair.

"I never doubted your strength, *enta habibi*," he chuckled softly. "I was just jealous of you holding her."

Rowena gently handed Eleadora to Christophe before giving both of their cheeks a kiss. Together the three of them walked through the garden that was slowly preparing for harvest, the cries of a farmer bringing in the cows across the fields echoing through the air.

"Happy?" Christophe asked as she placed her hand through his arm.

"Very," Rowena said.

9-12-22

good clean

romance

Aurora's Dilemma

Prelude to *Stepping Across the Desert*

It's 1827 and the Brayemore's are planning a return to London as Algeria creeps closer to the brink of war.

Aurora, the family's maid, longs to go home to Spain with her fiancée, Julian, but they lack the money. Desperate to stay together, the couple come up with a way to reunite in England.

When Lady Brayemore orders Aurora to stay in Algeria, however, the lovers struggle with the threat of separation. With political tensions mounting, Aurora and Julian are running out of options.

As the rumors of a blockade loom, a wealthy socialite offers the young lovers an enticing plan, but it has a dark twist. She will get them on the last ship sailing for Spain if they kidnap the young Miss Rowena Brayemore.

Is Aurora willing to forfeit her home and her love? Out of time and options, will Aurora choose honor and loyalty to the Brayemore's? Or will she commit this dark deed to get home?

Read the prelude to *Stepping Across the Desert* from the perspective of Rowena's maid Aurora in this brand-new historical novella!

Find it at Katcaldwell.com

Coffee Stains

OUT 2021!

Using a dead girl's name is just one of many things Ana Lopez is willing to do to graduate college. Secretly dating a professor and leaving her family in the dust are a few more. You name it, she'll do it, as long as it gets her closer to her dream of a better life and helps her escape her violent past.

But as much as she tries to outrun her past, it's catching up to her.

When Marlon, a friend from high school who's gotten more handsome, shows up in town, Ana finds herself attraction to him again. But Marlon knows her true identity, which threatens her precariously balanced schemes. When Marlon discovers some of her secrets, Ana has to choose to trust him or leave him behind as she did her family. Even if that means losing her chance at real love.

Distancing herself from Marlon won't solve everything. There are others searching for the truth and it's only a matter of time before everything Ana has worked so hard to bury is discovered.

Find it on Amazon, Kobo, Barnes&Noble, katcaldwell.com or anywhere you buy books!

An Audience with the King

The king says everyone is equal, but Nelia's life shows the opposite.

Once, she'd considered herself blessed; she has the ability to see the true character of others. Envy as green slime, evil as tar. Shame as rubies sparkling bright enough that men would fight over them.

But then war took her husband's kindness. Famine took her beloved grandfather. Plague took her only son. Now an outcast in her hometown, Nelia is at a breaking point. Her gift has brought her pain more often than not and it, like her own life, seems to have no purpose anymore.

With nothing left to lose, she sets out on a journey to see the king, the man who claims she possesses the same right to a life of purpose as everyone else. Let him prove it.

But the journey itself promises hardship. And if the king can't give her the answer she needs, then the despair that threatens to consume her will finally have its victory.

ABOUT KAT CALDWELL

Kat Caldwell believes that everyone on earth has a story worth telling and she is passionate about helping those who want to write their story get the tools and support they need. She decided to pursue the indie author route, publishing her historical romance, *Stepping Across the Desert* in 2017 and her magical realism novel, *An Audience with the King,* in 2019. Her third novel, a contemporary women's fiction, *Coffee Stains,* will be out September of 2021. She started the Creative Writing Community in March of 2021 as a place where writers of all levels can find support, community and industry tips and tools to be successful in their writing careers.

Facebook @katcaldwellauthor
Instagram @katcaldwell.author
Locals @Kat_Caldwell

Joining Kat's newsletter by scanning the QR code below:

SCAN ME

ARE YOU A WRITER?

No matter what you're level, you're invited to check out the Creative Writing Community. As group of writers commited to each other's success in the creative world, we:

• Write together — Every week there are up to three writing sprints where we show up together and write in 20 minute sprints.

• Brainstorm together — There are so many things to learn and do as a writer. We get together to talk about the latest trick, tools and tips that can help us all be successful.

• Learn together — Every month Kat invites an expert to come and teach us something more about writing, publishing, marketing, mindset, etc.

• Help — We trust each other with our work, feedback and help.

Want to learn more? Go to https://katcaldwell.com and click on Creative Writing Community.